797,885 Books
are available to read at

www.ForgottenBooks.com

Forgotten Books' App
Available for mobile, tablet & eReader

ISBN 978-1-331-50137-4
PIBN 10198659

This book is a reproduction of an important historical work. Forgotten Books uses state-of-the-art technology to digitally reconstruct the work, preserving the original format whilst repairing imperfections present in the aged copy. In rare cases, an imperfection in the original, such as a blemish or missing page, may be replicated in our edition. We do, however, repair the vast majority of imperfections successfully; any imperfections that remain are intentionally left to preserve the state of such historical works.

Forgotten Books is a registered trademark of FB &c Ltd.
Copyright © 2015 FB &c Ltd.
FB &c Ltd, Dalton House, 60 Windsor Avenue, London, SW19 2RR.
Company number 08720141. Registered in England and Wales.

For support please visit www.forgottenbooks.com

1 MONTH OF FREE READING

at

www.ForgottenBooks.com

By purchasing this book you are eligible for one month membership to ForgottenBooks.com, giving you unlimited access to our entire collection of over 700,000 titles via our web site and mobile apps.

To claim your free month visit: www.forgottenbooks.com/free198659

* Offer is valid for 45 days from date of purchase. Terms and conditions apply.

Similar Books Are Available from
www.forgottenbooks.com

Emma: A Novel, Vol. 1 of 3
by Jane Austen

A Tale of Two Cities
by Charles Dickens

The Jungle Book
by Rudyard Kipling

Neæra
A Tale of Ancient Rome, by John W. Graham

A Selection from the World's Greatest Short Stories
Illustrative of the History of Short Story Writing, by Sherwin Cody

And Quiet Flows the Don, Vol. 1 of 4
A Novel, by Mikhail Aleksandrovich Sholokhov

Les Misérables (The Wretched)
A Novel, by Victor Hugo

Agatha Webb
by Anna Katharine Green

The Alhambra
Tales and Sketches of the Moors and Spaniards, by Washington Irving

All Shakespeare's Tales
by Charles Lamb

Anna Karénina
by Leo Tolstoy

At the Foot of Sinai
by Georges Clemenceau

The Case of Mr. Lucraft, and Other Tales, Vol. 1
by Walter Besant

The Chartreuse of Parma
by Stendhal

Cheveley, Vol. 1 of 2
Or The Man of Honour, by Rosina Bulwer Lytton

Children of the Mist
by Eden Phillpotts

A Cornish Droll
A Novel, by Eden Phillpotts

Dark Hollow
by Anna Katharine Green

The Deaf Shoemaker
by Philip Barrett

Doctor Hathern's Daughters
A Story of Virginia, in Four Parts, by Mrs. Mary Jane Holmes

The Social Cancer

A Complete English Version of NOLI ME TANGERE
from the Spanish of

José Rizal

By

Charles Derbyshire

Manila
Philippine Education Company
1912

THE NOVELS OF JOSÉ RIZAL

Translated from Spanish into English
By Charles Derbyshire

THE SOCIAL CANCER (NOLI ME TANGERE)
THE REIGN OF GREED (EL FILIBUSTERISMO)

*Copyright, 1912, by Philippine Education Company.
Entered at Stationers' Hall. Registrado en las Islas
Filipinas. All rights reserved.*

TRANSLATOR'S INTRODUCTION

I

" We travel rapidly in these historical sketches. The reader flies in his express train in a few minutes through a couple of centuries. The centuries pass more slowly to those to whom the years are doled out day by day. Institutions grow and beneficently develop themselves, making their way into the hearts of generations which are shorter-lived than they, attracting love and respect, and winning loyal obedience; and then as gradually forfeiting by their shortcomings the allegiance which had been honorably gained in worthier periods. We see wealth and greatness; we see corruption and vice; and one seems to follow so close upon the other, that we fancy they must have always co-existed. We look more steadily, and we perceive long periods of time, in which there is first a growth and then a decay, like what we perceive in a tree of the forest."
FROUDE, *Annals of an English Abbey.*

Monasticism's record in the Philippines presents no new general fact to the eye of history. The attempt to eliminate the eternal feminine from her natural and normal sphere in the scheme of things there met with the same certain and signal disaster that awaits every perversion of human activity. Beginning with a band of zealous, earnest men, sincere in their convictions, to whom the cause was all and their personalities nothing, it there, as elsewhere, passed through its usual cycle of usefulness, stagnation, corruption, and degeneration.

To the unselfish and heroic efforts of the early friars Spain in large measure owed her dominion over the Philippine Islands and the Filipinos a marked advance on the road to civilization and nationality. In fact, after the dreams of sudden wealth from gold and spices had faded, the islands were retained chiefly as a missionary conquest and a stepping-stone to the broader fields of Asia, with Manila as a depot for the Oriental trade. The records of those early years are filled with tales of courage and heroism worthy of Spain's proudest years, as the missionary fathers labored with unflagging zeal in disinterested endeavor for the spread of the Faith and the betterment of the condition of the Malays among whom they found themselves. They won the confidence of the native peoples, gathered them into settlements and villages, led them into the ways of peace, and became their protectors, guides, and counselors.

In those times the cross and the sword went hand in hand, but in the Philippines the latter was rarely needed or used. The lightness and vivacity of the Spanish character, with its strain of Orientalism, its fertility of resource in meeting new conditions, its adaptability in dealing with the dwellers in warmer lands, all played their part in this as in the other conquests. Only on occasions when some stubborn resistance was met with, as in Manila and the surrounding country, where the most advanced of the native peoples dwelt and where some of the forms and beliefs of Islam had been established, was it necessary to resort to violence to destroy the native leaders and replace them with the missionary fathers. A few sallies by young Salcedo, the Cortez of the Philippine conquest, with a company of the splendid infantry which was at that time the admiration and despair of martial Europe, soon effectively exorcised any idea of resistance that even the boldest and most intransigent of the native leaders might have entertained.

For the most part, no great persuasion was needed to turn a simple, imaginative, fatalistic people from a few vague animistic deities to the systematic iconology and the elaborate ritual of the Spanish Church. An obscure *Bathala* or a dim *Malyari* was easily superseded by or transformed into a clearly defined *Diós,* and in the case of any especially tenacious "demon," he could without much difficulty be merged into a Christian saint or devil. There was no organized priesthood to be overcome, the primitive religious observances consisting almost entirely of occasional orgies presided over by an old woman, who filled the priestly offices of interpreter for the unseen powers and chief eater at the sacrificial feast. With their unflagging zeal, their organization, their elaborate forms and ceremonies, the missionaries were enabled to win the confidence of the natives, especially as the greater part of them learned the local language and identified their lives with the communities under their care. Accordingly, the people took kindly to their new teachers and rulers, so that in less than a generation Spanish authority was generally recognized in the settled portions of the Philippines, and in the succeeding years the missionaries gradually extended this area by forming settlements from among the wilder peoples, whom they persuaded to abandon the more objectionable features of their old roving, often predatory, life and to group themselves into towns and villages "under the bell."

The tactics employed in the conquest and the subsequent behavior of the conquerors were true to the old Spanish nature, so succinctly characterized by a plain-spoken Englishman of Mary's reign, when the war-cry of Castile encircled the globe and even hovered ominously near the "sceptered isle," when in the intoxication of power character stands out so sharply defined: "They be verye wyse and politicke, and can, thorowe ther wysdome, reform and brydell theyr owne natures for a tyme, and applye ther conditions to the manners of those men with whom they meddell gladlye by friendshippe; whose mischievous maners a man shall never know untyll he come under ther subjection; but then shall he parfectlye parceve and fele them: for in dissimulations untyll they have ther purposes, and afterwards in oppression and tyrannye, when they can obtain them, they do exceed all other nations upon the earthe."[1]

In the working out of this spirit, with all the indomitable courage and fanatical ardor derived from the long contests with the Moors, they reduced the native peoples to submission, but still not to the galling yoke which they fastened upon the aborigines of America, to make one Las Casas shine amid the horde of Pizarros. There was some compulsory labor in timber-cutting and ship-building, with enforced military service as rowers and soldiers for expeditions to the Moluccas and the coasts of Asia, but nowhere the unspeakable atrocities which in Mexico, Hispaniola, and South America drove mothers to strangle their babes at birth and whole tribes to prefer self-immolation to the living death in the mines and slave-pens. Quite differently from the case in America, where entire islands and districts were depopulated, to bring on later the curse of negro slavery, in the Philippines the fact appears that the

[1] Quoted by Macaulay: *Essay on the Succession in Spain.*

native population really increased and the standard of living was raised under the stern, yet beneficent, tutelage of the missionary fathers. The great distance and the hardships of the journey precluded the coming of many irresponsible adventurers from Spain and, fortunately for the native population, no great mineral wealth was ever discovered in the Philippine Islands.

The system of government was, in its essential features, a simple one. The missionary priests drew the inhabitants of the towns and villages about themselves or formed new settlements, and with profuse use of symbol and symbolism taught the people the Faith, laying particular stress upon "the fear of God," as administered by them, reconciling the people to their subjection by inculcating the Christian virtues of patience and humility. When any recalcitrants refused to accept the new order, or later showed an inclination to break away from it, the military forces, acting usually under secret directions from the padre, made raids in the disaffected parts with all the unpitying atrocity the Spanish soldiery were ever capable of displaying in their dealings with a weaker people. After sufficient punishment had been inflicted and a wholesome fear inspired, the padre very opportunely interfered in the natives' behalf, by which means they were convinced that peace and security lay in submission to the authorities, especially to the curate of their town or district. A single example will suffice to make the method clear: not an isolated instance but a typical case chosen from among the mass of records left by the chief actors themselves.

Fray Domingo Perez, evidently a man of courage and conviction, for he later lost his life in the work of which he wrote, was the Dominican vicar on the Zambales coast when that Order temporarily took over the district from the Recollects. In a report written for his superior in 1680 he outlines the method clearly: "In order that those whom we have assembled in the three villages may persevere in their settlements, the most efficacious fear and the one most suited to their nature is that the Spaniards of the fort and presidio of Paynaven[1] of whom

---

[1] The ruins of the *Fuerza de Playa Honda, ó Real de Paynavén*, are still to be seen in the present municipality of Botolan, Zambales. The walls are overgrown with rank vegetation, but are well preserved,

TRANSLATOR'S INTRODUCTION ix

they have a very great fear, may come very often to the said villages and overrun the land, and penetrate even into their old recesses where they formerly lived; and if perchance they should find anything planted in the said recesses that they would destroy it and cut it down without leaving them anything. And so that they may see the father protects them, when the said Spaniards come to the village, the father opposes them and takes the part of the Indians. But it is always necessary in this matter for the soldiers to conquer, and the father is always very careful always to inform the Spaniards by whom and where anything is planted which it may be necessary to destroy, and that the edicts which his Lordship, the governor, sent them be carried out. . . . But at all events said Spaniards are to make no trouble for the Indians whom they find in the villages, but rather must treat them well." [1]

This in 1680: the Dominican transcriber of the record in 1906 has added a very illuminating note, revealing the immutability of the system and showing that the rulers possessed in a superlative degree the Bourbonesque trait of learning nothing and forgetting nothing: "Even when I was a missionary to the heathens from 1882 to 1892, I had occasion to observe the said policy, to inform the chief of the fortress of the measures that he ought to take, and to make a false show on the other side so that it might have no influence on the fortress."

[Thus it stands out in bold relief as a system built up and maintained by fraud and force, bound in the course of nature to last only as long as the deception could be carried on and the repressive force kept up to sufficient strength.] Its maintenance required that the different sections be isolated from each other so that there could be no growth toward a common understanding and coöperation, and its permanence depended upon keeping the people ignorant and contented with their lot, held under strict control by religious and political fear.

Yet it was a vast improvement over their old mode of life

with the exception of a portion looking toward the Bankal River, which has been undermined by the currents and has fallen intact into the stream.

[1] *Relation of the Zambals*, by Domingo Perez, O. P.; manuscript dated 1680. The excerpts are taken from the translation in Blair and Robertson, *The Philippine Islands*, Vol. XLVII, by courtesy of the Arthur H. Clark Company, Cleveland, Ohio.

and their condition was bettered as they grew up to such a system. Only with the passing of the years and the increase of wealth and influence, the ease and luxury invited by these, and the consequent corruption so induced, with the insatiable longing ever for more wealth and greater influence, did the poison of greed and grasping power enter the system to work its insidious way into every part, slowly transforming the beneficent institution of the sixteenth and seventeenth centuries into an incubus weighing upon all the activities of the people in the nineteenth, an unyielding bar to the development of the country, a hideous anachronism in these modern times.

It must be remembered also that Spain, in the years following her brilliant conquests of the fifteenth and sixteenth centuries, lost strength and vigor through the corruption at home induced by the unearned wealth that flowed into the mother country from the colonies, and by the draining away of her best blood. Nor did her sons ever develop that economic spirit which is the permanent foundation of all empire, but they let the wealth of the Indies flow through their country, principally to London and Amsterdam, there to form in more practical hands the basis of the British and Dutch colonial empires.

The priest and the soldier were supreme, so her best sons took up either the cross or the sword to maintain her dominion in the distant colonies, a movement which, long continued, spelled for her a form of national suicide. The soldier expended his strength and generally laid down his life on alien soil, leaving no fit successor of his own stock to carry on the work according to his standards. The priest under the celibate system, in its better days left no offspring at all and in the days of its corruption none bred and reared under the influences that make for social and political progress. The dark chambers of the Inquisition stifled all advance in thought, so the civilization and the culture of Spain, as well as her political system, settled into rigid forms to await only the inevitable process of stagnation and decay. In her proudest hour an old soldier, who had lost one of his hands fighting her battles against the Turk at Lepanto, employed the other in writing the masterpiece of her literature, which is really a caricature of the nation.

There is much in the career of Spain that calls to mind the

dazzling beauty of her "dark-glancing daughters," with its early bloom, its startling — almost morbid — brilliance, and its premature decay. Rapid and brilliant was her rise, gradual and inglorious her steady decline, from the bright morning when the banners of Castile and Aragon were flung triumphantly from the battlements of the Alhambra, to the short summer, not so long gone, when at Cavite and Santiago with swift, decisive havoc the last ragged remnants of the once world-dominating power were blown into space and time, to hover disembodied there, a lesson and a warning to future generations. Whatever her final place in the records of mankind, whether as the pioneer of modern civilization or the buccaneer of the nations or, as would seem most likely, a goodly mixture of both, she has at least — with the exception only of her great mother, Rome — furnished the most instructive lessons in political pathology yet recorded, and the advice to students of world progress to familiarize themselves with her history is even more apt today than when it first issued from the encyclopedic mind of Macaulay nearly a century ago. Hardly had she reached the zenith of her power when the disintegration began, and one by one her brilliant conquests dropped away, to leave her alone in her faded splendor, with naught but her vaunting pride left, another "Niobe of nations." In the countries more in contact with the trend of civilization and more susceptible to revolutionary influences from the mother country this separation came from within, while in the remoter parts the archaic and outgrown system dragged along until a stronger force from without destroyed it.

Nowhere was the crystallization of form and principle more pronounced than in religious life, which fastened upon the mother country a deadening weight that hampered all progress, and in the colonies, notably in the Philippines, virtually converted her government into a hagiarchy that had its face toward the past and either could not or would not move with the current of the times. So, when "the shot heard round the world," the declaration of humanity's right to be and to become, in its all-encircling sweep, reached the lands controlled by her it was coldly received and blindly rejected by the governing powers, and there was left only the slower, subtler, but none the less sure, process of working its way among the people to burst in time in rebellion and the destruction of the conservative forces that would repress it.

In the opening years of the nineteenth century the friar orders in the Philippines had reached the apogee of their power and usefulness. Their influence was everywhere felt and acknowledged, while the country still prospered under the effects of the vigorous and progressive administrations of Anda and Vargas in the preceding century. Native levies had fought loyally under Spanish leadership against Dutch and British invaders, or in suppressing local revolts among their own people, which were always due to some specific grievance, never directed definitely against the Spanish sovereignty. The Philippines were shut off from contact with any country but Spain, and even this communication was restricted and carefully guarded. There was an elaborate central government which, however, hardly touched the life of the native peoples, who were guided and governed by the parish priests, each town being in a way an independent entity.

Of this halcyon period, just before the process of disintegration began, there has fortunately been left a record which may be characterized as the most notable Spanish literary production relating to the Philippines, being the calm, sympathetic, judicial account of one who had spent his manhood in the work there and who, full of years and experience, sat down to tell the story of their life.[1] In it there are no puerile whinings, no querulous curses that tropical Malays do not order their lives as did the people of the Spanish village where he may have been reared, no selfish laments of ingratitude over blessings unasked and only imperfectly understood by the natives, no fatuous self-deception as to the real conditions, but a patient consideration of the difficulties encountered, the

---

[1] "*Estadismo de las Islas Filipinas, ó Mis Viages por Este Pais*, por Fray Joaquin Martinez de Zuñiga, Agustino calzado." Padre Zuñiga was a parish priest in several towns and later Provincial of his Order. He wrote a history of the conquest, and in 1800 accompanied Alava, the *General de Marina*, on his tours of investigation looking toward preparations for the defense of the islands against another attack of the British, with whom war threatened. The *Estadismo*, which is a record of these journeys, with some account of the rest of the islands, remained in manuscript until 1893, when it was published in Madrid.

good accomplished, and the unavoidable evils incident to any human work. The country and the people, too, are described with the charming simplicity of the eyes that see clearly, the brain that ponders deeply, and the heart that beats sympathetically. Through all the pages of his account runs the quiet strain of peace and contentment, of satisfaction with the existing order, for he had looked upon the creation and saw that it was good. There is "neither haste, nor hate, nor anger," but the deliberate recital of the facts warmed and illumined by the geniality of a soul to whom age and experience had brought, not a sour cynicism, but the mellowing influence of a ripened philosophy. He was such an old man as may fondly be imagined walking through the streets of Parañaque in stately benignity amid the fear and respect of the brown people over whom he watched.

But in all his chronicle there is no suggestion of anything more to hope for, anything beyond. Beautiful as the picture is, it is that of a system which had reached maturity: a condition of stagnation, not of growth. In less than a decade, the terrific convulsions in European politics made themselves felt even in the remote Philippines, and then began the gradual drawing away of the people from their rulers — blind gropings and erratic wanderings at first, but nevertheless persistent and vigorous tendencies.

The first notable influence was the admission of representatives for the Philippines into the Spanish Cortes under the revolutionary governments and the abolition of the trade monopoly with Mexico. The last galleon reached Manila in 1815, and soon foreign commercial interests were permitted, in a restricted way, to enter the country. Then with the separation of Mexico and the other American colonies from Spain a more marked change was brought about in that direct communication was established with the mother country, and the absolutism of the hagiarchy first questioned by the numbers of Peninsular Spaniards who entered the islands to trade, some even to settle and rear families there. These also affected the native population in the larger centers by the spread of their ideas, which were not always in conformity with those that for several centuries the friars had been inculcating into their wards. Moreover, there was a not-inconsiderable portion of the population, sprung from the friars themselves, who were eager to adopt the customs and ideas of the Spanish immigrants.

The suppression of many of the monasteries in Spain in 1835 caused a large influx of the disestablished monks into the Philippines in search for a haven and a home, thus bringing about a conflict with the native clergy, who were displaced from their best holdings to provide berths for the newcomers. At the same time, the increase of education among the native priests brought the natural demand for more equitable treatment by the Spanish friar, so insistent that it even broke out into open rebellion in 1843 on the part of a young Tagalog who thought himself aggrieved in this respect.

Thus the struggle went on, with stagnation above and some growth below, so that the governors were ever getting further away from the governed, and for such a movement there is in the course of nature but one inevitable result, especially when outside influences are actively at work penetrating the social system and making for better things. Among these influences four cumulative ones may be noted: the spread of journalism, the introduction of steamships into the Philippines, the return of the Jesuits, and the opening of the Suez Canal.

The printing-press entered the islands with the conquest, but its use had been strictly confined to religious works until about the middle of the past century, when there was a sudden awakening and within a few years five journals were being published. In 1848 appeared the first regular newspaper of importance, *El Diario de Manila,* and about a decade later the principal organ of the Spanish-Filipino population, *El Comercio,* which, with varying vicissitudes, has continued down to the present. While rigorously censored, both politically and religiously, and accessible to only an infinitesimal portion of the people, they still performed the service of letting a few rays of light into the Cimmerian intellectual gloom of the time and place.

With the coming of steam navigation communication between the different parts of the islands was facilitated and trade encouraged, with all that such a change meant in the way of breaking up the old isolation and tending to a common understanding. Spanish power, too, was for the moment more firmly established, and Moro piracy in Luzon and the Bisayan

Islands, which had been so great a drawback to the development of the country, was forever ended.

The return of the Jesuits produced two general results tending to dissatisfaction with the existing order. To them was assigned the missionary field of Mindanao, which meant the displacement of the Recollect Fathers in the missions there, and for these other berths had to be found. Again the native clergy were the losers in that they had to give up their best parishes in Luzon, especially around Manila and Cavite, so the breach was further widened and the soil sown with discontent. But more far-reaching than this immediate result was the educational movement inaugurated by the Jesuits. The native, already feeling the vague impulses from without and stirred by the growing restlessness of the times, here saw a new world open before him. A considerable portion of the native population in the larger centers, who had shared in the economic progress of the colony, were enabled to look beyond their daily needs and to afford their children an opportunity for study and advancement — a condition and a need met by the Jesuits for a time.

With the opening of the Suez Canal in 1869 communication with the mother country became cheaper, quicker, surer, so that large numbers of Spaniards, many of them in sympathy with the republican movements at home, came to the Philippines in search of fortunes and generally left half-caste families who had imbibed their ideas. Native boys who had already felt the intoxication of such learning as the schools of Manila afforded them began to dream of greater wonders in Spain, now that the journey was possible for them. So began the definite movements that led directly to the disintegration of the friar régime.

In the same year occurred the revolution in the mother country, which had tired of the old corrupt despotism. Isabella II was driven into exile and the country left to waver about uncertainly for several years, passing through all the stages of government from red radicalism to absolute conservatism, finally adjusting itself to the middle course of constitutional monarchism. During the effervescent and ephemeral republic there was sent to the Philippines a governor who set to work to modify the old system and establish a government more in harmony with modern ideas and more democratic in form. His changes were hailed with delight by the growing class of Filipinos who were striving for more consideration in their own country, and who, in their enthusiasm and the intoxication of the moment, perhaps became more radical than was safe under the conditions — surely too radical for their religious guides watching and waiting behind the veil of the temple.

In January, 1872, an uprising occurred in the naval arsenal at Cavite, with a Spanish non-commissioned officer as one of the leaders. From the meager evidence now obtainable, this would seem to have been purely a local mutiny over the service questions of pay and treatment, but in it the friars saw their opportunity. It was blazoned forth, with all the wild panic that was to characterize the actions of the governing powers from that time on, as the premature outbreak of a general insurrection under the leadership of the native clergy, and rigorous repressive measures were demanded. Three native priests, notable for their popularity among their own people, one an octogenarian and the other two young canons of the Manila Cathedral, were summarily garroted, along with the renegade Spanish officer who had participated in the mutiny. No record of any trial of these priests has ever been brought to light. The Archbishop, himself a secular [1] clergyman, stoutly refused to degrade them from their holy office, and they wore their sacerdotal robes at the execution, which was conducted in a hurried, fearful manner. At the same time a number of young Manilans who had taken conspicuous part in the "liberal" demonstrations were deported to the Ladrone Islands or to remote islands of the Philippine group itself.

This was the beginning of the end. Yet there immediately followed the delusive calm which ever precedes the fatal outburst, lulling those marked for destruction to a delusive security. The two decades following were years of quiet, unobtrusive growth, during which the Philippine Islands made the greatest economic progress in their history. But this in itself was preparing the final catastrophe, for if there be any fact well established in human experience it is that with

[1] Secular, as distinguished from the regulars, i. e., members of the monastic orders.

economic development the power of organized religion begins to wane — the rise of the merchant spells the decline of the priest. A sordid change, from masses and mysteries to sugar and shoes, this is often said to be, but it should be noted that the epochs of greatest economic activity have been those during which the generality of mankind have lived fuller and freer lives, and above all that in such eras the finest intellects and the grandest souls have been developed.

Nor does an institution that has been slowly growing for three centuries, molding the very life and fiber of the people, disintegrate without a violent struggle, either in its own constitution or in the life of the people trained under it. Not only the ecclesiastical but also the social and political system of the country was controlled by the religious orders, often silently and secretly, but none the less effectively. This is evident from the ceaseless conflict that went on between the religious orders and the Spanish political administrators, who were at every turn thwarted in their efforts to keep the government abreast of the times.

The shock of the affair of 1872 had apparently stunned the Filipinos, but it had at the same time brought them to the parting of the ways and induced a vague feeling that there was something radically wrong, which could only be righted by a closer union among themselves. They began to consider that their interests and those of the governing powers were not the same. In these feelings of distrust toward the friars they were stimulated by the great numbers of immigrant Spaniards who were then entering the country, many of whom had taken part in the republican movements at home and who, upon the restoration of the monarchy, no doubt thought it safer for them to be at as great a distance as possible from the throne. The young Filipinos studying in Spain came from different parts of the islands, and by their association there in a foreign land were learning to forget their narrow sectionalism; hence the way was being prepared for some concerted action. Thus, aided and encouraged by the anti-clerical Spaniards in the mother country, there was growing up a new generation of native leaders, who looked toward something better than the old system.

It is with this period in the history of the country — the

author's boyhood — that the story of *Noli Me Tangere* deals. Typical scenes and characters are sketched from life with wonderful accuracy, and the picture presented is that of a master-mind, who knew and loved his subject. Terror and repression were the order of the day, with ever a growing unrest in the higher circles, while the native population at large seemed to be completely cowed — "brutalized" is the term repeatedly used by Rizal in his political essays. Spanish writers of the period, observing only the superficial movements, — some of which were indeed fantastical enough, for

> "they,
> Who in oppression's darkness caved have dwelt,
> They are not eagles, nourished with the day;
> What marvel, then, at times, if they mistake their way?"

— and not heeding the currents at work below, take great delight in ridiculing the pretensions of the young men seeking advancement, while they indulge in coarse ribaldry over the wretched condition of the great mass of the "Indians." The author, however, himself a "miserable Indian," vividly depicts the unnatural conditions and dominant characters produced under the outworn system of fraud and force, at the same time presenting his people as living, feeling, struggling individuals, with all the frailties of human nature and all the possibilities of mankind, either for good or evil; incidentally he throws into marked contrast the despicable depreciation used by the Spanish writers in referring to the Filipinos, making clear the application of the self-evident proposition that no ordinary human being in the presence of superior force can very well conduct himself as a man unless he be treated as such.

The friar orders, deluded by their transient triumph and secure in their pride of place, became more arrogant, more domineering than ever. In the general administration the political rulers were at every turn thwarted, their best efforts frustrated, and if they ventured too far their own security threatened; for in the three-cornered wrangle which lasted throughout the whole of the Spanish domination, the friar orders had, in addition to the strength derived from their organization and their wealth, the Damoclean weapon of control over the natives to hang above the heads of both governor and archbishop. The curates in the towns, always the real rulers, became veritable despots, so that no voice dared to raise itself against them, even in the midst of conditions which the humblest *indio* was beginning to feel dumbly to be perverted and unnatural, and that, too, after three centuries of training under the system that he had ever been taught to accept as "the will of God."

The friars seemed long since to have forgotten those noble aims that had meant so much to the founders and early workers of their orders, if indeed the great majority of those of the later day had ever realized the meaning of their office, for the Spanish writers of the time delight in characterizing them as the meanest of the Spanish peasantry, when not something worse, who had been "lassoed," taught a few ritualistic prayers, and shipped to the Philippines to be placed in isolated towns as lords and masters of the native population, with all the power and prestige over a docile people that the sacredness of their holy office gave them. These writers treat the matter lightly, seeing in it rather a huge joke on the "miserable Indians," and give the friars great credit for "patriotism," a term which in this connection they dragged from depth to depth until it quite aptly fitted Dr. Johnson's famous definition, "the last refuge of a scoundrel."

In their conduct the religious corporations, both as societies and as individuals, must be estimated according to their own standards — the application of any other criterion would be palpably unfair. They undertook to hold the native in subjection, to regulate the essential activities of his life according to their ideas, so upon them must fall the responsibility for the conditions finally attained: to destroy the freedom of the subject and then attempt to blame him for his conduct is a paradox into which the learned men often fell, perhaps inadvertently through their deductive logic. They endeavored to shape the lives of their Malay wards not only in this existence but also in the next. Their vows were poverty, chastity, and obedience.

The vow of poverty was early relegated to the limbo of neglect. Only a few years after the founding of Manila royal decrees began to issue on the subject of complaints received by the King over the usurpation of lands on the part of the priests. Using the same methods so familiar in the heyday of the institution of monasticism in Europe — pious gifts, death-bed bequests, pilgrims' offerings — the friar orders gradually secured the richest of the arable lands in the more thickly settled portions of the Philippines, notably the part of Luzon occupied by the Tagalogs. Not always, however, it must in justice be recorded, were such doubtful means resorted to, for there were instances where the missionary was the pioneer, gathering about himself a band of devoted natives and plunging into the unsettled parts to build up a town with its fields around it, which would later become a friar estate. With the accumulated incomes from these estates and the fees for religious observances that poured into their treasuries, the orders in their nature of perpetual corporations became the masters of the situation, the lords of the country. But this condition was not altogether objectionable; it was in the excess of their greed that they went astray, for the native peoples had been living under this system through generations and not until they began to feel that they were not receiving fair treatment did they question the authority of a power which not only secured them a peaceful existence in this life but also assured them eternal felicity in the next.

With only the shining exceptions that are produced in any system, no matter how false its premises or how decadent it may become, to uphold faith in the intrinsic soundness of human nature, the vow of chastity was never much more than a myth. Through the tremendous influence exerted over a fanatically religious people, who implicitly followed the teachings of the reverend fathers, once their confidence had been secured, the curate was seldom to be gainsaid in his desires. By means of the secret influence in the confessional and the more open political power wielded by him, the fairest was his to command, and the favored one and her people looked upon the choice more as an honor than otherwise, for besides the social standing that it gave her there was the proud prospect of becoming the mother of children who could claim kinship with the dominant race. The curate's "companion" or the sacristan's wife was a power in the community, her family was raised to a place of importance and influence among their own people, while she and her ecclesiastical offspring were well cared for. On the death or removal of the curate, it was almost invariably found that she had been provided with a husband or protector and a not inconsiderable amount of property — an arrangement rather appealing to a people among whom the means of living have ever been so insecure.

That this practise was not particularly offensive to the people among whom they dwelt may explain the situation, but to claim that it excuses the friars approaches dangerously close to casuistry. Still, as long as this arrangement was decently and moderately carried out, there seems to have been no great objection, nor from a worldly point of view, with all the conditions considered, could there be much. But the old story of excess, of unbridled power turned toward bad ends, again recurs, at the same time that the ideas brought in by the Spaniards who came each year in increasing numbers and the principles observed by the young men studying in Europe cast doubt upon the fitness of such a state of affairs. As they approached their downfall, like all mankind, the friars became more open, more insolent, more shameless, in their conduct.

The story of Maria Clara, as told in *Noli Me Tangere,* is by no means an exaggerated instance, but rather one of the few clean enough to bear the light, and her fate, as depicted in the epilogue, is said to be based upon an actual occurrence with which the author must have been familiar.

The vow of obedience — whether considered as to the Pope, their highest religious authority, or to the King of Spain, their political liege — might not always be so callously disregarded, but it could be evaded and defied. From the Vatican came bull after bull, from the Escorial decree after decree, only to be archived in Manila, sometimes after a hollow pretense of compliance. A large part of the records of Spanish domination is taken up with the wearisome quarrels that went on between the Archbishop, representing the head of the Church, and the friar orders, over the questions of the episcopal visitation and the enforcement of the provisions of the Council of Trent relegating the monks to their original status of missionaries, with the friars invariably victorious in their contentions. Royal decrees ordering inquiries into the titles to the estates of the men of poverty and those providing for the education of the natives in Spanish were merely sneered at and left to molder in harmless quiet. Not without good grounds for his contention, the friar claimed that the Spanish dominion over the Philippines depended upon him, and he therefore confidently set himself up as the best judge of how that dominion should be maintained.

Thus there are presented in the Philippines of the closing quarter of the century just past the phenomena so frequently met with in modern societies, so disheartening to the people who must drag out their lives under them, of an old system which has outworn its usefulness and is being called into question, with forces actively at work disintegrating it, yet with the unhappy folk bred and reared under it unprepared for a new order of things. The old faith was breaking down, its forms and beliefs, once so full of life and meaning, were being sharply examined, doubt and suspicion were the order of the day. Moreover, it must ever be borne in mind that in the Philippines this unrest, except in the parts where the friars were the landlords, was not general among the people, the masses of whom were still sunk in their "loved Egyptian night," but affected only a very small proportion of the poulation — for the most part young men who were groping their way toward something better, yet without any very clearly conceived idea of what that better might be, and among whom was to be found the usual sprinkling of "sunshine patriots" and omnipresent opportunists ready for any kind of trouble that will afford them a chance to rise.

Add to the apathy of the masses dragging out their vacant lives amid the shadows of religious superstition and to the unrest of the few, the fact that the orders were in absolute control of the political machinery of the country, with the best part of the agrarian wealth amortized in their hands; add also the ever-present jealousies, petty feuds, and racial hatreds, for which Manila and the Philippines, with their medley of creeds and races, offer such a fertile field, all fostered by the governing class for the maintenance of the old Machiavelian principle of "divide and rule," and the sum is about the most miserable condition under which any portion of mankind ever tried to fulfil nature's inexorable laws of growth.

II

> And third came she who gives dark creeds their power,
> Silabbat-paramasa, sorceress,
> Draped fair in many lands as lowly Faith,
> But ever juggling souls with rites and prayers;
> The keeper of those keys which lock up Hells
> And open Heavens. "Wilt thou dare," she said,
> "Put by our sacred books, dethrone our gods,
> Unpeople all the temples, shaking down
> That law which feeds the priests and props the realm?"
> But Buddha answered, "What thou bidd'st me keep
> Is form which passes, but the free Truth stands;
> Get thee unto thy darkness."
> SIR EDWIN ARNOLD, *The Light of Asia.*

"Ah, simple people, how little do you know the blessing that you enjoy! Neither hunger, nor nakedness, nor inclemency of the weather troubles you. With the payment of seven reals per year, you remain free of contributions. You do not have to close your houses with bolts. You do not fear that the district troopers will come in to lay waste your fields, and trample you under foot at your own firesides. You call 'father' the one who is in command over you. Perhaps there will come a time when you will be more civilized, and you will break out in revolution; and you will wake terrified at the tumult of the riots, and will see blood flowing through these quiet fields, and gallows and guillotines erected in these squares, which never yet have seen an execution."[1] Thus moralized a Spanish traveler in 1842, just as that *dolce far niente* was drawing to its close. Already far-seeing men had begun to raise in the Spanish parliament the question of the future of the Philippines, looking toward some definite program for their care under modern conditions and for the adjustment of their

---

[1] Sinibaldo de Mas, *Informe sobre el estado de las Islas Filipinas en 1842*, translated in Blair and Robertson's *The Philippine Islands*, Vol. XXVIII, p. 254.

xxiv TRANSLATOR'S INTRODUCTION

relations with the mother country. But these were mere Cassandra-voices — the horologe of time was striking for Rome's successor, as it did for Rome herself.

Just where will come the outbreak after three centuries of mind-repression and soul-distortion, of forcing a growing subjcet into the strait-jacket of medieval thought and action, of natural selection reversed by the constant elimination of native initiative and leadership, is indeed a curious study. That there will be an outbreak somewhere is as certain as that the plant will grow toward the light, even under the most unfavorable conditions, for man's nature is but the resultant of eternal forces that ceaselessly and irresistibly interplay about and upon him, and somewhere this resultant will express itself in thought or deed.

After three centuries of Spanish ecclesiastical domination in the Philippines, it was to be expected that the wards would turn against their mentors the methods that had been used upon them, nor is it especially remarkable that there was a decided tendency in some parts to revert to primitive barbarism, but that concurrently a creative genius — a bard or seer — should have been developed among a people who, as a whole, have hardly passed through the clan or village stage of society, can be regarded as little less than a psychological phenomenon, and provokes the perhaps presumptuous inquiry as to whether there may not be some things about our common human nature that the learned doctors have not yet included in their anthropometric diagrams.

On the western shore of the Lake of Bay in the heart of the Philippines clusters the village of Kalamba, first established by the Jesuit Fathers in the early days of the conquest, and upon their expulsion in 1767 taken over by the Crown, which later transferred it to the Dominicans, under whose care the fertile fields about it became one of the richest of the friar estates. It can hardly be called a town, even for the Philippines, but is rather a market-village, set as it is at the outlet of the rich country of northern Batangas on the open waterway to Manila and the outside world. Around it flourish the green rice-fields, while Mount Makiling towers majestically near in her moods of cloud and sunshine, overlooking the picturesque curve of the shore and the rippling waters of the lake. Shadowy to the eastward gleam the purple crests of Banahao and Cristobal, and but a few miles to the southwestward dim-thundering, seething, earth-rocking Taal mutters and moans of the world's birth-throes. It is the center of a region rich in native lore and legend, as it sleeps through the dusty noons when the cacao leaves droop with the heat and dreams through the silvery nights, waking twice or thrice a week to the endless babble and ceaseless chatter of an Oriental market where the noisy throngs make of their trading as much a matter of pleasure and recreation as of business.

Directly opposite this market-place, in a house facing the village church, there was born in 1861 into the already large family of one of the more prosperous tenants on the Dominican estate a boy who was to combine in his person the finest traits of the Oriental character with the best that Spanish and European culture could add, on whom would fall the burden of his people's woes to lead him over the *via dolorosa* of struggle and sacrifice, ending in his own destruction amid the crumbling ruins of the system whose disintegration he himself had done so much to compass.

José Rizal-Mercado y Alonso, as his name emerges from the confusion of Filipino nomenclature, was of Malay extraction, with some distant strains of Spanish and Chinese blood. His genealogy reveals several persons remarkable for intellect and independence of character, notably a Philippine Eloise and Abelard, who, drawn together by their common enthusiasm for study and learning, became his maternal grandparents, as well as a great-uncle who was a traveler and student and who directed the boy's early studies. Thus from the beginning his training was exceptional, while his mind was stirred by the trouble already brewing in his community, and from the earliest hours of consciousness he saw about him the wrongs and injustices which overgrown power will ever develop in dealing with a weaker subject. One fact of his childhood, too, stands out clearly, well worthy of record: his mother seems to have been a woman of more than ordinary education for the time and place, and, pleased with the boy's quick intelligence, she taught him to read Spanish from a copy of the Vulgate in that language, which she had somehow managed to secure and keep in her possession — the old, old

omnivorous reading. He was associated with the other Filipinos who were working in a somewhat spectacular way, misdirected rather than led by what may be styled the Spanish liberals, for more considerate treatment of the Philippines. But while he was among them he was not of them, as his studious habits and reticent disposition would hardly have made him a favorite among those who were enjoying the broader and gayer life there. Moreover, he soon advanced far beyond them in thought by realizing that they were beginning at the wrong end of the labor, for even at that time he seems to have caught, by what must almost be looked upon as an inspiration of genius, since there was nothing apparent in his training that would have suggested it, the realization of the fact that hope for his people lay in bettering their condition, that any real benefit must begin with the benighted folk at home, that the introduction of reforms for which they were unprepared would be useless, even dangerous to them. This was not at all the popular idea among his associates and led to serious disagreements with their leaders, for it was the way of toil and sacrifice without any of the excitement and glamour that came from drawing up magnificent plans and sending them back home with appeals for funds to carry on the propaganda — for the most part banquets and entertainments to Spain's political leaders.

His views, as revealed in his purely political writings, may be succinctly stated, for he had that faculty of expression which never leaves any room for doubt as to the meaning. His people had a natural right to grow and to develop, and any obstacles to such growth and development were to be removed. He realized that the masses of his countrymen were sunk deep in poverty and ignorance, cringing and crouching before political authority, crawling and groveling before religious superstition, but to him this was no subject for jest or indifferent neglect — it was a serious condition which should be ameliorated, and hope lay in working into the inert social mass the leaven of conscious individual effort toward the development of a distinctive, responsible personality. He was profoundly appreciative of all the good that Spain had done, but saw in this no inconsistency with the desire that this gratitude might be given cause to be ever on the increase, thereby uniting the Philippines with the mother country by

Sue's *The Wandering Jew,* while he was a student in Madrid, although the model for the greater part of it is plainly the delectable sketches in *Don Quixote,* for the author himself possessed in a remarkable degree that Cervantic touch which raises the commonplace, even the mean, into the highest regions of art. Not, however, until he had spent some time in Paris continuing his medical studies, and later in Germany, did anything definite result. But in 1887 *Noli Me Tangere* was printed in Berlin, in an establishment where the author is said to have worked part of his time as a compositor in order to defray his expenses while he continued his studies. A limited edition was published through the financial aid extended by a Filipino associate, and sent to Hongkong, thence to be surreptitiously introduced into the Philippines.

Noli Me Tangere ("Touch Me Not") at the time the work was written had a peculiar fitness as a title. Not only was there an apt suggestion of a comparison with the common flower of that name, but the term is also applied in pathology to a malignant cancer which affects every bone and tissue in the body, and that this latter was in the author's mind would appear from the dedication and from the summing-up of the Philippine situation in the final conversation between Ibarra and Elias. But in a letter written to a friend in Paris at the time, the author himself says that it was taken from the Gospel scene where the risen Savior appears to the Magdalene, to whom He addresses these words, a scene that has been the subject of several notable paintings.

In this connection it is interesting to note what he himself thought of the work, and his frank statement of what he had tried to accomplish, made just as he was publishing it: "*Noli Me Tangere,* an expression taken from the Gospel of St. Luke,[1] means *touch me not.* The book contains things of which no one up to the present time has spoken, for they are so sensitive that they have never suffered themselves to be touched by any one whomsoever. For my own part, I have attempted to do what no one else has been willing to do: I have dared to answer the calumnies that have for centuries been heaped upon us and our country. I have written of the social condition and the life,

---

[1] *Sic.* St. John xx, 17.

of our beliefs, our hopes, our longings, our complaints, and our sorrows; I have unmasked the hypocrisy which, under the cloak of religion, has come among us to impoverish and to brutalize us; I have distinguished the true religion from the false, from the superstition that traffics with the holy word to get money and to make us believe in absurdities for which Catholicism would blush, if ever it knew of them. I have unveiled that which has been hidden behind the deceptive and dazzling words of our governments. I have told our countrymen of our mistakes, our vices, our faults, and our weak complaisance with our miseries there. Where I have found virtue I have spoken of it highly in order to render it homage; and if I have not wept in speaking of our misfortunes, I have laughed over them, for no one would wish to weep with me over our woes, and laughter is ever the best means of concealing sorrow. The deeds that I have related are true and have actually occurred; I can furnish proof of this. My book may have (and it does have) defects from an artistic and esthetic point of view — this I do not deny — but no one can dispute the veracity of the facts presented." [1]

But while the primary purpose and first effect of the work was to crystallize anti-friar sentiment, the author has risen above a mere personal attack, which would give it only a temporary value, and by portraying in so clear and sympathetic a way the life of his people has produced a piece of real literature, of especial interest now as they are being swept into the newer day. Any fool can point out errors and defects, if they are at all apparent, and the persistent searching them out for their own sake is the surest mark of the vulpine mind, but the author has cast aside all such petty considerations and, whether consciously or not, has left a work of permanent value to his own people and of interest to all friends of humanity. If ever a fair land has been cursed with the wearisome breed of fault-finders, both indigenous and exotic, that land is the Philippines, so it is indeed refreshing to turn from the dreary waste of carping criticisms, pragmatical " scientific " analyses, and sneering half-truths to a story pulsating with life, present-

[1] This letter in the original French in which it was written is reproduced in the *Vida y Escritos del Dr. José Rizal*, by W. E. Retana (Madrid, 1907).

ing the Filipino as a human being, with his virtues and his vices, his loves and hates, his hopes and fears.

The publication of *Noli Me Tangere* suggests the reflection that the story of Achilles' heel is a myth only in form. The belief that any institution, system, organization, or arrangement has reached an absolute form is about as far as human folly can go. The friar orders looked upon themselves as the sum of human achievement in man-driving and God-persuading, divinely appointed to rule, fixed in their power, far above suspicion. Yet they were obsessed by the sensitive, covert dread of exposure that ever lurks spectrally under pharisaism's specious robe, so when there appeared this work of a " miserable Indian," who dared to portray them and the conditions that their control produced exactly as they were — for the indefinable touch by which the author gives an air of unimpeachable veracity to his story is perhaps its greatest artistic merit — the effect upon the mercurial Spanish temperament was, to say the least, electric. The very audacity of the thing left the friars breathless.

A committee of learned doctors from Santo Tomas, who were appointed to examine the work, unmercifully scored it as attacking everything from the state religion to the integrity of the Spanish dominions, so the circulation of it in the Philippines was, of course, strictly prohibited, which naturally made the demand for it greater. Large sums were paid for single copies, of which, it might be remarked in passing, the author himself received scarcely any part; collections have ever had a curious habit of going astray in the Philippines.

Although the possession of a copy by a Filipino usually meant summary imprisonment or deportation, often with the concomitant confiscation of property for the benefit of some " patriot," the book was widely read among the leading families and had the desired effect of crystallizing the sentiment against the friars, thus to pave the way for concerted action. At last the idol had been flouted, so all could attack it. Within a year after it had begun to circulate in the Philippines a memorial was presented to the Archbishop by quite a respectable part of the Filipinos in Manila, requesting that the friar orders be expelled from the country, but this resulted only in the deportation of every signer of the petition upon whom the government could lay hands. They were scattered literally to the four corners of the earth: some to the Ladrone Islands, some to Fernando Po off the west coast of Africa, some to Spanish prisons, others to remote parts of the Philippines.

Meanwhile, the author had returned to the Philippines for a visit to his family, during which time he was constantly attended by an officer of the Civil Guard, detailed ostensibly as a body-guard. All his movements were closely watched, and after a few months the Captain-General "advised" him to leave the country, at the same time requesting a copy of *Noli Me Tangere,* saying that the excerpts submitted to him by the censor had awakened a desire to read the entire work. Rizal returned to Europe by way of Japan and the United States, which did not seem to make any distinct impression upon him, although it was only a little later that he predicted that when Spain lost control of the Philippines, an eventuality he seemed to consider certain not far in the future, the United States would be a probable successor.[1]

Returning to Europe, he spent some time in London preparing an edition of Morga's *Sucesos de las Filipinas,* a work published in Mexico about 1606 by the principal actor in some of the most stirring scenes of the formative period of the Philippine government. It is a record of prime importance in Philippine history, and the resuscitation of it was no small service to the country. Rizal added notes tending to show that the Filipinos had been possessed of considerable culture and civilization before the Spanish conquest, and he even intimated that they had retrograded rather than advanced under Spanish tutelage. But such an extreme view must be ascribed to patriotic ardor, for Rizal himself, though possessed of that intangible quality commonly known as genius and partly trained in northern Europe, is still in his own personality the strongest refutation of such a contention.

Later, in Ghent, he published *El Filibusterismo,* called by him a continuation of *Noli Me Tangere,* but with which it really has no more connection than that some of the characters

[1] *Filipinas dentro de Cien Años,* published in the organ of the Filipinos in Spain, *La Solidaridad,* in 1889-90. This is the most studied of Rizal's purely political writings, and the completest exposition of his views concerning the Philippines.

reappear and are disposed of.[1] There is almost no connected plot in it and hardly any action, but there is the same incisive character-drawing and clear etching of conditions that characterize the earlier work. It is a maturer effort and a more forceful political argument, hence it lacks the charm and simplicity which assign *Noli Me Tangere* to a preëminent place in Philippine literature. The light satire of the earlier work is replaced by bitter sarcasm delivered with deliberate intent, for the iron had evidently entered his soul with broadening experience and the realization that justice at the hands of decadent Spain had been an iridescent dream of his youth. Nor had the Spanish authorities in the Philippines been idle; his relatives had been subjected to all the annoyances and irritations of petty persecution, eventually losing the greater part of their property, while some of them suffered deportation.

In 1891 he returned to Hongkong to practise medicine, in which profession he had remarkable success, even coming to be looked upon as a wizard by his simple countrymen, among whom circulated wonderful accounts of his magical powers. He was especially skilled in ophthalmology, and his first operation after returning from his studies in Europe was to restore his mother's sight by removing a cataract from one of her eyes, an achievement which no doubt formed the basis of marvelous tales. But the misfortunes of his people were ever the paramount consideration, so he wrote to the Captain-General requesting permission to remove his numerous relatives to Borneo to establish a colony there, for which purpose liberal concessions had been offered him by the British government. The request was denied, and further stigmatized as an "unpatriotic" attempt to lessen the population of the Philippines, when labor was already scarce. This was the answer he received to a reasonable petition after the homes of his family, including his own birthplace, had been ruthlessly destroyed by military force, while a quarrel over ownership and rents was still pending in the courts. The Captain-General at the time was Valeriano Weyler, the pitiless instrument of the reactionary forces manipulated by the monastic orders, he who

[1] An English version of *El Filibusterismo*, under the title *The Reign of Greed*, has been prepared to accompany the present work.

was later sent to Cuba to introduce there the repressive measures which had apparently been so efficacious in the Philippines, thus to bring on the interference of the United States to end Spain's colonial power — all of which induces the reflection that there may still be deluded casuists who doubt the reality of Nemesis.

Weyler was succeeded by Eulogio Despujols, who made sincere attempts to reform the administration, and was quite popular with the Filipinos. In reply to repeated requests from Rizal to be permitted to return to the Philippines unmolested a passport was finally granted to him and he set out for Manila. For this move on his part, in addition to the natural desire to be among his own people, two special reasons appear: he wished to investigate and stop if possible the unwarranted use of his name in taking up collections that always remained mysteriously unaccounted for, and he was drawn by a ruse deliberately planned and executed in that his mother was several times officiously arrested and hustled about as a common criminal in order to work upon the son's filial feelings and thus get him back within reach of the Spanish authority, which, as subsequent events and later researches have shown, was the real intention in issuing the passport. Entirely unsuspecting any ulterior motive, however, in a few days after his arrival he convoked a motley gathering of Filipinos of all grades of the population, for he seems to have been only slightly acquainted among his own people and not at all versed in the mazy Walpurgis dance of Philippine politics, and laid before it the constitution for a *Liga Filipina* (Philippine League), an organization looking toward greater unity among the Filipinos and coöperation for economic progress. This *Liga* was no doubt the result of his observations in England and Germany, and, despite its questionable form as a secret society for political and economic purposes, was assuredly a step in the right direction, but unfortunately its significance was beyond the comprehension of his countrymen, most of whom saw in it only an opportunity for harassing the Spanish government, for which all were ready enough.

All his movements were closely watched, and a few days after his return he was arrested on the charge of having seditious literature in his baggage. The friars were already clamoring for his blood, but Despujols seems to have been more in sympathy with Rizal than with the men whose tool he found himself forced to be. Without trial Rizal was ordered deported to Dapitan, a small settlement on the northern coast of Mindanao. The decree ordering this deportation and the destruction of all copies of his books to be found in the Philippines is a marvel of sophistry, since, in the words of a Spanish writer of the time, " in this document we do not know which to wonder at most: the ingenuousness of the Governor-General, for in this decree he implicitly acknowledges his weakness and proneness to error, or the candor of Rizal, who believed that all the way was strewn with roses."[1] But it is quite evident that Despujols was playing a double game, of which he seems to have been rather ashamed, for he gave strict orders that copies of the decree should be withheld from Rizal.

In Dapitan Rizal gave himself up to his studies and such medical practice as sought him out in that remote spot, for the fame of his skill was widely extended, and he was allowed to live unmolested under parole that he would make no attempt to escape. In company with a Jesuit missionary he gathered about him a number of native boys and conducted a practical school on the German plan, at the same time indulging in religious polemics with his Jesuit acquaintances by correspondence and working fitfully on some compositions which were never completed, noteworthy among them being a study in English of the Tagalog verb.

But while he was living thus quietly in Dapitan, events that were to determine his fate were misshaping themselves in Manila. The stone had been loosened on the mountain-side and was bounding on in mad career, far beyond his control.

---

[1] "Que todo el monte era orégano." W. E. Retana, in the appendix to Fray Martinez de Zuñiga's *Estadismo*, Madrid, 1893, where the decree is quoted. The rest of this comment of Retana's deserves quotation as an estimate of the living man by a Spanish publicist who was at the time in the employ of the friars and contemptuously hostile to Rizal, but who has since 1898 been giving quite a spectacular demonstration of waving a red light after the wreck, having become his most enthusiastic, almost hysterical, biographer: "Rizal is what is commonly called a character, but he has repeatedly demonstrated very great inexperience in the affairs of life. I believe him to be now about thirty-two years old. He is the Indian of most ability among those who have written."

III

> He who of old would rend the oak,
> Dream'd not of the rebound;
> Chain'd by the trunk he vainly broke —
> Alone — how look'd he round?
>
> BYRON.

Reason and moderation in the person of Rizal scorned and banished, the spirit of Jean Paul Marat and John Brown of Ossawatomie rises to the fore in the shape of one Andres Bonifacio, warehouse porter, who sits up o' nights copying all the letters and documents that he can lay hands on; composing grandiloquent manifestoes in Tagalog; drawing up magnificent appointments in the names of prominent persons who would later suffer even to the shedding of their life's blood through his mania for writing history in advance; spelling out Spanish tales of the French Revolution; babbling of Liberty, Equality, and Fraternity; hinting darkly to his confidants that the President of France had begun life as a blacksmith. Only a few days after Rizal was so summarily hustled away, Bonifacio gathered together a crowd of malcontents and ignorant dupes, some of them composing as choice a gang of cutthroats as ever slit the gullet of a Chinese or tied mutilated prisoners in ant hills, and solemnly organized the *Kataastaasang Kagalanggalang Katipunan ñg mga Anak ñg Bayan,* " Supreme Select Association of the Sons of the People," for the extermination of the ruling race and the restoration of the Golden Age. It was to bring the people into concerted action for a general revolt on a fixed date, when they would rise simultaneously, take possession of the city of Manila, and — the rest were better left to the imagination, for they had been reared under the Spanish colonial system and imitativeness has ever been pointed out as a cardinal trait in the Filipino character. No quarter was to be asked or given, and the most sacred ties, even of consanguinity, were to be disregarded in the general slaughter. To the inquiry of a curious neophyte as to how the Spaniards were to be distinguished from the other Europeans, in order to avoid international complications, dark Andres replied that in case of doubt they should proceed with due caution but should take good care that they made no mistakes about letting any of the *Castilas* escape their vengeance. The higher officials of the government were to be taken alive as hostages, while the friars were to be reserved for a special holocaust on Bagumbayan Field, where over their incinerated remains a heaven-kissing monument would be erected.

This Katipunan seems to have been an outgrowth from Spanish freemasonry, introduced into the Philippines by a Spaniard named Morayta and Marcelo H. del Pilar, a native of Bulacan Province who was the practical leader of the Filipinos in Spain, but who died there in 1896 just as he was setting out for Hongkong to mature his plans for a general uprising to expel the friar orders. There had been some masonic societies in the islands for some time, but the membership had been limited to Peninsulars, and they played no part in the politics of the time. But about 1888 Filipinos began to be admitted into some of them, and later, chiefly through the exertions of Pilar, lodges exclusively for them were instituted. These soon began to display great activity, especially in the transcendental matter of collections, so that their existence became a source of care to the government and a nightmare to the religious orders. From them, and with a perversion of the idea in Rizal's still-born *Liga,* it was an easy transition to the Katipunan, which was to put aside all pretense of reconciliation with Spain, and at the appointed time rise to exterminate not only the friars but also all the Spaniards and Spanish sympathizers, thus to bring about the reign of Liberty, Equality, and Fraternity, under the benign guidance of Patriot Bonifacio, with his bolo for a scepter.

With its secrecy and mystic forms, its methods of threats and intimidation, the Katipunan spread rapidly, especially among the Tagalogs, the most intransigent of the native peoples, and, it should be noted, the ones in whose territory the friars were the principal landlords. It was organized on the triangle plan, so that no member might know or communicate with more than three others — the one above him from whom he received his information and instructions and two below to whom he transmitted them. The initiations were conducted with great secrecy and solemnity, calculated to inspire the new members with awe and fear. The initiate, after a series of blood-curdling ordeals to try out his courage and resolution, swore on a human skull a terrific oath to devote his life and energies to the extermination of the white race, regardless of age or sex, and later affixed to it his signature or mark, usually the latter, with his own blood taken from an incision in the left arm or left breast. This was one form of the famous "blood compact," which, if history reads aright, played so important a part in the assumption of sovereignty over the Philippines by Legazpi in the name of Philip II.

Rizal was made the honorary president of the association, his portrait hung in all the meeting-halls, and the magic of his name used to attract the easily deluded masses, who were in a state of agitated ignorance and growing unrest, ripe for any movement that looked anti-governmental, and especially anti-Spanish. Soon after the organization had been perfected, collections began to be taken up — those collections were never overlooked — for the purpose of chartering a steamer to rescue him from Dapitan and transport him to Singapore, whence he might direct the general uprising, the day and the hour for which were fixed by Bonifacio for August twenty-sixth, 1896, at six o'clock sharp in the evening, since lack of precision in his magnificent programs was never a fault of that bold patriot, his logic being as severe as that of the Filipino policeman who put the flag at half-mast on Good Friday.

Of all this Rizal himself was, of course, entirely ignorant, until in May, 1896, a Filipino doctor named Pio Valenzuela, a creature of Bonifacio's, was despatched to Dapitan, taking along a blind man as a pretext for the visit to the famous oculist, to lay the plans before him for his consent and approval. Rizal expostulated with Valenzuela for a time over such a mad and hopeless venture, which would only bring ruin and misery upon the masses, and then is said to have very humanly lost his patience, ending the interview "in so bad a humor and with words so offensive that the deponent, who had gone with the intention of remaining there a month, took the steamer on the following day, for return to Manila."[1] He reported secretly to Bonifacio, who bestowed several choice Tagalog epithets on Rizal, and charged his envoy to say nothing about the failure of his mission, but rather to give the impression that he had been successful. Rizal's name continued to be used as the shibboleth of the insurrection, and the masses were made to believe that he would appear as their leader at the appointed hour.

Vague reports from police officers, to the effect that something unusual in the nature of secret societies was going on among the people, began to reach the government, but no great attention was paid to them, until the evening of August nineteenth, when the parish priest of Tondo was informed by the mother-superior of one of the convent-schools that she had just learned of a plot to massacre all the Spaniards. She had the information from a devoted pupil, whose brother was a compositor in the office of the *Diario de Manila.* As is so frequently the case in Filipino families, this elder sister was the purse-holder, and the brother's insistent requests for money, which was needed by him to meet the repeated assessments made on the members as the critical hour approached, awakened her curiosity and suspicion to such an extent that she forced him to confide the whole plan to her. Without delay she divulged it to her patroness, who in turn notified the curate of Tondo, where the printing-office was located. The priest called in two officers of the Civil Guard, who arrested the young printer, frightened a confession out of him, and that night, in company with the friar, searched the printing-office, finding secreted there several lithographic plates for printing receipts and certificates of membership in the Katipunan, with a number of documents giving some account of the plot.

Then the Spanish population went wild. General Ramon Blanco was governor and seems to have been about the only person who kept his head at all. He tried to prevent giving so irresponsible a movement a fictitious importance, but was utterly powerless to stay the clamor for blood which at once arose, loudest on the part of those alleged ministers of the gentle Christ. The gates of the old Walled City, long fallen

[1] From Valenzuela's deposition before the military tribunal, September sixth, 1896.

into disuse, were cleaned and put in order, martial law was declared, and wholesale arrests made. Many of the prisoners were confined in Fort Santiago, one batch being crowded into a dungeon for which the only ventilation was a grated opening at the top, and one night a sergeant of the guard carelessly spread his sleeping-mat over this, so the next morning some fifty-five asphyxiated corpses were hauled away. On the twenty-sixth armed insurrection broke out at Caloocan, just north of Manila, from time immemorial the resort of bad characters from all the country round and the center of brigandage, while at San Juan del Monte, on the outskirts of the city, several bloody skirmishes were fought a few days later with the *Guardia Civil Veterana,* the picked police force.

Bonifacio had been warned of the discovery of his schemes in time to make his escape and flee to the barrio, or village, of Balintawak, a few miles north of Manila, thence to lead the attack on Caloocan and inaugurate the reign of Liberty, Equality, and Fraternity in the manner in which Philippine insurrections have generally had a habit of starting — with the murder of Chinese merchants and the pillage of their shops. He had from the first reserved for himself the important office of treasurer in the Katipunan, in addition to being on occasions president and at all times its ruling spirit, so he now established himself as dictator and proceeded to appoint a magnificent staff, most of whom contrived to escape as soon as they were out of reach of his bolo. Yet he drew considerable numbers about him, for this man, though almost entirely unlettered, seems to have been quite a personality among his own people, especially possessed of that gift of oratory in his native tongue to which the Malay is so preëminently susceptible.

In Manila a special tribunal was constituted and worked steadily, sometimes through the siesta-hour, for there were times, of which this was one, when even Spanish justice could be swift. Bagumbayan began to be a veritable field of blood, as the old methods of repression were resorted to for the purpose of striking terror into the native population by wholesale executions, nor did the ruling powers realize that the time for such methods had passed. It was a case of sixteenth-century colonial methods fallen into fretful and frantic senility, so in all this wretched business it is doubtful which to pity the more: the blind stupidity of the fossilized conservatives incontinently throwing an empire away, forfeiting their influence over a people whom they, by temperament and experience, should have been fitted to control and govern; or the potential cruelty of perverted human nature in the dark Frankenstein who would wreak upon the rulers in their decadent days the most hideous of the methods in the system that produced him, as he planned his festive holocaust and carmagnole on the spot where every spark of initiative and leadership among his people, both good and bad, had been summarily and ruthlessly extinguished. There is at least a world of reflection in it for the rulers of men.

In the meantime Rizal, wearying of the quiet life in Dapitan and doubtless foreseeing the impending catastrophe, had requested leave to volunteer his services as a physician in the military hospitals of Cuba, of the horrors and sufferings in which he had heard. General Blanco at once gladly acceded to this request and had him brought to Manila, but unfortunately the boat carrying him arrived there a day too late for him to catch the regular August mail-steamer to Spain, so he was kept in the cruiser a prisoner of war, awaiting the next transportation. While he was thus detained, the Katipunan plot was discovered and the rebellion broke out. He was accused of being the head of it, but Blanco gave him a personal letter completely exonerating him from any complicity in the outbreak, as well as a letter of recommendation to the Spanish minister of war. He was placed on the *Isla de Panay* when it left for Spain on September third and traveled at first as a passenger. At Singapore he was advised to land and claim British protection, as did some of his fellow travelers, but he refused to do so, saying that his conscience was clear.

As the name of Rizal had constantly recurred during the trials of the Katipunan suspects, the military tribunal finally issued a formal demand for him. The order of arrest was cabled to Port Said and Rizal there placed in solitary confinement for the remainder of the voyage. Arrived at Barcelona, he was confined in the grim fortress of Montjuich, where, by a curious coincidence, the governor was the same Despujols who had issued the decree of banishment in 1892. Shortly afterwards, he was placed on the transport *Colon,* which was bound for the Philippines with troops, Blanco having at last been stirred to action. Strenuous efforts were now made by Rizal's friends in London to have him removed from the ship at Singapore, but the British authorities declined to take any action, on the ground that he was on a Spanish warship and therefore beyond the jurisdiction of their courts. The *Colon* arrived at Manila on November third and Rizal was imprisoned in Fort Santiago, while a special tribunal was constituted to try him on the charges of carrying on anti-patriotic and anti-religious propaganda, rebellion, sedition, and the formation of illegal associations. Some other charges may have been overlooked in the hurry and excitement.

It would be almost a travesty to call a trial the proceedings which began early in December and dragged along until the twenty-sixth. Rizal was defended by a young Spanish officer selected by him from among a number designated by the tribunal, who chivalrously performed so unpopular a duty as well as he could. But the whole affair was a mockery of justice, for the Spanish government in the Philippines had finally and hopelessly reached the condition graphically pictured by Mr. Kipling:

> Panic that shells the drifting spar
> Loud waste with none to check
> Mad fear that rakes a scornful star
> Or sweeps a consort's deck!

The clamor against Blanco had resulted in his summary removal by royal decree and the appointment of a real " pacificator," Camilo Polavieja.

While in prison Rizal prepared an address to those of his countrymen who were in armed rebellion, repudiating the use of his name and deprecating the resort to violence. The closing words are a compendium of his life and beliefs: " Countrymen: I have given proofs, as well as the best of you, of desiring liberty for our country, and I continue to desire it. But I place as a premise the education of the people, so that by means of instruction and work they may have a personality of their own and that they may make themselves worthy of that same liberty. In my writings I have recommended the study of the civic virtues, without which there can be no redemption. I have also written (and my words have been repeated) that reforms, to be fruitful, must come from *above,* that those which spring from *below* are uncertain and insecure movements. Imbued with these ideas, I cannot do less than condemn, and I do condemn, this absurd, savage rebellion, planned behind my back, which dishonors the Filipinos and discredits those who can speak for us. I abominate all criminal actions and refuse any kind of participation in them, pitying with all my heart the dupes who have allowed themselves to be deceived. Go back, then, to your homes, and may God forgive those who have acted in bad faith." This address, however, was not published by the Spanish authorities, since they did not consider it " patriotic " enough; instead, they killed the writer!

Rizal appeared before the tribunal bound, closely guarded by two Peninsular soldiers, but maintained his serenity throughout and answered the charges in a straightforward way. He pointed out the fact that he had never taken any great part in politics, having even quarreled with Marcelo del Pilar, the active leader of the anti-clericals, by reason of those perennial "subscriptions," and that during the time he was accused of being the instigator and organizer of armed rebellion he had been a close prisoner in Dapitan under strict surveillance by both the military and ecclesiastical authorities. The prosecutor presented a lengthy document, which ran mostly to words, about the only definite conclusion laid down in it being that the Philippines " are, and always must remain, Spanish territory." What there may have been in Rizal's career to hang such a conclusion upon is not quite clear, but at any rate this learned legal light was evidently still thinking in colors on the map serenely unconscious in his European pseudo-prescience of the new and wonderful development in the Western Hemisphere — humanity militant, Lincolnism.

The death sentence was asked, but the longer the case dragged on the more favorable it began to look for the accused, so the president of the tribunal, after deciding, Jeffreys-like, that the charges had been proved, ordered that no further evidence be taken. Rizal betrayed some surprise when his doom was thus foreshadowed, for, dreamer that he was, he seems not to have anticipated such a fatal eventuality for himself. He did not lose his serenity, however, even when the tribunal promptly brought in a verdict of guilty and imposed the death sentence,

xlvi   TRANSLATOR'S INTRODUCTION

upon which Polavieja the next day placed his *Cúmplase,* fixing the morning of December thirtieth for the execution.

So Rizal's fate was sealed. The witnesses against him, in so far as there was any substantial testimony at all, had been his own countrymen, coerced or cajoled into making statements which they have since repudiated as false, and which in some cases were extorted from them by threats and even torture. But he betrayed very little emotion, even maintaining what must have been an assumed cheerfulness. Only one reproach is recorded: that he had been made a dupe of, that he had been deceived by every one, even the *bankeros* and *cocheros.* His old Jesuit instructors remained with him in the *capilla,* or death-cell,[1] and largely through the influence of an image of the Sacred Heart, which he had carved as a schoolboy, it is claimed that a reconciliation with the Church was effected. There has been considerable pragmatical discussion as to what form of retraction from him was necessary, since he had been, after studying in Europe, a frank freethinker, but such futile polemics may safely be left to the learned doctors. That he was reconciled with the Church would seem to be evidenced by the fact that just before the execution he gave legal status as his wife to the woman, a rather remarkable Eurasian adventuress, who had lived with him in Dapitan, and the religious ceremony was the only one then recognized in the islands.[2] The greater part of his last night on earth was

[1] *Capilla:* the Spanish practise is to place a condemned person for the twenty-four hours preceding his execution in a *chapel,* or a cell fitted up as such, where he may devote himself to religious exercises and receive the final ministrations of the Church.

[2] But even this conclusion is open to doubt: there is no proof beyond the unsupported statement of the Jesuits that he made a written retraction, which was later destroyed, though why a document so interesting, and so important in support of their own point of view, should not have been preserved furnishes an illuminating commentary on the whole confused affair. The only unofficial witness present was the condemned man's sister, and her declaration, that she was at the time in such a state of excitement and distress that she is unable to affirm positively that there was a real marriage ceremony performed, can readily be accepted. It must be remembered that the Jesuits were themselves under the official and popular ban for the part they had played in Rizal's education and development and that they were seeking to set themselves right in order to maintain their prestige. Add to this the persistent and systematic effort made to destroy every scrap

spent in composing a chain of verse; no very majestic flight of poesy, but a pathetic monody throbbing with patient resignation and inextinguishable hope, one of the sweetest, saddest swan-songs ever sung.

Thus he was left at the last, entirely alone. As soon as his doom became certain the Patriots had all scurried to cover, one gentle poetaster even rushing into doggerel verse to condemn him as a reversion to barbarism; the wealthier suspects betook themselves to other lands or made judicious use of their money-bags among the Spanish officials; the better classes of the population floundered hopelessly, leaderless, in the confused whirl of opinions and passions; while the voiceless millions for whom he had spoken moved on in dumb, uncomprehending silence. He had lived in that higher dreamland of the future, ahead of his countrymen, ahead even of those who assumed to be the mentors of his people, and he must learn, as does every noble soul that labors "to make the bounds of freedom wider yet," the bitter lesson that nine-tenths, if not all, the woes that afflict humanity spring from man's own stupid selfishness, that the wresting of the scepter from the tyrant is often the least of the task, that the bondman comes to love his bonds — like Chillon's prisoner, his very chains and he grow friends, — but that the struggle for human freedom must go on, at whatever cost, in ever-widening circles, "wave after wave, each mightier than the last," for as long as one body toils in fetters or one mind welters in blind ignorance, either of the slave's base delusion or the despot's specious illusion, there can be no final security for any free man, or his children, or his children's children.

of record relating to the man — the sole gleam of shame evidenced in the impolitic, idiotic, and pusillanimous treatment of him — and the whole question becomes such a puzzle that it may just as well be left in darkness, with a throb of pity for the unfortunate victim caught in such a maelstrom of panic-stricken passion and selfish intrigue.

IV

> "God save thee, ancient Mariner!
> From the fiends, that plague thee thus!
> Why look'st thou so?" — "With my cross-bow
> I shot the Albatross!"
>
> COLERIDGE.

It was one of those magic December mornings of the tropics — the very nuptials of earth and sky, when great Nature seems to fling herself incontinently into creation, wrapping the world in a brooding calm of light and color, that Spain chose for committing political suicide in the Philippines. Bagumbayan Field was crowded with troops, both regulars and militia, for every man capable of being trusted with arms was drawn up there, excepting only the necessary guards in other parts of the city. Extra patrols were in the streets, double guards were placed over the archiepiscopal and gubernatorial palaces. The calmest man in all Manila that day was he who must stand before the firing-squad.

Two special and unusual features are to be noted about this execution. All the principal actors were Filipinos: the commander of the troops and the officer directly in charge of the execution were native-born, while the firing-squad itself was drawn from a local native regiment, though it is true that on this occasion a squad of Peninsular *cazadores,* armed with loaded Mausers, stood directly behind them to see that they failed not in their duty. Again, there was but one victim; for it seems to have ever been the custom of the Spanish rulers to associate in these gruesome affairs some real criminals with the political offenders, no doubt with the intentional purpose of confusing the issue in the general mind. Rizal standing alone, the occasion of so much hurried preparation and fearful precaution, is a pathetic testimonial to the degree of incapacity into which the ruling powers had fallen, even in chicanery.

After bidding good-by to his sister and making final disposition regarding some personal property, the doomed man, under close guard, walked calmly, even cheerfully, from Fort Santiago along the Malecon to the Luneta, accompanied by his Jesuit confessors. Arrived there, he thanked those about him for their kindness and requested the officer in charge to allow him to face the firing-squad, since he had never been a traitor to Spain. This the officer declined to permit, for the order was to shoot him in the back. Rizal assented with a slight protest, pointed out to the soldiers the spot in his back at which they should aim, and with a firm step took his place in front of them.

Then occurred an act almost too hideous to record. There he stood, expecting a volley of Remington bullets in his back — Time was, and Life's stream ebbed to Eternity's flood — when the military surgeon stepped forward and asked if he might feel his pulse! Rizal extended his left hand, and the officer remarked that he could not understand how a man's pulse could beat normally at such a terrific moment! The victim shrugged his shoulders and let the hand fall again to his side — Latin refinement could be no further refined!

A moment later there he lay, on his right side, his life-blood spurting over the Luneta curb, eyes wide open, fixedly staring at that Heaven where the priests had taught all those centuries agone that Justice abides. The troops filed past the body, for the most part silently, while desultory cries of "*Viva España!*" from among the "patriotic" Filipino volunteers were summarily hushed by a Spanish artillery-officer's stern rebuke: "Silence, you rabble!" To drown out the fitful cheers and the audible murmurs, the bands struck up Spanish national airs. Stranger death-dirge no man and system ever had. Carnival revelers now dance about the scene and Filipino schoolboys play baseball over that same spot.

A few days later another execution was held on that spot, of members of the *Liga,* some of them characters that would have richly deserved shooting at any place or time, according to existing standards, but notable among them there knelt, torture-crazed, as to his orisons, Francisco Roxas, millionaire capitalist, who may be regarded as the social and economic head of the Filipino people, as Rizal was fitted to be their intellectual leader. Shades of Anda and Vargas! Out there

TRANSLATOR'S INTRODUCTION

at Balintawak — rather fitly, "the home of the snake-demon," — not three hours' march from this same spot, on the very edge of the city, Andres Bonifacio and his literally sansculottic gangs of cutthroats were, almost with impunity, soiling the fair name of Freedom with murder and mutilation, rape and rapine, awakening the worst passions of an excitable, impulsive people, destroying that essential respect for law and order, which to restore would take a holocaust of fire and blood, with a generation of severe training. Unquestionably did Rizal demonstrate himself to be a seer and prophet when he applied to such a system the story of Babylon and the fateful handwriting on the wall!

But forces had been loosed that would not be so suppressed, the time had gone by when such wild methods of repression would serve. The destruction of the native leaders, culminating in the executions of Rizal and Roxas, produced a counter-effect by rousing the Tagalogs, good and bad alike, to desperate fury, and the aftermath was frightful. The better classes were driven to take part in the rebellion, and Cavite especially became a veritable slaughter-pen, as the contest settled down into a hideous struggle for mutual extermination. Dark Andres went his wild way to perish by the violence he had himself invoked, a prey to the rising ambition of a young leader of considerable culture and ability, a schoolmaster named Emilio Aguinaldo. His Katipunan hovered fitfully around Manila, for a time even drawing to itself in their desperation some of the better elements of the population, only to find itself sold out and deserted by its leaders, dying away for a time; but later, under changed conditions, it reappeared in strange metamorphosis as the rallying-center for the largest number of Filipinos who have ever gathered together for a common purpose, and then finally went down before those thin grim lines in khaki with sharp and sharpest shot clearing away the wreck of the old, blazing the way for the new: the broadening sweep of "Democracy announcing, in rifle-volleys death-winged, under her Star Banner, to the tune of Yankee-doodle-do, that she is born, and, whirlwind-like, will envelop the whole world!"

MANILA, December 1, 1909

What? Does no Cæsar, does no Achilles, appear on your stage now?
   Not an Andromache e'en, not an Orestes, my friend?

No! there is nought to be seen there but parsons, and syndics of commerce,
   Secretaries perchance, ensigns and majors of horse.

But, my good friend, pray tell, what can such people e'er meet with
   That can be truly call'd great?—what that is great can they do?

SCHILLER: *Shakespeare's Ghost.*
(*Bowring's translation.*)

CONTENTS

Author's Dedication

Chapter		Page
I	A Social Gathering	1
II	Crisostomo Ibarra	15
III	The Dinner	19
IV	Heretic and Filibuster	25
V	A Star in a Dark Night	33
VI	Capitan Tiago	36
VII	An Idyl on an Azotea	50
VIII	Recollections	60
IX	Local Affairs	66
X	The Town	72
XI	The Rulers	76
XII	All Saints	82
XIII	Signs of Storm	87
XIV	Tasio: Lunatic or Sage	91
XV	The Sacristans	101
XVI	Sisa	106
XVII	Basilio	112
XVIII	Souls in Torment	118
XIX	A Schoolmaster's Difficulties	125
XX	The Meeting in the Town Hall	136
XXI	The Story of a Mother	149

CONTENTS

Chapter		Page
XXII	Lights and Shadows	157
XXIII	Fishing	161
XXIV	In the Wood	175
XXV	In the House of the Sage	188
XXVI	The Eve of the Fiesta	201
XXVII	In the Twilight	210
XXVIII	Correspondence	218
XXIX	The Morning	225
XXX	In the Church	231
XXXI	The Sermon	236
XXXII	The Derrick	247
XXXIII	Free Thought	258
XXXIV	The Dinner	262
XXXV	Comments	273
XXXVI	The First Cloud	280
XXXVII	His Excellency	284
XXXVIII	The Procéssion	294
XXXIX	Doña Consolación	300
XL	Right and Might	312
XLI	Two Visits	321
XLII	The Espadañas	324
XLIII	Plans	337
XLIV	An Examination of Conscience	341
XLV	The Hunted	348
XLVI	The Cockpit	355
XLVII	The Two Señoras	366
XLVIII	The Enigma	372
XLIX	The Voice of the Hunted	375

CONTENTS

Chapter		Page
L	Elias's Story	386
LI	Exchanges	395
LII	The Cards of the Dead and the Shadows	399
LIII	Il Buon Dí si Conosce da Mattina	405
LIV	Revelations	412
LV	The Catastrophe	419
LVI	Rumors and Belief	426
LVII	Vae Victis!	434
LVIII	The Accursed	443
LIX	Patriotism and Private Interests	447
LX	Maria Clara Weds	459
LXI	The Chase on the Lake	472
LXII	Padre Damaso Explains	480
LXIII	Christmas Eve	484
Epilogue		493
Glossary		499

AUTHOR'S DEDICATION

To My Fatherland:

Recorded in the history of human sufferings is a cancer of so malignant a character that the least touch irritates it and awakens in it the sharpest pains. Thus, how many times, when in the midst of modern civilizations I have wished to call thee before me, now to accompany me in memories, now to compare thee with other countries, hath thy dear image presented itself showing a social cancer like to that other!

Desiring thy welfare, which is our own, and seeking the best treatment, I will do with thee what the ancients did with their sick, exposing them on the steps of the temple so that every one who came to invoke the Divinity might offer them a remedy.

And to this end, I will strive to reproduce thy condition faithfully, without discriminations; I will raise a part of the veil that covers the evil, sacrificing to truth everything, even vanity itself, since, as thy son, I am conscious that I also suffer from thy defects and weaknesses.

THE AUTHOR

Europe, 1886

THE SOCIAL CANCER

CHAPTER I

A SOCIAL GATHERING

ON the last of October Don Santiago de los Santos, popularly known as Capitan Tiago, gave a dinner. In spite of the fact that, contrary to his usual custom, he had made the announcement only that afternoon, it was already the sole topic of conversation in Binondo and adjacent districts, and even in the Walled City, for at that time Capitan Tiago was considered one of the most hospitable of men, and it was well known that his house, like his country, shut its doors against nothing except commerce and all new or bold ideas. Like an electric shock the announcement ran through the world of parasites, bores, and hangers-on, whom God in His infinite bounty creates and so kindly multiplies in Manila. Some looked at once for shoe-polish, others for buttons and cravats, but all were especially concerned about how to greet the master of the house in the most familiar tone, in order to create an atmosphere of ancient friendship or, if occasion should arise, to excuse a late arrival.

This dinner was given in a house on Calle Anloague, and although we do not remember the number we will describe it in such a way that it may still be recognized, provided the earthquakes have not destroyed it. We do not believe that its owner has had it torn down, for such labors are generally entrusted to God or nature — which Powers hold the contracts also for many of the projects of our government. It is a rather large building, in the style of many in the country, and fronts upon the arm of the Pasig which is known to some as the Binondo River, and which, like all the streams in Manila, plays the varied rôles of bath, sewer, laundry, fishery, means of transportation and communication, and even drinking water if the Chinese water-carrier finds it convenient. It is worthy of note that in the distance of nearly a mile this important artery of the district, where traffic is most dense and movement most deafening, can boast of only one wooden bridge, which is out of repair on one side for six months and impassable on the other for the rest of the year, so that during the hot season the ponies take advantage of this permanent *status quo* to jump off the bridge into the water, to the great surprise of the abstracted mortal who may be dozing inside the carriage or philosophizing upon the progress of the age.

The house of which we are speaking is somewhat low and not exactly correct in all its lines: whether the architect who built it was afflicted with poor eyesight or whether the earthquakes and typhoons have twisted it out of shape, no one can say with certainty. A wide staircase with green newels and carpeted steps leads from the tiled entrance up to the main floor between rows of flower-pots set upon pedestals of motley-colored and fantastically decorated Chinese porcelain. Since there are neither porters nor servants who demand invitation cards, we will go in, O you who read this, whether friend or foe, if you are attracted by the strains of the orchestra, the lights, or the suggestive rattling of dishes, knives, and forks, and if you wish to see what such a gathering is like in the distant Pearl of the Orient. Gladly, and for my own comfort, I should spare you this description of the house, were it not of great importance, since we mortals in general are very much like tortoises: we are esteemed and classified according to our shells; in this and still other respects the mortals of the Philippines in particular also resemble tortoises.

If we go up the stairs, we immediately find ourselves in

·a spacious hallway, called there, for some unknown reason, the *caida*, which tonight serves as the dining-room and at the same time affords a place for the orchestra. In the center a large table profusely and expensively decorated seems to beckon to the hanger-on with sweet promises, while it threatens the bashful maiden, the simple *dalaga*, with two mortal hours in the company of strangers whose language and conversation usually have a very restricted and special character.

Contrasted with these terrestrial preparations are the motley paintings on the walls representing religious matters, such as "Purgatory," "Hell," "The Last Judgment," "The Death of the Just," and "The Death of the Sinner." At the back of the room, fastened in a splendid and elegant framework, in the Renaissance style, possibly by Arévalo, is a glass case in which are seen the figures of two old women. The inscription on this reads: "Our Lady of Peace and Prosperous Voyages, who is worshiped in Antipolo, visiting in the disguise of a beggar the holy and renowned Capitana Inez during her sickness."[1] While the work reveals little taste or art, yet it possesses in compensation an extreme realism, for to judge from the yellow and bluish tints of her face the sick woman seems to be already a decaying corpse, and the glasses and other objects, accompaniments of long illness, are so minutely reproduced that even their contents may be distinguished. In looking at these pictures, which excite the appetite and inspire gay bucolic ideas, one may perhaps be led to think that the malicious host is well acquainted with the characters of the majority of those who are to sit at his table and that, in order to conceal his own way of thinking, he has hung from the ceiling costly Chinese lanterns; bird-cages without birds; red, green, and blue globes of frosted glass; faded air-plants; and dried and inflated fishes, which they call *botetes*. The view is closed on the side of the river by curious wooden arches, half Chinese and half

[1] A similar picture is found in the convento at Antipolo. — *Author's note.*

European, affording glimpses of a terrace with arbors and bowers faintly lighted by paper lanterns of many colors.

In the sala, among massive mirrors and gleaming chandeliers, the guests are assembled. Here, on a raised platform, stands a grand piano of great price, which tonight has the additional virtue of not being played upon. Here, hanging on the wall, is an oil-painting of a handsome man in full dress, rigid, erect, straight as the tasseled cane he holds in his stiff, ring-covered fingers — the whole seeming to say, "Ahem! See how well dressed and how dignified I am!" The furnishings of the room are elegant and perhaps uncomfortable and unhealthful, since the master of the house would consider not so much the comfort and health of his guests as his own ostentation. "A terrible thing is dysentery," he would say to them, "but you are sitting in European chairs and that is something you don't find every day."

This room is almost filled with people, the men being separated from the women as in synagogues and Catholic churches. The women consist of a number of Filipino and Spanish maidens, who, when they open their mouths to yawn, instantly cover them with their fans and who murmur only a few words to each other, any conversation ventured upon dying out in monosyllables like the sounds heard in a house at night, sounds made by the rats and lizards. Is it perhaps the different likenesses of Our Lady hanging on the walls that force them to silence and a religious demeanor or is it that the women here are an exception?

A cousin of Capitan Tiago, a sweet-faced old woman, who speaks Spanish quite badly, is the only one receiving the ladies. To offer to the Spanish ladies a plate of cigars and *buyos,* to extend her hand to her countrywomen to be kissed, exactly as the friars do, — this is the sum of her courtesy, her policy. The poor old lady soon became bored, and taking advantage of the noise of a plate breaking, rushed precipitately away, muttering, "*Jesús!* Just wait, you rascals!" and failed to reappear.

The men, for their part, are making more of a stir. Some

A SOCIAL GATHERING

cadets in one corner are conversing in a lively manner but in low tones, looking around now and then to point out different persons in the room while they laugh more or less openly among themselves. In contrast, two foreigners dressed in white are promenading silently from one end of the room to the other with their hands crossed behind their backs, like the bored passengers on the deck of a ship. All the interest and the greatest animation proceed from a group composed of two priests, two civilians, and a soldier who are seated around a small table on which are seen bottles of wine and English biscuits.

The soldier, a tall, elderly lieutenant with an austere countenance — a Duke of Alva straggling behind in the roster of the Civil Guard — talks little, but in a harsh, curt way. One of the priests, a youthful Dominican friar, handsome, graceful, polished as the gold-mounted eyeglasses he wears, maintains a premature gravity. He is the curate of Binondo and has been in former years a professor in the college of San Juan de Letran,[1] where he enjoyed the reputation of being a consummate dialectician, so much so that in the days when the sons of Guzman[2] still dared to match themselves in subtleties with laymen, the able disputant B. de Luna had never been able either to catch or to confuse him, the distinctions made by Fray Sibyla leaving his opponent in the situation of a fisherman who tries to catch eels with a lasso. The Dominican says little, appearing to weigh his words.

Quite in contrast, the other priest, a Franciscan, talks much and gesticulates more. In spite of the fact that his hair is beginning to turn gray, he seems to be preserving

---

[1] A school of secondary instruction conducted by the Dominican Fathers, by whom it was taken over in 1640. "It had its first beginning in the house of a pious Spaniard, called Juan Geronimo Guerrero, who had dedicated himself, with Christian piety, to gathering orphan boys in his house, where he raised, clothed, and sustained them, and taught them to read and to write, and much more, to live in the fear of God." — Blair and Robertson, *The Philippine Islands*, Vol. XLV, p. 208. — TR.

[2] The Dominican friars, whose order was founded by Dominic de Guzman. — TR.

well his robust constitution, while his regular features, his rather disquieting glance, his wide jaws and herculean frame give him the appearance of a Roman noble in disguise and make us involuntarily recall one of those three monks of whom Heine tells in his "Gods in Exile," who at the September equinox in the Tyrol used to cross a lake at midnight and each time place in the hand of the poor boatman a silver piece, cold as ice, which left him full of terror.[1] But Fray Damaso is not so mysterious as they were. He is full of merriment, and if the tone of his voice is rough like that of a man who has never had occasion to correct himself and who believes that whatever he says is holy and above improvement, still his frank, merry laugh wipes out this disagreeable impression and even obliges us to pardon his showing to the room bare feet and hairy legs that would make the fortune of a Mendieta in the Quiapo fairs.[2]

One of the civilians is a very small man with a black beard, the only thing notable about him being his nose, which, to judge from its size, ought not to belong to him. The other is a rubicund youth, who seems to have arrived but recently in the country. With him the Franciscan is carrying on a lively discussion.

"You'll see," the friar was saying, "when you've been here a few months you'll be convinced of what I say. It's one thing to govern in Madrid and another to live in the Philippines."

"But—"

"I, for example," continued Fray Damaso, raising his voice still higher to prevent the other from speaking, "I, for example, who can look back over twenty-three years of bananas and *morisqueta*, know whereof I speak. Don't

---

[1] In the story mentioned, the three monks were the old Roman god Bacchus and two of his satellites, in the disguise of Franciscan friars. — TR.

[2] According to a note to the Barcelona edition of this novel, Mendieta was a character well known in Manila, doorkeeper at the Alcaldía, impresario of children's theaters, director of a merry-go-round, etc. — TR.

come at me with theories and fine speeches, for I know the
Indian.[1] Mark well that the moment I arrived in the country I was assigned to a town, small it is true, but especially
devoted to agriculture. I didn't understand Tagalog very
well then, but I was soon confessing the women, and we understood one another and they came to like me so well that
three years later, when I was transferred to another and
larger town, made vacant by the death of the native curate,
all fell to weeping, they heaped gifts upon me, they escorted
me with music — "

"But that only goes to show — "

"Wait, wait! Don't be so hasty! My successor remained
a shorter time, and when he left he had more attendance,
more tears, and more music. Yet he had been more given
to whipping and had raised the fees in the parish to almost
double."

"But you will allow me — "

"But that is n't all. I stayed in the town of San Diego
twenty years and it has been only a few months since I —
left it."

Here he showed signs of chagrin.

"Twenty years, no one can deny, are more than sufficient
to get acquainted with a town. San Diego has a population
of six thousand souls and I knew every inhabitant as well as
if I had been his mother and wet-nurse. I knew in which
foot this one was lame, where the shoe pinched that one, who
was courting that girl, what affairs she had had and with
whom, who was the real father of the child, and so on —
for I was the confessor of every last one, and they took care
not to fail in their duty. Our host, Santiago, will tell you
whether I am speaking the truth, for he has a lot of land
there and that was where we first became friends. Well
then, you may see what the Indian is: when I left I was
escorted by only a few old women and some of the tertiary
brethren — and that after I had been there twenty years!"

"But I don't see what that has to do with the abolition

[1] See Glossary.

of the tobacco monopoly," [1] ventured the rubicund youth, taking advantage of the Franciscan's pausing to drink a glass of sherry.

Fray Damaso was so greatly surprised that he nearly let his glass fall. He remained for a moment staring fixedly at the young man.

"What? How's that?" he was finally able to exclaim in great wonderment. "Is it possible that you don't see it as clear as day? Don't you see, my son, that all this proves plainly that the reforms of the ministers are irrational?"

It was now the youth's turn to look perplexed. The lieutenant wrinkled his eyebrows a little more and the small man nodded toward Fray Damaso equivocally. The Dominican contented himself with almost turning his back on the whole group.

"Do you really believe so?" the young man at length asked with great seriousness, as he looked at the friar with curiosity.

"Do I believe so? As I believe the Gospel! The Indian is so indolent!"

"Ah, pardon me for interrupting you," said the young man, lowering his voice and drawing his chair a little closer. "but you have said something that awakens all my interest. Does this indolence actually, naturally, exist among the natives or is there some truth in what a foreign traveler says: that with this indolence we excuse our own, as well as our backwardness and our colonial system. He referred to other colonies whose inhabitants belong to the same race —"

---

[1] The "tobacco monopoly" was established during the administration of Basco de Vargas (1778–1787), one of the ablest governors Spain sent to the Philippines, in order to provide revenue for the local government and to encourage agricultural development. The operation of the monopoly, however, soon degenerated into a system of "graft" and petty abuse which bore heavily upon the natives (see Zuñiga's *Estadismo*), and the abolition of it in 1881 was one of the heroic efforts made by the Spanish civil administrators to adjust the archaic colonial system to the changing conditions in the Archipelago. — TR.

"Bah, jealousy! Ask Señor Laruja, who also knows this country. Ask him if there is any equal to the ignorance and indolence of the Indian."

"It's true," affirmed the little man, who was referred to as Señor Laruja. "In no part of the world can you find any one more indolent than the Indian, in no part of the world."

"Nor more vicious, nor more ungrateful!"

"Nor more unmannerly!"

The rubicund youth began to glance about nervously. "Gentlemen," he whispered, "I believe that we are in the house of an Indian. Those young ladies —"

"Bah, don't be so apprehensive! Santiago does n't consider himself an Indian — and besides, he's not here. And what if he were! These are the nonsensical ideas of the newcomers. Let a few months pass and you will change your opinion, after you have attended a lot of fiestas and *bailúhan*, slept on cots, and eaten your fill of *tinola*."

"Ah, is this thing that you call *tinola* a variety of lotus which makes people — er — forgetful?"

"Nothing of the kind!" exclaimed Fray Damaso with a smile. "You're getting absurd. *Tinola* is a stew of chicken and squash. How long has it been since you got here?"

"Four days," responded the youth, rather offended.

"Have you come as a government employee?"

"No, sir, I've come at my own expense to study the country."

"Man, what a rare bird!" exclaimed Fray Damaso, staring at him with curiosity. "To come at one's own expense and for such foolishness! What a wonder! When there are so many books! And with two fingerbreadths of forehead! Many have written books as big as that! With two fingerbreadths of forehead!"

The Dominican here brusquely broke in upon the conversation. "Did your Reverence, Fray Damaso, say that you had been twenty years in the town of San Diego and that you had left it? Wasn't your Reverence satisfied with the town?"

At this question, which was put in a very natural and almost negligent tone, Fray Damaso suddenly lost all his merriment and stopped laughing. "No!" he grunted dryly, and let himself back heavily against the back of his chair.

The Dominican went on in a still more indifferent tone. "It must be painful to leave a town where one has been for twenty years and which he knows as well as the clothes he wears. I certainly was sorry to leave Kamiling and that after I had been there only a few months. But my superiors did it for the good of the Order — for my own good."

Fray Damaso, for the first time that evening, seemed to be very thoughtful. Suddenly he brought his fist down on the arm of his chair and with a heavy breath exclaimed: "Either Religion is a fact or it is not! That is, either the curates are free or they are not! The country is going to ruin, it is lost!" And again he struck the arm of his chair.

Everybody in the sala turned toward the group with astonished looks. The Dominican raised his head to stare at the Franciscan from under his glasses. The two foreigners paused a moment, stared with an expression of mingled severity and reproof, then immediately continued their promenade.

"He's in a bad humor because you have n't treated him with deference," murmured Señor Laruja into the ear of the rubicund youth.

"What does your Reverence mean? What's the trouble?" inquired the Dominican and the lieutenant at the same time, but in different tones.

"That's why so many calamities come! The ruling powers support heretics against the ministers of God!" continued the Franciscan, raising his heavy fists.

"What do you mean?" again inquired the frowning lieutenant, half rising from his chair.

"What do I mean?" repeated Fray Damaso, raising his voice and facing the lieutenant. "I'll tell you what I mean. I, yes I, mean to say that when a priest throws out of his cemetery the corpse of a heretic, no one, not even the King himself, has any right to interfere and much less to impose any punishment! But a little General — a little General Calamity —"

"Padre, his Excellency is the Vice-Regal Patron!" shouted the soldier, rising to his feet.

"Excellency! Vice-Regal Patron! What of that!" retorted the Franciscan, also rising. "In other times he would have been dragged down a staircase as the religious orders once did with the impious Governor Bustamente.[1] Those were indeed the days of faith."

"I warn you that I can't permit this! His Excellency represents his Majesty the King!"

"King or rook! What difference does that make? For us there is no king other than the legitimate [2] —"

"Halt!" shouted the lieutenant in a threatening tone, as if he were commanding his soldiers. "Either you withdraw what you have said or tomorrow I will report it to his Excellency!"

"Go ahead — right now — go on!" was the sarcastic

[1] As a result of his severity in enforcing the payment of sums due the royal treasury on account of the galleon trade, in which the religious orders were heavily interested, Governor Fernando de Bustillos Bustamente y Rueda met a violent death at the hands of a mob headed by friars, October 11, 1719. See Blair and Robertson, *The Philippine Islands*, Vol. XLIV; Montero y Vidal, *Historia General de Filipinas*, Vol. I, Chap. XXXV. — TR.

[2] A reference to the fact that the clerical party in Spain refused to accept the decree of Ferdinand VII setting aside the Salic law and naming his daughter Isabella as his successor, and, upon the death of Ferdinand, supported the claim of the nearest male heir, Don Carlos de Bourbon, thus giving rise to the Carlist movement. Some writers state that severe measures had to be adopted to compel many of the friars in the Philippines to use the feminine pronoun in their prayers for the sovereign, just whom the reverend gentlemen expected to deceive not being explained. — TR.

rejoinder of Fray Damaso as he approached the officer with clenched fists. "Do you think that because I wear the cloth, I'm afraid? Go now, while I can lend you my carriage!"

The dispute was taking a ludicrous turn, but fortunately the Dominican intervened. "Gentlemen," he began in an authoritative tone and with the nasal twang that so well becomes the friars, "you must not confuse things or seek for offenses where there are none. We must distinguish in the words of Fray Damaso those of the man from those of the priest. The latter, as such, *per se,* can never give offense, because they spring from absolute truth, while in those of the man there is a secondary distinction to be made: those which he utters *ab irato,* those which he utters *ex ore,* but not *in corde,* and those which he does utter *in corde.* These last are the only ones that can really offend, and only according to whether they preexisted as a motive *in mente,* or arose solely *per accidens* in the heat of the discussion, if there really exist —"

"But I, by *accidens* and for my own part, understand his motives, Padre Sibyla," broke in the old soldier, who saw himself about to be entangled in so many distinctions that he feared lest he might still be held to blame. "I understand the motives about which your Reverence is going to make distinctions. During the absence of Padre Damaso from San Diego, his coadjutor buried the body of an extremely worthy individual — yes, sir, extremely worthy, for I had had dealings with him many times and had been entertained in his house. What if he never went to confession, what does that matter? Neither do I go to confession! But to say that he committed suicide is a lie, a slander! A man such as he was, who has a son upon whom he centers his affection and hopes, a man who has faith in God, who recognizes his duties to society, a just and honorable man, does not commit suicide. This much I will say and will refrain from expressing the rest of my thoughts here, so please your Reverence."

A SOCIAL GATHERING

Then, turning his back on the Franciscan, he went on: "Now then, this priest on his return to the town, after maltreating the poor coadjutor, had the corpse dug up and taken away from the cemetery to be buried I don't know where. The people of San Diego were cowardly enough not to protest, although it is true that few knew of the outrage. The dead man had no relatives there and his only son was in Europe. But his Excellency learned of the affair and as he is an upright man asked for some punishment — and Padre Damaso was transferred to a better town. That's all there is to it. Now your Reverence can make your distinctions."

So saying, he withdrew from the group.

"I'm sorry that I inadvertently brought up so delicate a subject," said Padre Sibyla sadly. "But, after all, if there has been a gain in the change of towns —"

"How is there to be a gain? And what of all the things that are lost in moving, the letters, and the — and everything that is mislaid?" interrupted Fray Damaso, stammering in the vain effort to control his anger.

Little by little the party resumed its former tranquillity. Other guests had come in, among them a lame old Spaniard of mild and inoffensive aspect leaning on the arm of an elderly Filipina, who was resplendent in frizzes and paint and a European gown. The group welcomed them heartily, and Doctor De Espadaña and his señora, the *Doctora* Doña Victorina, took their seats among our acquaintances. Some newspaper reporters and shopkeepers greeted one another and moved about aimlessly without knowing just what to do.

"But can you tell me, Señor Laruja, what kind of man our host is?" inquired the rubicund youth. "I haven't been introduced to him yet."

"They say that he has gone out. I haven't seen him either."

"There's no need of introductions here," volunteered Fray Damaso. "Santiago is made of the right stuff."

"No, he's not the man who invented gunpowder,"[1] added Laruja.

"You too, Señor Laruja," exclaimed Doña Victorina in mild reproach, as she fanned herself. "How could the poor man invent gunpowder if, as is said, the Chinese invented it centuries ago?"

"The Chinese! Are you crazy?" cried Fray Damaso. "Out with you! A Franciscan, one of my Order, Fray What-do-you-call-him Savalls,[2] invented it in the — ah — the seventh century!"

"A Franciscan? Well, he must have been a missionary in China, that Padre Savalls," replied the lady, who did not thus easily part from her beliefs.

"Schwartz,[3] perhaps you mean, señora," said Fray Sibyla, without looking at her.

"I don't know. Fray Damaso said a Franciscan and I was only repeating."

"Well, Savalls or Chevas, what does it matter? The difference of a letter doesn't make him a Chinaman," replied the Franciscan in bad humor.

"And in the fourteenth century, not the seventh," added the Dominican in a tone of correction, as if to mortify the pride of the other friar.

"Well, neither does a century more or less make him a Dominican."

"Don't get angry, your Reverence," admonished Padre Sibyla, smiling. "So much the better that he did invent it so as to save his brethren the trouble."

"And did you say, Padre Sibyla, that it was in the fourteenth century?" asked Doña Victorina with great interest. "Was that before or after Christ?"

Fortunately for the individual questioned, two persons entered the room.

[1] An apothegm equivalent to the English, "He'll never set any rivers on fire." — TR.

[2] The name of a Carlist leader in Spain. — TR.

[3] A German Franciscan monk who is said to have invented gunpowder about 1330.

CHAPTER II

CRISOSTOMO IBARRA

IT was not two beautiful and well-gowned young women that attracted the attention of all, even including Fray Sibyla, nor was it his Excellency the Captain-General with his staff, that the lieutenant should start from his abstraction and take a couple of steps forward, or that Fray Damaso should look as if turned to stone; it was simply the original of the oil-painting leading by the hand a young man dressed in deep mourning.

"Good evening, gentlemen! Good evening, Padre!" were the greetings of Capitan Tiago as he kissed the hands of the priests, who forgot to bestow upon him their benediction. The Dominican had taken off his glasses to stare at the newly arrived youth, while Fray Damaso was pale and unnaturally wide-eyed.

"I have the honor of presenting to you Don Crisostomo Ibarra, the son of my deceased friend," went on Capitan Tiago. "The young gentleman has just arrived from Europe and I went to meet him."

At the mention of the name exclamations were heard. The lieutenant forgot to pay his respects to his host and approached the young man, looking him over from head to foot. The young man himself at that moment was exchanging the conventional greetings with all in the group, nor did there seem to be any thing extraordinary about him except his mourning garments in the center of that brilliantly lighted room. Yet in spite of them his remarkable stature, his features, and his movements breathed forth an air of healthy youthfulness in which both body and mind had equally developed. There might have been noticed in his frank, pleasant face some faint traces of Spanish blood showing through a beautiful brown color, slightly flushed at the cheeks as a result perhaps of his residence in cold countries.

"What!" he exclaimed with joyful surprise, "the curate of my native town! Padre Damaso, my father's intimate friend!"

Every look in the room was directed toward the Franciscan, who made no movement.

"Pardon me, perhaps I'm mistaken," added Ibarra, embarrassed.

"You are not mistaken," the friar was at last able to articulate in a changed voice, "but your father was never an intimate friend of mine."

Ibarra slowly withdrew his extended hand, looking greatly surprised, and turned to encounter the gloomy gaze of the lieutenant fixed on him.

"Young man, are you the son of Don Rafael Ibarra?" he asked.

The youth bowed. Fray Damaso partly rose in his chair and stared fixedly at the lieutenant.

"Welcome back to your country! And may you be happier in it than your father was!" exclaimed the officer in a trembling voice. "I knew him well and can say that he was one of the worthiest and most honorable men in the Philippines."

"Sir," replied Ibarra, deeply moved, "the praise you bestow upon my father removes my doubts about the manner of his death, of which I, his son, am yet ignorant."

The eyes of the old soldier filled with tears and turning away hastily he withdrew. The young man thus found himself alone in the center of the room. His host having disappeared, he saw no one who might introduce him to the young ladies, many of whom were watching him with interest. After a few moments of hesitation he started toward them in a simple and natural manner.

"Allow me," he said, "to overstep the rules of strict

etiquette. It has been seven years since I have been in my own country and upon returning to it I cannot suppress my admiration and refrain from paying my respects to its most precious ornaments, the ladies."

But as none of them ventured a reply, he found himself obliged to retire. He then turned toward a group of men who, upon seeing him approach, arranged themselves in a semicircle.

"Gentlemen," he addressed them, "it is a custom in Germany, when a stranger finds himself at a function and there is no one to introduce him to those present, that he give his name and so introduce himself. Allow me to adopt this usage here, not to introduce foreign customs when our own are so beautiful, but because I find myself driven to it by necessity. I have already paid my respects to the skies and to the ladies of my native land; now I wish to greet its citizens, my fellow-countrymen. Gentlemen, my name is Juan Crisostomo Ibarra y Magsalin."

The others gave their names, more or less obscure, and unimportant here.

"My name is A——," said one youth dryly, as he made a slight bow.

"Then I have the honor of addressing the poet whose works have done so much to keep up my enthusiasm for my native land. It is said that you do not write any more, but I could not learn the reason."

"The reason? Because one does not seek inspiration in order to debase himself and lie. One writer has been imprisoned for having put a very obvious truth into verse. They may have called me a poet but they sha'n't call me a fool."

"And may I enquire what that truth was?"

"He said that the lion's son is also a lion. He came very near to being exiled for it," replied the strange youth, moving away from the group.

A man with a smiling face, dressed in the fashion of the natives of the country, with diamond studs in his shirt-bosom, came up at that moment almost running. He went directly to Ibarra and grasped his hand, saying, "Señor Ibarra, I've been eager to make your acquaintance. Capitan Tiago is a friend of mine and I knew your respected father. I am known as Capitan Tinong and live in Tondo, where you will always be welcome. I hope that you will honor me with a visit. Come and dine with us tomorrow." He smiled and rubbed his hands.

"Thank you," replied Ibarra, warmly, charmed with such amiability, "but tomorrow morning I must leave for San Diego."

"How unfortunate! Then it will be on your return."

"Dinner is served!" announced a waiter from the café La Campana, and the guests began to file out toward the table, the women, especially the Filipinas, with great hesitation.

CHAPTER III

THE DINNER

Jele, jele, bago quiere.[1]

FRAY SIBYLA seemed to be very content as he moved along tranquilly with the look of disdain no longer playing about his thin, refined lips. He even condescended to speak to the lame doctor, De Espadaña, who answered in monosyllables only, as he was somewhat of a stutterer. The Franciscan was in a frightful humor, kicking at the chairs and even elbowing a cadet out of his way. The lieutenant was grave while the others talked vivaciously, praising the magnificence of the table. Doña Victorina, however, was just turning up her nose in disdain when she suddenly became as furious as a trampled serpent — the lieutenant had stepped on the train of her gown.

"Have n't you any eyes?" she demanded.

"Yes, señora, two better than yours, but the fact is that I was admiring your frizzes," retorted the rather ungallant soldier as he moved away from her.

As if from instinct the two friars both started toward the head of the table, perhaps from habit, and then, as might have been expected, the same thing happened that occurs with the competitors for a university position, who openly exalt the qualifications and superiority of their opponents, later giving to understand that just the contrary was meant, and who murmur and grumble when they do not receive the appointment.

[1] "He says that he does n't want it when it is exactly what he does want." An expression used in the mongrel Spanish-Tagalog 'market language' of Manila and Cavite, especially among the children, — somewhat akin to the English 'sour grapes.' — TR.

"For you, Fray Damaso."

"For you, Fray Sibyla."

"An older friend of the family — confessor of the deceased lady — age, dignity, and authority —"

"Not so very old, either! On the other hand, you are the curate of the district," replied Fray Damaso sourly without taking his hand from the back of the chair.

"Since you command it, I obey," concluded Fray Sibyla, disposing himself to take the seat.

"I don't command it!" protested the Franciscan. "I don't command it!"

Fray Sibyla was about to seat himself without paying any more attention to these protests when his eyes happened to encounter those of the lieutenant. According to clerical opinion in the Philippines, the highest secular official is inferior to a friar-cook: *cedant arma togae*, said Cicero in the Senate — *cedant arma cottae*, say the friars in the Philippines.[1]

But Fray Sibyla was a well-bred person, so he said, "Lieutenant, here we are in the world and not in the church. The seat of honor belongs to you." To judge from the tone of his voice, however, even in the world it really did belong to him, and the lieutenant, either to keep out of trouble or to avoid sitting between two friars, curtly declined.

None of the claimants had given a thought to their host. Ibarra noticed him watching the scene with a smile of satisfaction.

"How's this, Don Santiago, are n't you going to sit down with us?"

But all the seats were occupied; Lucullus was not to sup in the house of Lucullus.

"Sit still, don't get up!" said Capitan Tiago, placing his hand on the young man's shoulder. "This fiesta is for the special purpose of giving thanks to the Virgin for your

---

[1] Arms should yield to the toga (military to civil power). Arms should yield to the surplice (military to religious power). — TR.

THE DINNER

safe arrival. *Oy!* Bring on the *tinola!* I ordered *tinola* as you doubtless have not tasted any for so long a time."

A large steaming tureen was brought in. The Dominican, after muttering the benedicite, to which scarcely any one knew how to respond, began to serve the contents. But whether from carelessness or other cause, Padre Damaso received a plate in which a bare neck and a tough wing of chicken floated about in a large quantity of soup amid lumps of squash, while the others were eating legs and breasts, especially Ibarra, to whose lot fell the second joints. Observing all this, the Franciscan mashed up some pieces of squash, barely tasted the soup, dropped his spoon noisily, and roughly pushed his plate away. The Dominican was very busy talking to the rubicund youth.

"How long have you been away from the country?" Laruja asked Ibarra.

"Almost seven years."

"Then you have probably forgotten all about it."

"Quite the contrary. Even if my country does seem to have forgotten me, I have always thought about it."

"How do you mean that it has forgotten you?" inquired the rubicund youth.

"I mean that it has been a year since I have received any news from here, so that I find myself a stranger who does not yet know how and when his father died."

This statement drew a sudden exclamation from the lieutenant.

"And where were you that you didn't telegraph?" asked Doña Victorina. "When we were married we telegraphed to the Peñinsula."[1]

"Señora, for the past two years I have been in the northern part of Europe, in Germany and Russian Poland."

Doctor De Espadaña, who until now had not ventured upon any conversation, thought this a good opportunity to say something. "I — I knew in S-spain a P-pole from

[1] For *Peninsula*, i. e., Spain. The change of *n* to *ñ* was common among ignorant Filipinos. — TR.

W-warsaw, c-called S-stadtnitzki, if I r-remember c-correctly. P-perhaps you s-saw him?" he asked timidly and almost blushingly.

"It's very likely," answered Ibarra in a friendly manner, "but just at this moment I don't recall him."

"B-but you c-could n't have c-confused him with any one else," went on the Doctor, taking courage. "He was r-ruddy as gold and t-talked Spanish very b-badly."

"Those are good clues, but unfortunately while there I talked Spanish only in a few consulates."

"How then did you get along?" asked the wondering Doña Victorina.

"The language of the country served my needs, madam."

"Do you also speak English?" inquired the Dominican, who had been in Hongkong, and who was a master of pidgin-English, that adulteration of Shakespeare's tongue used by the sons of the Celestial Empire.

"I stayed in England a year among people who talked nothing but English."

"Which country of Europe pleased you the most?" asked the rubicund youth.

"After Spain, my second fatherland, any country of free Europe."

"And you who seem to have traveled so much, tell us — what do you consider the most notable thing that you have seen?" inquired Laruja.

Ibarra appeared to reflect. "Notable — in what way?"

"For example, in regard to the life of the people — the social, political, religious life — in general, in its essential features — as a whole."

Ibarra paused thoughtfully before replying. "Frankly, I like everything in those people, setting aside the national pride of each one. But before visiting a country, I tried to familiarize myself with its history, its Exodus, if I may so speak, and afterwards I found everything quite natural. I have observed that the prosperity or misery of each people is in direct proportion to its liberties or its prejudices and,

THE DINNER

accordingly, to the sacrifices or the selfishness of its forefathers."

"And haven't you observed anything more than that?" broke in the Franciscan with a sneer. Since the beginning of the dinner he had not uttered a single word, his whole attention having been taking up, no doubt, with the food. "It wasn't worth while to squander your fortune to learn so trifling a thing. Any schoolboy knows that."

Ibarra was placed in an embarrassing position, and the rest looked from one to the other as if fearing a disagreeable scene. He was about to say, "The dinner is nearly over and his Reverence is now satiated," but restrained himself and merely remarked to the others, "Gentlemen, don't be surprised at the familiarity with which our former curate treats me. He treated me so when I was a child, and the years seem to make no difference in his Reverence. I appreciate it, too, because it recalls the days when his Reverence visited our home and honored my father's table."

The Dominican glanced furtively at the Franciscan, who was trembling visibly. Ibarra continued as he rose from the table: "You will now permit me to retire, since, as I have just arrived and must go away tomorrow morning, there remain some important business matters for me to attend to. The principal part of the dinner is over and I drink but little wine and seldom touch cordials. Gentlemen, all for Spain and the Philippines!" Saying this, he drained his glass, which he had not before touched. The old lieutenant silently followed his example.

"Don't go!" whispered Capitan Tiago. "Maria Clara will be here. Isabel has gone to get her. The new curate of your town, who is a saint, is also coming."

"I'll call tomorrow before starting. I've a very important visit to make now." With this he went away.

Meanwhile the Franciscan had recovered himself. "Do you see?" he said to the rubicund youth, at the same time flourishing his dessert spoon. "That comes from pride. They can't stand to have the curate correct them.

They even think that they are respectable persons. It's the evil result of sending young men to Europe. The government ought to prohibit it."

"And how about the lieutenant?" Doña Victorina chimed in upon the Franciscan, "he did n't get the frown off his face the whole evening. He did well to leave us — so old and still only a lieutenant!" The lady could not forget the allusion to her frizzes and the trampled ruffles of her gown.

That night the rubicund youth wrote down, among other things, the following title for a chapter in his *Colonial Studies:* "Concerning the manner in which the neck and wing of a chicken in a friar's plate of soup may disturb the merriment of a feast." Among his notes there appeared these observations: "In the Philippines the most unnecessary person at a dinner is he who gives it, for they are quite capable of beginning by throwing the host into the street and then everything will go on smoothly. Under present conditions it would perhaps be a good thing not to allow the Filipinos to leave the country, and even not to teach them to read."

CHAPTER IV

HERETIC AND FILIBUSTER

IBARRA stood undecided for a moment. The night breeze, which during those months blows cool enough in Manila, seemed to drive from his forehead the light cloud that had darkened it. He took off his hat and drew a deep breath. Carriages flashed by, public rigs moved along at a sleepy pace, pedestrians of many nationalities were passing. He walked along at that irregular pace which indicates thoughtful abstraction or freedom from care, directing his steps toward Binondo Plaza and looking about him as if to recall the place. There were the same streets and the identical houses with their white and blue walls, whitewashed, or frescoed in bad imitation of granite; the church continued to show its illuminated clock face; there were the same Chinese shops with their soiled curtains and their iron gratings, in one of which was a bar that he, in imitation of the street urchins of Manila, had twisted one night; it was still unstraightened. "How slowly everything moves," he murmured as he turned into Calle Sacristia. The ice-cream venders were repeating the same shrill cry, "*Sorbeteee!*" while the smoky lamps still lighted the identical Chinese stands and those of the old women who sold candy and fruit.

"Wonderful!" he exclaimed. "There's the same Chinese who was here seven years ago, and that old woman — the very same! It might be said that tonight I've dreamed of a seven years' journey in Europe. Good heavens, that pavement is still in the same unrepaired condition as when I left!" True it was that the stones of the sidewalk on the corner of San Jacinto and Sacristia were still loose.

While he was meditating upon this marvel of the city's

stability in a country where everything is so unstable, a hand was placed lightly on his shoulder. He raised his head to see the old lieutenant gazing at him with something like a smile in place of the hard expression and the frown which usually characterized him.

"Young man, be careful! Learn from your father!" was the abrupt greeting of the old soldier.

"Pardon me, but you seem to have thought a great deal of my father. Can you tell me how he died?" asked Ibarra, staring at him.

"What! Don't you know about it?" asked the officer.

"I asked Don Santiago about it, but he would n't promise to tell me until tomorrow. Perhaps you know?"

"I should say I do, as does everybody else. He died in prison!"

The young man stepped backward a pace and gazed searchingly at the lieutenant. "In prison? Who died in prison?"

"Your father, man, since he was in confinement," was the somewhat surprised answer.

"My father — in prison — confined in a prison? What are you talking about? Do you know who my father was? Are you — ?" demanded the young man, seizing the officer's arm.

"I rather think that I'm not mistaken. He was Don Rafael Ibarra."

"Yes, Don Rafael Ibarra," echoed the youth weakly.

"Well, I thought you knew about it," muttered the soldier in a tone of compassion as he saw what was passing in Ibarra's mind. "I supposed that you — but be brave! Here one cannot be honest and keep out of jail."

"I must believe that you are not joking with me," replied Ibarra in a weak voice, after a few moments' silence. "Can you tell me why he was in prison?"

The old man seemed to be perplexed. "It's strange to me that your family affairs were not made known to you."

"His last letter, a year ago, said that I should not be

HERETIC AND FILIBUSTER

uneasy if he did not write, as he was very busy. He charged me to continue my studies and — sent me his blessing."

"Then he wrote that letter to you just before he died. It will soon be a year since we buried him."

"But why was my father a prisoner?"

"For a very honorable reason. But come with me to the barracks and I'll tell you as we go along. Take my arm."

They moved along for some time in silence. The elder seemed to be in deep thought and to be seeking inspiration from his goatee, which he stroked continually.

"As you well know," he began, "your father was the richest man in the province, and while many loved and respected him, there were also some who envied and hated him. We Spaniards who come to the Philippines are unfortunately not all we ought to be. I say this as much on account of one of your ancestors as on account of your father's enemies. The continual changes, the corruption in the higher circles, the favoritism, the low cost and the shortness of the journey, are to blame for it all. The worst characters of the Peninsula come here, and even if a good man does come, the country soon ruins him. So it was that your father had a number of enemies among the curates and other Spaniards."

Here he hesitated for a while. "Some months after your departure the troubles with Padre Damaso began, but I am unable to explain the real cause of them. Fray Damaso accused him of not coming to confession, although he had not done so formerly and they had nevertheless been good friends, as you may still remember. Moreover, Don Rafael was a very upright man, more so than many of those who regularly attend confession and than the confessors themselves. He had framed for himself a rigid morality and often said to me, when he talked of these troubles, 'Señor Guevara, do you believe that God will pardon any crime, a murder for instance, solely by a man's telling it to a priest — a man after all and one whose duty it is to keep quiet about it — by his fearing that he will roast in hell as a penance — by being cowardly and certainly shameless into the bargain? I have another conception of God,' he used to say, 'for in my opinion one evil does not correct another, nor is a crime to be expiated by vain lamentings or by giving alms to the Church. Take this example: if I have killed the father of a family, if I have made of a woman a sorrowing widow and destitute orphans of some happy children, have I satisfied eternal Justice by letting myself be hanged, or by entrusting my secret to one who is obliged to guard it for me, or by giving alms to priests who are least in need of them, or by buying indulgences and lamenting night and day? What of the widow and the orphans? My conscience tells me that I should try to take the place of him whom I killed, that I should dedicate my whole life to the welfare of the family whose misfortunes I caused. But even so, who can replace the love of a husband and a father?' Thus your father reasoned and by this strict standard of conduct regulated all his actions, so that it can be said that he never injured anybody. On the contrary, he endeavored by his good deeds to wipe out some injustices which he said your ancestors had committed. But to get back to his troubles with the curate — these took /on a serious aspect. Padre Damaso denounced him from the pulpit, and that he did not expressly name him was a miracle, since anything might have been expected of such a character. I foresaw that sooner or later the affair would have serious results."

Again the old lieutenant paused. "There happened to be wandering about the province an ex-artilleryman who has been discharged from the army on account of his stupidity and ignorance. As the man had to live and he was not permitted to engage in manual labor, which would injure our prestige, he somehow or other obtained a position as collector of the tax on vehicles. The poor devil had no education at all, a fact of which the natives soon became aware, as it was a marvel for them to see a Spaniard who didn't know how to read and write. Every one ridiculed him and the payment of the tax was the occasion of broad smiles. He knew that he was an object of ridicule and this tended to sour his disposition even more, rough and bad as it had formerly been. They would purposely hand him the papers upside down to see his efforts to read them, and wherever he found a blank space he would scribble a lot of pothooks which rather fitly passed for his signature. The natives mocked while they paid him. He swallowed his pride and made the collections, but was in such a state of mind that he had no respect for any one. He even came to have some hard words with your father.

"One day it happened that he was in a shop turning a document over and over in the effort to get it straight when a schoolboy began to make signs to his companions and to point laughingly at the collector with his finger. The fellow heard the laughter and saw the joke reflected in the solemn faces of the bystanders. He lost his patience and, turning quickly, started to chase the boys, who ran away shouting *ba, be, bi, bo, bu.*[1] Blind with rage and unable to catch them, he threw his cane and struck one of the boys on the head, knocking him down. He ran up and began to kick the fallen boy, and none of those who had been laughing had the courage to interfere. Unfortunately, your father happened to come along just at that time. He ran forward indignantly, caught the collector by the arm, and reprimanded him severely. The artilleryman, who was no doubt beside himself with rage, raised his hand, but your father was too quick for him, and with the strength of a descendant of the Basques — some say that he struck him, others that he merely pushed him, but at any rate the man staggered and fell a little way off, striking his head against a stone. Don Rafael quietly picked the wounded boy up and carried him to the town hall. The artilleryman bled freely from the mouth and died a few moments later without recovering consciousness.

[1] The syllables which constitute the first reading lesson in Spanish primers. — TR.

"As was to be expected, the authorities intervened and arrested your father. All his hidden enemies at once rose up and false accusations came from all sides. He was accused of being a heretic and a filibuster. To be a heretic is a great danger anywhere, but especially so at that time when the province was governed by an alcalde who made a great show of his piety, who with his servants used to recite his rosary in the church in a loud voice, perhaps that all might hear and pray with him. But to be a filibuster is worse than to be a heretic and to kill three or four tax-collectors who know how to read, write, and attend to business. Every one abandoned him, and his books and papers were seized. He was accused of subscribing to *El Correo de Ultramar,* and to newspapers from Madrid, of having sent you to Germany, of having in his possession letters and a photograph of a priest who had been legally executed, and I don't know what not. Everything served as an accusation, even the fact that he, a descendant of Peninsulars, wore a camisa. Had it been any one but your father, it is likely that he would soon have been set free, as there was a physician who ascribed the death of the unfortunate collector to a hemorrhage. But his wealth, his confidence in the law, and his hatred of everything that was not legal and just, wrought his undoing. In spite of my repugnance to asking for mercy from any one, I applied personally to the Captain-General — the predecessor of our present one — and urged upon him that there could not be anything of the filibuster about a man who took up with all the Spaniards, even the poor emigrants, and gave them food and shelter, and in whose veins yet flowed the generous blood of Spain. It was in vain that I pledged my life and swore by my poverty and my military honor. I succeeded only in being coldly listened to and roughly sent away with the epithet of *chiflado.*" [1]

---

[1] A Spanish colloquial term ("cracked"), applied to a native of Spain who was considered to be mentally unbalanced from too long residence in the islands. — TR.

The old man paused to take a deep breath, and after noticing the silence of his companion, who was listening with averted face, continued: "At your father's request I prepared the defense in the case. I went first to the celebrated Filipino lawyer, young A——, but he refused to take the case. 'I should lose it,' he told me, 'and my defending him would furnish the motive for another charge against him and perhaps one against me. Go to Señor M——, who is a forceful and fluent speaker and a Peninsular of great influence.' I did so, and the noted lawyer took charge of the case and conducted it with mastery and brilliance. But your father's enemies were numerous, some of them hidden and unknown. False witnesses abounded, and their calumnies, which under other circumstances would have melted away before a sarcastic phrase from the defense, here assumed shape and substance. If the lawyer succeeded in destroying the force of their testimony by making them contradict each other and even perjure themselves, new charges were at once preferred. They accused him of having illegally taken possession of a great deal of land and demanded damages. They said that he maintained relations with the tulisanes in order that his crops and animals might not be molested by them. At last the case became so confused that at the end of a year no one understood it. The alcalde had to leave and there came in his place one who had the reputation of being honest, but unfortunately he stayed only a few months, and his successor was too fond of good horses.

"The sufferings, the worries, the hard life in the prison, or the pain of seeing so much ingratitude, broke your father's iron constitution and he fell ill with that malady which only the tomb can cure. When the case was almost finished and he was about to be acquitted of the charge of being an enemy of the fatherland and of being the murderer of the tax-collector, he died in the prison with no one at his side. I arrived just in time to see him breathe his last."

The old lieutenant became silent, but still Ibarra said nothing. They had arrived meanwhile at the door of the barracks, so the soldier stopped and said, as he grasped the youth's hand, "Young man, for details ask Capitan Tiago. Now, good night, as I must return to duty and see that all's well."

Silently, but with great feeling, Ibarra shook the lieutenant's bony hand and followed him with his eyes until he disappeared. Then he turned slowly and signaled to a passing carriage. "To Lala's Hotel," was the direction he gave in a scarcely audible voice.

"This fellow must have just got out of jail," thought the cochero as he whipped up his horses.

CHAPTER V

A STAR IN A DARK NIGHT

IBARRA went to his room, which overlooked the river, and dropping into a chair gazed out into the vast expanse of the heavens spread before him through the open window. The house on the opposite bank was profusely lighted, and gay strains of music, largely from stringed instruments, were borne across the river even to his room.

If the young man had been less preoccupied, if he had had more curiosity and had cared to see with his opera glasses what was going on in that atmosphere of light, he would have been charmed with one of those magical and fantastic spectacles, the like of which is sometimes seen in the great theaters of Europe. To the subdued strains of the orchestra there seems to appear in the midst of a shower of light, a cascade of gold and diamonds in an Oriental setting, a deity wrapped in misty gauze, a sylph enveloped in a luminous halo, who moves forward apparently without touching the floor. In her presence the flowers bloom, the dance awakens, the music bursts forth, and troops of devils, nymphs, satyrs, demons, angels, shepherds and shepherdesses, dance, shake their tambourines, and whirl about in rhythmic evolutions, each one placing some tribute at the feet of the goddess. Ibarra would have seen a beautiful and graceful maiden, clothed in the picturesque garments of the daughters of the Philippines, standing in the center of a semicircle made up of every class of people, Chinese, Spaniards, Filipinos, soldiers, curates, old men and young, all gesticulating and moving about in a lively manner. Padre Damaso stood at the side of the beauty, smiling like one especially blessed. Fray Sibyla — yes, Fray Sibyla himself — was talking to her. Doña Victorina was arranging in the magnificent hair of the maiden a string of pearls and diamonds which threw out all the beautiful tints of the rainbow. She was white, perhaps too much so, and whenever she raised her downcast eyes there shone forth a spotless soul. When she smiled so as to show her small white teeth the beholder realized that the rose is only a flower and ivory but the elephant's tusk. From out the filmy piña draperies around her white and shapely neck there blinked, as the Tagalogs say, the bright eyes of a collar of diamonds. One man only in all the crowd seemed insensible to her radiant influence — a young Franciscan, thin, wasted, and pale, who watched her from a distance, motionless as a statue and scarcely breathing.

But Ibarra saw nothing of all this — his eyes were fixed on other things. A small space was enclosed by four bare and grimy walls, in one of which was an iron grating. On the filthy and loathsome floor was a mat upon which an old man lay alone in the throes of death, an old man breathing with difficulty and turning his head from side to side as amid his tears he uttered a name. The old man was alone, but from time to time a groan or the rattle of a chain was heard on the other side of the wall. Far away there was a merry feast, almost an orgy; a youth was laughing, shouting, and pouring wine upon the flowers amid the applause and drunken laughter of his compauions. The old man had the features of *his* father, the youth was himself, and the name that the old man uttered with tears was *his own* name! This was what the wretched young man saw before him. The lights in the house opposite were extinguished, the music and the noises ceased, but Ibarra still heard the anguished cry of his father calling upon his son in the hour of his death.

Silence had now blown its hollow breath over the city, and all things seemed to sleep in the embrace of nothingness. The cock-crow alternated with the strokes of the clocks in the church towers and the mournful cries of the weary

A STAR IN A DARK NIGHT

sentinels. A waning moon began to appear, and everything seemed to be at rest; even Ibarra himself, worn out by his sad thoughts or by his journey, now slept.

Only the young Franciscan whom we saw not so long ago standing motionless and silent in the midst of the gaiety of the ballroom slept not, but kept vigil. In his cell, with his elbow upon the window sill and his pale, worn cheek resting on the palm of his hand, he was gazing silently into the distance where a bright star glittered in the dark sky. The star paled and disappeared, the dim light of the waning moon faded, but the friar did not move from his place — he was gazing out over the field of Bagumbayan and the sleeping sea at the far horizon wrapped in the morning mist.

CHAPTER VI

CAPITAN TIAGO

Thy will be done on earth.

WHILE our characters are deep in slumber or busy with their breakfasts, let us turn our attention to Capitan Tiago. We have never had the honor of being his guest, so it is neither our right nor our duty to pass him by slightingly, even under the stress of important events.

Low in stature, with a clear complexion, a corpulent figure and a full face, thanks to the liberal supply of fat which according to his admirers was the gift of Heaven and which his enemies averred was the blood of the poor, Capitan Tiago appeared to be younger than he really was; he might have been thought between thirty and thirty-five years of age. At the time of our story his countenance always wore a sanctified look; his little round head, covered with ebony-black hair cut long in front and short behind, was reputed to contain many things of weight; his eyes, small but with no Chinese slant, never varied in expression; his nose was slender and not at all inclined to flatness; and if his mouth had not been disfigured by the immoderate use of tobacco and buyo, which, when chewed and gathered in one cheek, marred the symmetry of his features, we would say that he might properly have considered himself a handsome man and have passed for such. Yet in spite of this bad habit he kept marvelously white both his natural teeth and also the two which the dentist furnished him at twelve pesos each.

He was considered one of the richest landlords in Binondo and a planter of some importance by reason of his

CAPITAN TIAGO

estates in Pampanga and Laguna, principally in the town of San Diego, the income from which increased with each year. San Diego, on account of its agreeable baths, its famous cockpit, and his cherished memories of the place, was his favorite town, so that he spent at least two months of the year there. His holdings of real estate in the city were large, and it is superfluous to state that the opium monopoly controlled by him and a Chinese brought in large profits. They also had the lucrative contract of feeding the prisoners in Bilibid and furnished zacate to many of the stateliest establishments in Manila — through the medium of contracts, of course. Standing well with all the authorities, clever, cunning, and even bold in speenlating upon the wants of others, he was the only formidable rival of a certain Perez in the matter of the farming-out of revenues and the sale of offices and appointments, which the Philippine government always confides to private persons. Thus, at the time of the events here narrated, Capitan Tiago was a happy man in so far as it is possible for a narrow-brained individual to be happy in such a land: he was rich, and at peace with God, the government, and men.

That he was at peace with God was beyond doubt, — almost like religion itself. There is no need to be on bad terms with the good God when one is prosperous on earth, when one has never had any direct dealings with Him and has never lent Him any money. Capitan Tiago himself had never offered any prayers to Him, even in his greatest difficulties, for he was rich and his gold prayed for him. For masses and supplications high and powerful priests had been created; for novenas and rosaries God in His infinite bounty had created the poor for the service of the rich — the poor who for a peso could be secured to recite sixteen mysteries and to read all the sacred books, even the Hebrew Bible, for a little extra. If at any time in the midst of pressing difficulties he needed celestial aid and had not at hand even a red Chinese taper, he would call upon his most adored saints, promising them many things for the purpose of putting them under obligation to him and ultimately convincing them of the righteouness of his desires.

The saint to whom he promised the most, and whose promises he was the most faithful in fulfilling, was the Virgin of Antipolo, Our Lady of Peace and Prosperous Voyages.[1] With many of the lesser saints he was not very punctual or even decent; and sometimes, after having his petitions granted, he thought no more about them, though of course after such treatment he did not bother them again, when occasion arose. Capitan Tiago knew that the calendar was full of idle saints who perhaps had nothing wherewith to occupy their time up there in heaven. Furthermore, to the Virgin of Antipolo he ascribed greater power and efficiency than to all the other Virgins combined, whether they carried silver canes, naked or richly clothed images of the Christ Child, scapularies, rosaries, or girdles. Perhaps this reverence was owing to the fact that she was a very strict Lady, watchful of her name, and, according to the senior sacristan of Antipolo, an enemy of photography. When she was angered she turned black as ebony, while

[1] This celebrated Lady was first brought from Acapulco, Mexico, by Juan Niño de Tabora, when he came to govern the Philippines in 1626. By reason of her miraculous powers of allaying the storms she was carried back and forth in the state galleons on a number of voyages, until in 1672 she was formally installed in a church in the hills northeast of Manila, under the care of the Augustinian Fathers. While her shrine was building she is said to have appeared to the faithful in the top of a large breadfruit tree, which is known to the Tagalogs as "antipolo"; hence her name. Hers is the best known and most frequented shrine in the country, while she disputes with the Holy Child of Cebu the glory of being the wealthiest individual in the whole archipelago.

There has always existed a pious rivalry between her and the Dominicans' Lady of the Rosary as to which is the patron saint of the Philippines, the contest being at times complicated by counterclaims on the part of St. Francis, although the entire question would seem to have been definitely settled by a royal decree, published about 1650, officially conferring that honorable post upon St. Michael the Archangel (San Miguel). A rather irreverent sketch of this celebrated queen of the skies appears in Chapter XI of Foreman's *The Philippine Islands.* — TR.

CAPITAN TIAGO

the other Virgins were softer of heart and more indulgent. It is a well-known fact that some minds love an absolute monarch rather than a constitutional one, as witness Louis XIV and Louis XVI, Philip II and Amadeo I. This fact perhaps explains why infidel Chinese and even Spaniards may be seen kneeling in the famous sanctuary; what is not explained is why the priests run away with the money of the terrible Image, go to America, and get married there.

In the sala of Capitan Tiago's house, that door hidden by a silk curtain leads to a small chapel or oratory such as must be lacking in no Filipino home. There were placed his household gods — and we say "gods" because he was inclined to polytheism rather than to monotheism, which he had never come to understand. There could be seen images of the Holy Family with busts and extremities of ivory, glass eyes, long eyelashes, and curly blond hair — masterpieces of Santa Cruz sculpture. Paintings in oil by artists of Paco and Ermita [1] represented martyrdoms of saints and miracles of the Virgin; St. Lucy gazing at the sky and carrying in a plate an extra pair of eyes with lashes and eyebrows, such as are seen painted in the triangle of the Trinity or on Egyptian tombs; St. Pascual Bailon; St. Anthony of Padua in a *guingón* habit looking with tears upon a Christ Child dressed as a Captain-General with the three-cornered hat, sword, and boots, as in the children's ball at Madrid that character is represented — which signified for Capitan Tiago that while God might include in His omnipotence the power of a Captain-General of the Philippines, the Franciscans would nevertheless play with Him as with a doll. There might also be seen a St. Anthony the Abbot with a hog by his side, a hog that for the worthy Capitan was as miraculous as the saint himself, for which reason he never dared to refer to it as the *hog,* but as the *creature of holy St. Anthony;* a St. Francis

[1] Santa Cruz, Paco, and Ermita are districts of Manila, outside the Walled City. — TR.

of Assisi in a coffee-colored robe and with seven wings, placed over a St. Vincent who had only two but in compensation carried a trumpet; a St. Peter the Martyr with his head split open by the talibon of an evil-doer and held fast by a kneeling infidel, side by side with another St. Peter cutting off the ear of a Moro, Malchus[1] no doubt, who was gnawing his lips and writhing with pain, while a fighting-cock on a doric column crowed and flapped his wings — from all of which Capitan Tiago deduced that in order to be a saint it was just as well to smite as to be smitten.

Who could enumerate that army of images and recount the virtues and perfections that were treasured there! A whole chapter would hardly suffice. Yet we must not pass over in silence a beautiful St. Michael of painted and gilded wood almost four feet high. The Archangel is biting his lower lip and with flashing eyes, frowning forehead, and rosy cheeks is grasping a Greek shield and brandishing in his right hand a Sulu kris, ready, as would appear from his attitude and expression, to smite a worshiper or any one else who might approach, rather than the horned and tailed devil that had his teeth set in his girlish leg.

Capitan Tiago never went near this image from fear of a miracle. Had not other images, even those more rudely carved ones that issue from the carpenter shops of Paete,[2] many times come to life for the confusion and punishment of incredulous sinners? It is a well-known fact that a certain image of Christ in Spain, when invoked as a witness of promises of love, had assented with a movement of the head in the presence of the judge, and that another such image had reached out its right arm to embrace St. Lutgarda. And furthermore, had he not himself read a booklet recently published about a mimic sermon preached

---

[1] John xviii. 10.
[2] A town in Laguna Province, noted for the manufacture of furniture. — TR.

by an image of St. Dominic in Soriano? True, the saint had not said a single word, but from his movements it was inferred, at any rate the author of the booklet inferred, that he was announcing the end of the world.[1] Was it not reported, too, that the Virgin of Luta in the town of Lipa had one cheek swollen larger than the other and that there was mud on the borders of her gown? Does not this prove mathematically that the holy images also walk about without holding up their skirts and that they even suffer from the toothache, perhaps for our sake? Had he not seen with his own eyes, during the regular Good-Friday sermon, all the images of Christ move and bow their heads thrice in unison, thereby calling forth wails and cries from the women and other sensitive souls destined for Heaven? More? We ourselves have seen the preacher show to the congregation at the moment of the descent from the cross a handkerchief stained with blood, and were ourselves on the point of weeping piously, when, to the sorrow of our soul, a sacristan assured us that it was all a joke, that the blood was that of a chicken which had been roasted and eaten on the spot in spite of the fact that it was Good Friday — and the sacristan was fat! So Capitan Tiago, even though he was a prudent and pious individual, took care not to approach the kris of St. Michael. "Let's take no chances," he would say to himself, "I know that he's an archangel, but I don't trust him, no, I don't trust him."

Not a year passed without his joining with an orchestra in the pilgrimage to the wealthy shrine of Antipolo. He paid for two thanksgiving masses of the many that make up the three novenas, and also for the days when there are no novenas, and washed himself afterwards in the famous *bátis*, or pool, where the sacred Image herself had bathed. Her votaries can even yet discern the tracks of her feet and the traces of her locks in the hard rock, where she dried them, resembling exactly those made by any

---

[1] God grant that this prophecy may soon be fulfilled for the author of the booklet and all of us who believe it. Amen. — *Author's note.*

woman who uses coconut-oil, and just as if her hair had been steel or diamonds and she had weighed a thousand tons. We should like to see the terrible Image once shake her sacred hair in the eyes of those credulous persons and put her foot upon their tongues or their heads. There at the very edge of the pool Capitan Tiago made it his duty to eat roast pig, *sinigang* of *dalag* with *alibambang* leaves, and other more or less appetizing dishes. The two masses would cost him over four hundred pesos, but it was cheap, after all, if one considered the glory that the Mother of the Lord would acquire from the pin-wheels, rockets, bombs, and mortars, and also the increased profits which, thanks to these masses, would come to one during the year.

But Antipolo was not the only theater of his ostentatious devotion. In Binondo, in Pampanga, and in the town of San Diego, when he was about to put up a fighting-cock with large wagers, he would send gold moneys to the curate for propitiatory masses and, just as the Romans consulted the augurs before a battle, giving food to the sacred fowls, so Capitan Tiago would also consult his augurs, with the modifications befitting the times and the new truths. He would watch closely the flame of the tapers, the smoke from the incense, the voice of the priest, and from it all attempt to forecast his luck. It was an admitted fact that he lost very few wagers, and in those cases it was due to the unlucky circumstance that the officiating priest was hoarse, or that the altar-candles were few or contained too much tallow, or that a bad piece of money had slipped in with the rest. The warden of the Brotherhood would then assure him that such reverses were tests to which he was subjected by Heaven to receive assurance of his fidelity and devotion. So, beloved by the priests, respected by the sacristans, humored by the Chinese chandlers and the dealers in fireworks, he was a man happy in the religion of this world, and persons of discernment and great piety even claimed for him great influence in the celestial court.

CAPITAN TIAGO

That he was at peace with the government cannot be doubted, however difficult an achievement it may seem. Incapable of any new idea and satisfied with his *modus vivendi,* he was ever ready to gratify the desires of the last official of the fifth class in every one of the offices, to make presents of hams, capons, turkeys, and Chinese fruits at all seasons of the year. If he heard any one speak ill of the natives, he, who did not consider himself as such, would join in the chorus and speak worse of them; if any one aspersed the Chinese or Spanish mestizos, he would do the same, perhaps because he considered himself become a full-blooded Iberian. He was ever first to talk in favor of any new imposition of taxes, or special assessment, especially when he smelled a contract or a farming assignment behind it. He always had an orchestra ready for congratulating and serenading the governors, judges, and other officials on their name-days and birthdays, at the birth or death of a relative, and in fact at every variation from the usual monotony. For such occasions he would secure laudatory poems and hymns in which were celebrated "the kind and loving governor," "the brave and courageous judge for whom there awaits in heaven the palm of the just," with many other things of the same kind.

He was the president of the rich guild of mestizos in spite of the protests of many of them, who did not regard him as one of themselves. In the two years that he held this office he wore out ten frock coats, an equal number of high hats, and half a dozen canes. The frock coat and the high hat were in evidence at the Ayuntamiento, in the governor-general's palace, and at military headquarters; the high hat and the frock coat might have been noticed in the cockpit, in the market, in the processions, in the Chinese shops, and under the hat and within the coat might have been seen the perspiring Capitan Tiago, waving his tasseled cane, directing, arranging, and throwing everything into disorder with marvelous activity and a gravity even more marvelous.

So the authorities saw in him a safe man, gifted with the best of dispositions, peaceful, tractable, and obsequious, who read no books or newspapers from Spain, although he spoke Spanish well. Indeed, they rather looked upon him with the feeling with which a poor student contemplates the worn-out heel of his old shoe, twisted by his manner of walking. In his case there was truth in both the Christian and profane proverbs: *beati pauperes spiritu* and *beati possidentes*,[1] and there might well be applied to him that translation, according to some people incorrect, from the Greek, "Glory to God in the highest and peace to men of good-will on earth!" even though we shall see further along that it is not sufficient for men to have good-will in order to live in peace.

The irreverent considered him a fool, the poor regarded him as a heartless and cruel exploiter of misery and want, and his inferiors saw in him a despot and a tyrant. As to the women, ah, the women! Accusing rumors buzzed through the wretched nipa huts, and it was said that wails and sobs might be heard mingled with the weak cries of an infant. More than one young woman was pointed out by her neighbors with the finger of scorn: she had a downcast glance and a faded cheek. But such things never robbed him of sleep nor did any maiden disturb his peace. It was an old woman who made him suffer, an old woman who was his rival in piety and who had gained from many curates such enthusiastic praises and eulogies as he in his best days had never received.

Between Capitan Tiago and this widow, who had inherited from brothers and cousins, there existed a holy rivalry which redounded to the benefit of the Church as the competition among the Pampanga steamers then redounded to the benefit of the public. Did Capitan Tiago present to some Virgin a silver wand ornamented with emeralds and topazes? At once Doña Patrocinio had ordered another

---

[1] "Blessed are the poor in spirit" and "blessed are the possessors." — TR.

CAPITAN TIAGO

of gold set with diamonds! If at the time of the Naval procession [1] Capitan Tiago erected an arch with two façades, covered with ruffled cloth and decorated with mirrors, glass globes, and chandeliers, then Doña Patrocinio would have another with four façades, six feet higher, and more gorgeous hangings. Then he would fall back on his reserves, his strong point, his specialty — masses with bombs and fireworks; whereat Doña Patrocinia could only gnaw at her lips with her toothless gums, because, being exceedingly nervous, she could not endure the chiming of the bells and still less the explosions of the bombs. While he smiled in triumph, she would plan her revenge and pay the money of others to secure the best orators of the five Orders in Manila, the most famous preachers of the Cathedral, and even the Paulists,[2] to preach on the holy days upon profound theological subjects to the sinners who understood only the vernacular of the markets. The partizans of Capitan Tiago would observe that she slept during the sermon; but her adherents would answer that the sermon was paid for in advance, and by her, and that in any affair payment was the prime requisite. At length, she had driven him from the field completely by presenting to the church three *andas* of gilded silver, each one of which cost her over three thousand pesos. Capitan Tiago hoped that the old woman would breathe her last almost any day, or that she would lose five or six of her lawsuits, so that he might be alone in serving God; but unfortunately the best lawyers of the *Real Audiencia* looked after her interests, and as to her health, there was no part of her that could be attacked by sickness; she seemed to be a steel wire, no

---

[1] The annual celebration of the Dominican Order held in October in honor of its patroness, the Virgin of the Rosary, to whose intervention was ascribed the victory over a Dutch fleet in 1646, whence the name. See *Guia Oficial de Filipinas*, 1885, pp. 138. 139; Montero y Vidal, *Historia General de Filipinas*, Vol. I, Chap. XXIII; Blair, and Robertson, *The Philippine Islands*, Vol. XXXV, pp. 249, 250. — Tr.

[2] Members of the Society of St. Vincent de Paul, whose chief business is preaching and teaching. They entered the Philippines in 1862. — Tr.

doubt for the edification of souls, and she hung on in this vale of tears with the tenacity of a boil on the skin. Her adherents were secure in the belief that she would be canonized at her death and that Capitan Tiago himself would have to worship her at the altars — all of which he agreed to and cheerfully promised, provided only that she die soon.

Such was Capitan Tiago in the days of which we write. As for the past, he was the only son of a sugar-planter of Malabon, wealthy enough, but so miserly that he would not spend a cent to educate his son, for which reason the little Santiago had been the servant of a good Dominican, a worthy man who had tried to train him in all of good that he knew and could teach. When he had reached the happy stage of being known among his acquaintances as a *logician,* that is, when he began to study logic, the death of his protector, soon followed by that of his father, put an end to his studies and he had to turn his attention to business affairs. He married a pretty young woman of Santa Cruz, who gave him social position and helped him to make his fortune. Doña Pia Alba was not satisfied with buying and selling sugar, indigo, and coffee, but wished to plant and reap, so the newly-married couple bought land in San Diego. From this time dated their friendship with Padre Damoso and with Don Rafael Ibarra, the richest capitalist of the town.

The lack of an heir in the first six years of their wedded life made of that eagerness to accumulate riches almost a censurable ambition. Doña Pia was comely, strong, and healthy, yet it was in vain that she offered novenas and at the advice of the devout women of San Diego made a pilgrimage to the Virgin of Kaysaysay[1] in Taal, distrib-

---

[1] "Kaysaysay: A celebrated sanctuary in the island of Luzon, province of Batangas, jurisdiction of Taal, so called because there is venerated in it a Virgin who bears that name. . . .

"The image is in the center of the high altar, where there is seen an eagle in half-relief, whose abdomen is left open in order to afford a tabernacle for the Virgin: an idea enchanting to many of the Spaniards

CAPITAN TIAGO

uted alms to the poor, and danced at midday in May in the procession of the Virgin of Turumba [1] in Pakil. But it was all with no result until Fray Damaso advised her to go to Obando to dance in the fiesta of St. Pascual Bailon and ask him for a son. Now it is well known that there is in Obando a trinity which grants sons or daughters according to request — Our Lady of Salambaw, St. Clara, and St. Pascual. Thanks to this wise advice, Doña Pia soon recognized the signs of approaching motherhood. But alas! like the fisherman of whom Shakespeare tells in *Macbeth*, who ceased to sing when he had found a treasure, she at once lost all her mirthfulness, fell into melancholy, and was never seen to smile again " Capricious-

established in the Philippines during the last century, but which in our opinion any sensible person will characterize as extravagant.

"This image of the Virgin of Kaysaysay enjoys the fame of being very miraculous, so that the Indians gather from great distances to hear mass in her sanctuary every Saturday. Her discovery, over two and a half centuries ago, is notable in that she was found in the sea during some fisheries, coming up in a drag-net with the fish. It is thought that this venerable image of the Filipinos may have been in some ship which was wrecked and that the currents carried her up to the coast, where she was found in the manner related.

"The Indians, naturally credulous and for the most part quite superstitious, in spite of the advancements in civilization and culture, relate that she appeared afterwards in some trees, and in memory of these manifestations an arch representing them was erected at a short distance from the place where her sanctuary is now located." — Buzeta and Bravo's *Diccionario*, Madrid, 1850, but copied " with proper modifications for the times and the new truths " from Zuñiga's *Estadismo*, which, though written in 1803 and not published until 1893, was yet used by later writers, since it was preserved in manuscript in the convent of the Augustinians in Manila, Buzeta and Bravo, as well as Zuñiga, being members of that order.

So great was the reverence for this Lady that the Acapulco galleons on their annual voyages were accustomed to fire salutes in her honor as they passed along the coast near her shrine. — Foreman. *The Philippine Islands*, quoting from the account of an eruption of Taal Volcano in 1749, by Fray Francisco Vencuchillo.

This Lady's sanctuary, where she is still " enchanting " in her " eagle in half-relief," stands out prominently on the hill above the town of Taal, plainly visible from Balayan Bay. — TR. .

[1] A Tagalog term meaning " to tumble," or " to caper about," doubtless from the actions of the Lady's devotees. Pakil is a town in Laguna Province. — TR.

ness, natural in her condition," commented all, even Capitan Tiago. A puerperal fever put an end to her hidden grief, and she died, leaving behind a beautiful girl baby for whom Fray Damaso himself stood sponsor. As St. Pascual had not granted the son that was asked, they gave the child the name of Maria Clara, in honor of the Virgin of Salambaw and St. Clara, punishing the worthy St. Pascual with silence.

The little girl grew up under the care of her aunt Isabel, that good old lady of monkish urbanity whom we met at the beginning of the story. For the most part, her early life was spent in San Diego, on account of its healthful climate, and there Padre Damaso was devoted to her.

Maria Clara had not the small eyes of her father; like her mother, she had eyes large, black, long-lashed, merry and smiling when she was playing but sad, deep, and pensive in moments of repose. As a child her hair was curly and almost blond, her straight nose was neither too pointed nor too flat, while her mouth with the merry dimples at the corners recalled the small and pleasing one of her mother. Her skin had the fineness of an onion-cover and was white as cotton, according to her perplexed relatives, who found the traces of Capitan Tiago's paternity in her small and shapely ears. Aunt Isabel ascribed her half-European features to the longings of Doña Pia, whom she remembered to have seen many times weeping before the image of St. Anthony. Another cousin was of the same opinion, differing only in the choice of the saint, as for her it was either the Virgin herself or St. Michael. A famous philosopher, who was the cousin of Capitan Tinong and who had memorized the "Amat,"[1] sought for the true explanation in planetary influences.

The idol of all, Maria Clara grew up amidst smiles and love. The very friars showered her with attentions when she appeared in the processions dressed in white, her

---

[1] A work on scholastic philosophy, by a Spanish prelate of that name. — TR.

CAPITAN TIAGO

abundant hair interwoven with tuberoses and sampaguitas, with two diminutive wings of silver and gold fastened on the back of her gown, and carrying in her hands a pair of white doves tied with blue ribbons. Afterwards, she would be so merry and talk so sweetly in her childish simplicity that the enraptured Capitan Tiago could do nothing but bless the saints of Obando and advise every one to purchase beautiful works of sculpture.

In southern countries the girl of thirteen or fourteen years changes into a woman as the bud of the night becomes a flower in the morning. At this period of change, so full of mystery and romance, Maria Clara was placed, by the advice of the curate of Binondo, in the nunnery of St. Catherine [1] in order to receive strict religious training from the Sisters. With tears she took leave of Padre Damaso and of the only lad who had been a friend of her childhood, Crisostomo Ibarra, who himself shortly afterward went away to Europe. There in that convent, which communicates with the world through double bars, even under the watchful eyes of the nuns, she spent seven years.

Each having his own particular ends in view and knowing the mutual inclinations of the two young persons, Don Rafael and Capitan Tiago agreed upon the marriage of their children and the formation of a business partnership. This agreement, which was concluded some years after the younger Ibarra's departure, was celebrated with equal joy by two hearts in widely separated parts of the world and under very different circumstances.

[1] The nunnery and college of St. Catherine of Sienna ("Santa Catalina de la Sena") was founded by the Dominican Fathers in 1696. — Tr.

CHAPTER VII

AN IDYL ON AN AZOTEA

The Song of Songs, which is Solomon's.

THAT morning Aunt Isabel and Maria Clara went early to mass, the latter elegantly dressed and wearing a rosary of blue beads, which partly served as a bracelet for her, and the former with her spectacles in order to read her *Anchor of Salvation* during the holy communion. Scarcely had the priest disappeared from the altar when the maiden expressed a desire for returning home, to the great surprise and displeasure of her good aunt, who believed her niece to be as pious and devoted to praying as a nun, at least. Grumbling and crossing herself, the good old lady rose. " The good Lord will forgive me, Aunt Isabel, since He must know the hearts of girls better than you do," Maria Clara might have said to check the severe yet maternal chidings.

After they had breakfasted, Maria Clara consumed her impatience in working at a silk purse while her aunt was trying to clean up the traces of the former night's revelry by swinging a feather duster about. Capitan Tiago was busy looking over some papers. Every noise in the street, every carriage that passed, caused the maiden to tremble and quickened the beatings of her heart. Now she wished that she were back in the quiet convent among her friends; there she could have seen him without emotion and agitation! But was he not the companion of her infancy, had they not played together and even quarreled at times? The reason for all this I need not explain; if you, O reader, have ever loved, you will understand; and if you

AN IDYL ON AN AZOTEA

have not, it is useless for me to tell you, as the uninitiated do not comprehend these mysteries.

"I believe, Maria, that the doctor is right," said Capitan Tiago. "You ought to go into the country, for you are pale and need fresh air. What do you think of Malabon — or San Diego?" At the mention of the latter place Maria Clara blushed like a poppy and was unable to answer.

"You and Isabel can go at once to the convent to get your clothes and to say good-by to your friends," he continued, without raising his head "You will not stay there any longer."

The girl felt the vague sadness that possesses the mind when we leave forever a place where we have been happy, but another thought softened this sorrow.

"In four or five days, after you get some new clothes made, we'll go to Malabon. Your godfather is no longer in San Diego. The priest that you may have noticed here last night, that young padre, is the new curate whom we have there, and he is a saint."

"I think that San Diego would be better, cousin," observed Aunt Isabel. "Besides, our house there is better and the time for the fiesta draws near."

Maria Clara wanted to embrace her aunt for this speech, but hearing a carriage stop, she turned pale.

"Ah, very true," answered Capitan Tiago, and then in a different tone he exclaimed, "Don Crisostomo!"

The maiden let her sewing fall from her hands and wished to move but could not — a violent tremor ran through her body. Steps were heard on the stairway and then a fresh, manly voice. As if that voice had some magic power, the maiden controlled her emotion and ran to hide in the oratory among the saints. The two cousins laughed, and Ibarra even heard the noise of the door closing. Pale and breathing rapidly, the maiden pressed her beating heart and tried to listen. She heard his voice, that beloved voice that for so long a time she had heard only in her dreams — he was asking for her! Overcome with joy, she kissed the nearest saint, which happened to be St. Anthony the Abbot, a saint happy in flesh and in wood, ever the object of pleasing temptations! Afterwards she sought the keyhole in order to see and examine him. She smiled, and when her aunt snatched her from that position she unconsciously threw her arms around the old lady's neck and rained kisses upon her.

"Foolish child, what's the matter with you?" the old lady was at last able to say as she wiped a tear from her faded eyes. Maria Clara felt ashamed and covered her eyes with her plump arm.

"Come on, get ready, come!" added the old aunt fondly. "While he is talking to your father about you. Come, don't make him wait." Like a child the maiden obediently followed her and they shut themselves up in her chamber.

Capitan Tiago and Ibarra were conversing in a lively manner when Aunt Isabel appeared half dragging her niece, who was looking in every direction except toward the persons in the room.

What said those two souls communicating through the language of the eyes, more perfect than that of the lips, the language given to the soul in order that sound may not mar the ecstasy of feeling? In such moments, when the thoughts of two happy beings penetrate into each other's souls through the eyes, the spoken word is halting, rude, and weak — it is as the harsh, slow roar of the thunder compared with the rapidity of the dazzling lightning flash, expressing feelings already recognized, ideas already understood, and if words are made use of it is only because the heart's desire, dominating all the being and flooding it with happiness, wills that the whole human organism with all its physical and psychical powers give expression to the song of joy that rolls through the soul. To the questioning glance of love, as it flashes out and then conceals itself, speech has no reply; the smile, the kiss, the sigh answer.

AN IDYL ON AN AZOTEA

Soon the two lovers, fleeing from the dust raised by Aunt Isabel's broom, found themselves on the azotea where they could commune in liberty among the little arbors. What did they tell each other in murmurs that you nod your heads, O little red cypress flowers? Tell it, you who have fragrance in your breath and color on your lips. And thou, O zephyr, who learnest rare harmonies in the stillness of the dark night amid the hidden depths of our virgin forests! Tell it, O sunbeams, brilliant manifestation upon earth of the Eternal, sole immaterial essence in a material world, you tell it, for I only know how to relate prosaic commonplaces. But since you seem unwilling to do so, I am going to try myself.

The sky was blue and a fresh breeze, not yet laden with the fragrance of roses, stirred the leaves and flowers of the vines; that is why the cypresses, the orchids, the dried fishes, and the Chinese lanterns were trembling. The splash of paddles in the muddy waters of the river and the rattle of carriages and carts passing over the Binondo bridge came up to them distinctly, although they did not hear what the old aunt murmured as she saw where they were: "That's better, there you'll be watched by the whole neighborhood." At first they talked nonsense, giving utterance only to those sweet inanities which are so much like the boastings of the nations of Europe — pleasing and honey-sweet at home, but causing foreigners to laugh or frown.

She, like a sister of Cain, was of course jealous and asked her sweetheart, "Have you always thought of me? Have you never forgotten me on all your travels in the great cities among so many beautiful women?"

He, too, was a brother of Cain, and sought to evade such questions, making use of a little fiction. "Could I forget you?" he answered as he gazed enraptured into her dark eyes. "Could I be faithless to my oath, my sacred oath? Do you remember that stormy night when you saw me weeping alone by the side of my dead mother and, drawing near to me, you put your hand on my shoulder, that hand which for so long a time you had not allowed me to touch, saying to me, 'You have lost your mother while I never had one,' and you wept with me? You loved her and she looked upon you as a daughter. Outside it rained and the lightning flashed, but within I seemed to hear music and to see a smile on the pallid face of the dead. Oh, that my parents were alive and might behold you now! I then caught your hand along with the hand of my mother and swore to love you and to make you happy, whatever fortune Heaven might have in store for me; and that oath, which has never weighed upon me as a burden, I now renew!

"Could I forget you? The thought of you has ever been with me, strengthening me amid the dangers of travel, and has been a comfort to my soul's loneliness in foreign lands. The thoughts of you have neutralized the lotus-effect of Europe, which erases from the memories of so many of our countrymen the hopes and misfortunes of our fatherland. In dreams I saw you standing on the shore at Manila, gazing at the far horizon wrapped in the warm light of the early dawn. I heard the slow, sad song that awoke in me sleeping affections and called back to the memory of my heart the first years of our childhood, our joys, our pleasures, and all that happy past which you gave life to while you were in our town. It seemed to me that you were the fairy, the spirit, the poetic incarnation of my fatherland, beautiful, unaffected, lovable, frank, a true daughter of the Philippines, that beautiful land which unites with the imposing virtues of the mother country, Spain, the admirable qualities of a young people, as you unite in your being all that is beautiful and lovely, the inheritance of both races: so indeed the love of you and that of my fatherland have become fused into one.

"Could I forget you? Many times have I thought that I heard the sound of your piano and the accents of your voice. When in Germany, as I wandered at twi-

light in the woods, peopled with the fantastic creations
of its poets and the mysterious legends of past generations, always I called upon your name, imagining that
I saw you in the mists that rose from the depths of the
valley, or I fancied that I heard your voice in the rustling
of the leaves. When from afar I heard the songs of the
peasants as they returned from their labors, it seemed
to me that their tones harmonized with my inner voices,
that they were singing for you, and thus they lent reality
to my illusions and dreams. At times I became lost among
the mountain paths and while the night descended slowly,
as it does there, I would find myself still wandering, seeking my way among the pines and beeches and oaks. Then
when some scattering rays of moonlight slipped down into
the clear spaces left in the dense foliage, I seemed to see
you in the heart of the forest as a dim, loving shade wavering about between the spots of light and shadow. If perhaps the nightingale poured forth his varied trills, I fancied
it was because he saw you and was inspired by you.

"Have I thought of you? The fever of love not only
gave warmth to the snows but colored the ice! The beautiful skies of Italy with their clear depths reminded me
of your eyes, its sunny landscape spoke to me of your smile;
the plains of Andalusia with their scent-laden airs, peopled
with oriental memories, full of romance and color, told me
of your love! On dreamy, moonlit nights, while boating
on the Rhine, I have asked myself if my fancy did not
deceive me as I saw you among the poplars on the banks,
on the rocks of the Lorelei, or in the midst of the waters,
singing in the silence of the night as if you were a com-
forting fairy maiden sent to enliven the solitude and sadness
of those ruined castles!"

"I have not traveled like you, so I know only your town
and Manila and Antipolo," she answered with a smile
which showed that she believed all he said. "But since
I said good-by to you and entered the convent, I have always thought of you and have only put you out of my mind

when ordered to do so by my confessor, who imposed many
penances upon me. I recalled our games and our quarrels
when we were children. You used to pick up the most beautiful shells and search in the river for the roundest and
smoothest pebbles of different colors that we might play
games with them. You were very stupid and always lost,
and by way of a forfeit I would slap you with the palm of
my hand, but I always tried not to strike you hard, for
I had pity on you. In those games you cheated much,
even more than I did, and we used to finish our play in
a quarrel. Do you remember that time when you became
really angry at me? Then you made me suffer, but afterwards, when I thought of it in the convent, I smiled and
longed for you so that we might quarrel again — so that
we might once more make up. We were still children
and had gone with your mother to bathe in the brook
under the shade of the thick bamboo. On the banks grew
many flowers and plants whose strange names you told me
in Latin and Spanish, for you were even then studying
in the Ateneo.[1] I paid no attention, but amused myself
by running after the needle-like dragon-flies and the butterflies with their rainbow colors and tints of mother-of-
pearl as they swarmed about among the flowers. Sometimes
I tried to surprise them with my hands or to catch the little
fishes that slipped rapidly about amongst the moss and
stones in the edge of the water. Once you disappeared
suddenly and when you returned you brought a crown
of leaves and orange blossoms, which you placed upon my
head, calling me Chloe. For yourself you made one of
vines. But your mother snatched away my crown, and
after mashing it with a stone mixed it with the *gogo* with
which she was going to wash our heads. The tears came
into your eyes and you said that she did not understand
mythology. 'Silly boy,' your mother exclaimed, 'you'll

---

[1] The "Ateneo Municipal," where the author, as well as nearly every other Filipino of note in the past generation, received his early education, was founded by the Jesuits shortly after their return to the islands in 1859. — TR.

see how sweet your hair will smell afterwards.' I laughed, but you were offended and would not talk with me, and for the rest of the day appeared so serious that then I wanted to cry. On our way back to the town through the hot sun, I picked some sage leaves that grew beside the path and gave them to you to put in your hat so that you might not get a headache. You smiled and caught my hand, and we made up."

Ibarra smiled with happiness as he opened his pocket-book and took from it a piece of paper in which were wrapped some dry, blackened leaves which gave off a sweet odor. " Your sage leaves," he said, in answer to her inquiring look. " This is all that you have ever given me."

She in turn snatched from her bosom a little pouch of white satin. " You must not touch this," she said, tapping the palm of his hand lightly. " It's a letter of farewell."

" The one I wrote to you before leaving?"

" Have you ever written me any other, sir?"

" And what did I say to you then?"

" Many fibs, excuses of a delinquent debtor," she answered smilingly, thus giving him to understand how sweet to her those fibs were. " Be quiet now and I'll read it to you. I'll leave out your fine phrases in order not to make a martyr of you."

Raising the paper to the height of her eyes so that the youth might not see her face, she began: " '*My*' — but I'll not read what follows that because it's not true."

Her eyes ran along some lines.

" ' My father wishes me to go away, in spite of all my pleadings. ' You are a man now,' he told me, ' and you must think about your future and about your duties. You must learn the science of life, a thing which your fatherland cannot teach you, so that you may some day be useful to it. If you remain here in my shadow, in this environment of business affairs, you will not learn to look far ahead. The day in which you lose me you will find yourself like the plant of which our poet Baltazar tells: grown in the water, its leaves wither at the least scarcity of moisture and a moment's heat dries it up. Don't you understand? You are almost a young man, and yet you weep!' These reproaches hurt me and I confessed that I loved you. My father reflected for a time in silence and then, placing his hand on my shoulder, said in a trembling voice, 'Do you think that you alone know how to love, that your father does not love you, and that he will not feel the separation from you? It is only a short time since we lost your mother, and I must journey on alone toward old age, toward the very time of life when I would seek help and comfort from your youth, yet I accept my loneliness, hardly knowing whether I shall ever see you again. But you must think of other and greater things; the future lies open before you, while for me it is already passing behind; your love is just awakening, while mine is dying; fire burns in your blood, while the chill is creeping into mine. Yet you weep and cannot sacrifice the present for the future, useful as it may be alike to yourself and to your country.' My father's eyes filled with tears and I fell upon my knees at his feet, I embraced him, I begged his forgiveness, and I assured him that I was ready to set out —'"

Ibarra's growing agitation caused her to suspend the reading, for he had grown pale and was pacing back and forth.

"What's the matter? What is troubling you?" she asked him.

"You have almost made me forget that I have my duties, that I must leave at once for the town. Tomorrow is the day for commemorating the dead."

Maria Clara silently fixed her large dreamy eyes upon him for a few moments and then, picking some flowers, she said with emotion, "Go, I won't detain you longer! In a few days we shall see each other again. Lay these flowers on the tomb of your parents."

A few moments later the youth descended the stairway accompanied by Capitan Tiago and Aunt Isabel, while Maria Clara shut herself up in the oratory.

"Please tell Andeng to get the house ready, as Maria and Isabel are coming. A pleasant journey!" said Capi-

AN IDYL ON AN AZOTEA

tan Tiago as Ibarra stepped into the carriage, which at once started in the direction of the plaza of San Gabriel.

Afterwards, by way of consolation, her father said to Maria Clara, who was weeping beside an image of the Virgin, " Come, light two candles worth two reals each, one to St. Roch,[1] and one to St. Raphael, the protector of travelers. Light the lamp of Our Lady of Peace and Prosperous Voyages, since there are so many tulisanes. It's better to spend four reals for wax and six cuartos for oil now than to pay a big ransom later."

[1] The patron saint of Tondo, Manila's Saint-Antoine. He is invoked for aid in driving away plagues. — TR.

CHAPTER VIII

RECOLLECTIONS

IBARRA'S carriage was passing through a part of the busiest district in Manila, the same which the night before had made him feel sad, but which by daylight caused him to smile in spite of himself. The movement in every part, so many carriages coming and going at full speed, the carromatas and calesas, the Europeans, the Chinese, the natives, each in his own peculiar costume, the fruit-venders, the money-changers, the naked porters, the grocery stores, the lunch stands and restaurants, the shops, and even the carts drawn by the impassive and indifferent carabao, who seems to amuse himself in carrying burdens while he patiently ruminates, all this noise and confusion, the very sun itself, the distinctive odors and the motley colors, awoke in the youth's mind a world of sleeping recollections.

Those streets had not yet been paved, and two successive days of sunshine filled them with dust which covered everything and made the passer-by cough while it nearly blinded him. A day of rain formed pools of muddy water, which at night reflected the carriage lights and splashed mud a distance of several yards away upon the pedestrians on the narrow sidewalks. And how many women have left their embroidered slippers in those waves of mud!

Then there might have been seen repairing those streets the lines of convicts with their shaven heads, dressed in short-sleeved camisas and pantaloons that reached only to their knees, each with his letter and number in blue. On their legs were chains partly wrapped in dirty rags to ease the chafing or perhaps the chill of the iron. Joined two by two, scorched in the sun, worn out by the heat and fatigue, they were lashed and goaded by a whip in the hands of one of their own number, who perhaps consoled himself with this power of maltreating others. They were tall men with somber faces, which he had never seen brightened with the light of a smile. Yet their eyes gleamed when the whistling lash fell upon their shoulders or when a passer-by threw them the chewed and broken stub of a cigar, which the nearest would snatch up and hide in his salakot, while the rest remained gazing at the passers-by with strange looks.

The noise of the stones being crushed to fill the puddles and the merry clank of the heavy fetters on the swollen ankles seemed to remain with Ibarra. He shuddered as he recalled a scene that had made a deep impression on his childish imagination. It was a hot afternoon, and the burning rays of the sun fell perpendicularly upon a large cart by the side of which was stretched out one of those unfortunates, lifeless, yet with his eyes half opened. Two others were silently preparing a bamboo bier, showing no signs of anger or sorrow or impatience, for such is the character attributed to the natives: today it is you, tomorrow it will be I, they say to themselves. The people moved rapidly about without giving heed, women came up and after a look of curiosity continued unconcerned on their way — it was such a common sight that their hearts had become callous. Carriages passed, flashing back from their varnished sides the rays of the sun that burned in a cloudless sky. Only he, a child of eleven years and fresh from the country, was moved, and to him alone it brought bad dreams on the following night.

There no longer existed the useful and honored *Puente de Barcas,* the good Filipino pontoon bridge that had done its best to be of service in spite of its natural imperfections and its rising and falling at the caprice of the Pasig, which had more than once abused it and finally destroyed it. The almond trees in the plaza of San Gabriel [1] had not grown; they were still in the same feeble and stunted condition. The Escolta appeared less beautiful in spite of the fact that an imposing building with caryatids carved on its front now occupied the place of the old row of shops. The new Bridge of Spain caught his attention, while the houses on the right bank of the river among the clumps of bamboo and trees where the Escolta ends and the Isla de Romero begins, reminded him of the cool mornings when he used to pass there in a boat on his way to the baths of Uli-Uli.

He met many carriages, drawn by beautiful pairs of dwarfish ponies, within which were government clerks who seemed yet half asleep as they made their way to their offices, or military officers, or Chinese in foolish and ridiculous attitudes, or grave friars and canons. In an elegant victoria he thought he recognized Padre Damaso, grave and frowning, but he had already passed. Now he was pleasantly greeted by Capitan Tinong, who was passing in a carretela with his wife and two daughters.

As they went down off the bridge the horses broke into a trot along the Sabana Drive.[2] On the left the Arroceros Cigar Factory resounded with the noise of the cigar-makers pounding the tobacco leaves, and Ibarra was unable to restrain a smile as he thought of the strong odor which about five o'clock in the afternoon used to float all over the *Puente de Barcas* and which had made him sick when he was a child. The lively conversations and the repartee of the crowds from the cigar factories carried him back to the district of Lavapiés in Madrid, with its riots of cigar-makers, so fatal for the unfortunate policemen.

The Botanical Garden drove away these agreeable recollections; the demon of comparison brought before his mind the Botanical Gardens of Europe, in countries where great labor and much money are needed to make a single

---

[1] Now Plaza Cervantes. — TR.
[2] Now Plaza Lawton and Bagumbayan; see note, *infra*. — TR.

leaf grow or one flower open its calyx; he recalled those of the colonies, where they are well supplied and tended, and all open to the public. Ibarra turned away his gaze toward the old Manila surrounded still by its walls and moats like a sickly girl wrapped in the garments of her grandmother's better days.

Then the sight of the sea losing itself in the distance! "On the other shore lies Europe," thought the young man, — "Europe, with its attractive peoples in constant movement in the search for happiness, weaving their dreams in the morning and disillusioning themselves at the setting of the sun, happy even in the midst of their calamities. Yes, on the farther shore of the boundless sea are the really spiritual nations, those who, even though they put no restraints on material development, are still more spiritual than those who pride themselves on adoring only the spirit!"

But these musings were in turn banished from his mind as he came in sight of the little mound in Bagumbayan Field.[1] This isolated knoll at the side of the Luneta now caught his attention and made him reminiscent. He thought of the man who had awakened his intellect and made him understand goodness and justice. The ideas which that man had impressed upon him were not many, to be sure, but they were not meaningless repetitions, they were convictions which had not paled in the light of the most brilliant foci of progress. That man was an old priest whose words of farewell still resounded in his ears: "Do

---

[1] The Field of Bagumbayan, adjoining the Luneta, was the place where political prisoners were shot or garroted, and was the scene of the author's execution on December 30, 1906. It is situated just outside and east of the old Walled City (Manila proper), being the location to which the natives who had occupied the site of Manila moved their town after having been driven back by the Spaniards — hence the name, which is a Tagalog compound meaning "new town." This place is now called Wallace Field, the name Bagumbayan being applied to the driveway which was known to the Spaniards as the *Paseo de las Aguadas*, or *de Vidal*, extending from the Luneta to the Bridge of Spain, just outside the moat that formerly encircled the Walled City. — TR.

not forget that if knowledge is the heritage of mankind, it is only the courageous who inherit it," he had reminded him. "I have tried to pass on to you what I got from my teachers, the sum of which I have endeavored to increase and transmit to the coming generation as far as in me lay. You will now do the same for those who come after you, and you can treble it, since you are going to rich countries." Then he had added with a smile, "They come here seeking wealth, go you to their country to seek also that other wealth which we lack! But remember that all that glitters is not gold." The old man had died on that spot.

At these recollections the youth murmured audibly: "No, in spite of everything, the fatherland first, first the Philippines, the child of Spain, first the Spanish fatherland! No, that which is decreed by fate does not tarnish the honor of the fatherland, no!"

He gave little heed to Ermita, the phenix of nipa that had rearisen from its ashes under the form of blue and white houses with red-painted roofs of corrugated iron. Nor was his attention caught by Malate, neither by the cavalry barracks with the spreading trees in front, nor by the inhabitants or their little nipa huts, pyramidal or prismatic in shape, hidden away among the banana plants and areca palms, constructed like nests by each father of a family.

The carriage continued on its way, meeting now and then carromatas drawn by one or two ponies whose abaka harness indicated that they were from the country. The drivers would try to catch a glimpse of the occupant of the fine carriage, but would pass on without exchanging a word, without a single salute. At times a heavy cart drawn by a slow and indifferent carabao would appear on the dusty road over which beat the brilliant sunlight of the tropics. The mournful and monotonous song of the driver mounted on the back of the carabao would be mingled at one time with the screechings of a dry wheel on the huge axle of the heavy vehicle or at another time with the dull scraping of worn-out runners on a sledge which was dragged heavily through the dust and over the ruts in the road. In the fields and wide meadows the herds were grazing, attended ever by the white buffalo-birds which roosted peacefully on the backs of the animals while these chewed their cuds or browsed in lazy contentment upon the rich grass. In the distance ponies frisked, jumping and running about, pursued by the lively colts with long tails and abundant manes who whinnied and pawed the ground with their hard hoofs.

Let us leave the youth dreaming or dozing, since neither the sad nor the animated poetry of the open country held his attention. For him there was no charm in the sun that gleamed upon the tops of the trees and caused the rustics, with feet burned by the hot ground in spite of their callousness, to hurry along, or that made the villager pause beneath the shade of an almond tree or a bamboo brake while he pondered upon vague and inexplicable things. While the youth's carriage sways along like a drunken thing on account of the inequalities in the surface of the road when passing over a bamboo bridge or going up an incline or descending a steep slope, let us return to Manila.

CHAPTER IX

LOCAL AFFAIRS

IBARRA had not been mistaken about the occupant of the victoria, for it was indeed Padre Damaso, and he was on his way to the house which the youth had just left.

"Where are you going?" asked the friar of Maria Clara and Aunt Isabel, who were about to enter a silver-mounted carriage. In the midst of his preoccupation Padre Damaso stroked the maiden's cheek lightly.

"To the convent to get my things," answered the latter.

"Ahaa! Aha! We'll see who's stronger, we'll see," muttered the friar abstractedly, as with bowed head and slow step he turned to the stairway, leaving the two women not a little amazed.

"He must have a sermon to preach and is memorizing it," commented Aunt Isabel. "Get in, Maria, or we'll be late."

Whether or not Padre Damaso was preparing a sermon we cannot say, but it is certain that some grave matter filled his mind, for he did not extend his hand to Capitan Tiago, who had almost to get down on his knees to kiss it.

"Santiago," said the friar at once, "I have an important matter to talk to you about. Let's go into your office."

Capitan Tiago began to feel uneasy, so much so that he did not know what to say; but he obeyed, following the heavy figure of the priest, who closed the door behind him.

While they confer in secret, let us learn what Fray

Sibyla has been doing. The astute Dominican is not at the rectory, for very soon after celebrating mass he had gone to the convent of his order, situated just inside the gate of Isabel II, or of Magellan, according to what family happened to be reigning in Madrid. Without paying any attention to the rich odor of chocolate, or to the rattle of boxes and coins which came from the treasury, and scarcely acknowledging the respectful and deferential salute of the procurator-brother, he entered, passed along several corridors, and knocked at a door.

"Come in," sighed a weak voice.

"May God restore health to your Reverence," was the young Dominican's greeting as he entered.

Seated in a large armchair was an aged priest, wasted and rather sallow, like the saints that Rivera painted. His eyes were sunken in their hollow sockets, over which his heavy eyebrows were almost always contracted, thus accentuating their brilliant gleam. Padre Sibyla, with his arms crossed under the venerable scapulary of St. Dominic, gazed at him feelingly, then bowed his head and waited in silence.

"Ah," sighed the old man, "they advise an operation, an operation, Hernando, at my age! This country, O this terrible country! Take warning from my case, Hernando!"

Fray Sibyla raised his eyes slowly and fixed them on the sick man's face. "What has your Reverence decided to do?" he asked.

"To die! Ah, what else can I do? I am suffering too much, but — I have made many suffer, I am paying my debt! And how are you? What has brought you here?"

"I've come to talk about the business which you committed to my care."

"Ah! What about it?"

"Pish!" answered the young man disgustedly, as he seated himself and turned away his face with a contemptuous expression, " They 've been telling us fairy tales. Young Ibarra is a youth of discernment; he does n't seem to be a fool, but I believe that he is a good lad."

" You believe so ? "

" Hostilities began last night."

" Already ? How ? "

Fray Sibyla then recounted briefly what had taken place between Padre Damaso and Ibarra. " Besides," he said in conclusion, " the young man is going to marry Capitan Tiago's daughter, who was educated in the college of our Sisterhood. He 's rich, and won't care to make enemies and to run the risk of ruining his fortune and his happiness."

The sick man nodded in agreement. " Yes, I think as you do. With a wife like that and such a father-in-law, we 'll own him body and soul. If not, so much the better for him to declare himself an enemy of ours."

Fray Sibyla looked at the old man in surprise.

" For the good of our holy Order, I mean, of course," he added, breathing heavily. " I prefer open attacks to the silly praises and flatteries of friends, which are really paid for."

" Does your Reverence think — "

The old man regarded him sadly. " Keep it clearly before you," he answered, gasping for breath. " Our power will last as long as it is believed in. If they attack us, the government will say, ' They attack them because they see in them an obstacle to their liberty, so then let us preserve them.' "

" But if it should listen to them ? Sometimes the government — "

" It will not listen ! "

" Nevertheless, if, led on by cupidity, it should come to wish for itself what we are taking in — if there should be some bold and daring one — "

" Then woe unto that one ! "

Both remained silent for a time, then the sick man continued: "Besides, we need their attacks, to keep us awake; that makes us see our weaknesses so that we may remedy them. Exaggerated flattery will deceive us and put us to sleep, while outside our walls we shall be laughed at, and the day in which we become an object of ridicule, we shall fall as we fell in Europe. Money will not flow into our churches, no one will buy our scapularies or girdles or anything else, and when we cease to be rich we shall no longer be able to control consciences."

"But we shall always have our estates, our property."

"All will be lost as we lost them in Europe! And the worst of it is that we are working toward our own ruin. For example, this unrestrained eagerness to raise arbitrarily the rents on our lands each year, this eagerness which I have so vainly combated in all the chapters, this will ruin us! The native sees himself obliged to purchase farms in other places, which bring him as good returns as ours, or better. I fear that we are already on the decline; *quos vult perdere Jupiter dementat prius.*[1] For this reason we should not increase our burden; the people are already murmuring. You have decided well: let us leave the others to settle their accounts in that quarter; let us preserve the prestige that remains to us, and as we shall soon appear before God, let us wash our hands of it — and may the God of mercy have pity on our weakness!"

"So your Reverence thinks that the rent or tax —"

"Let's not talk any more about money," interrupted the sick man with signs of disgust. "You say that the lieutenant threatened to Padre Damaso that —"

"Yes, Padre," broke in Fray Sibyla with a faint smile, "but this morning I saw him and he told me that he was sorry for what occurred last night, that the sherry had gone to his head, and that he believed that Padre Damaso was in the same condition. 'And your threat?' I asked him jokingly. 'Padre,' he answered me, 'I know how to keep my word when my honor is affected, but I am not nor have

[1] Whom the gods would destroy, they first make mad. — Tr.

ever been an informer — for that reason I wear only two stars.'"

After they had conversed a while longer on unimportant subjects, Fray Sibyla took his departure.

It was true that the lieutenant had not gone to the Palace, but the Captain-General heard what had occurred. While talking with some of his aides about the allusions that the Manila newspapers were making to him under the names of comets and celestial apparitions, one of them told him about the affair of Padre Damaso, with a somewhat heightened coloring although substantially correct as to matter.

"From whom did you learn this?" asked his Excellency, smiling.

"From Laruja, who was telling it this morning in the office."

The Captain-General again smiled and said: "A woman or a friar can't insult one. I contemplate living in peace for the time that I shall remain in this country and I don't want any more quarrels with men who wear skirts. Besides, I've learned that the Provincial has scoffed at my orders. I asked for the removal of this friar as a punishment and they transferred him to a better town — 'monkish tricks,' as we say in Spain."

But when his Excellency found himself alone he stopped smiling. "Ah, if this people were not so stupid, I would put a curb on their Reverences," he sighed to himself. "But every people deserves its fate, so let's do as everybody else does."

Capitan Tiago, meanwhile, had concluded his interview with Padre Damaso, or rather, to speak more exactly, Padre Damaso had concluded with him.

"So now you are warned!" said the Franciscan on leaving. "All this could have been avoided if you had consulted me beforehand, if you had not lied when I asked you. Try not to play any more foolish tricks, and trust your protector."

Capitan Tiago walked up and down the sala a few times, meditating and sighing. Suddenly, as if a happy thought had occurred to him, he ran to the oratory and extinguished the candles and the lamp that had been lighted for Ibarra's safety. "The way is long and there's yet time," he muttered.

CHAPTER X

THE TOWN

ALMOST on the margin of the lake, in the midst of meadows and paddy-fields, lies the town of San Diego.[1] From it sugar, rice, coffee, and fruits are either exported or sold for a small part of their value to the Chinese, who exploit the simplicity and vices of the native farmers.

When on a clear day the boys ascend to the upper part of the church tower, which is beautified by moss and creeping plants, they break out into joyful exclamations at the beauty of the scene spread out before them. In the midst of the clustering roofs of nipa, tiles, corrugated iron, and palm leaves, separated by groves and gardens, each one is able to discover his own home, his little nest. Everything serves as a mark: a tree, that tamarind with its light foliage, that coco palm laden with nuts, like the Astarte Genetrix, or the Diana of Ephesus with her numerous breasts, a bending bamboo, an areca palm, or a cross. Yonder is the river, a huge glassy serpent sleeping on a green carpet, with rocks, scattered here and there along its sandy channel, that break its current into ripples. There, the bed is narrowed between high banks to which the gnarled trees cling with bared roots; here, it becomes a gentle slope where the stream widens and eddies about. Farther away, a small hut built on the edge of the high bank seems to defy the winds, the heights and the depths, presenting

[1] We have been unable to find any town of this name, but many of these conditions. — *Author's note.*
San Diego and Santiago are variant forms of the name of the patron saint of Spain, St. James. — TR.

with its slender posts the appearance of a huge, long-legged bird watching for a reptile to seize upon. Trunks of palm or other trees with their bark still on them unite the banks by a shaky and infirm foot-bridge which, if not a very secure crossing, is nevertheless a wonderful contrivance for gymnastic exercises in preserving one's balance, a thing not to be despised. The boys bathing in the river are amused by the difficulties of the old woman crossing with a basket on her head or by the antics of the old man who moves tremblingly and loses his staff in the water.

But that which always attracts particular notice is what might be called a peninsula of forest in the sea of cultivated fields. There in that wood are century-old trees with hollow trunks, which die only when their high tops are struck and set on fire by the lightning — and it is said that the fire always checks itself and dies out in the same spot. There are huge points of rock which time and nature are clothing with velvet garments of moss. Layer after layer of dust settles in the hollows, the rains beat it down, and the birds bring seeds. The tropical vegetation spreads out luxuriantly in thickets and underbrush, while curtains of interwoven vines hang from the branches of the trees and twine about their roots or spread along the ground, as if Flora were not yet satisfied but must place plant above plant. Mosses and fungi live upon the cracked trunks, and orchids — graceful guests — twine in loving embrace with the foliage of the hospitable trees.

Strange legends exist concerning this wood, which is held in awe by the country folk. The most credible account, and therefore the one least known and believed, seems to be this. When the town was still a collection of miserable huts with the grass growing abundantly in the so-called streets, at the time when the wild boar and deer roamed about during the nights, there arrived in the place one day an old, hollow-eyed Spaniard, who spoke Tagalog rather well. After looking about and inspecting the land, he finally inquired for the owners of this wood, in which there were hot springs. Some persons who claimed to be such presented themselves, and the old man acquired it in exchange for clothes, jewels, and a sum of money. Soon afterward he disappeared mysteriously. The people thought that he had been spirited away, when a bad odor from the neighboring wood attracted the attention of some herdsmen. Tracing this, they found the decaying corpse of the old Spaniard hanging from the branch of a balete tree.[1] In life he had inspired fear by his deep, hollow voice, his sunken eyes, and his mirthless laugh, but now, dead by his own act, he disturbed the sleep of the women. Some threw the jewels into the river and burned the clothes, and from the time that the corpse was buried at the foot of the balete itself, no one willingly ventured near the spot. A belated herdsman looking for some of his strayed charges told of lights that he had seen there, and when some venturesome youths went to the place they heard mournful cries. To win the smiles of his disdainful lady, a forlorn lover agreed to spend the night there and in proof to wrap around the trunk a long piece of rattan, but he died of a quick fever that seized him the very next day. Stories and legends still cluster about the place.

A few months after the finding of the old Spaniard's body there appeared a youth, apparently a Spanish mestizo, who said that he was the son of the deceased. He established himself in the place and devoted his attention to agriculture, especially the raising of indigo. Don Saturnino was a silent young man with a violent disposition, even cruel at times, yet he was energetic and industrious. He surrounded the grave of his father with a

---

[1] The "sacred tree" of Malaya, being a species of banyan that begins life as a vine twining on another tree, which it finally strangles, using the dead trunk as a support until it is able to stand alone. When old it often covers a large space with gnarled and twisted trunks of varied shapes and sizes, thus presenting a weird and grotesque appearance. This tree was held in reverent awe by the primitive Filipinos, who believed it to be the abode of the *nono*, or ancestral ghosts, and is still the object of superstitious beliefs. — TR.

wall, but visited it only at rare intervals. When he was along in years, he married a young woman from Manila, and she became the mother of Don Rafael, the father of Crisostomo. From his youth Don Rafael was a favorite with the country people. The agricultural methods introduced and encouraged by his father spread rapidly, new settlers poured in, the Chinese came, and the settlement became a village with a native priest. Later the village grew into a town, the priest died, and Fray Damaso came.

All this time the tomb and the land around it remained unmolested. Sometimes a crowd of boys armed with clubs and stones would become bold enough to wander into the place to gather guavas, papayas, lomboy, and other fruits, but it frequently happened that when their sport was at its height, or while they gazed in awed silence at the rotting piece of rope which still swung from the branch, stones would fall, coming from they knew not where. Then with cries of "The old man! The old man!" they would throw away fruit and clubs, jump from the trees, and hurry between the rocks and through the thickets; nor would they stop running until they were well out of the wood, some pale and breathless, others weeping, and only a few laughing.

CHAPTER XI

THE RULERS

Divide and rule.
(*The New Machiavelli.*)

WHO were the caciques of the town? Don Rafael, when alive, even though he was the richest, owned more land, and was the patron of nearly everybody, had not been one of them. As he was modest and depreciated the value of his own deeds, no faction in his favor had ever been formed in the town, and we have already seen how the people all rose up against him when they saw him hesitate upon being attacked.

Could it be Capitan Tiago? True it was that when he went there he was received with an orchestra by his debtors, who banqueted him and heaped gifts upon him. The finest fruits burdened his table and a quarter of deer or wild boar was his share of the hunt. If he found the horse of a debtor beautiful, half an hour afterwards it was in his stable. All this was true, but they laughed at him behind his back and in secret called him "Sacristan Tiago."

Perhaps it was the gobernadorcillo?[1] No, for he was

---

[1] "Petty governor," the chief municipal official, chosen annually from among their own number, with the approval of the parish priest and the central government, by the *principalia*, i. e., persons who owned considerable property or who had previously held some municipal office. The manner of his selection is thus described by a German traveler (Jagor) in the Philippines in 1860: "The election is held in the town hall. The governor or his representative presides, having on his right the parish priest and on his left a clerk, who also acts as interpreter. All the cabezas de barangay, the gobernadorcillo, and those who have formerly occupied the latter position, seat themselves on benches. First, there are chosen by lot six cabezas de barangay and six ex-gobernadorcillos as electors, the actual gobernadorcillo being the thirteenth. The

only an unhappy mortal who commanded not, but obeyed; who ordered not, but was ordered; who drove not, but was driven. Nevertheless, he had to answer to the alcalde for having commanded, ordered, and driven, just as if he were the originator of everything. Yet be it said to his credit that he had never presumed upon or usurped such honors, which had cost him five thousand pesos and many humiliations. But considering the income it brought him, it was cheap.

Well then, might it be God? Ah, the good God disturbed neither the consciences nor the sleep of the inhabitants. At least, He did not make them tremble, and if by chance He might have been mentioned in a sermon, surely they would have sighed longingly, "Oh, that only there were a God!" To the good Lord they paid little attention, as the saints gave them enough to do. For those poor folk God had come to be like those unfortunate monarchs who are surrounded by courtiers to whom alone the people render homage.

San Diego was a kind of Rome: not the Rome of the time when the cunning Romulus laid out its walls with a plow, nor of the later time when, bathed in its own and others' blood, it dictated laws to the world — no, it was a Rome of our own times with the difference that in place of marble monuments and colosseums it had its monuments of sawali and its cockpit of nipa. The curate was the Pope in the Vatican; the alferez of the Civil Guard, the King of Italy on the Quirinal: all, it must be understood, on a scale of nipa and bamboo. Here, as there, continual quarreling went on, since each wished to be the master

rest leave the hall. After the presiding officer has read the statutes in a loud voice and reminded the electors of their duty to act in accordance with their consciences and to heed only the welfare of the town, the electors move to a table and write three names on a slip of paper. The person receiving a majority of votes is declared elected gobernadorcillo for the ensuing year, provided that there is no protest from the curate or the electors, and always conditioned upon the approval of the superior authority in Manila, which is never withheld, since the influence of the curate is enough to prevent an unsatisfactory election." — Tr.

and considered the other an intruder. Let us examine the characteristics of each.

Fray Bernardo Salvi was that silent young Franciscan of whom we have spoken before. In his habits and manners he was quite different from his brethren and even from his predecessor, the violent Padre Damaso. He was thin and sickly, habitually pensive, strict in the fulfilment of his religious duties, and careful of his good name. In a month after his arrival nearly every one in the town had joined the Venerable Tertiary Order, to the great distress of its rival, the Society of the Holy Rosary. His soul leaped with joy to see about each neck four or five scapularies and around each waist a knotted girdle, and to behold the procession of corpses and ghosts in *guingón* habits. The senior sacristan made a small fortune selling — or giving away as alms, we should say — all things necessary for the salvation of the soul and the warfare against the devil, as it is well known that this spirit, which formerly had the temerity to contradict God himself face to face and to doubt His words, as is related in the holy book of Job, who carried our Lord Christ through the air as afterwards in the Dark Ages he carried the ghosts, and continues, according to report, to carry the *asuang* of the Philippines, now seems to have become so shamefaced that he cannot endure the sight of a piece of painted cloth and that he fears the knots on a cord. But all this proves nothing more than that there is progress on this side also and that the devil is backward, or at least a conservative, as are all who dwell in darkness. Otherwise, we must attribute to him the weakness of a fifteen-year-old girl.

As we have said, Fray Salvi was very assiduous in the fulfilment of his duties, too assiduous, the alferez thought. While he was preaching — he was very fond of preaching — the doors of the church were closed, wherein he was like Nero, who allowed no one to leave the theater while he was singing. But the former did it for the salvation and the latter for the corruption of souls. Fray Salvi

THE RULERS

rarely resorted to blows, but was accustomed to punish every shortcoming of his subordinates with fines. In this respect he was very different from Padre Damaso, who had been accustomed to settle everything with his fists or a cane, administering such chastisement with the greatest good-will. For this, however, he should not be judged too harshly, as he was firm in the belief that the Indian could be managed only by beating him, just as was affirmed by a friar who knew enough to write books, and Padre Damaso never disputed anything that he saw in print, a credulity of which many might have reason to complain. Although Fray Salvi made little use of violence, yet, as an old wiseacre of the town said, what he lacked in quantity he made up in quality. But this should not be counted against him, for the fasts and abstinences thinned his blood and unstrung his nerves and, as the people said, the wind got into his head. Thus it came about that it was not possible to learn from the condition of the sacristans' backs whether the curate was fasting or feasting.

The only rival of this spiritual power, with tendencies toward the temporal, was, as we have said, the alferez: the only one, since the women told how the devil himself would flee from the curate, because, having one day dared to tempt him, he was caught, tied to a bedpost, soundly whipped with a rope, and set at liberty only after nine days. As a consequence, any one who after this would still be the enemy of such a man, deserved to fall into worse repute than even the weak and unwary devils.

But the alferez deserved his fate. His wife was an old Filipina of abundant rouge and paint, known as Doña Consolacion — although her husband and some others called her by quite another name. The alferez revenged his conjugal misfortunes on his own person by getting so drunk that he made a tank of himself, or by ordering his soldiers to drill in the sun while he remained in the shade, or, more frequently, by beating up his consort, who, if she was not a lamb of God to take away one's sins, at least served to lay up for her spouse many torments in Purgatory — if perchance he should get there, a matter of doubt to the devout women. As if for the fun of it, these two used to beat each other up beautifully, giving free shows to the neighborhood with vocal and instrumental accompaniments, four-handed, soft, loud, with pedal and all.

Whenever these scandals reached the ears of Padre Salvi, he would smile, cross himself, and recite a paternoster. They called him a grafter, a hypocrite, a Carlist, and a miser: he merely smiled and recited more prayers. The alferez had a little anecdote which he always related to the occasional Spaniards who visited him:

"Are you going over to the convento to visit the sanctimonious rascal there, the little curate? Yes! Well, if he offers you chocolate — which I doubt — but if he offers it remember this: if he calls to the servant and says, 'Juan, make a cup of chocolate, *eh!*' then stay without fear; but if he calls out, 'Juan, make a cup of chocolate, *ah!*' then take your hat and leave on a run."

"What!" the startled visitor would ask, "does he poison people? *Carambas!*"

"No, man, not at all!"

"What then?"

"'Chocolate, *eh!*' means thick and rich, while 'chocolate, *ah!*' means watered and thin."

But we are of the opinion that this was a slander on the part of the alferez, since the same story is told of many curates. At least, it may be a thing peculiar to the Order.

To make trouble for the curate, the soldier, at the instigation of his wife, would prohibit any one from walking abroad after nine o'clock at night. Doña Consolacion would then claim that she had seen the curate, disguised in a piña camisa and salakot, walking about late. Fray Salvi would take his revenge in a holy manner. Upon seeing the alferez enter the church he would innocently order the sacristan to close all the doors, and would then go

THE RULERS

up into the pulpit and preach until the very saints closed their eyes and even the wooden dove above his head, the image of the Holy Ghost, murmured for mercy. But the alferez, like all the unregenerate, did not change his ways for this; he would go away cursing, and as soon as he was able to catch a sacristan, or one of the curate's servants, he would arrest him, give him a beating, and make him scrub the floor of the barracks and that of his own house, which at such times was put in a decent condition. On going to pay the fine imposed by the curate for his absence, the sacristan would explain the cause. Fray Salvi would listen in silence, take the money, and at once turn out his goats and sheep so that they might graze in the alferez's garden, while he himself looked up a new text for another longer and more edifying sermon. But these were only little pleasantries, and if the two chanced to meet they would shake hands and converse politely.

When her husband was sleeping off the wine he had drunk, or was snoring through the siesta, and she could not quarrel with him, Doña Consolacion, in a blue flannel camisa, with a big cigar in her mouth, would take her stand at the window. She could not endure the young people, so from there she would scrutinize and mock the passing girls, who, being afraid of her, would hurry by in confusion, holding their breath the while, and not daring to raise their eyes. One great virtue Doña Consolacion possessed, and this was that she had evidently never looked in a mirror.

These were the rulers of the town of San Diego.

CHAPTER XII

ALL SAINTS

THE one thing perhaps that indisputably distinguishes man from the brute creation is the attention which he pays to those who have passed away and, wonder of wonders! this characteristic seems to be more deeply rooted in proportion to the lack of civilization. Historians relate that the ancient inhabitants of the Philippines venerated and deified their ancestors; but now the contrary is true, and the dead have to entrust themselves to the living. It is also related that the people of New Guinea preserve the bones of their dead in chests and maintain communication with them. The greater part of the peoples of Asia, Africa, and America offer them the finest products of their kitchens or dishes of what was their favorite food when alive, and give banquets at which they believe them to be present. The Egyptians raised up palaces and the Mussulmans built shrines, but the masters in these things, those who have most clearly read the human heart, are the people of Dahomey. These negroes know that man is revengeful, so they consider that nothing will more content the dead than to sacrifice all his enemies upon his grave, and, as man is curious and may not know how to entertain himself in the other life, each year they send him a newsletter under the skin of a beheaded slave.

We ourselves differ from all the rest. In spite of the inscriptions on the tombs, hardly any one believes that the dead rest, and much less, that they rest in peace. The most optimistic fancies his forefathers still roasting in purgatory and, if it turns out that he himself be not completely damned, he will yet be able to associate with them for many

ALL SAINTS

years. If any one would contradict let him visit the churches and cemeteries of the country on All Saints' day and he will be convinced.

Now that we are in San Diego let us visit its cemetery, which is located in the midst of paddy-fields, there toward the west — not a city, merely a village of the dead, approached by a path dusty in dry weather and navigable on rainy days. A wooden gate and a fence half of stone and half of bamboo stakes, appear to separate it from the abode of the living but not from the curate's goats and some of the pigs of the neighborhood, who come and go making explorations among the tombs and enlivening the solitude with their presence. In the center of this enclosure rises a large wooden cross set on a stone pedestal. The storms have doubled over the tin plate for the inscription INRI, and the rains have effaced the letters. At the foot of the cross, as on the real Golgotha, is a confused heap of skulls and bones which the indifferent grave-digger has thrown from the graves he digs, and there they will probably await, not the resurrection of the dead, but the coming of the animals to defile them. Round about may be noted signs of recent excavations; here the earth is sunken, there it forms a low mound. There grow in all their luxuriance the *tarambulo* to prick the feet with its spiny berries and the *pandakaki* to add its odor to that of the cemetery, as if the place did not have smells enough already. Yet the ground is sprinkled with a few little flowers which, like those skulls, are known only to their Creator; their petals wear a pale smile and their fragrance is the fragrance of the tombs. The grass and creepers fill up the corners or climb over the walls and niches to cover and beautify the naked ugliness and in places even penetrate into the fissures made by the earthquakes, so as to hide from sight the revered hollowness of the sepulcher.

At the time we enter, the people have driven the animals away, with the single exception of some old hog, an animal that is hard to convince, who shows his small eyes and pulling back his head from a great gap in the fence, sticks up his snout and seems to say to a woman praying near, "Don't eat it all, leave something for me, won't you?"

Two men are digging a grave near one of the tottering walls. One of them, the grave-digger, works with indifference, throwing about bones as a gardener does stones and dry branches, while the other, more intent on his work, is perspiring, smoking, and spitting at every moment.

"Listen," says the latter in Tagalog, "wouldn't it be better for us to dig in some other place? This is too recent."

"One grave is as recent as another."

"I can't stand it any longer! That bone you've just cut in two has blood oozing from it — and those hairs?"

"But how sensitive you are!" was the other's reproach. "Just as if you were a town clerk! If, like myself, you had dug up a corpse of twenty days, on a dark and rainy night — ! My lantern went out — "

His companion shuddered.

"The coffin burst open, the corpse fell half-way out, it stunk — and supposing you had to carry it — the rain wet us both — "

"Ugh! And why did you dig it up?"

The grave-digger looked at him in surprise. "Why? How do I know? I was ordered to do so."

"Who ordered you?"

The grave-digger stepped backward and looked his companion over from head to foot. "Man, you're like a Spaniard, for afterwards a Spaniard asked me the same questions, but in secret. So I'm going to answer you as I answered the Spaniard: the fat curate ordered me to do so."

"Ah! And what did you do with the corpse afterwards?" further questioned the sensitive one.

"The devil! If I didn't know you and was not sure that you are a *man* I would say that you were certainly a Spaniard of the Civil Guard, since you ask questions just as he did. Well, the fat curate ordered me to bury it in the Chinamen's cemetery, but the coffin was heavy and the Chinese cemetery far away —"

"No, no! I'm not going to dig any more!" the other interrupted in horror as he threw away his spade and jumped out of the hole. "I've cut a skull in two and I'm afraid that it won't let me sleep tonight." The old grave-digger laughed to see how the chicken-hearted fellow left, crossing himself.

The cemetery was filling up with men and women dressed in mourning. Some sought a grave for a time, disputing among themselves the while, and as if they were unable to agree, they scattered about, each kneeling where he thought best. Others, who had niches for their deceased relatives, lighted candles and fell to praying devoutly. Exaggerated or suppressed sighs and sobs were heard amid the hum of prayers, *orapreo, orapreiss, requiem-aeternams,* that arose from all sides.

A little old man with bright eyes entered bareheaded. Upon seeing him many laughed, and some women knitted their eyebrows. The old man did not seem to pay any attention to these demonstrations as he went toward a pile of skulls and knelt to look earnestly for something among the bones. Then he carefully removed the skulls one by one, but apparently without finding what he sought, for he wrinkled his brow, nodded his head from side to side, looked all about him, and finally rose and approached the grave-digger, who raised his head when the old man spoke to him.

"Do you know where there is a beautiful skull, white as the meat of a coconut, with a complete set of teeth, which I had there at the foot of the cross under those leaves?"

The grave-digger shrugged his shoulders.

"Look!" added the old man, showing a silver coin, "I have only this, but I'll give it to you if you find the skull for me."

The gleam of the silver caused the grave-digger to consider, and staring toward the heap of bones he said, " Is n't it there? No? Then I don't know where it is."

" Don't you know? When those who owe me pay me, I 'll give you more," continued the old man " It was the skull of my wife, so if you find it for me —"

" Is n't it there? Then I don't know! But if you wish, I can give you another."

" You 're like the grave you 're digging," apostrophized the old man nervously. " You don't know the value of what you lose. For whom is that grave?"

" How should I know?" replied the other in bad humor. " For a corpse!"

" Like the grave, like the grave!" repeated the old man with a dry smile. " You don't know what you throw away nor what you receive! Dig, dig on!" And he turned away in the direction of the gate.

Meanwhile, the grave-digger had completed his task, attested by the two mounds of fresh red earth at the sides of the grave. He took some buyo from his salakot and began to chew it while he stared stupidly at what was going on around him.

CHAPTER XIII

SIGNS OF STORM

AS the old man was leaving the cemetery there stopped at the head of the path a carriage which, from its dust-covered appearance and sweating horses, seemed to have come from a great distance. Followed by an aged servant, Ibarra left the carriage and dismissed it with a wave of his hand, then gravely and silently turned toward the cemetery.

"My illness and my duties have not permitted me to return," said the old servant timidly. "Capitan Tiago promised that he would see that a niche was constructed, but I planted some flowers on the grave and set up a cross carved by my own hands." Ibarra made no reply. "There behind that big cross, sir," he added when they were well inside the gate, as he pointed to the place.

Ibarra was so intent upon his quest that he did not notice the movement of surprise on the part of the persons who recognized him and suspended their prayers to watch him curiously. He walked along carefully to avoid stepping on any of the graves, which were easily distinguishable by the hollow places in the soil. In other times he had walked on them carelessly, but now they were to be respected: his father lay among them. When he reached the large cross he stopped and looked all around. His companion stood confused and confounded, seeking some mark in the ground, but nowhere was any cross to be seen.

"Was it here?" he murmured through his teeth. "No, there! But the ground has been disturbed."

Ibarra gave him a look of anguish.

"Yes," he went on, "I remember that there was a stone

near it. The grave was rather short. The grave-digger was sick, so a farmer had to dig it. But let's ask that man what has become of the cross."

They went over to where the grave-digger was watching them with curiosity. He removed his salakot respectfully as they approached.

"Can you tell me which is the grave there that had a cross over it?" asked the servant.

The grave-digger looked toward the place and reflected. "A big cross?"

"Yes, a big one!" affirmed the servant eagerly, with a significant look at Ibarra, whose face lighted up.

"A carved cross tied up with rattan?" continued the grave-digger.

"That's it, that's it, like this!" exclaimed the servant in answer as he drew on the ground the figure of a Byzantine cross.

"Were there flowers scattered on the grave?"

"Oleanders and tuberoses and forget-me-nots, yes!" the servant added joyfully, offering the grave-digger a cigar.

"Tell us which is the grave and where the cross is."

The grave-digger scratched his ear and answered with a yawn: "Well, as for the cross, I burned it."

"Burned it? Why did you burn it?"

"Because the fat curate ordered me to do so."

"Who is the fat curate?" asked Ibarra.

"Who? Why, the one that beats people with a big cane."

Ibarra drew his hand across his forehead. "But at least you can tell us where the grave is. You must remember that."

The grave-digger smiled as he answered quietly, "But the corpse is no longer there."

"What's that you're saying?"

"Yes," continued the grave-digger in a half-jesting tone. "I buried a woman in that place a week ago."

"Are you crazy?" cried the servant. "It has n't been a year since we buried him."

"That 's very true, but a good many months ago I dug the body up. The fat curate ordered me to do so and to take it to the cemetery of the Chinamen. But as it was heavy and there was rain that night —"

He was stopped by the threatening attitude of Ibarra, who had caught him by the arm and was shaking him. "Did you do that?" demanded the youth in an indescribable tone.

"Don't be angry, sir," stammered the pale and trembling grave-digger. "I did n't bury him among the Chinamen. Better be drowned than lie among Chinamen, I said to myself, so I threw the body into the lake."

Ibarra placed both his hands on the grave-digger's shoulders and stared at him for a long time with an indefinable expression. Then, with the ejaculation, "You are only a miserable slave!" he turned away hurriedly, stepping upon bones, graves, and crosses, like one beside himself.

The grave-digger patted his arm and muttered, "All the trouble dead men cause! The fat padre caned me for allowing it to be buried while I was sick, and this fellow almost tore my arm off for having dug it up. That 's what these Spaniards are! I 'll lose my job yet!"

Ibarra walked rapidly with a far-away look in his eyes, while the aged servant followed him weeping. The sun was setting, and over the eastern sky was flung a heavy curtain of clouds. A dry wind shook the tree-tops and made the bamboo clumps creak. Ibarra went bareheaded, but no tear wet his eyes nor did any sigh escape from his breast. He moved as if fleeing from something, perhaps the shade of his father, perhaps the approaching storm. He crossed through the town to the outskirts on the opposite side and turned toward the old house which he had not entered for so many years. Surrounded by a cactus-covered wall it seemed to beckon to him with its open windows, while the ilang-ilang waved its flower-laden branches joyfully and the doves circled about the conical roof of their cote in the middle of the garden.

But the youth gave no heed to these signs of welcome back to his old home, his eyes being fixed on the figure of a priest approaching from the opposite direction. It was the curate of San Diego, the pensive Franciscan whom we have seen before, the rival of the alferez. The breeze folded back the brim of his wide hat and blew his *guingón* habit closely about him, revealing the outlines of his body and his thin, curved thighs. In his right hand he carried an ivory-headed *palasan* cane.

This was the first time that he and Ibarra had met. When they drew near each other Ibarra stopped and gazed at him from head to foot; Fray Salvi avoided the look and tried to appear unconcerned. After a moment of hesitation Ibarra went up to him quickly and dropping a heavy hand on his shoulder, asked in a husky voice, " What did you do with my father ? "

Fray Salvi, pale and trembling as he read the deep feelings that flushed the youth's face, could not answer; he seemed paralyzed.

" What did you do with my father ? " again demanded the youth in a choking voice.

The priest, who was gradually being forced to his knees by the heavy hand that pressed upon his shoulder, made a great effort and answered, " You are mistaken, I did nothing to your father."

" You did n't ? " went on the youth, forcing him down upon his knees.

" No, I assure you ! It was my predecessor, it was Padre Damaso ! "

" Ah ! " exclaimed the youth, releasing his hold, and clapping his hand desperately to his brow; then, leaving poor Fray Salvi, he turned away and hurried toward his house. The old servant came up and helped the friar to his feet.

CHAPTER XIV

TASIO: LUNATIC OR SAGE

THE peculiar old man wandered about the streets aimlessly. A former student of philosophy, he had given up his career in obedience to his mother's wishes and not from any lack of means or ability. Quite the contrary, it was because his mother was rich and he was said to possess talent. The good woman feared that her son would become learned and forget God, so she had given him his choice of entering the priesthood or leaving college. Being in love, he chose the latter course and married. Then having lost both his wife and his mother within a year, he sought consolation in his books in order to free himself from sorrow, the cockpit, and the dangers of idleness. He became so addicted to his studies and the purchase of books, that he entirely neglected his fortune and gradually ruined himself. Persons of culture called him Don Anastasio, or Tasio the Sage, while the great crowd of the ignorant knew him as Tasio the Lunatic, on account of his peculiar ideas and his eccentric manner of dealing with others.

As we said before, the evening threatened to be stormy. The lightning flashed its pale rays across the leaden sky, the air was heavy and the slight breeze excessively sultry. Tasio had apparently already forgotten his beloved skull, and now he was smiling as he looked at the dark clouds. Near the church he met a man wearing an alpaca coat, who carried in one hand a large bundle of candles and in the other a tasseled cane, the emblem of his office as gobernadorcillo.

"You seem to be merry?" he greeted Tasio in Tagalog.

"Truly I am, señor capitan, I'm merry because I hope for something."

"Ah? What do you hope for?"

"The storm!"

"The storm? Are you thinking of taking a bath?" asked the gobernadorcillo in a jesting way as he stared at the simple attire of the old man.

"A bath? That's not a bad idea, especially when one has just stumbled over some trash!" answered Tasio in a similar, though somewhat more offensive tone, staring at the other's face. "But I hope for something better."

"What, then?"

"Some thunderbolts that will kill people and burn down houses," returned the Sage seriously.

"Why don't you ask for the deluge at once?"

"We all deserve it, even you and I! You, señor gobernadorcillo, have there a bundle of tapers that came from some Chinese shop, yet this now makes the tenth year that I have been proposing to each new occupant of your office the purchase of lightning-rods. Every one laughs at me, and buys bombs and rockets and pays for the ringing of bells. Even you yourself, on the day after I made my proposition, ordered from the Chinese founders a bell in honor of St. Barbara,[1] when science has shown that it is dangerous to ring the bells during a storm. Explain to me why in the year '70, when lightning struck in Biñan, it hit the very church tower and destroyed the clock and altar. What was the bell of St. Barbara doing then?"

At the moment there was a vivid flash. "*Jesús, María, y José!* Holy St. Barbara!" exclaimed the gobernadorcillo, turning pale and crossing himself.

Tasio burst out into a loud laugh. "You are worthy of your patroness," he remarked dryly in Spanish as he turned his back and went toward the church.

Inside, the sacristans were preparing a catafalque, bor-

---

[1] St. Barbara is invoked during thunder-storms as the special protectress against lightning. —Tr.

dered with candles placed in wooden sockets. Two large tables had been placed one above the other and covered with black cloth across which ran white stripes, with here and there a skull painted on it.

"Is that for the souls or for the candles?" inquired the old man, but noticing two boys, one about ten and the other seven, he turned to them without awaiting an answer from the sacristans.

"Won't you come with me, boys?" he asked them. "Your mother has prepared a supper for you fit for a curate."

"The senior sacristan will not let us leave until eight o'clock, sir," answered the larger of the two boys. "I expect to get my pay to give it to our mother."

"Ah! And where are you going now?"

"To the belfry, sir, to ring the knell for the souls."

"Going to the belfry! Then take care! Don't go near the bells during the storm!"

Tasio then left the church, not without first bestowing a look of pity on the two boys, who were climbing the stairway into the organ-loft. He passed his hand over his eyes, looked at the sky again, and murmured, "Now I should be sorry if thunderbolts should fall." With his head bowed in thought he started toward the outskirts of the town.

"Won't you come in?" invited a voice in Spanish from a window.

The Sage raised his head and saw a man of thirty or thirty-five years of age smiling at him.

"What are you reading there?" asked Tasio, pointing to a book the man held in his hand.

"A work just published: 'The Torments Suffered by the Blessed Souls in Purgatory,'" the other answered with a smile.

"Man, man, man!" exclaimed the Sage in an altered tone as he entered the house. "The author must be a very clever person."

Upon reaching the top of the stairway, he was cordially received by the master of the house, Don Filipo Lino, and his young wife, Doña Teodora Viña. Don Filipo was the teniente-mayor of the town and leader of one of the parties — the liberal faction, if it be possible to speak so, and if there exist parties in the towns of the Philippines.

"Did you meet in the cemetery the son of the deceased Don Rafael, who has just returned from Europe?"

"Yes, I saw him as he alighted from his carriage."

"They say that he went to look for his father's grave. It must have been a terrible blow."

The Sage shrugged his shoulders.

"Does n't such a misfortune affect you?" asked the young wife.

"You know very well that I was one of the six who accompanied the body, and it was I who appealed to the Captain-General when I saw that no one, not even the authorities, said anything about such an outrage, although I always prefer to honor a good man in life rather than to worship him after his death."

"Well?"

"But, madam, I am not a believer in hereditary monarchy. By reason of the Chinese blood which I have received from my mother I believe a little like the Chinese: I honor the father on account of the son and not the son on account of the father. I believe that each one should receive the reward or punishment for his own deeds, not for those of another."

"Did you order a mass said for your dead wife, as I advised you yesterday?" asked the young woman, changing the subject of conversation.

"No," answered the old man with a smile.

"What a pity!" she exclaimed with unfeigned regret. "They say that until ten o'clock tomorrow the souls will wander at liberty, awaiting the prayers of the living, and that during these days one mass is equivalent to five on other days of the year, or even to six, as the curate said this morning."

"What! Does that mean that we have a period without paying, which we should take advantage of?"

"But, Doray," interrupted Don Filipo, "you know that Don Anastasio does n't believe in purgatory."

"I don't believe in purgatory!" protested the old man, partly rising from his seat. "Even when I know something of its history!"

"The history of purgatory!" exclaimed the couple, full of surprise. "Come, relate it to us."

"You don't know it and yet you order masses and talk about its torments? Well, as it has begun to rain and threatens to continue, we shall have time to relieve the monotony," replied Tasio, falling into a thoughtful mood.

Don Filipo closed the book which he held in his hand and Doray sat down at his side determined not to believe anything that the old man was about to say.

The latter began in the following manner: "Purgatory existed long before Our Lord came into the world and must have been located in the center of the earth, according to Padre Astete; or somewhere near Cluny, according to the monk of whom Padre Girard tells us. But the location is of least importance here. Now then, who were scorching in those fires that had been burning from the beginning of the world? Its very ancient existence is proved by Christian philosophy, which teaches that God has created nothing new since he rested."

"But it could have existed *in potentia* and not *in actu*,"[1] observed Don Filipo.

"Very well! But yet I must answer that some knew of it and as existing *in actu*. One of these was Zarathustra, or Zoroaster, who wrote part of the Zend-Avesta and founded a religion which in some points resembles ours, and Zarathustra, according to the scholars, flourished at least eight hundred years before Christ. I say 'at least,'

[1] In possibility (i. e., latent) and not in fact. — TR.

since Gaffarel, after examining the testimony of Plato, Xanthus of Lydia, Pliny, Hermippus, and Eudoxus, believes it to have been two thousand five hundred years before our era. However that may be, it is certain that Zarathustra talked of a kind of purgatory and showed ways of getting free from it. The living could redeem the souls of those who died in sin by reciting passages from the Avesta and by doing good works, but under the condition that the person offering the petitions should be a relative, up to the fourth generation. The time for this occurred every year and lasted five days. Later, when this belief had become fixed among the people, the priests of that religion saw in it a chance of profit and so they exploited 'the deep and dark prison where remorse reigns,' as Zarathustra called it. They declared that by the payment of a small coin it was possible to save a soul from a year of torture, but as in that religion there were sins punishable by three hundred to a thousand years of suffering, such as lying, faithlessness, failure to keep one's word, and so on, it resulted that the rascals took in countless sums. Here you will observe something like our purgatory, if you take into account the differences in the religions."

A vivid flash of lightning, followed by rolling thunder, caused Doray to start up and exclaim, as she crossed herself: "*Jesús, María, y José!* I'm going to leave you, I'm going to burn some sacred palm and light candles of penitence."

The rain began to fall in torrents. The Sage Tasio, watching the young woman leave, continued: "Now that she is not here, we can consider this matter more rationally. Doray, even though a little superstitious, is a good Catholic, and I don't care to root out the faith from her heart. A pure and simple faith is as distinct from fanaticism as the flame from smoke or music from discords: only the fools and the deaf confuse them. Between ourselves we can say that the idea of purgatory is good, holy, and rational. It perpetuates the union of those who were and those who are, leading thus to greater purity of life. The evil is in its abuse.

"But let us how see where Catholicism got this idea, which does not exist in the Old Testament nor in the Gospels. Neither Moses nor Christ made the slightest mention of it, and the single passage which is cited from Maccabees is insufficient. Besides, this book was declared apocryphal by the Council of Laodicea and the holy Catholic Church accepted it only later. Neither have the pagan religions anything like it. The oft-quoted passage in Virgil, *Aliae panduntur inanes*,[1] which probably gave occasion for St. Gregory the Great to speak of drowned souls, and to Dante for another narrative in his *Divine Comedy*, cannot have been the origin of this belief. Neither the Brahmins, the Buddhists, nor the Egyptians, who may have given Rome her Charon and her Avernus, had anything like this idea. I won't speak now of the religions of northern Europe, for they were religions of warriors, bards, and hunters, and not of philosophers. While they yet preserve their beliefs and even their rites under Christian forms, they were unable to accompany the hordes in the spoliation of Rome or to seat themselves on the Capitoline; the religions of the mists were dissipated by the southern sun. Now then, the early Christians did not believe in a purgatory but died in the blissful confidence of shortly seeing God face to face. Apparently the first fathers of the Church who mentioned it were St. Clement of Alexandria, Origen, and St. Irenaeus, who were all perhaps influenced by Zarathustra's religion, which still flourished and was widely spread throughout the East, since at every step we read reproaches against Origen's Orientalism. St. Irenaeus proved its existence by the fact that Christ remained 'three days in the depths of the

---

[1] "For this are various penances enjoined;
And some are hung to bleach upon the wind;
Some plunged in waters, others purged in fires,
Till all the dregs are drained, and all the rust expires."
                    Dryden, *Virgil's Aeneid*, VI.

earth,' three days of purgatory, and deduced from this that every soul must remain there until the resurrection of the body, although the '*Hodie mecum eris in Paradiso*' [1] seems to contradict it. St. Augustine also speaks of purgatory and, if not affirming its existence, yet he did not believe it impossible, conjecturing that in another existence there might continue the punishments that we receive in this life for our sins."

"The devil with St. Augustine!" ejaculated Don Filipo. "He wasn't satisfied with what we suffer here but wished a continuance."

"Well, so it went: some believed it and others didn't. Although St. Gregory finally came to admit it in his *de quibusdam levibus culpis esse ante judicium purgatorius ignis credendus est*,[2] yet nothing definite was done until the year 1439, that is, eight centuries later, when the Council of Florence declared that there must exist a purifying fire for the souls of those who have died in the love of God but without having satisfied divine Justice. Lastly, the Council of Trent under Pius IV in 1563, in the twenty-fifth session, issued the purgatorial decree beginning *Cum catholica ecclesia, Spiritu Santo edocta,* wherein it deduces that, after the office of the mass, the petitions of the living, their prayers, alms, and other pious works are the surest means of freeing the souls. Nevertheless, the Protestants do not believe in it nor do the Greek Fathers, since they reject any Biblical authority for it and say that our responsibility ends with death, and that the '*Quodcumque ligaberis in terra*,'[3] does not mean '*usque ad purgatorium*,'[4] but to this the answer can be made that since purgatory is located in the center of the earth it fell naturally under the control of St. Peter. But I should never get through if I had to relate all that

[1] "Today shalt thou be with me in paradise." — Luke xxiii, 43.
[2] It should be believed that for some light faults there is a purgatorial fire before the judgment.
[3] Whatsoever thou shalt bind on earth. — Matt. xvi, 19.
[4] Even up to purgatory.

TASIO: LUNATIC OR SAGE 99

has been said on the subject. Any day that you wish to discuss the matter with me, come to my house and there we will consult the books and talk freely and quietly.

"Now I must go. I don't understand why Christian piety permits robbery on this night — and you, the authorities, allow it — and I fear for my books. If they should steal them to read I would n't object, but I know that there are many who wish to burn them in order to do for me an act of charity, and such charity, worthy of the Caliph Omar, is to be dreaded. Some believe that on account of those books I am already damned —"

"But I suppose that you do believe in damnation?" asked Doray with a smile, as she appeared carrying in a brazier the dry palm leaves, which gave off a peculiar smoke and an agreeable odor.

"I don't know, madam, what God will do with me," replied the old man thoughtfully. "When I die I will commit myself to Him without fear and He may do with me what He wishes. But a thought strikes me!"

"What thought is that?"

"If the only ones who can be saved are the Catholics, and of them only five per cent — as many curates say — and as the Catholics form only a twelfth part of the population of the world — if we believe what statistics show — it would result that after damning millions and millions of men during the countless ages that passed before the Saviour came to the earth, after a Son of God has died for us, it is now possible to save only five in every twelve hundred. That cannot be so! I prefer to believe and say with Job: 'Wilt thou break a leaf driven to and fro, and wilt thou pursue the dry stubble?' No, such a calamity is impossible and to believe it is blasphemy!"

"What do you wish? Divine Justice, divine Purity —"

"Oh, but divine Justice and divine Purity saw the future before the creation," answered the old man, as he rose shuddering. "Man is an accidental and not a necessary part of creation, and that God cannot have created him, no indeed, only to make a few happy and condemn hundreds to eternal misery, and all in a moment, for hereditary faults! No! If that be true, strangle your baby son sleeping there! If such a belief were not a blasphemy against that God, who must be the Highest Good, then the Phenician Moloch, which was appeased with human sacrifices and innocent blood, and in whose belly were burned the babes torn from their mothers' breasts, that bloody deity, that horrible divinity, would be by the side of Him a weak girl, a friend, a mother of humanity!"

Horrified, the Lunatic — or the Sage — left the house and ran along the street in spite of the rain and the darkness. A lurid flash, followed by frightful thunder and filling the air with deadly currents, lighted the old man as he stretched his hand toward the sky and cried out: "Thou protestest! I know that Thou art not cruel, I know that I must only name Thee Good!"

The flashes of lightning became more frequent and the storm increased in violence.

CHAPTER XV

THE SACRISTANS

THE thunder resounded, roar following close upon roar, each preceded by a blinding flash of zigzag lightning, so that it might have been said that God was writing his name in fire and that the eternal arch of heaven was trembling with fear. The rain, whipped about in a different direction each moment by the mournfully whistling wind, fell in torrents. With a voice full of fear the bells sounded their sad supplication, and in the brief pauses between the roars of the unchained elements tolled forth sorrowful peals, like plaintive groans.

On the second floor of the church tower were the two boys whom we saw talking to the Sage. The younger, a child of seven years with large black eyes and a timid countenance, was huddling close to his brother, a boy of ten, whom he greatly resembled in features, except that the look on the elder's face was deeper and firmer.

Both were meanly dressed in clothes full of rents and patches. They sat upon a block of wood, each holding the end of a rope which extended upward and was lost amid the shadows above. The wind-driven rain reached them and snuffed the piece of candle burning dimly on the large round stone that was used to furnish the thunder on Good Friday by being rolled around the gallery.

"Pull on the rope, Crispin, pull!" cried the elder to his little brother, who did as he was told, so that from above was heard a faint peal, instantly drowned out by the re-echoing thunder.

"Oh, if we were only at home now with mother," sighed

the younger, as he gazed at his brother. "There I should n't be afraid."

The elder did not answer; he was watching the melting wax of the candle, apparently lost in thought.

"There no one would say that I stole," went on Crispin. "Mother would n't allow it. If she knew that they whip me —"

The elder took his gaze from the flame, raised his head, and clutching the thick rope pulled violently on it so that a sonorous peal of the bells was heard.

"Are we always going to live this way, brother?" continued Crispin. "I'd like to get sick at home tomorrow, I'd like to fall into a long sickness so that mother might take care of me and not let me come back to the convento. So I'd not be called a thief nor would they whip me. And you too, brother, you must get sick with me."

"No," answered the older, "we should all die: mother of grief and we of hunger."

Crispin remained silent for a moment, then asked, "How much will you get this month?"

"Two pesos. They've fined me twice."

"Then pay what they say I've stolen, so that they won't call us thieves. Pay it, brother!"

"Are you crazy, Crispin? Mother would n't have anything to eat. The senior sacristan says that you've stolen two gold pieces, and they're worth thirty-two pesos."

The little one counted on his fingers up to thirty-two. "Six hands and two fingers over and each finger a peso!" he murmured thoughtfully. "And each peso, how many cuartos?"

"A hundred and sixty."

"A hundred and sixty cuartos? A hundred and sixty times a cuarto? Goodness! And how many are a hundred and sixty?"

"Thirty-two hands," answered the older.

Crispin looked hard at his little hands. "Thirty-two hands," he repeated, "six hands and two fingers over and each finger thirty-two hands and each finger a cuarto — goodness, what a lot of cuartos! I could hardly count them in three days; and with them could be bought shoes for our feet, a hat for my head when the sun shines hot, a big umbrella for the rain, and food, and clothes for you and mother, and — " He became silent and thoughtful again.

"Now I'm sorry that I didn't steal!" he soon exclaimed.

"Crispin!" reproached his brother.

"Don't get angry! The curate has said that he'll beat me to death if the money does n't appear, and if I had stolen it I could make it appear. Anyhow, if I died you and mother would at least have clothes. Oh, if I had only stolen it!"

The elder pulled on the rope in silence. After a time he replied with a sigh: "What I'm afraid of is that mother will scold you when she knows about it."

"Do you think so?" asked the younger with astonishment. "You will tell her that they've whipped me and I'll show the welts on my back and my torn pocket. I had only one cuarto, which was given to me last Easter, but the curate took that away from me yesterday. I never saw a prettier cuarto! No, mother won't believe it."

"If the curate says so — "

Crispin began to cry, murmuring between his sobs, "Then go home alone! I don't want to go. Tell mother that I'm sick. I don't want to go."

"Crispin, don't cry!" pleaded the elder. "Mother won't believe it — don't cry! Old Tasio told us that a fine supper is waiting for us."

"A fine supper! And I have n't eaten for a long time. They won't give me anything to eat until the two gold pieces appear. But, if mother believes it? You must tell her that the senior sacristan is a liar but that the curate believes him and that all of them are liars, that they say that we're thieves because our father is a vagabond who — "

At that instant a head appeared at the top of the stairway leading down to the floor below, and that head, like Medusa's, froze the words on the child's lips. It was a long, narrow head covered with black hair, with blue glasses concealing the fact that one eye was sightless. The senior sacristan was accustomed to appear thus without noise or warning of any kind. The two brothers turned cold with fear.

"On you, Basilio, I impose a fine of two reals for not ringing the bells in time," he said in a voice so hollow that his throat seemed to lack vocal chords. "You, Crispin, must stay tonight, until what you stole reappears."

Crispin looked at his brother as if pleading for protection.

"But we already have permission — mother expects us at eight o'clock," objected Basilio timidly.

"Neither shall you go home at eight, you'll stay until ten."

"But, sir, after nine o'clock no one is allowed to be out and our house is far from here."

"Are you trying to give me orders?" growled the man irritably, as he caught Crispin by the arm and started to drag him away.

"Oh, sir, it's been a week now since we've seen our mother," begged Basilio, catching hold of his brother as if to defend him.

The senior sacristan struck his hand away and jerked at Crispin, who began to weep as he fell to the floor, crying out to his brother, "Don't leave me, they're going to kill me!"

The sacristan gave no heed to this and dragged him on to the stairway. As they disappeared among the shadows below Basilio stood speechless, listening to the sounds of his brother's body striking against the steps. Then followed the sound of a blow and heartrending cries that died away in the distance.

The boy stood on tiptoe, hardly breathing and listening

fixedly, with his eyes unnaturally wide and his fists clenched. "When shall I be strong enough to plow a field?" he muttered between his teeth as he started below hastily. Upon reaching the organ-loft he paused to listen; the voice of his brother was fast dying away in the distance and the cries of "Mother! Brother!" were at last completely cut off by the sound of a closing door. Trembling and perspiring, he paused for a moment with his fist in his mouth to keep down a cry of anguish. He let his gaze wander about the dimly lighted church where an oil-lamp gave a ghostly light, revealing the catafalque in the center. The doors were closed and fastened, and the windows had iron bars on them. Suddenly he reascended the stairway to the place where the candle was burning and then climbed up into the third floor of the belfry. After untying the ropes from the bell-clappers he again descended. He was pale and his eyes glistened, but not with tears.

Meanwhile, the rain was gradually ceasing and the sky was clearing. Basilio knotted the ropes together, tied one end to a rail of the balustrade, and without even remembering to put out the light let himself down into the darkness outside. A few moments later voices were heard on one of the streets of the town, two shots resounded, but no one seemed to be alarmed and silence again reigned.

CHAPTER XVI

SISA

THROUGH the dark night the villagers slept. The families who had remembered their dead gave themselves up to quiet and satisfied sleep, for they had recited their requiems, the novena of the souls, and had burned many wax tapers before the sacred images. The rich and powerful had discharged the duties their positions imposed upon them. On the following day they would hear three masses said by each priest and would give two pesos for another, besides buying a bull of indulgences for the dead. Truly, divine justice is not nearly so exacting as human.

But the poor and indigent who earn scarcely enough to keep themselves alive and who also have to pay tribute to the petty officials, clerks, and soldiers, that they may be allowed to live in peace, sleep not so tranquilly as gentle poets who have perhaps not felt the pinches of want would have us believe. The poor are sad and thoughtful, for on that night, if they have not recited many prayers, yet they have prayed much — with pain in their eyes and tears in their hearts. They have not the novenas, nor do they know the responsories, versicles, and prayers which the friars have composed for those who lack original ideas and feelings, nor do they understand them. They pray in the language of their misery: their souls weep for them and for those dead beings whose love was their wealth. Their lips may proffer the salutations, but their minds cry out complaints, charged with lamentations. Wilt Thou be satisfied, O Thou who blessedst poverty, and you, O suffering souls, with the simple prayers of the poor, offered before a rude picture in the light of a dim wick, or do you perhaps desire wax tapers before bleeding Christs and Virgins with small mouths and crystal eyes, and masses in Latin recited mechanically by priests? And thou, Religion preached for suffering humanity, hast thou forgotten thy mission of consoling the oppressed in their misery and of humiliating the powerful in their pride? Hast thou now promises only for the rich, for those who can pay thee?

The poor widow watches among the children who sleep at her side. She is thinking of the indulgences that she ought to buy for the repose of the souls of her parents and of her dead husband. "A peso," she says, "a peso is a week of happiness for my children, a week of laughter and joy, my savings for a month, a dress for my daughter who is becoming a woman." "But it is necessary that you put aside these worldly desires," says the voice that she heard in the pulpit, "it is necessary that you make sacrifices." Yes, it is necessary. The Church does not gratuitously save the beloved souls for you nor does it distribute indulgences without payment. You must buy them, so tonight instead of sleeping you should work. Think of your daughter, so poorly clothed! Fast, for heaven is dear! Decidedly, it seems that the poor enter not into heaven. Such thoughts wander through the space enclosed between the rough mats spread out on the bamboo floor and the ridge of the roof, from which hangs the hammock wherein the baby swings. The infant's breathing is easy and peaceful, but from time to time he swallows and smacks his lips; his hungry stomach, which is not satisfied with what his older brothers have given him, dreams of eating.

The cicadas chant monotonously, mingling their ceaseless notes with the trills of the cricket hidden in the grass, or the chirp of the little lizard which has come out in search of food, while the big gekko, no longer fearing the water, disturbs the concert with its ill-omened voice as it shows its head from out the hollow of the decayed tree-trunk.

The dogs howl mournfully in the streets and superstitious folk, hearing them, are convinced that they see spirits and ghosts. But neither the dogs nor the other animals see the sorrows of men — yet how many of these exist!

Distant from the town an hour's walk lives the mother of Basilio and Crispin. The wife of a heartless man, she struggles to live for her sons, while her husband is a vagrant gamester with whom her interviews are rare but always painful. He has gradually stripped her of her few jewels to pay the cost of his vices, and when the suffering Sisa no longer had anything that he might take to satisfy his whims, he had begun to maltreat her. Weak in character, with more heart than intellect, she knew only how to love and to weep. Her husband was a god and her sons were his angels, so he, knowing to what point he was loved and feared, conducted himself like all false gods: daily he became more cruel, more inhuman, more wilful. Once when he had appeared with his countenance gloomier than ever before, Sisa had consulted him about the plan of making a sacristan of Basilio, and he had merely continued to stroke his game-cock, saying neither yes nor no, only asking whether the boy would earn much money. She had not dared to insist, but her needy situation and her desire that the boys should learn to read and write in the town school forced her to carry out the plan. Still her husband had said nothing.

That night, between ten and eleven o'clock, when the stars were glittering in a sky now cleared of all signs of the storm of the early evening, Sisa sat on a wooden bench watching some fagots that smouldered upon the fireplace fashioned of rough pieces of natural rock. Upon a tripod, or *tunko,* was a small pot of boiling rice and upon the red coals lay three little dried fishes such as are sold at three for two cuartos. Her chin rested in the palm of her hand while she gazed at the weak yellow glow peculiar to the cane, which burns rapidly and leaves embers that quickly grow pale. A sad smile lighted up her face as she recalled a funny riddle about the pot and the fire which Crispin had once propounded to her. The boy said· "The black man sat down and the red man looked at him, a moment passed, and çock-a-doodle-doo rang forth."

Sisa was still young, and it was plain that at one time she had been pretty and attractive. Her eyes, which, like her disposition, she had given to her sons, were beautiful, with long lashes and a deep look. Her nose was regular and her pale lips curved pleasantly. She was what the Tagalogs call *kayumanguing-kaligátan;* that is, her color was a clear, pure brown. In spite of her youthfulness, pain and perhaps even hunger had begun to make hollow her pallid cheeks, and if her abundant hair, in other times the delight and adornment of her person, was even yet simply and neatly arranged, though without pins or combs, it was not from coquetry but from habit.

Sisa had been for several days confined to the house sewing upon some work which had been ordered for the earliest possible time. In order to earn the money, she had not attended mass that morning, as it would have taken two hours at least to go to the town and return: poverty obliges one to sin! She had finished the work and delivered it but had received only a promise of payment. All that day she had been anticipating the pleasures of the evening, for she knew that her sons were coming and she had intended to make them some presents. She had bought some small fishes, picked the most beautiful tomatoes in her little garden, as she knew that Crispin was very fond of them, and begged from a neighbor, old Tasio the Sage, who lived half a mile away, some slices of dried wild boar's meat and a leg of wild duck, which Basilio especially liked. Full of hope, she had cooked the whitest of rice, which she herself had gleaned from the threshing-floors. It was indeed a curate's meal for the poor boys.

But by an unfortunate chance her husband came and ate the rice, the slices of wild boar's meat, the duck leg, five of the little fishes, and the tomatoes. Sisa said nothing, although she felt as if she herself were being eaten. His hunger at length appeased, he remembered to ask for the boys. Then Sisa smiled happily and resolved that she would not eat that night, because what remained was not enough for three. The father had asked for their sons and that for her was better than eating.

Soon he picked up his game-cock and started away.

"Don't you want to see them?" she asked tremulously. "Old Tasio told me that they would be a little late. Crispin now knows how to read and perhaps Basilio will bring his wages."

This last reason caused the husband to pause and waver, but his good angel triumphed. "In that case keep a peso for me," he said as he went away.

Sisa wept bitterly, but the thought of her sons soon dried her tears. She cooked some more rice and prepared the only three fishes that were left: each would have one and a half. "They'll have good appetites," she mused, "the way is long and hungry stomachs have no heart."

So she sat, he ear strained to catch every sound, listening to the lightest footfalls: strong and clear, Basilio; light and irregular, Crispin — thus she mused. The *kalao* called in the woods several times after the rain had ceased, but still her sons did not come. She put the fishes inside the pot to keep them warm and went to the threshold of the hut to look toward the road. To keep herself company, she began to sing in a low voice, a voice usually so sweet and tender that when her sons listened to her singing the *kundíman* they wept without knowing why, but tonight it trembled and the notes were halting. She stopped singing and gazed earnestly into the darkness, but no one was coming from the town — that noise was only the wind shaking the raindrops from the wide banana leaves.

Suddenly a black dog appeared before her dragging something along the path. Sisa was frightened but caught up a stone and threw it at the dog, which ran away howling mournfully. She was not superstitious, but she had heard so much about presentiments and black dogs that terror seized her. She shut the door hastily and sat down by the light. Night favors credulity and the imagination peoples the air with specters. She tried to pray, to call upon the Virgin and upon God to watch over her sons, especially her little Crispin. Then she forgot her prayers as her thoughts wandered to think about them, to recall the features of each, those features that always wore a smile for her both asleep and awake. Suddenly she felt her hair rise on her head and her eyes stared wildly; illusion or reality, she saw Crispin standing by the fireplace, there where he was wont to sit and prattle to her, but now he said nothing as he gazed at her with those large, thoughtful eyes, and smiled.

"Mother, open the door! Open, mother!" cried the voice of Basilio from without.

Sisa shuddered violently and the vision disappeared.

CHAPTER XVII

BASILIO

La vida es sueño.

BASILIO was scarcely inside when he staggered and fell into his mother's arms. An inexplicable chill seized Sisa as she saw him enter alone. She wanted to speak but could make no sound; she wanted to embrace her son but lacked the strength; to weep was impossible. At sight of the blood which covered the boy's forehead she cried in a tone that seemed to come from a breaking heart, "My sons!"

"Don't be afraid, mother," Basilio reassured her. "Crispin stayed at the convento."

"At the convento? He stayed at the convento? Is he alive?"

The boy raised his eyes to her. "Ah!" she sighed, passing from the depths of sorrow to the heights of joy. She wept and embraced her son, covering his bloody forehead with kisses.

"Crispin is alive! You left him at the convento! But why are you wounded, my son? Have you had a fall?" she inquired, as she examined him anxiously.

"The senior sacristan took Crispin away and told me that I could not leave until ten o'clock, but it was already late and so I ran away. In the town the soldiers challenged me, I started to run, they fired, and a bullet grazed my forehead. I was afraid they would arrest me and beat me and make me scrub out the barracks, as they did with Pablo, who is still sick from it."

"My God, my God!" murmured his mother, shuddering. "Thou hast saved him!" Then while she sought for bandages, water, vinegar, and a feather, she went on, "A finger's breadth more and they would have killed you, they would have killed my boy! The civil-guards do not think of the mothers."

"You must say that I fell from a tree so that no one will know they chased me," Basilio cautioned her.

"Why did Crispin stay?" asked Sisa, after dressing her son's wound.

Basilio hesitated a few moments, then with his arms about her and their tears mingling, he related little by little the story of the gold pieces, without speaking, however, of the tortures they were inflicting upon his young brother.

"My good Crispin! To accuse my good Crispin! It's because we're poor and we poor people have to endure everything!" murmured Sisa, staring through her tears at the light of the lamp, which was now dying out from lack of oil. So they remained silent for a while.

"Haven't you had any supper yet? Here are rice and fish."

"I don't want anything, only a little water."

"Yes," answered his mother sadly, "I know that you don't like dried fish. I had prepared something else, but your father came."

"Father came?" asked Basilio, instinctively examining the face and hands of his mother.

The son's questioning gaze pained Sisa's heart, for she understood it only too well, so she added hastily: "He came and asked a lot about you and wanted to see you, and he was very hungry. He said that if you continued to be so good he would come back to stay with us."

An exclamation of disgust from Basilio's contracted lips interrupted her. "Son!" she reproached him.

"Forgive me, mother," he answered seriously. "But aren't we three better off — you, Crispin, and I? You're crying — I haven't said anything."

Sisa sighed and asked, "Aren't you going to eat? Then

let's go to sleep, for it's now very late." She then closed up the hut and covered the few coals with ashes so that the fire would not die out entirely, just as a man does with his inner feelings; he covers them with the ashes of his life, which he calls indifference, so that they may not be deadened by daily contact with his fellows.

Basilio murmured his prayers and lay down near his mother, who was upon her knees praying. He felt hot and cold, he tried to close his eyes as he thought of his little brother who that night had expected to sleep in his mother's lap and who now was probably trembling with terror and weeping in some dark corner of the convento. His ears were again pierced with those cries he had heard in the church tower. But wearied nature soon began to confuse his ideas and the veil of sleep descended upon his eyes.

He saw a bedroom where two dim tapers burned. The curate, with a rattan whip in his hand, was listening gloomily to something that the senior sacristan was telling him in a strange tongue with horrible gestures. Crispin quailed and turned his tearful eyes in every direction as if seeking some one or some hiding-place. The curate turned toward him and called to him irritably, the rattan whistled. The child ran to hide himself behind the sacristan, who caught and held him, thus exposing him to the curate's fury. The unfortunate boy fought, kicked, screamed, threw himself on the floor and rolled about. He picked himself up, ran, slipped, fell, and parried the blows with his hands, which, wounded, he hid quickly, all the time shrieking with pain. Basilio saw him twist himself, strike the floor with his head, he saw and heard the rattan whistle. In desperation his little brother rose. Mad with pain he threw himself upon his tormentor and bit him on the hand. The curate gave a cry and dropped the rattan — the sacristan caught up a heavy cane and struck the boy a blow on the head so that he fell stunned — the curate, seeing him down, trampled him with his feet.

But the child no longer defended himself nor did he cry out; he rolled along the floor, a lifeless mass that left a damp track.[1]

Sisa's voice brought him back to reality. "What's the matter? Why are you crying?"

"I dreamed— O God!" exclaimed Basilio, sitting up, covered with perspiration. "It was a dream! Tell me, mother, that it was only a dream! Only a dream!"

"What did you dream?"

The boy did not answer, but sat drying his tears and wiping away the perspiration. The hut was in total darkness.

"A dream, a dream!" repeated Basilio in subdued tones.

"Tell me what you dreamed. I can't sleep," said his mother when he lay down again.

"Well," he said in a low voice, "I dreamed that we had gone to glean the rice-stalks — in a field where there were many flowers — the women had baskets full of rice-stalks — the men too had baskets full of rice-stalks — and the children too — I don't remember any more, mother, I don't remember the rest."

Sisa had no faith in dreams, so she did not insist.

"Mother, I've thought of a plan tonight," said Basilio after a few moments' silence.

---

[1] Dream or reality, we do not know whether this may have happened to any Franciscan, but something similar is related of the Augustinian Padre Piernavieja. — *Author's note.*

Fray Antonio Piernavieja, O.S.A., was a parish curate in the province of Bulacan when this work was written. Later, on account of alleged brutality similar to the incident used here, he was transferred to the province of Cavite, where, in 1896, he was taken prisoner by the insurgents and by them made "bishop" of their camp. Having taken advantage of this position to collect and forward to the Spanish authorities in Manila information concerning the insurgents' preparations and plans, he was tied out in an open field and left to perish of hunger and thirst under the tropical sun. See *Guia Oficial de Filipinas*, 1885, p. 195; *El Katipunan ó El Filibusterismo en Filipinas* (Madrid, 1897), p. 347; Foreman's *The Philippine Islands*, Chap. XII. — Tr.

"What is your plan?" she asked. Sisa was humble in everything, even with her own sons, trusting their judgment more than her own.

"I don't want to be a sacristan any longer."

"What?"

"Listen, mother, to what I've been thinking about. Today there arrived from Spain the son of the dead Don Rafael, and he will be a good man like his father. Well now, mother, tomorrow you will get Crispin, collect my wages, and say that I will not be a sacristan any longer. As soon as I get well I'll go to see Don Crisostomo and ask him to hire me as a herdsman of his cattle and carabaos — I'm now big enough. Crispin can study with old Tasio, who does not whip and who is a good man, even if the curate does not believe so. What have we to fear now from the padre? Can he make us any poorer than we are? You may believe it, mother, the old man is good. I've seen him often in the church when no one else was about, kneeling and praying, believe it. So, mother, I'll stop being a sacristan. I earn but little and that little is taken away from me in fines. Every one complains of the same thing. I'll be a herdsman and by performing my tasks carefully I'll make my employer like me. Perhaps he'll let us milk a cow so that we can drink milk — Crispin likes milk so much. Who can tell! Maybe they'll give us a little calf if they see that I behave well and we'll take care of it and fatten it like our hen. I'll pick fruits in the woods and sell them in the town along with the vegetables from our garden, so we'll have money. I'll set snares and traps to catch birds and wild cats,[1] I'll fish in the river, and when I'm bigger, I'll hunt. I'll be able also to cut firewood to sell or to present to the owner of the cows, and so he'll be satisfied with us. When I'm able to plow, I'll ask him to let me have a piece of land to plant in sugar-cane or corn and you won't have to sew until midnight. We'll

---

[1] The Philippine civet-cat, quite rare, and the only wild carnivore in the Philippine Islands. — Tr.

have new clothes for every fiesta, we'll eat meat and big fish, we'll live free, seeing each other every day and eating together. Old Tasio says that Crispin has a good head and so we'll send him to Manila to study. I'll support him by working hard. Isn't that fine, mother? Perhaps he'll be a doctor, what do you say?"

"What can I say but yes?" said Sisa as she embraced her son. She noted, however, that in their future the boy took no account of his father, and shed silent tears.

Basilio went on talking of his plans with the confidence of the years that see only what they wish for. To everything Sisa said yes — everything appeared good.

Sleep again began to weigh down upon the tired eyelids of the boy, and this time Ole-Luk-Oie, of whom Andersen tells us, spread over him his beautiful umbrella with its pleasing pictures. Now he saw himself with his little brother as they picked guavas, alpay, and other fruits in the woods; they clambered from branch to branch, light as butterflies; they penetrated into the caves and saw the shining rocks; they bathed in the springs where the sand was gold-dust and the stones like the jewels in the Virgin's crown. The little fishes sang and laughed, the plants bent their branches toward them laden with golden fruit. Then he saw a bell hanging in a tree with a long rope for ringing it; to the rope was tied a cow with a bird's nest between her horns and Crispin was inside the bell.

Thus he went on dreaming, while his mother, who was not of his age and who had not run for an hour, slept not.

CHAPTER XVIII

SOULS IN TORMENT

IT was about seven o'clock in the morning when Fray Salvi finished celebrating his last mass, having offered up three in the space of an hour. "The padre is ill," commented the pious women. "He does n't move about with his usual slowness and elegance of manner."

He took off his vestments without the least comment, without saying a word or looking at any one. "Attention!" whispered the sacristans among themselves. "The devil's to pay! It's going to rain fines, and all on account of those two brothers."

He left the sacristy to go up into the rectory, in the hallway of which there awaited him some seven or eight women seated upon benches and a man who was pacing back and forth. Upon seeing him approach, the women arose and one of them pressed forward to kiss his hand, but the holy man made a sign of impatience that stopped her short.

"Can it be that you've lost a real, *kuriput*?" exclaimed the woman with a jesting laugh, offended at such a reception. "Not to give his hand to me, Matron of the Sisterhood, Sister Rufa!" It was an unheard-of proceeding.

"He did n't go into the confessional this morning," added Sister Sipa, a toothless old woman. "I wanted to confess myself so as to receive communion and get the indulgences."

"Well, I'm sorry for you," commented a young woman with a frank face. "This week I earned three plenary indulgences and dedicated them to the soul of my husband."

"Badly done, Sister Juana," said the offended Rufa.

"One plenary indulgence was enough to get him out of purgatory. You ought not to squander the holy indulgences. Do as I do."

"I thought, so many more the better," answered the simple Sister Juana, smiling. "But tell me what you do."

Sister Rufa did not answer at once. First, she asked for a buyo and chewed at it, gazed at her audience, which was listening attentively, then spat to one side and commenced, chewing at the buyo meanwhile: "I don't misspend one holy day! Since I've belonged to the Sisterhood I've earned four hundred and fifty-seven plenary indulgences, seven hundred sixty thousand five hundred and ninety-eight years of indulgence. I set down all that I earn, for I like to have clean accounts. I don't want to cheat or be cheated."

Here Sister Rufa paused to give more attention to her chewing. The women gazed at her in admiration, but the man who was pacing back and forth remarked with some disdain, "Well, this year I've gained four plenary indulgences more than you have, Sister Rufa, and a hundred years more, and that without praying much either."

"More than I? More than six hundred and eighty-nine plenary indulgences or nine hundred ninety-four thousand eight hundred and fifty-six years?" queried Rufa, somewhat disgruntled.

"That's it, eight indulgences and a hundred fifteen years more and a few months over," answered the man, from whose neck hung soiled scapularies and rosaries.

"That's not strange!" admitted Rufa, at last admitting defeat. "You're an expert, the best in the province."

The flattered man smiled and continued, "It isn't so wonderful that I earn more than you do. Why, I can almost say that even when sleeping I earn indulgences."

"And what do you do with them, sir?" asked four or five voices at the same time.

"Pish!" answered the man with a gesture of proud disdain. "I have them to throw away!"

"But in that I can't commend you, sir," protested Rufa. "You'll go to purgatory for wasting the indulgences. You know very well that for every idle word one must suffer forty days in fire, according to the curate; for every span of thread uselessly wasted, sixty days; and for every drop of water spilled, twenty. You'll go to purgatory."

"Well, I'll know how to get out," answered Brother Pedro with sublime confidence. "How many souls have I saved from the flames! How many saints have I made! Besides, even *in articulo mortis* I can still earn, if I wish, at least seven plenary indulgences and shall be able to save others as I die." So saying, he strode proudly away.

Sister Rufa turned to the others: "Nevertheless, you must do as I do, for I don't lose a single day and I keep my accounts well. I don't want to cheat or be cheated."

"Well, what do you do?" asked Juana.

"You must imitate what I do. For example, suppose I earn a year of indulgence: I set it down in my account-book and say, 'Most Blessed Father and Lord St. Dominic, please see if there is anybody in purgatory who needs exactly a year — neither a day more nor a day less.' Then I play heads and tails: if it comes heads, no; if tails, yes. Let's suppose that it comes tails, then I write down *paid;* if it comes heads, then I keep the indulgence. In this way I arrange groups of a hundred years each, of which I keep a careful account. It's a pity that we can't do with them as with money — put them out at interest, for in that way we should be able to save more souls. Believe me, and do as I do."

"Well, I do it a better way," remarked Sister Sipa.

"What? Better?" demanded the astonished Rufa. "That can't be! My system can't be improved upon!"

"Listen a moment and you'll be convinced, Sister," said old Sipa in a tone of vexation.

"How is it? Let's hear!" exclaimed the others.

After coughing ceremoniously the old woman began with

great care· "You know very well that by saying the *Bendita sea tu pureza* and the *Señor mío Jesucristo, Padre dulcísimo por el gozo*, ten years are gained for each letter—"

"Twenty!" "No, less!" "Five!" interrupted several voices.

"A few years more or less make no difference. Now, when a servant breaks a plate, a glass, or a cup, I make him pick up the pieces; and for every scrap, even the very smallest, he has to recite for me one of those prayers. The indulgences that I earn in this way I devote to the souls. Every one in my house, except the cats, understands this system."

"But those indulgences are earned by the servants and not by you, Sister Sipa," objected Rufa.

"And my cups and plates, who pays for them? The servants are glad to pay for them in that way and it suits me also. I never resort to blows, only sometimes a pinch, or a whack on the head."

"I'm going to do as you do!" "I'll do the same!" "And I!" exclaimed the women.

"But suppose the plate is only broken into two or three pieces, then you earn very few," observed the obstinate Rufa.

"*Abá!*" answered old Sipa. "I make them recite the prayers anyhow. Then I glue the pieces together again and so lose nothing."

Sister Rufa had no more objections left.

"Allow me to ask about a doubt of mine," said young Juana timidly. "You ladies understand so well these matters of heaven, purgatory, and hell, while I confess that I'm ignorant. Often I find in the novenas and other books this direction: three paternosters, three Ave Marias, and three Gloria Patris—"

"Yes, well?"

"Now I want to know how they should be recited: whether three paternosters in succession, three Ave Marias in succession, and three Gloria Patris in succession; or a paternoster, an Ave Maria, and a Gloria Patri together, three times?"

"This way: a paternoster three times —"

"Pardon me, Sister Sipa," interrupted Rufa, "they must be recited in the other way. You must n't mix up males and females. The paternosters are males, the Ave Marias are females, and the Gloria Patris are the children."

"Eh? Excuse me, Sister Rufa: paternoster, Ave Maria, and Gloria are like rice, meat, and sauce — a mouthful for the saints —"

"You 're wrong! You 'll see, for you who pray that way will never get what you ask for."

"And you who pray the other way won't get anything from your novenas," replied old Sipa.

"Who won't?" asked Rufa, rising. "A short time ago I lost a little pig, I prayed to St. Anthony and found it, and then I sold it for a good price. *Abá!*"

"Yes? Then that 's why one of your neighbors was saying that you sold a pig of hers."

"Who? The shameless one! Perhaps I 'm like you —"

Here the expert had to interfere to restore peace, for no one was thinking any more about paternosters — the talk was all about pigs. "Come, come, there must n't be any quarrel over a pig, Sisters! The Holy Scriptures give us an example to follow. The heretics and Protestants did n't quarrel with Our Lord for driving into the water a herd of swine that belonged to them, and we that are Christians and besides, Brethren of the Holy Rosary, shall we have hard words on account of a little pig! What would our rivals, the Tertiary Brethren, say?"

All became silent before such wisdom, at the same time fearing what the Tertiary Brethren might say. The expert, well satisfied with such acquiescence, changed his tone and continued: "Soon the curate will send for us. We must tell him which preacher we 've chosen of the three that he suggested yesterday, whether Padre Damaso, Padre Martin, or the coadjutor. I don't know whether the Tertiary Brethren have yet made any choice, so we must decide."

"The coadjutor," murmured Juana timidly.

"Ahem! The coadjutor doesn't know how to preach," declared Sipa. "Padre Martin is better."

"Padre Martin!" exclaimed another disdainfully. "He hasn't any voice. Padre Damaso would be better."

"That's right!" cried Rufa. "Padre Damaso surely does know how to preach! He looks like a comedian!"

"But we don't understand him," murmured Juana.

"Because he's very deep! And as he preaches well —"

This speech was interrupted by the arrival of Sisa, who was carrying a basket on her head. She saluted the Sisters and went on up the stairway.

"She's going in! Let's go in too!" they exclaimed.

Sisa felt her heart beating violently as she ascended the stairs. She did not know just what to say to the padre to placate his wrath or what reasons she could advance in defense of her son. That morning at the first flush of dawn she had gone into her garden to pick the choicest vegetables, which she placed in a basket among bananaleaves and flowers; then she had looked along the bank of the river for the *pakó* which she knew the curate liked for salads. Putting on her best clothes and without awakening her son, she had set out for the town with the basket on her head. As she went up the stairway she tried to make as little noise as possible and listened attentively in the hope that she might hear a fresh, childish voice, so well known to her. But she heard nothing nor did she meet any one as she made her way to the kitchen. There she looked into all the corners. The servants and sacristans received her coldly, scarcely acknowledging her greeting.

"Where can I put these vegetables?" she asked, not taking any offense at their coldness.

"There, anywhere!" growled the cook, hardly looking

at her as he busied himself in picking the feathers from a capon.

With great care Sisa arranged the vegetables and the salad leaves on the table, placing the flowers above them. Smiling, she then addressed one of the servants, who seemed to be more approachable than the cook: "May I speak with the padre?"

"He's sick," was the whispered answer.

"And Crispin? Do you know if he is in the sacristy?"

The servant looked surprised and wrinkled his eyebrows. "Crispin? Isn't he at your house? Do you mean to deny it?"

"Basilio is at home, but Crispin stayed here," answered Sisa, "and I want to see him."

"Yes, he stayed, but afterwards he ran away, after stealing a lot of things. Early this morning the curate ordered me to go and report it to the Civil Guard. They must have gone to your house already to hunt for the boys."

Sisa covered her ears and opened her mouth to speak, but her lips moved without giving out any sound.

"A pretty pair of sons you have!" exclaimed the cook. "It's plain that you're a faithful wife, the sons are so like the father. Take care that the younger doesn't surpass him."

Sisa broke out into bitter weeping and let herself fall upon a bench.

"Don't cry here!" yelled the cook. "Don't you know that the padre's sick? Get out in the street and cry!"

The unfortunate mother was almost shoved down the stairway at the very time when the Sisters were coming down, complaining and making conjectures about the curate's illness, so she hid her face in her pañuelo and suppressed the sounds of her grief. Upon reaching the street she looked about uncertainly for a moment and then, as if having reached a decision, walked rapidly away.

CHAPTER XIX

A SCHOOLMASTER'S DIFFICULTIES

El vulgo es necio y pues lo paga, es justo
Hablarle en necio para darle el gusto.[1]
LOPE DE VEGA.

THE mountain-encircled lake slept peacefully with that hypocrisy of the elements which gave no hint of how its waters had the night before responded to the fury of the storm. As the first reflections of light awoke on its surface the phosphorescent spirits, there were outlined in the distance, almost on the horizon, the gray silhouettes of the little bankas of the fishermen who were taking in their nets and of the larger craft spreading their sails. Two men dressed in deep mourning stood gazing at the water from a little elevation: one was Ibarra and the other a youth of humble aspect and melancholy features.

"This is the place," the latter was saying. "From here your father's body was thrown into the water. Here's where the grave-digger brought Lieutenant Guevara and me."

Ibarra warmly grasped the hand of the young man, who went on: "You have no occasion to thank me. I owed many favors to your father, and the only thing that I could do for him was to accompany his body to the grave. I came here without knowing any one, without recommendation, and having neither name nor fortune, just as at present. My predecessor had abandoned the school to engage in the tobacco trade. Your father protected me, secured me a house, and furnished whatever was necessary

[1] The common crowd is a fool and since it pays for it, it is proper to talk to it foolishly to please it.

for running the school. He used to visit the classes and distribute pictures among the poor but studious children, as well as provide them with books and paper. But this, like all good things, lasted only a little while."

Ibarra took off his hat and seemed to be praying for a time. Then he turned to his companion: "Did you say that my father helped the poor children? And now?"

"Now they get along as well as possible and write when they can," answered the youth.

"What is the reason?"

"The reason lies in their torn camisas and their downcast eyes."

"How many pupils have you now?" asked Ibarra with interest, after a pause.

"More than two hundred on the roll but only about twenty-five in actual attendance."

"How does that happen?"

The schoolmaster smiled sadly as he answered, "To tell you the reasons would make a long and tiresome story."

"Don't attribute my question to idle curiosity," replied Ibarra gravely, while he stared at the distant horizon. "I've thought better of it and believe that to carry out my father's ideas will be more fitting than to weep for him, and far better than to revenge him. Sacred nature has become his grave, and his enemies were the people and a priest. The former I pardon on account of their ignorance and the latter because I wish that Religion, which elevated society, should be respected. I wish to be inspired with the spirit of him who gave me life and therefore desire to know about the obstacles encountered here in educational work."

"The country will bless your memory, sir," said the schoolmaster, "if you carry out the beautiful plans of your dead father! You wish to know the obstacles which the progress of education meets? Well then, under present circumstances, without substantial aid education will never amount to much; in the very first place because, even when we have the pupils, lack of suitable means, and other things that attract them more, kill off their interest. It is said that in Germany a peasant's son studies for eight years in the town school, but who here would spend half that time when such poor results are to be obtained? They read, write, and memorize selections, and sometimes whole books, in Spanish, without understanding a single word.[1] What benefit does our country child get from the school?"

"And why have you, who see the evil, not thought of remedying it?"

The schoolmaster shook his head sadly. "A poor teacher struggles not only against prejudices but also against certain influences. First, it would be necessary to have a suitable place and not to do as I must at present — hold the classes under the convento by the side of the padre's carriage. There the children, who like to read aloud, very naturally disturb the padre, and he often comes down, nervous, especially when he has his attacks, yells at them, and even insults me at times. You know that no one can either teach or learn under such circumstances, for the child will not respect his teacher when he sees him abused without standing up for his rights. In order to be heeded and to maintain his authority the teacher needs prestige, reputation, moral strength, and some freedom of action.

---

[1] "The schools are under the inspection of the parish priests. Reading and writing in Spanish are taught, or at least it is so ordered; but the schoolmaster himself usually does not know it, and on the other hand the Spanish government employees do not understand the vernacular. Besides, the curates, in order to preserve their influence intact, do not look favorably upon the spread of Castilian. About the only ones who know Spanish are the Indians who have been in the service of Europeans. The first reading exercise is some devotional book, then the catechism; the reader is called *Casuysayan*. On the average half of the children between seven and ten years attend school; they learn to read fairly well and some to write a little, but they soon forget it." — Jagor, *Viajes por Filipinas* (Vidal's Spanish version). Jagor was speaking particularly of the settled parts of the Bicol region. Referring to the islands generally, his "half of the children" would be a great exaggeration. — TR.

"Now let me recount to you even sadder details. I have wished to introduce reforms and have been laughed at. In order to remedy the evil of which I just spoke to you, I tried to teach Spanish to the children because, in addition to the fact that the government so orders, I thought also that it would be of advantage for everybody. I used the simplest method of words and phrases without paying any attention to long rules, expecting to teach them grammar when they should understand the language. At the end of a few weeks some of the brightest were almost able to understand me and could use a few phrases."

The schoolmaster paused and seemed to hesitate, then, as if making a resolution, he went on: "I must not be ashamed of the story of my wrongs, for any one in my place would have acted the same as I did. As I said, it was a good beginning, but a few days afterwards Padre Damaso, who was the curate then, sent for me by the senior sacristan. Knowing his disposition and fearing to make him wait, I went up-stairs at once, saluted him, and wished him good-morning in Spanish. His only greeting had been to put out his hand for me to kiss, but at this he drew it back and without answering me began to laugh loud and mockingly. I was very much embarrassed, as the senior sacristan was present. At the moment I did n't know just what to say, for the curate continued his laughter and I stood staring at him. Then I began to get impatient and saw that I was about to do something indiscreet, since to be a good Christian and to preserve one's dignity are not incompatible. I was going to put a question to him when suddenly, passing from ridicule to insult, he said sarcastically, 'So it's *buenos dias, eh? Buenos dias!* How nice that you know how to talk Spanish!' Then again he broke out into laughter."

Ibarra was unable to repress a smile.

"You smile," continued the schoolmaster, following Ibarra's example, "but I must confess that at the time I had very little desire to laugh. I was still standing — I

A SCHOOLMASTER'S DIFFICULTIES

felt the blood rush to my head and lightning seemed to flash through my brain. The curate I saw far, far away. I advanced to reply to him without knowing just what I was going to say, but the senior sacristan put himself between us. Padre Damaso arose and said to me in Tagalog: 'Don't try to shine in borrowed finery. Be content to talk your own dialect and don't spoil Spanish, which is n't meant for you. Do you know the teacher Ciruela?[1] Well, Ciruela was a teacher who did n't know how to read, and he had a school.' I wanted to detain him, but he went into his bedroom and slammed the door.

"What was I to do with only my meager salary, to collect which I have to get the curate's approval and make a trip to the capital of the province, what could I do against him, the foremost religious and political power in the town, backed up by his Order, feared by the government, rich, powerful, sought after and listened to, always believed and heeded by everybody? Although he insulted me, I had to remain silent, for if I replied he would have had me removed from my position, by which I should lose all hope in my chosen profession. Nor would the cause of education gain anything, but the opposite, for everybody would take the curate's side, they would curse me and call me presumptuous, proud, vain, a bad Christian, uncultured, and if not those things, then anti-Spanish and a filibuster. Of a schoolmaster neither learning nor zeal is expected; resignation, humility, and inaction only are asked. May God pardon me if I have gone against my conscience and my judgment, but I was born in this country, I have to live, I have a mother, so I have abandoned myself to my fate like a corpse tossed about by the waves."

"Did this difficulty discourage you for all time? Have you lived so since?"

"Would that it had been a warning to me! If only

---

[1] A delicate bit of sarcasm is lost in the translation here. The reference to *Maestro Ciruela* in Spanish is somewhat similar to a mention in English of Mr. Squeers, of Dotheboys Hall fame. — TR.

my troubles had been limited to that! It is true that from that time I began to dislike my profession and thought of seeking some other occupation, as my predecessor had done, because any work that is done in disgust and shame is a kind of martyrdom and because every day the school recalled the insult to my mind, causing me hours of great bitterness. But what was I to do? I could not undeceive my mother, I had to say to her that her three years of sacrifice to give me this profession now constituted my happiness. It is necessary to make her believe that this profession is most honorable, the work delightful, the way strewn with flowers, that the performance of my duties brings me only friendship, that the people respect me and show me every consideration. By doing otherwise, without ceasing to be unhappy myself, I should have caused more sorrow, which besides being useless would also be a sin. I stayed on, therefore, and tried not to feel discouraged. I tried to struggle on."

Here he paused for a while, then resumed: "From the day on which I was so grossly insulted I began to examine myself and I found that I was in fact very ignorant. I applied myself day and night to the study of Spanish and whatever concerned my profession. The old Sage lent me some books, and I read and pondered over everything that I could get hold of. With the new ideas that I have been acquiring in one place and another my point of view has changed and I have seen many things under a different aspect from what they had appeared to me before. I saw error where before I had seen only truth, and truth in many things where I had formerly seen only error. Corporal punishment, for example, which from time immemorial has been the distinctive feature in the schools and which has heretofore been considered as the only efficacious means of making pupils learn — so we have been accustomed to believe — soon appeared to me to be a great hindrance rather than in any way an aid to the child's progress. I became convinced that it was impossible to use one's mind properly when blows, or similar punishment, were in prospect. Fear and terror disturb the most serene, and a child's imagination, besides being very lively, is also very impressionable. As it is on the brain that ideas are impressed, it is necessary that there be both inner and outer calm, that there be serenity of spirit, physical and moral repose, and willingness, so I thought that before everything else I should cultivate in the children confidence, assurance, and some personal pride. Moreover, I comprehended that the daily sight of floggings destroyed kindness in their hearts and deadened all sense of dignity, which is such a powerful lever in the world. At the same time it caused them to lose their sense of shame, which is a difficult thing to restore. I have also observed that when one pupil is flogged, he gets comfort from the fact that the others are treated in the same way, and that he smiles with satisfaction upon hearing the wails of the others. As for the person who does the flogging, while at first he may do it with repugnance, he soon becomes hardened to it and even takes delight in his gloomy task. The past filled me with horror, so I wanted to save the present by modifying the old system. I endeavored to make study a thing of love and joy, I wished to make the primer not a black book bathed in the tears of childhood but a friend who was going to reveal wonderful secrets, and of the schoolroom not a place of sorrows but a scene of intellectual refreshment. So, little by little, I abolished corporal punishment, taking the instruments of it entirely away from the school and replacing them with emulation and personal pride. If one was careless about his lesson, I charged it to lack of desire and never to lack of capacity. I made them think that they were more capable than they really were, which urged them on to study just as any confidence leads to notable achievements. At first it seemed that the change of method was impracticable; many ceased their studies, but I persisted and observed that little by little their minds were being elevated and that more children came, that they came with more regularity, and that he who was praised in the presence of the others studied with double diligence on the next day.

"It soon became known throughout the town that I did not whip the children. The curate sent for me, and fearing another scene I greeted him curtly in Tagalog. On this occasion he was very serious with me. He said that I was exposing the children to destruction, that I was wasting time, that I was not fulfilling my duties, that the father who spared the rod was spoiling the child — according to the Holy Ghost — that learning enters with blood, and so on. He quoted to me sayings of barbarous times just as if it were enough that a thing had been said by the ancients to make it indisputable; according to which we ought to believe that there really existed those monsters which in past ages were imaged and sculptured in the palaces and temples. Finally, he charged me to be more careful and to return to the old system, otherwise he would make unfavorable report about me to the alcalde of the province. Nor was this the end of my troubles. A few days afterward some of the parents of the children presented themselves under the convento and I had to call to my aid all my patience and resignation. They began by reminding me of former times when teachers had character and taught as their grandfathers had. 'Those indeed were the times of the wise men,' they declared, 'they whipped, and straightened the bent tree. They were not boys but old men of experience, gray-haired and severe. Don Catalino, king of them all and founder of this very school, used to administer no less than twenty-five blows and as a result his pupils became wise men and priests. Ah, the old people were worth more than we ourselves, yes, sir, more than we ourselves!' Some did not content themselves with such indirect rudeness, but told me plainly that if I continued my system their children would learn nothing and that they would be obliged to take them from the school. It was useless to argue with them, for as a

A SCHOOLMASTER'S DIFFICULTIES

young man they thought me incapable of sound judgment. What would I not have given for some gray hairs! They cited the authority of the curate, of this one and that one, and even called attention to themselves, saying that if it had not been for the whippings they had received from their teachers they would never have learned anything. Only a few persons showed any sympathy to sweeten for me the bitterness of such a disillusioning.

"In view of all this I had to give up my system, which, after so much toil, was just beginning to produce results. In desperation I carried the whips back to the school the next day and began the barbarous practice again. Serenity disappeared and sadness reigned in the faces of the children, who had just begun to care for me, and who were my only kindred and friends. Although I tried to spare the whippings and to administer them with all the moderation possible, yet the children felt the change keenly, they became discouraged and wept bitterly. It touched my heart, and even though in my own mind I was vexed with the stupid parents, still I was unable to take any spite out on those innocent victims of their parents' prejudices. Their tears burned me, my heart seemed bursting from my breast, and that day I left the school before closing-time to go home and weep alone. Perhaps my sensitiveness may seem strange to you, but if you had been in my place you would understand it. Old Don Anastasio said to me, 'So the parents want floggings? Why not inflict them on themselves?' As a result of it all I became sick."

Ibarra was listening thoughtfully.

"Scarcely had I recovered when I returned to the school to find the number of my pupils reduced to a fifth. The better ones had run away upon the return to the old system, and of those who remained — mostly those who came to school to escape work at home — not one showed any joy, not one congratulated me on my recovery. It would have been the same to them whether I got well or not, or they might have preferred that I continue sick since my substitute, although he whipped them more, rarely went to the school. My other pupils, those whose parents had obliged them to attend school, had gone to other places. Their parents blamed me for having spoiled them and heaped reproaches on me for it. One, however, the son of a country woman who visited me during my illness, had not returned on account of having been made a sacristan, and the senior sacristan says that the sacristans must not attend school: they would be dismissed."

"Were you resigned in looking after your new pupils?" asked Ibarra.

"What else could I do?" was the queried reply. "Nevertheless, during my illness many things had happened, among them a change of curates, so I took new hope and made another attempt to the end that the children should not lose all their time and should, in so far as possible, get some benefit from the floggings, that such things might at least have some good result for them. I pondered over the matter, as I wished that even if they could not love me, by getting something useful from me, they might remember me with less bitterness. You know that in nearly all the schools the books are in Spanish, with the exception of the catechism in Tagalog, which varies according to the religious order to which the curate belongs. These books are generally novenas, canticles, and the Catechism of Padre Astete,[1] from which they learn about as much piety as they would from the books of heretics. Seeing the impossibility of teaching the pupils in Spanish or of translating so many books, I tried to substitute short passages from useful works in Tagalog, such as the Treatise on Manners by Hortensio y Feliza, some manuals of Agriculture, and so forth. Sometimes I would myself translate simple works, such as Padre Barranera's

[1] By one of the provisions of a royal decree of December 20, 1863, the *Catecismo de la Doctrina Cristina*, by Gaspar Astete, was prescribed as the text-book for primary schools in the Philippines. See Blair and Robertson's *The Philippine Islands*, Vol. XLVI, p. 98; *Census of the Philippine Islands* (*Washington, 1905*), p. 584. — TR.

A SCHOOLMASTER'S DIFFICULTIES

History of the Philippines, which I then dictated to the children, with at times a few observations of my own, so that they might make note-books. As I had no maps for teaching geography, I copied one of the province that I saw at the capital and with this and the tiles of the floor I gave them some idea of the country. This time it was the women who got excited. The men contented themselves with smiling, as they saw in it only one of my vagaries. The new curate sent for me, and while he did not reprimand me, yet he said that I should first take care of religion, that before learning such things the children must pass an examination to show that they had memorized the mysteries, the canticles, and the catechism of Christian Doctrine.

"So then, I am now working to the end that the children become changed into parrots and know by heart so many things of which they do not understand a single word. Many of them now know the mysteries and the canticles, but I fear that my efforts will come to grief with the Catechism of Padre Astete, since the greater part of the pupils do not distinguish between the questions and the answers, nor do they understand what either may mean. Thus we shall die, thus those unborn will do, while in Europe they will talk of progress."

"Let's not be so pessimistic," said Ibarra. "The teniente-mayor has sent me an invitation to attend a meeting in the town hall. Who knows but that there you may find an answer to your questions?"

The schoolmaster shook his head in doubt as he answered: "You'll see how the plan of which they talked to me meets the same fate as mine has. But yet, let us see!"

CHAPTER XX

THE MEETING IN THE TOWN HALL

THE hall was about twelve to fifteen meters long by eight to ten wide. Its whitewashed walls were covered with drawings in charcoal, more or less ugly and obscene, with inscriptions to complete their meanings. Stacked neatly against the wall in one corner were to be seen about a dozen old flint-locks among rusty swords and talibons, the armament of the cuadrilleros.[1] At one end of the hall there hung, half hidden by soiled red curtains, a picture of his Majesty, the King of Spain. Underneath this picture, upon a wooden platform, an old chair spread out its broken arms. In front of the chair was a wooden table spotted with ink stains and whittled and carved with inscriptions and initials like the tables in the German taverns frequented by students. Benches and broken chairs completed the furniture.

This is the hall of council, of judgment, and of torture, wherein are now gathered the officials of the town and its dependent villages. The faction of old men does not mix with that of the youths, for they are mutually hostile. They represent respectively the conservative and the liberal

---

[1] The municipal police of the old régime. They were thus described by a Spanish writer, W. E. Retana, in a note to Ventura F. Lopez's *El Filibustero* (Madrid, 1893): "Municipal guards, whose duties are principally rural. Their uniform is a disaster; they go barefoot; on horseback, they hold the reins in the right hand and a lance in the left. They are usually good-for-nothing, but to their credit it must be said that they do no damage. Lacking military instruction, provided with fire-arms of the first part of the century, of which one in a hundred might go off in case of need, and for other arms bolos, talibons, old swords, etc., the cuadrilleros are truly a parody on armed force." — TR.

THE MEETING IN THE TOWN HALL 137

parties, save that their disputes assume in the towns an extreme character.

"The conduct of the gobernadorcillo fills me with distrust," Don Filipo, the teniente-mayor and leader of the liberal faction, was saying to his friends. "It was a deep-laid scheme, this thing of putting off the discussion of expenses until the eleventh hour. Remember that we have scarcely eleven days left."

"And he has stayed at the convento to hold a conference with the curate, who is sick," observed one of the youths.

"It doesn't matter," remarked another. "We have everything prepared. Just so the plan of the old men does n't receive a majority —"

"I don't believe it will," interrupted Don Filipo, "as I shall present the plan of the old men myself!"

"What! What are you saying?" asked his surprised hearers.

"I said that if I speak first I shall present the plan of our rivals."

"But what about our plan?"

"I shall leave it to you to present ours," answered Don Filipo with a smile, turning toward a youthful cabeza de barangay.[1] "You will propose it after I have been defeated."

"We don't understand you, sir," said his hearers, staring at him with doubtful looks.

"Listen," continued the liberal leader in a low voice to several near him. "This morning I met old Tasio and the old man said to me: 'Your rivals hate you more than they do your ideas. Do you wish that a thing shall

---

[1] Headman and tax-collector of a district, generally including about fifty families, for whose annual tribute he was personally responsible. The "barangay" is a Malay boat of the kind supposed to have been used by the first emigrants to the Philippines. Hence, at first, the "head of a barangay" meant the leader or chief of a family or group of families. This office, quite analogous to the old Germanic or Anglo-Saxon "head of a hundred," was adopted and perpetuated by the Spaniards in their system of local administration. — TR.

not be done? Then propose it yourself, and though it were more useful than a miter, it would be rejected. Once they have defeated you, have the least forward person in the whole gathering propose what you want, and your rivals, in order to humiliate you, will accept it.' But keep quiet about it."

" But — "

" So I will propose the plan of our rivals and exaggerate it to the point of making it ridiculous. Ah, here come Señor Ibarra and the schoolmaster."

These two young men saluted each of the groups without joining either. A few moments later the gobernadorcillo, the very same individual whom we saw yesterday carrying a bundle of candles, entered with a look of disgust on his face. Upon his entrance the murmurs ceased, every one sat down, and silence was gradually established, as he took his seat under the picture of the King, coughed four or five times, rubbed his hand over his face and head, rested his elbows on the table, then withdrew them, coughed once more, and then the whole thing over again.

" Gentlemen," he at last began in an unsteady voice, " I have been so bold as to call you together here for this meeting — ahem! Ahem! We have to celebrate the fiesta of our patron saint, San Diego, on the twelfth of this month — ahem! — today is the second — ahem! Ahem!" At this point a slow, dry cough cut off his speech.

A man of proud bearing, apparently about forty years of age, then arose from the bench of the elders. He was the rich Capitan Basilio, the direct contrast of Don Rafael, Ibarra's father. He was a man who maintained that after the death of St. Thomas Aquinas the world had made no more progress, and that since St. John Lateran had left it, humanity had been retrograding.

" Gentlemen, allow me to speak a few words about such an interesting matter," he began. " I speak first even though there are others here present who have more right to do so than I have, but I speak first because in these

THE MEETING IN THE TOWN HALL 139

matters it seems to me that by speaking first one does not take the first place — no more than that by speaking last does one become the least. Besides, the things that I have to say are of such importance that they should not be put off or last spoken of, and accordingly I wish to speak first in order to give them due weight. So you will allow me to speak first in this meeting where I see so many notable persons, such as the present señor capitan; the former capitan; my distinguished friend, Don Valentin, a former capitan; the friend of my infancy, Don Julio; our celebrated captain of cuadrilleros, Don Melchor; and many other personages, whom, for the sake of brevity, I must omit to enumerate — all of whom you see present here. I beg of you that I may be allowed a few words before any one else speaks. Have I the good fortune to see my humble request granted by the meeting?"

Here the orator with a faint smile inclined his head respectfully. "Go on, you have our undivided attention!" said the notables alluded to and some others who considered Capitan Basilio a great orator. The elders coughed in a satisfied way and rubbed their hands. After wiping the perspiration from his brow with a silk handkerchief, he then proceeded:

"Now that you have been so kind and complaisant with my humble self as to grant me the use of a few words before any one else of those here present, I shall take advantage of this permission, so generously granted, and shall talk. In imagination I fancy myself in the midst of the august Roman senate, *senatus populusque romanus,* as was said in those happy days which, unfortunately for humanity, will nevermore return. I propose to the *Patres Conscripti,* as the learned Cicero would say if he were in my place, I propose, in view of the short time left, and time is money as Solomon said, that concerning this important matter each one set forth his opinion clearly, briefly, and simply."

Satisfied with himself and flattered by the attention in

the hall, the orator took his seat, not without first casting a glance of superiority toward Ibarra, who was seated in a corner, and a significant look at his friends as if to say, "Aha! Have n't I spoken well?" His friends reflected both of these expressions by staring at the youths as though to make them die of envy.

"Now any one may speak who wishes that — ahem!" began the gobernadorcillo, but a repetition of the cough and sighs cut short the phrase.

To judge from the silence, no one wished to consider himself called upon as one of the Conscript Fathers, since no one rose. Then Don Filipo seized the opportunity and rose to speak. The conservatives winked and made significant signs to each other.

"I rise, gentlemen, to present my estimate of expenses for the fiesta," he began.

"We can't allow it," commented a consumptive old man, who was an irreconcilable conservative.

"We'll vote against it," corroborated others.

"Gentlemen!" exclaimed Don Filipo, repressing a smile, "I have n't yet made known the plan which we, *the younger men,* bring here. We feel *sure* that this great plan will be preferred by all over any other that our opponents think of or are capable of conceiving."

This presumptuous exordium so thoroughly irritated the minds of the conservatives that they swore in their hearts to offer determined opposition.

"We have estimated three thousand five hundred pesos for the expenses," went on Don Filipo. "Now then, with such a sum we shall be able to celebrate a fiesta that will eclipse in magnificence any that has been seen up to this time in our own or neighboring provinces."

"Ahem!" coughed some doubters. "The town of A—— has five thousand, B—— has four thousand, ahem! Humbug!"

"Listen to me, gentlemen, and I'll convince you," continued the unterrified speaker. "I propose that we erect

THE MEETING IN THE TOWN HALL 141

a theater in the middle of the plaza, to cost one hundred and fifty pesos."

"That won't be enough! It'll take one hundred and sixty," objected a confirmed conservative.

"Write it down, Señor Director, two hundred pesos for the theater," said Don Filipo. "I further propose that we contract with a troupe of comedians from Tondo for seven performances on seven successive nights. Seven performances at two hundred pesos a night make fourteen hundred pesos. Write down fourteen hundred pesos, Señor Director!"

Both the elders and the youths stared in amazement. Only those in the secret gave no sign.

"I propose besides that we have magnificent fireworks; no little lights and pin-wheels such as please children and old maids, nothing of the sort. We want big bombs and immense rockets. I propose two hundred big bombs at two pesos each and two hundred rockets at the same price. We'll have them made by the pyrotechnists of Malabon."

"Huh!" grunted an old man, "a two-peso bomb does n't frighten or deafen me! They ought to be three-peso ones."

"Write down one thousand pesos for two hundred bombs and two hundred rockets."

The conservatives could no longer restrain themselves. Some of them rose and began to whisper together.

"Moreover, in order that our visitors may see that we are a liberal people and have plenty of money," continued the speaker, raising his voice and casting a rapid glance at the whispering group of elders, "I propose: first, four *hermanos mayores*[1] for the two days of the fiesta; and second, that each day there be thrown into the lake two hundred fried chickens, one hundred stuffed capons, and

[1] The *hermano mayor* was a person appointed to direct the ceremonies during the fiesta, an appointment carrying with it great honor and importance, but also entailing considerable expense, as the appointee was supposed to furnish a large share of the entertainments. Hence, the greater the number of *hermanos mayores* the more splendid the fiesta. — TR.

forty roast pigs, as did Sylla, a contemporary of that Cicero, of whom Capitan Basilio just spoke."

"That's it, like Sylla," repeated the flattered Capitan Basilio.

The surprise steadily increased.

"Since many rich people will attend and each one will bring thousands of pesos, his best game-cocks, and his playing-cards, I propose that the cockpit run for fifteen days and that license be granted to open all gambling houses —"

The youths interrupted him by rising, thinking that he had gone crazy. The elders were arguing heatedly.

"And, finally, that we may not neglect the pleasures of the soul —"

The murmurs and cries which arose all over the hall drowned his voice out completely, and tumult reigned.

"No!" yelled an irreconcilable conservative. "I don't want him to flatter himself over having run the whole fiesta, no! Let me speak! Let me speak!"

"Don Filipo has deceived us," cried the liberals. "We'll vote against his plan. He has gone over to the old men. We'll vote against him!"

The gobernadorcillo, more overwhelmed than ever, did nothing to restore order, but rather was waiting for them to restore it themselves.

The captain of the cuadrilleros begged to be heard and was granted permission to speak, but he did not open his mouth and sat down again confused and ashamed.

By good fortune, Capitan Valentin, the most moderate of all the conservatives, arose and said: "We cannot agree to what the teniente-mayor has proposed, as it appears to be exaggerated. So many bombs and so many nights of theatrical performances can only be desired by a young man, such as he is, who can spend night after night sitting up and listening to so many explosions without becoming deaf. I have consulted the opinion of the sensible persons here and all of them unanimously disapprove Don Filipo's plan. Is it not so, gentlemen?"

THE MEETING IN THE TOWN HALL

"Yes, yes!" cried the youths and elders with one voice. The youths were delighted to hear an old man speak so.

"What are we going to do with four *hermanos mayores?*" went on the old man. "What is the meaning of those chickens, capons, and roast pigs, thrown into the lake? 'Humbug!' our neighbors would say. And afterwards we should have to fast for six months! What have we to do with Sylla and the Romans? Have they ever invited us to any of their festivities, I wonder? I, at least, have never received any invitation from them, and you can all see that I'm an old man!"

"The Romans live in Rome, where the Pope is," Capitan Basilio prompted him in a low voice.

"Now I understand!" exclaimed the old man calmly. "They would make of their festivals watch-meetings, and the Pope would order them to throw their food into the sea so that they might commit no sin. But, in spite of all that, your plan is inadmissible, impossible, a piece of foolishness!"

Being so stoutly opposed, Don Filipo had to withdraw his proposal. Now that their chief rival had been defeated, even the worst of the irreconcilable insurgents looked on with calmness while a young cabeza de barangay asked for the floor.

"I beg that you excuse the boldness of one so young as I am in daring to speak before so many persons respected for their age and prudence and judgment in affairs, but since the eloquent orator, Capitan Basilio, has requested every one to express his opinion, let the authoritative words spoken by him excuse my insignificance."

The conservatives nodded their heads with satisfaction, remarking to one another: "This young man talks sensibly." "He's modest." "He reasons admirably."

"What a pity that he does n't know very well how to gesticulate," observed Capitan Basilio. "But there's time yet! He hasn't studied Cicero and he's still a young man!"

"If I present to you, gentlemen, any program or plan," the young man continued, "I don't do so with the thought that you will find it perfect or that you will accept it, but at the same time that I once more bow to the judgment of all of you, I wish to prove to our elders that our thoughts are always like theirs, since we take as our own those ideas so eloquently expressed by Capitan Basilio."

"Well spoken! Well spoken!" cried the flattered conservatives. Capitan Basilio made signs to the speaker showing him how he should stand and how he ought to move his arm. The only one remaining impassive was the gobernadorcillo, who was either bewildered or preoccupied; as a matter of fact, he seemed to be both. The young man went on with more warmth:

"My plan, gentlemen, reduces itself to this: invent new shows that are not common and ordinary, such as we see every day, and endeavor that the money collected may not leave the town, and that it be not wasted in smoke, but that it be used in some manner beneficial to all."

"That's right!" assented the youths. "That's what we want."

"Excellent!" added the elders.

"What should we get from a week of comedies, as the teniente-mayor proposes? What can we learn from the kings of Bohemia and Granada, who commanded that their daughters' heads be cut off, or that they should be blown from a cannon, which later is converted into a throne? We are not kings, neither are we barbarians; we have no cannon, and if we should imitate those people, they would hang us on Bagumbayan. What are those princesses who mingle in the battles, scattering thrusts and blows about in combat with princes, or who wander alone over mountains and through valleys as though seduced by the *tikbálang?* Our nature is to love sweetness and tenderness in woman, and we would shudder at the thought of

THE MEETING IN THE TOWN HALL 145

taking the blood-stained hand of a maiden, even when the blood was that of a Moro or a giant, so abhorred by us. We consider vile the man who raises his hand against a woman, be he prince or alferez or rude countryman. Would it not be a thousand times better to give a representation of our own customs in order to correct our defects and vices and to encourage our better qualities?"

"That's right! That's right!" exclaimed some of his faction.

"He's right," muttered several old men thoughtfully.

"I should never have thought of that," murmured Capitan Basilio.

"But how are you going to do it?" asked the irreconcilable.

"Very easily," answered the youth. "I have brought here two dramas which I feel sure the good taste and recognized judgment of the respected elders here assembled will find very agreeable and entertaining. One is entitled 'The Election of the Gobernadorcillo,' being a comedy in prose in five acts, written by one who is here present. The other is in nine acts for two nights and is a fantastical drama of a satirical nature, entitled 'Mariang Makiling,'[1] written by one of the best poets of the province. Seeing that the discussion of preparations for the fiesta has been postponed and fearing that there would not be time enough left, we have secretly secured the actors and had them learn their parts. We hope that with a week of rehearsal they will have plenty of time to know their parts thoroughly. This, gentlemen, besides being new, useful, and reasonable, has the great advantage of being economical; we shall not need costumes, as those of our daily life will be suitable."

[1] Mt. Makiling is a volcanic cone at the southern end of the Lake of Bay. At its base is situated the town of Kalamba, the author's birthplace. About this mountain cluster a number of native legends having as their principal character a celebrated sorceress or enchantress, known as "Mariang Makiling." — TR.

"I'll pay for the theater!" shouted Capitan Basilio enthusiastically.

"If you need cuadrilleros, I'll lend you mine," cried their captain.

"And I — and I — if an old man is needed —" stammered another one, swelling with pride.

"Accepted! Accepted!" cried many voices.

Don Filipo became pale with emotion and his eyes filled with tears.

"He's crying from spite," thought the irreconcilable, so he yelled, "Accepted! Accepted without discussion!" Thus satisfied with revenge and the complete defeat of his rival, this fellow began to praise the young man's plan.

The latter continued his speech: "A fifth of the money collected may be used to distribute a few prizes, such as to the best school child, the best herdsman, farmer, fisherman, and so on. We can arrange for boat races on the river and lake and for horse races on shore, we can raise greased poles and also have other games in which our country people can take part. I concede that on account of our long-established customs we must have some fireworks; wheels and fire castles are very beautiful and entertaining, but I don't believe it necessary to have bombs, as the former speaker proposed. Two bands of music will afford sufficient merriment and thus we shall avoid those rivalries and quarrels between the poor musicians who come to gladden our fiesta with their work and who so often behave like fighting-cocks, afterwards going away poorly paid, underfed, and even bruised and wounded at times. With the money left over we can begin the erection of a small building for a schoolhouse, since we can't wait until God Himself comes down and builds one for us, and it is a sad state of affairs that while we have a fine cockpit our children study almost in the curate's stable. Such are the outlines of my plan; the details can be worked out by all."

A murmur of pleasure ran through the hall, as nearly every one agreed with the youth.

THE MEETING IN THE TOWN HALL

Some few muttered, "Innovations! Innovations! When we were young—"

"Let's adopt it for the time being and humiliate that fellow," said others, indicating Don Filipo.

When silence was restored all were agreed. There was lacking only the approval of the gobernadorcillo. That worthy official was perspiring and fidgeting about. He rubbed his hand over his forehead and was at length able to stammer out in a weak voice: "I also agree, but—ahem!"

Every one in the hall listened in silence.

"But what?" asked Capitan Basilio.

"Very agreeable," repeated the gobernadorcillo, "that is to say—I don't agree—I mean—yes, but—" Here he rubbed his eyes with the back of his hand. "But the curate," the poor fellow went on, "the curate wants something else."

"Does the curate or do we ourselves pay for this fiesta? Has he given a cuarto for it?" exclaimed a penetrating voice. All looked toward the place whence these questions came and saw there the Sage Tasio.

Don Filipo remained motionless with his eyes fixed on the gobernadorcillo.

"What does the curate want?" asked Capitan Basilio.

"Well, the padre wants six processions, three sermons, three high masses, and if there is any money left, a comedy from Tondo with songs in the intermissions."

"But we don't want that," said the youths and some of the old men.

"The curate wants it," repeated the gobernadorcillo. "I've promised him that his wish shall be carried out."

"Then why did you have us assemble here?"

"F-for the very purpose of telling you this!"

"Why didn't you tell us so at the start?"

"I wanted to tell you, gentlemen, but Capitan Basilio spoke and I haven't had a chance. The curate must be obeyed."

"He must be obeyed," echoed several old men.

"He must be obeyed or else the alcalde will put us all in jail," added several other old men sadly.

"Well then, obey him, and run the fiesta yourselves," exclaimed the youths, rising. "We withdraw our contributions."

"Everything has already been collected," said the gobernadorcillo.

Don Filipo approached this official and said to him bitterly, "I sacrificed my pride in favor of a good cause; you are sacrificing your dignity as a man in favor of a bad one, and you've spoiled everything."

Ibarra turned to the schoolmaster and asked him, "Is there anything that I can do for you at the capital of the province? I leave for there immediately."

"Have you some business there?"

"*We* have business there!" answered Ibarra mysteriously.

On the way home, when Don Filipo was cursing his bad luck, old Tasio said to him: "The blame is ours! You didn't protest when they gave you a slave for a chief, and I, fool that I am, had forgotten it!"

CHAPTER XXI

THE STORY OF A MOTHER

Andaba incierto — volaba errante,
Un solo instante — sin descansar.[1]
      ALAEJOS.

SISA ran in the direction of her home with her thoughts in that confused whirl which is produced in our being when, in the midst of misfortunes, protection and hope alike are gone. It is then that everything seems to grow dark around us, and, if we do see some faint light shining from afar, we run toward it, we follow it, even though an abyss yawns in our path. The mother wanted to save her sons, and mothers do not ask about means when their children are concerned. Precipitately she ran, pursued by fear and dark forebodings. Had they already arrested her son Basilio? Whither had her boy Crispin fled?

As she approached her little hut she made out above the garden fence the caps of two soldiers. It would be impossible to tell what her heart felt: she forgot everything. She was not ignorant of the boldness of those men, who did not lower their gaze before even the richest people of the town. What would they do now to her and to her sons, accused of theft! The civil-guards are not men, they are civil-guards; they do not listen to supplications and they are accustomed to see tears.

Sisa instinctively raised her eyes toward the sky, that sky which smiled with brilliance indescribable, and in whose transparent blue floated some little fleecy clouds. She stopped to control the trembling that had seized her whole body. The soldiers were leaving the house and were alone,

---

[1] With uncertain pace, in wandering flight, for an instant only — without rest.

as they had arrested nothing more than the hen which Sisa had been fattening. She breathed more freely and took heart again. "How good they are and what kind hearts they have!" she murmured, almost weeping with joy. Had the soldiers burned her house but left her sons at liberty she would have heaped blessings upon them! She again looked gratefully toward the sky through which a flock of herons, those light clouds in the skies of the Philippines, were cutting their path, and with restored confidence she continued on her way. As she approached those fearful men she threw her glances in every direction as if unconcerned and pretended not to see her hen, which was cackling for help. Scarcely had she passed them when she wanted to run, but prudence restrained her steps.

She had not gone far when she heard herself called by an imperious voice. Shuddering, she pretended not to hear, and continued on her way. They called her again, this time with a yell and an insulting epithet. She turned toward them, pale and trembling in spite of herself. One of them beckoned to her. Mechanically Sisa approached them, her tongue paralyzed with fear and her throat parched.

"Tell us the truth or we'll tie you to that tree and shoot you," said one of them in a threatening tone.

The woman stared at the tree.

"You're the mother of the thieves, are n't you?" asked the other.

"Mother of the thieves!" repeated Sisa mechanically.

"Where's the money your sons brought you last night?"

"Ah! The money—"

"Don't deny it or it'll be the worse for you," added the other. "We've come to arrest your sons, and the older has escaped from us. Where have you hidden the younger?"

Upon hearing this Sisa breathed more freely and answered, "Sir, it has been many days since I've seen Crispin. I expected to see him this morning at the convento, but there they only told me—"

THE STORY OF A MOTHER 151

The two soldiers exchanged significant glances. "All right!" exclaimed one of them. "Give us the money and we'll leave you alone."

"Sir," begged the unfortunate woman, "my sons wouldn't steal even though they were starving, for we are used to that kind of suffering. Basilio didn't bring me a single cuarto. Search the whole house and if you find even a real, do with us what you will. Not all of us poor folks are thieves!"

"Well then," ordered the soldier slowly, as he fixed his gaze on Sisa's eyes, "come with us. Your sons will show up and try to get rid of the money they stole. Come on!"

"I — go with you?" murmured the woman, as she stepped backward and gazed fearfully at their uniforms.

"And why not?"

"Oh, have pity on me!" she begged, almost on her knees. "I'm very poor, so I've neither gold nor jewels to offer you. The only thing I had you've already taken, and that is the hen which I was thinking of selling. Take everything that you find in the house, but leave me here in peace, leave me here to die!"

"Go ahead! You've got to go, and if you don't move along willingly, we'll tie you."

Sisa broke out into bitter weeping, but those men were inflexible. "At least, let me go ahead of you some distance," she begged, when she felt them take hold of her brutally and push her along.

The soldiers seemed to be somewhat affected and, after whispering apart, one of them said: "All right, since from here until we get into the town, you might be able to escape, you'll walk between us. Once there you may walk ahead twenty paces, but take care that you don't delay and that you don't go into any shop, and don't stop. Go ahead, quickly!"

Vain were her supplications and arguments, useless her promises. The soldiers said that they had already compromised themselves by having conceded too much. Upon finding herself between them she felt as if she would die of shame. No one indeed was coming along the road, but how about the air and the light of day? True shame encounters eyes everywhere. She covered her face with her pañuelo and walked along blindly, weeping in silence at her disgrace. She had felt misery and knew what it was to be abandoned by every one, even her own husband, but until now she had considered herself honored and respected: up to this time she had looked with compassion on those boldly dressed women whom the town knew as the concubines of the soldiers. Now it seemed to her that she had fallen even a step lower than they in the social scale.

The sound of hoofs was heard, proceeding from a small train of men and women mounted on poor nags, each between two baskets hung over the back of his mount; it was a party carrying fish to the interior towns. Some of them on passing her hut had often asked for a drink of water and had presented her with some fishes. Now as they passed her they seemed to beat and trample upon her while their compassionate or disdainful looks penetrated through her pañuelo and stung her face. When these travelers had finally passed she sighed and raised the pañuelo an instant to see how far she still was from the town. There yet remained a few telegraph poles to be passed before reaching the *bantayan,* or little watch-house, at the entrance to the town. Never had that distance seemed so great to her.

Beside the road there grew a leafy bamboo thicket in whose shade she had rested at other times, and where her lover had talked so sweetly as he helped her carry her basket of fruit and vegetables. Alas, all that was past, like a dream! The lover had become her husband and a cabeza de barangay, and then trouble had commenced to knock at her door. As the sun was beginning to shine hotly, the soldiers asked her if she did not want to

THE STORY OF A MOTHER 153

rest there. "Thanks, no!" was the horrified woman's answer.

Real terror seized her when they neared the town. She threw her anguished gaze in all directions, but no refuge offered itself, only wide rice-fields, a small irrigating ditch, and some stunted trees; there was not a cliff or even a rock upon which she might dash herself to pieces! Now she regretted that she had come so far with the soldiers; she longed for the deep river that flowed by her hut, whose high and rock-strewn banks would have offered such a sweet death. But again the thought of her sons, especially of Crispin, of whose fate she was still ignorant, lightened the darkness of her night, and she was able to murmur resignedly, "Afterwards — afterwards — we'll go and live in the depths of the forest."

Drying her eyes and trying to look calm, she turned to her guards and said in a low voice, with an indefinable accent that was a complaint and a lament, a prayer and a reproach, sorrow condensed into sound, "Now we're in the town." Even the soldiers seemed touched as they answered her with a gesture. She struggled to affect a calm bearing while she went forward quickly.

At that moment the church bells began to peal out, announcing the end of the high mass. Sisa hurried her steps so as to avoid, if possible, meeting the people who were coming out, but in vain, for no means offered to escape encountering them. With a bitter smile she saluted two of her acquaintances, who merely turned inquiring glances upon her, so that to avoid further mortification she fixed her gaze on the ground, and yet, strange to say, she stumbled over the stones in the road! Upon seeing her, people paused for a moment and conversed among themselves as they gazed at her, all of which she saw and felt in spite of her downcast eyes.

She heard the shameless tones of a woman who asked from behind at the top of her voice, "Where did you catch her? And the money?" It was a woman without a tapis, or tunic, dressed in a green and yellow skirt and a camisa of blue gauze, easily recognizable from her costume as a *querida* of the soldiery. Sisa felt as if she had received a slap in the face, for that woman had exposed her before the crowd. She raised her eyes for a moment to get her fill of scorn and hate, but saw the people far, far away. Yet she felt the chill of their stares and heard their whispers as she moved over the ground almost without knowing that she touched it.

"Eh, this way!" a guard called to her. Like an automaton whose mechanism is breaking, she whirled about rapidly on her heels, then without seeing or thinking of anything ran to hide herself. She made out a door where a sentinel stood and tried to enter it, but a still more imperious voice called her aside. With wavering steps she sought the direction of that voice, then felt herself pushed along by the shoulders; she shut her eyes, took a couple of steps, and lacking further strength, let herself fall to the ground, first on her knees and then in a sitting posture. Dry and voiceless sobs shook her frame convulsively.

Now she was in the barracks among the soldiers, women, hogs, and chickens. Some of the men were sewing at their clothes while their thighs furnished pillows for their *queridas,* who were reclining on benches, smoking and gazing wearily at the ceiling. Other women were helping some of the men clean their ornaments and arms, humming doubtful songs the while.

"It seems that the chicks have escaped, for you've brought only the old hen!" commented one woman to the new arrivals, — whether alluding to Sisa or the still clucking hen is not certain.

"Yes, the hen is always worth more than the chicks," Sisa herself answered when she observed that the soldiers were silent.

"Where's the sergeant?" asked one of the guards in a disgusted tone. "Has report been made to the alferez yet?"

THE STORY OF A MOTHER

A general shrugging of shoulders was his answer, for no one was going to trouble himself inquiring about the fate of a poor woman.

There Sisa spent two hours in a state of semi-idiocy, huddled in a corner with her head hidden in her arms and her hair falling down in disorder. At noon the alferez was informed, and the first thing that he did was to discredit the curate's accusation.

"Bah! Tricks of that rascally friar," he commented, as he ordered that the woman be released and that no one should pay any attention to the matter. "If he wants to get back what he's lost, let him ask St. Anthony or complain to the nuncio. Out with her!"

Consequently, Sisa was ejected from the barracks almost violently, as she did not try to move herself. Finding herself in the street, she instinctively started to hurry toward her house, with her head bared, her hair disheveled, and her gaze fixed on the distant horizon. The sun burned in its zenith with never a cloud to shade its flashing disk; the wind shook the leaves of the trees lightly along the dry road, while no bird dared stir from the shade of their branches.

At last Sisa reached her hut and entered it in silence. She walked all about it and ran in and out for a time. Then she hurried to old Tasio's house and knocked at the door, but he was not at home. The unhappy woman then returned to her hut and began to call loudly for Basilio and Crispin, stopping every few minutes to listen attentively. Her voice came back in an echo, for the soft murmur of the water in the neighboring river and the rustling of the bamboo leaves were the only sounds that broke the stillness. She called again and again as she climbed the low cliffs, or went down into a gully, or descended to the river. Her eyes rolled about with a sinister expression, now flashing up with brilliant gleams, now becoming obscured like the sky on a stormy night; it might be said that the light of reason was flickering and about to be extinguished.

Again returning to her hut, she sat down on the mat where she had lain the night before. Raising her eyes, she saw a twisted remnant from Basilio's camisa at the end of the bamboo post in the *dinding,* or wall, that overlooked the precipice. She seized and examined it in the sunlight. There were blood stains on it, but Sisa hardly saw them, for she went outside and continued to raise and lower it before her eyes to examine it in the burning sunlight. The light was failing and everything beginning to grow dark around her. She gazed wide-eyed and unblinkingly straight at the sun.

Still wandering about here and there, crying and wailing, she would have frightened any listener, for her voice now uttered rare notes such as are not often produced in the human throat. In a night of roaring tempest, when the whirling winds beat with invisible wings against the crowding shadows that ride upon it, if you should find yourself in a solitary and ruined building, you would hear moans and sighs which you might suppose to be the soughing of the wind as it beats on the high towers and moldering walls to fill you with terror and make you shudder in spite of yourself; as mournful as those unknown sounds of the dark night when the tempest roars were the accents of that mother. In this condition night came upon her. Perhaps Heaven had granted some hours of sleep while the invisible wing of an angel, brushing over her pallid countenance, might wipe out the sorrows from her memory; perhaps such suffering was too great for weak human endurance, and Providence had intervened with its sweet remedy, forgetfulness. However that may be, the next day Sisa wandered about smiling, singing, and talking with all the creatures of wood and field.

CHAPTER XXII

LIGHTS AND SHADOWS

THREE days have passed since the events narrated, three days which the town of San Diego has devoted to making preparations for the fiesta, commenting and murmuring at the same time. While all were enjoying the prospect of the pleasures to come, some spoke ill of the gobernadorcillo, others of the teniente-mayor, others of the young men, and there were not lacking those who blamed everybody for everything.

There was a great deal of comment on the arrival of Maria Clara, accompanied by her Aunt Isabel. All rejoiced over it because they loved her and admired her beauty, while at the same time they wondered at the change that had come over Padre Salvi. "He often becomes inattentive during the holy services, nor does he talk much with us, and he is thinner and more taciturn than usual," commented his penitents. The cook noticed him getting thinner and thinner by minutes and complained of the little honor that was done to his dishes. But that which caused the most comment among the people was the fact that in the convento were to be seen more than two lights burning during the evening while Padre Salvi was on a visit to a private dwelling—the home of Maria Clara! The pious women crossed themselves but continued their comments.

Ibarra had telegraphed from the capital of the province welcoming Aunt Isabel and her niece, but had failed to explain the reason for his absence. Many thought him a prisoner on account of his treatment of Padre Salvi on the afternoon of All Saints, but the comments reached a climax when, on the evening of the third day, they saw him alight before the home of his fiancée and extend a polite greeting to the priest, who was just entering the same house.

Sisa and her sons were forgotten by all.

If we should now go into the home of Maria Clara, a beautiful nest set among trees of orange and ilang-ilang, we should surprise the two young people at a window overlooking the lake, shadowed by flowers and climbing vines which exhaled a delicate perfume. Their lips murmured words softer than the rustling of the leaves and sweeter than the aromatic odors that floated through the garden. It was the hour when the sirens of the lake take advantage of the fast falling twilight to show their merry heads above the waves to gaze upon the setting sun and sing it to rest. It is said that their eyes and hair are blue, and that they are crowned with white and red water plants; that at times the foam reveals their shapely forms, whiter than the foam itself, and that when night descends completely they begin their divine sports, playing mysterious airs like those of Æolian harps. But let us turn to our young people and listen to the end of their conversation. Ibarra was speaking to Maria Clara.

"Tomorrow before daybreak your wish shall be fulfilled. I'll arrange everything tonight so that nothing will be lacking."

"Then I'll write to my girl friends to come. But arrange it so that the curate won't be there."

"Why?"

"Because he seems to be watching me. His deep, gloomy eyes trouble me, and when he fixes them on me I'm afraid. When he talks to me, his voice — oh, he speaks of such odd, such strange, such incomprehensible things! He asked me once if I have ever dreamed of letters from my mother. I really believe that he is half-crazy. My friend Sinang and my foster-sister, Andeng, say that he is somewhat touched, because he neither eats nor bathes and lives in darkness. See to it that he does not come!"

"We can't do otherwise than invite him," answered Ibarra thoughtfully. "The customs of the country require it. He is in your house and, besides, he has conducted himself nobly toward me. When the alcalde consulted him about the business of which I've told you, he had only praises for me and did n't try to put the least obstacle in the way. But I see that you're serious about it, so cease worrying, for he won't go in the same boat with us."

Light footsteps were heard. It was the curate, who approached with a forced smile on his lips. "The wind is chilly," he said, "and when one catches cold one generally does n't get rid of it until the hot weather. Are n't you afraid of catching cold?" His voice trembled and his eyes were turned toward the distant horizon, away from the young people.

"No, we rather find the night pleasant and the breeze delicious," answered Ibarra. "During these months we have our autumn and our spring. Some leaves fall, but the flowers are always in bloom."

Fray Salvi sighed.

"I think the union of these two seasons beautiful, with no cold winter intervening," continued Ibarra. "In February the buds on the trees will burst open and in March we'll have the ripe fruit. When the hot months come we shall go elsewhere."

Fray Salvi smiled and began to talk of commonplace things, of the weather, of the town, and of the fiesta. Maria Clara slipped away on some pretext.

"Since we are talking of fiestas, allow me to invite you to the one that we are going to celebrate tomorrow. It is to be a picnic in the woods, which we and our friends are going to hold together."

"Where will it be held?"

"The young women wish to hold it by the brook in the neighboring wood, near to the old balete, so we shall rise early to avoid the sun."

The priest thought a moment and then answered: "The

invitation is very tempting and I accept it to prove to you that I hold no rancor against you. But I shall have to go late, after I've attended to my duties. Happy are you who are free, entirely free."

A few moments later Ibarra left in order to look after the arrangements for the picnic on the next day. The night was dark and in the street some one approached and saluted him respectfully.

"Who are you?" asked Ibarra.

"Sir, you don't know my name," answered the unknown, "but I've been waiting for you two days."

"For what purpose?"

"Because nowhere has any pity been shown me and they say that I'm an outlaw, sir. But I've lost my two sons, my wife is insane, and every one says that I deserve what has happened to me."

Ibarra looked at the man critically as he asked, "What do you want now?"

"To beg for your pity upon my wife and sons."

"I can't stop now," replied Ibarra. "If you wish to come, you can tell me as we go along what has happened to you."

The man thanked him, and the two quickly disappeared in the shadows along the dimly lighted street.

CHAPTER XXIII

FISHING

THE stars still glittered in the sapphire arch of heaven and the birds were still sleeping among the branches when a merry party, lighted by torches of resin, commonly called *huepes*, made its way through the streets toward the lake. There were five girls, who walked along rapidly with hands clasped or arms encircling one another's waists, followed by some old women and by servants who were carrying gracefully on their heads baskets of food and dishes. Looking upon the laughing and hopeful countenances of the young women and watching the wind blow about their abundant black hair and the wide folds of their garments, we might have taken them for goddesses of the night fleeing from the day, did we not know that they were Maria Clara and her four friends, the merry Sinang, the grave Victoria, the beautiful Iday, and the thoughtful Neneng of modest and timid beauty. They were conversing in a lively manner, laughing and pinching one another, whispering in one another's ears and then breaking out into loud laughter.

"You'll wake up the people who are still asleep," Aunt Isabel scolded. "When we were young, we did n't make so much disturbance."

"Neither would you get up so early nor would the old folks have been such sleepy-heads," retorted little Sinang.

They were silent for a short time, then tried to talk in low tones, but soon forgot themselves and again filled the street with their fresh young voices.

"Behave as if you were displeased and don't talk to him," Sinang was advising Maria Clara. "Scold him so he won't get into bad habits."

"Don't be so exacting," objected Iday.

"Be exacting! Don't be foolish! He must be made to obey while he's only engaged, for after he's your husband he'll do as he pleases," counseled little Sinang.

"What do you know about that, child?" her cousin Victoria corrected her.

"Sst! Keep quiet, for here they come!"

A group of young men, lighting their way with large bamboo torches, now came up, marching gravely along to the sound of a guitar.

"It sounds like a beggar's guitar," laughed Sinang.

When the two parties met it was the women who maintained a serious and formal attitude, just as if they had never known how to laugh, while on the other hand the men talked and laughed, asking six questions to get half an answer.

"Is the lake calm? Do you think we'll have good weather?" asked the mothers.

"Don't be alarmed, ladies, I know how to swim well," answered a tall, thin, emaciated youth.

"We ought to have heard mass first," sighed Aunt Isabel, clasping her hands.

"There's yet time, ma'am. Albino has been a theological student in his day and can say it in the boat," remarked another youth, pointing to the tall, thin one who had first spoken. The latter, who had a clownish countenance, threw himself into an attitude of contrition, caricaturing Padre Salvi. Ibarra, though he maintained his serious demeanor, also joined in the merriment.

When they arrived at the beach, there involuntarily escaped from the women exclamations of surprise and pleasure at the sight of two large bankas fastened together and picturesquely adorned with garlands of flowers, leaves, and ruffled cotton of many colors. Little paper lanterns hung from an improvised canopy amid flowers and fruits. Comfortable seats with rugs and cushions for the women had been provided by Ibarra. Even the paddles and oars were decorated, while in the more profusely decorated banka were a harp, guitars, accordions, and a trumpet made from a carabao horn. In the other banka fires burned on the clay *kalanes* for preparing refreshments of tea, coffee, and *salabat*.

"In this boat here the women, and in the other there the men," ordered the mothers upon embarking. "Keep quiet! Don't move about so or we'll be upset."

"Cross yourself first," advised Aunt Isabel, setting the example.

"Are we to be here all alone?" asked Sinang with a grimace. "Ourselves alone?" This question was opportunely answered by a pinch from her mother.

As the boats moved slowly away from the shore, the light of the lanterns was reflected in the calm waters of the lake, while in the eastern sky the first tints of dawn were just beginning to appear. A deep silence reigned over the party after the division established by the mothers, for the young people seemed to have given themselves up to meditation.

"Take care," said Albino, the ex-theological student, in a loud tone to another youth. "Keep your foot tight on the plug under you."

"What?"

"It might come out and let the water in. This banka has a lot of holes in it."

"Oh, we're going to sink!" cried the frightened women.

"Don't be alarmed, ladies," the ex-theological student reassured them to calm their fears. "The banka you are in is safe. It has only five holes in it and they are n't large."

"Five holes! *Jesús!* Do you want to drown us?" exclaimed the horrified women.

"Not more than five, ladies, and only about so large," the ex-theological student assured them, indicating the circle formed with his index finger and thumb. "Press hard on the plugs so that they won't come out."

"*María Santísima!* The water's coming in," cried an old woman who felt herself already getting wet.

There now arose a small tumult; some screamed, while others thought of jumping into the water.

"Press hard on the plugs there!" repeated Albino, pointing toward the place where the girls were.

"Where, where? *Diós!* We don't know how! For pity's sake come here, for we don't know how!" begged the frightened women.

It was accordingly necessary for five of the young men to get over into the other banka to calm the terrified mothers. But by some strange chance it seemed that there was danger by the side of each of the *dalagas;* all the old ladies together did not have a single dangerous hole near them! Still more strange it was that Ibarra had to be seated by the side of Maria Clara, Albino beside Victoria, and so on. Quiet was restored among the solicitous mothers but not in the circle of the young people.

As the water was perfectly still, the fish-corrals not far away, and the hour yet early, it was decided to abandon the oars so that all might partake of some refreshment. Dawn had now come, so the lanterns were extinguished.

"There's nothing to compare with *salabat,* drunk in the morning before going to mass," said Capitana Tika, mother of the merry Sinang. "Drink some *salabat* and eat a rice-cake, Albino, and you'll see that even you will want to pray."

"That's what I'm doing," answered the youth addressed. "I'm thinking of confessing myself."

"No," said Sinang, "drink some coffee to bring merry thoughts."

"I will, at once, because I feel a trifle sad."

"Don't do that," advised Aunt Isabel. "Drink some tea and eat a few crackers. They say that tea calms one's thoughts."

"I'll also take some tea and crackers," answered the complaisant youth, "since fortunately none of these drinks is Catholicism."

"But, can you — " Victoria began.

FISHING

"Drink some chocolate also? Well, I guess so, since breakfast is not so far off."

The morning was beautiful. The water began to gleam with the light reflected from the sky with such clearness that every object stood revealed without producing a shadow, a bright, fresh clearness permeated with color, such as we get a hint of in some marine paintings. All were now merry as they breathed in the light breeze that began to arise. Even the mothers, so full of cautions and warnings, now laughed and joked among themselves.

"Do you remember," one old woman was saying to Capitana Tika, "do you remember the time we went to bathe in the river, before we were married? In little boats made from banana-stalks there drifted down with the current fruits of many kinds and fragrant flowers. The little boats had banners on them and each of us could see her name on one of them."

"And when we were on our way back home?" added another, without letting her go on. "We found the bamboo bridges destroyed and so we had to wade the brooks. The rascals!"

"Yes, I know that I chose rather to let the borders of my skirt get wet than to uncover my feet," said Capitana Tika, "for I knew that in the thickets on the bank there were eyes watching us."

Some of the girls who heard these reminiscences winked and smiled, while the others were so occupied with their own conversations that they took no notice.

One man alone, he who performed the duty of pilot, remained silent and removed from all the merriment. He was a youth of athletic build and striking features, with large, sad eyes and compressed lips. His black hair, long and unkempt, fell over a stout neck. A dark striped shirt afforded a suggestion through its folds of the powerful muscles that enabled the vigorous arms to handle as if it were a pen the wide and unwieldy paddle which served as a rudder for steering the two bankas.

Maria Clara had more than once caught him looking at her, but on such occasions he had quickly turned his gaze toward the distant mountain or the shore. The young woman was moved with pity at his loneliness and offered him some crackers. The pilot gave her a surprised stare, which, however, lasted for only a second. He took a cracker and thanked her briefly in a scarcely audible voice. After this no one paid any more attention to him. The sallies and merry laughter of the young folks caused not the slightest movement in the muscles of his face. Even the merry Sinang did not make him smile when she received pinchings that caused her to wrinkle up her eyebrows for an instant, only to return to her former merry mood.

The lunch over, they proceeded on their way toward the fish-corrals, of which there were two situated near each other, both belonging to Capitan Tiago. From afar were to be seen some herons perched in contemplative attitude on the tops of the bamboo posts, while a number of white birds, which the Tagalogs call *kalaway,* flew about in different directions, skimming the water with their wings and filling the air with shrill cries. At the approach of the bankas the herons took to flight, and Maria Clara followed them with her gaze as they flew in the direction of the neighboring mountain.

"Do those birds build their nests on the mountain?" she asked the pilot, not so much from a desire to know as for the purpose of making him talk.

"Probably they do, señora," he answered, "but no one up to this time has ever seen their nests."

"Don't they have nests?"

"I suppose they must have them, otherwise they would be very unfortunate."

Maria Clara did not notice the tone of sadness with which he uttered these words. "Then —"

"It is said, señora," answered the strange youth, "that the nests of those birds are invisible and that they have the power of rendering invisible any one who possesses one of them. Just as the soul can only be seen in the pure mirror of the eyes, so also in the mirror of the water alone can their nests be looked upon."

Maria Clara became sad and thoughtful. Meanwhile, they had reached the first fish-corral and an aged boatman tied the craft to a post.

"Wait!" called Aunt Isabel to the son of the fisherman, who was getting ready to climb upon the platform of the corral with his *panalok,* or fish-net fastened on the end of a stout bamboo pole. "We must get the *sinigang* ready so that the fish may pass at once from the water into the soup."

"Kind Aunt Isabel!" exclaimed the ex-theological student. "She does n't want the fish to miss the water for an instant!"

Andeng, Maria Clara's foster-sister, in spite of her carefree and happy face, enjoyed the reputation of being an excellent cook, so she set about preparing a soup of rice and vegetables, helped and hindered by some of the young men, eager perhaps to win her favor. The other young women all busied themselves in cutting up and washing the vegetables.

In order to divert the impatience of those who were waiting to see the fishes taken alive and wriggling from their prison, the beautiful Iday got out the harp, for Iday not only played well on that instrument, but, besides, she had very pretty fingers. The young people applauded and Maria Clara kissed her, for the harp is the most popular instrument in that province, and was especially suited to this occasion.

"Sing the hymn about marriage," begged the old women. The men protested and Victoria, who had a fine voice, complained of hoarseness. The "Hymn of Marriage" is a beautiful Tagalog chant in which are set forth the cares and sorrows of the married state, yet not passing over its joys.

They then asked Maria Clara to sing, but she protested

that all her songs were sad ones. This protest, however, was overruled so she held back no longer. Taking the harp, she played a short prelude and then sang in a harmonious and vibrating voice full of feeling:

> Sweet are the hours in one's native land,
> Where all is dear the sunbeams bless;
> Life-giving breezes sweep the strand,
> And death is soften'd by love's caress.
>
> Warm kisses play on mother's lips,
> On her fond, tender breast awaking;
> When round her neck the soft arm slips,
> And bright eyes smile, all love partaking.
>
> Sweet is death for one's native land,
> Where all is dear the sunbeams bless;
> Dead is the breeze that sweeps the strand,
> Without a mother, home, or love's caress.

The song ceased, the voice died away, the harp became silent, and they still listened; no one applauded. The young women felt their eyes fill with tears, and Ibarra seemed to be unpleasantly affected. The youthful pilot stared motionless into the distance.

Suddenly a thundering roar was heard, such that the women screamed and covered their ears; it was the ex-theological student blowing with all the strength of his lungs on the *tambuli,* or carabao horn. Laughter and cheerfulness returned while tear-dimmed eyes brightened.

"Are you trying to deafen us, you heretic?" cried Aunt Isabel.

"Madam," replied the offender gravely, "I once heard of a poor trumpeter on the banks of the Rhine who, by playing on his trumpet, won in marriage a rich and noble maiden."

"That's right, the trumpeter of Sackingen!" exclaimed Ibarra, unable to resist taking part in the renewed merriment.

"Do you hear that?" went on Albino. "Now I want to see if I can't have the same luck." So saying, he began to blow with even more force into the resounding horn, holding it close to the ears of the girls who looked saddest. As might be expected, a small tumult arose and the mothers finally reduced him to silence by beating him with their slippers [1] and pinching him.

"My, oh my!" he complained as he felt of his smarting arms, "what a distance there is between the Philippines and the banks of the Rhine! *O tempora! O mores!* Some are given honors and others sanbenitos!"

All laughed at this, even the grave Victoria, while Sinang, she of the smiling eyes, whispered to Maria Clara, "Happy girl! I, too, would sing if I could!"

Andeng at length announced that the soup was ready to receive its guests, so the young fisherman climbed up into the pen placed at the narrower end of the corral, over which might be written for the fishes, were they able to read and understand Italian, "*Lasciate ogni speranza voi ch' entrante*," [2] for no fish that gets in there is ever released except by death. This division of the corral encloses a circular space so arranged that a man can stand on a platform in the upper part and draw the fish out with a small net.

"I should n't get tired fishing there with a pole and line," commented Sinang, trembling with pleasant anticipation.

All were now watching and some even began to believe that they saw the fishes wriggling about in the net and showing their glittering scales. But when the youth lowered his net not a fish leaped up.

"It must be full," whispered Albino, "for it has been over five days now since it was visited."

The fisherman drew in his net, but not even a single little fish adorned it. The water as it fell back in glitter-

---

[1] The *chinela*, the Philippine slipper, is a soft leather sole, heelless, with only a vamp, usually of plush or velvet, to hold it on. — Tr.

[2] "All hope abandon, ye who enter here." The words inscribed over the gate of Hell: Dante's *Inferno*, III, 9. — Tr.

ing drops reflecting the sunlight seemed to mock his efforts with a silvery smile. An exclamation of surprise, displeasure, and disappointment escaped from the lips of all. Again the youth repeated the operation, but with no better result.

"You don't understand your business," said Albino, climbing up into the pen of the corral and taking the net from the youth's hands. "Now you'll see! Andeng, get the pot ready!"

But apparently Albino did not understand the business either, for the net again came up empty. All broke out into laughter at him.

"Don't make so much noise that the fish can hear and so not let themselves be caught. This net must be torn." But on examination all the meshes of the net appeared to be intact.

"Give it to me," said Leon, Iday's sweetheart. He assured himself that the fence was in good condition, examined the net and being satisfied with it, asked, "Are you sure that it hasn't been visited for five days?"

"Very sure! The last time was on the eve of All Saints."

"Well then, either the lake is enchanted or I'll draw up something."

Leon then dropped the pole into the water and instantly astonishment was pictured on his countenance. Silently he looked off toward the mountain and moved the pole about in the water, then without raising it murmured in a low voice:

"A cayman!"

"A cayman!" repeated everyone, as the word ran from mouth to mouth in the midst of fright and general surprise.

"What did you say?" they asked him.

"I say that we've caught a cayman," Leon assured them and as he dropped the heavy end of the pole into the water, he continued: "Don't you hear that sound? That's not sand, but a tough hide, the back of a cayman. Don't you see how the posts shake? He's pushing against them even though he is all rolled up. Wait, he's a big one, his body is almost a foot or more across."

"What shall we do?" was the question.

"Catch him!" prompted some one.

"Heavens! And who'll catch him?"

No one offered to go down into the trap, for the water was deep.

"We ought to tie him to our banka and drag him along in triumph," suggested Sinang. "The idea of his eating the fish that we were going to eat!"

"I have never yet seen a live cayman," murmured Maria Clara.

The pilot arose, picked up a long rope, and climbed nimbly up on the platform, where Leon made room for him. With the exception of Maria Clara, no one had taken any notice of him, but now all admired his shapely figure. To the great surprise of all and in spite of their cries, he leaped down into the enclosure.

"Take this knife!" called Crisostomo to him, holding out a wide Toledo blade, but already the water was splashing up in a thousand jets and the depths closed mysteriously.

"*Jesús, María, y José!*" exclaimed the old women. "We're going to have an accident!"

"Don't be uneasy, ladies," said the old boatman, "for if there is any one in the province who can do it, he's the man."

"What's his name?" they asked.

"We call him 'The Pilot' and he's the best I've ever seen, only he doesn't like the business."

The water became disturbed, then broke into ripples, the fence shook; a struggle seemed to be going on in the depths. All were silent and hardly breathed. Ibarra grasped the handle of the sharp knife convulsively.

Now the struggle seemed to be at an end and the head of the youth appeared, to be greeted with joyful cries. The eyes of the old women filled with tears. The pilot climbed up with one end of the rope in his hand and once on the platform began to pull on it. The monster soon appeared above the water with the rope tied in a double band around its neck and underneath its front legs. It was a large one, as Leon had said, speckled, and on its back grew the green moss which is to the caymans what gray hairs are to men. Roaring like a bull and beating its tail against or catching hold of the sides of the corral, it opened its huge jaws and showed its long, sharp teeth. The pilot was hoisting it alone, for no one had thought to assist him.

Once out of the water and resting on the platform, he placed his foot upon it and with his strong hands forced its huge jaws together and tried to tie its snout with stout knots. With a last effort the reptile arched its body, struck the floor with its powerful tail, and jerking free, hurled itself with one leap into the water outside the corral, dragging its captor along with it. A cry of horror broke from the lips of all. But like a flash of lightning another body shot into the water so quickly that there was hardly time to realize that it was Ibarra. Maria Clara did not swoon only for the reason that the Filipino women do not yet know how to do so.

The anxious watchers saw the water become colored and dyed with blood. The young fisherman jumped down with his bolo in his hand and was followed by his father, but they had scarcely disappeared when Crisostomo and the pilot reappeared clinging to the dead body of the reptile, which had the whole length of its white belly slit open and the knife still sticking in its throat.

To describe the joy were impossible, as a dozen arms reached out to drag the young men from the water. The old women were beside themselves between laughter and prayers. Andeng forgot that her *sinigang* had boiled over three times, spilling the soup and putting out the fire. The only one who could say nothing was Maria Clara.

Ibarra was uninjured, while the pilot had only a slight

scratch on his arm. "I owe my life to you," said the latter to Ibarra, who was wrapping himself up in blankets and cloths. The pilot's voice seemed to have a note of sadness in it.

"You are too daring," answered Ibarra. "Don't tempt fate again."

"If you had not come up again — " murmured the still pale and trembling Maria Clara.

"If I had not come up and you had followed me," replied Ibarra, completing the thought in his own way, "in the bottom of the lake, *I should still have been with my family!*" He had not forgotten that there lay the bones of his father.

The old women did not want to visit the other corral but wished to return, saying that the day had begun inauspiciously and that many more accidents might occur.

"All because we did n't hear mass," sighed one.

"But what accident has befallen us, ladies?" asked Ibarra. "The cayman seems to have been the only unlucky one."

"All of which proves," concluded the ex-student of theology, "that in all its sinful life this unfortunate reptile has never attended mass — at least, I 've never seen him among the many other caymans that frequent the church."

So the boats were turned in the direction of the other corral and Andeng had to get her *sinigang* ready again. The day was now well advanced, with a fresh breeze blowing. The waves curled up behind the body of the cayman, raising "mountains of foam whereon the smooth, rich sunlight glitters," as the poet says. The music again resounded; Iday played on the harp, while the men handled the accordions and guitars with greater or less skill. The prize-winner was Albino, who actually scratched the instruments, getting out of tune and losing the time every moment or else forgetting it and changing to another tune entirely different.

The second corral was visited with some misgivings, as many expected to find there the mate of the dead cayman, but nature is ever a jester, and the nets came up full at each haul. Aunt Isabel superintended the sorting of the fish and ordered that some be left in the trap for decoys. "It's not lucky to empty the corral completely," she concluded.

Then they made their way toward the shore near the forest of old trees that belonged to Ibarra. There in the shade by the clear waters of the brook, among the flowers, they ate their breakfast under improvised canopies. The space was filled with music while the smoke from the fires curled up in slender wreaths. The water bubbled cheerfully in the hot dishes as though uttering sounds of consolation, or perchance of sarcasm and irony, to the dead fishes. The body of the cayman writhed about, sometimes showing its torn white belly and again its speckled greenish back, while man, Nature's favorite, went on his way undisturbed by what the Brahmins and vegetarians would call so many cases of fratricide.

CHAPTER XXIV

IN THE WOOD

EARLY, very early indeed, somewhat differently from his usual custom, Padre Salvi had celebrated mass and cleansed a dozen sinful souls in a few moments. Then it seemed that the reading of some letters which he had received firmly sealed and waxed caused the worthy curate to lose his appetite, since he allowed his chocolate to become completely cold.

"The padre is getting sick," commented the cook while preparing another cup. "For days he has n't eaten; of the six dishes that I set before him on the table he does n't touch even two."

"It 's because he sleeps badly," replied the other servant. "He has nightmares since he changed his bedroom. His eyes are becoming more sunken all the time and he 's getting thinner and yellower day by day."

Truly, Padre Salvi was a pitiable sight. He did not care to touch the second cup of chocolate nor to taste the sweet cakes of Cebu; instead, he paced thoughtfully about the spacious sala, crumpling in his bony hands the letters, which he read from time to time. Finally, he called for his carriage, got ready, and directed that he be taken to the wood where stood the fateful tree near which the picnic was being held.

Arriving at the edge of the wood, the padre dismissed his carriage and made his way alone into its depths. A gloomy pathway opened a difficult passage through the thickets and led to the brook formed by certain warm springs, like many that flow from the slopes of Mt. Makiling. Adorning its banks grow wild flowers, many of which have as yet no Latin names, but which are doubtless well-known to the gilded insects and butterflies of all shapes and colors, blue and gold, white and black, many-hued, glittering with iridescent spots, with rubies and emeralds on their wings, and to the countless beetles with their metallic lusters of powdered gold. The hum of the insects, the cries of the cicada, which cease not night or day, the songs of the birds, and the dry crashing of the rotten branch that falls and strikes all around against the trees, are the only sounds to break the stillness of that mysterious place.

For some time the padre wandered aimlessly among the thick underbrush, avoiding the thorns that caught at his *guingón* habit as though to detain him, and the roots of the trees that protruded from the soil to form stumbling-blocks at every step for this wanderer unaccustomed to such places. But suddenly his feet were arrested by the sound of clear voices raised in merry laughter, seeming to come from the brook and apparently drawing nearer.

"I'm going to see if I can find one of those nests," said a beautiful, sweet voice, which the curate recognized. "I'd like to see *him* without having him see me, so I could follow him everywhere."

Padre Salvi hid behind the trunk of a large tree and set himself to eavesdrop.

"Does that mean that you want to do with him what the curate does with you?" asked a laughing voice. "He watches you everywhere. Be careful, for jealousy makes people thin and puts rings around their eyes."

"No, no, not jealousy, it's pure curiosity," replied the silvery voice, while the laughing one repeated, "Yes, jealousy, jealousy!" and she burst out into merry laughter.

"If I were jealous, instead of making myself invisible, I'd make him so, in order that no one might see him."

"But neither would you see *him* and that would n't be nice. The best thing for us to do if we find the nest would be to present it to the curate so that he could watch over us without the necessity of our seeing him, don't you think so?"

"I don't believe in those herons' nests," interrupted another voice, "but if at any time I should be jealous, I'd know how to watch and still keep myself hidden."

"How, how? Perhaps like a *Sor Escucha?*"[1]

This reminiscence of school-days provoked another merry burst of laughter.

"And you know how she's fooled, the *Sor Escucha!*"

From his hiding-place Padre Salvi saw Maria Clara, Victoria, and Sinang wading along the border of the brook. They were moving forward with their eyes fixed on the crystal waters, seeking the enchanted nest of the heron, wet to their knees so that the wide folds of their bathing skirts revealed the graceful curves of their bodies. Their hair was flung loose, their arms bare, and they wore camisas with wide stripes of bright hues. While looking for something that they could not find they were picking flowers and plants which grew along the bank.

The religious Acteon stood pale and motionless gazing at that chaste Diana, but his eyes glittered in their dark circles, untired of staring at those white and shapely arms and at that elegant neck and bust, while the small rosy feet that played in the water awoke in his starved being strange sensations and in his burning brain dreams of new ideas.

The three charming figures disappeared behind a bamboo thicket around a bend in the brook, and their cruel allusions ceased to be heard. Intoxicated, staggering, covered with perspiration, Padre Salvi left his hiding-place and looked all about him with rolling eyes. He stood still as if in doubt, then took a few steps as though he would try to follow the girls, but turned again and made his way along the banks of the stream to seek the rest of the party.

At a little distance he saw in the middle of the brook a kind of bathing-place, well enclosed, decorated with

---

[1] "Listening Sister," the nun who acts as spy and monitor over the girls studying in a convent. — TR.

palm leaves, flowers, and streamers, with a leafy clump of bamboo for a covering, from within which came the sound of happy feminine voices. Farther on he saw a bamboo bridge and beyond it the men bathing. Near these a crowd of servants was busily engaged around improvised *kalanes* in plucking chickens, washing rice, and roasting a pig. On the opposite bank in a cleared space were gathered men and women under a canvas covering which was fastened partly to the hoary trees and partly to newly-driven stakes. There were gathered the alferez, the coadjutor, the gobernadorcillo, the teniente-mayor, the schoolmaster, and many other personages of the town, even including Sinang's father, Capitan Basilio, who had been the adversary of the deceased Don Rafael in an old lawsuit. Ibarra had said to him, " We are disputing over a point of law, but that does not mean that we are enemies," so the celebrated orator of the conservatives had enthusiastically accepted the invitation, sending along three turkeys and putting his servants at the young man's disposal.

The curate was received with respect and deference by all, even the alferez. " Why, where has your Reverence been ? " asked the latter, as he noticed the curate's scratched face and his habit covered with leaves and dry twigs. " Has your Reverence had a fall ? "

" No, I lost my way," replied Padre Salvi, lowering his gaze to examine his gown.

Bottles of lemonade were brought out and green coconuts were split open so that the bathers as they came from the water might refresh themselves with the milk and the soft meat, whiter than the milk itself. The girls all received in addition rosaries of sampaguitas, intertwined with roses and ilang-ilang blossoms, to perfume their flowing tresses. Some of the company sat on the ground or reclined in hammocks swung from the branches of the trees, while others amused themselves around a wide flat rock on which were to be seen playing-cards, a chess-board, booklets, cowry shells, and pebbles.

IN THE WOOD

They showed the cayman to the curate, but he seemed inattentive until they told him that the gaping wound had been inflicted by Ibarra. The celebrated and unknown pilot was no longer to be seen, as he had disappeared before the arrival of the alferez.

At length Maria Clara came from the bath with her companions, looking fresh as a rose on its first morning when the dew sparkling on its fair petals glistens like diamonds. Her first smile was for Crisostomo and the first cloud on her brow for Padre Salvi, who noted it and sighed.

The lunch hour was now come,. and the curate, the coadjutor, the gobernadorcillo, the teniente-mayor, and the other dignitaries took their seats at the table over which Ibarra presided. The mothers would not permit any of the men to eat at the table where the young women sat.

"This time, Albino, you can't invent holes as in the bankas," said Leon to the quondam student of theology.

"What! What's that?" asked the old women.

"The bankas, ladies, were as whole as this plate is," explained Leon.

"*Jesús!* The rascal!" exclaimed the smiling Aunt Isabel.

"Have you yet learned anything of the criminal who assaulted Padre Damaso?" inquired Fray Salvi of the alferez.

"Of what criminal, Padre?" asked the military man, staring at the friar over the glass of wine that he was emptying.

"What criminal! Why, the one who struck Padre Damaso in the road yesterday afternoon!"

"Struck Padre Damaso?" asked several voices.

The coadjutor seemed to smile, while Padre Salvi went on "Yes, and Padre Damaso is now confined to his bed. It's thought that he may be the very same Elias who threw you into the mudhole, señor alferez."

Either from shame or wine the alferez's face became very red.

"Of course, I thought," continued Padre Salvi in a joking manner, "that you, the alferez of the Civil Guard, would be informed about the affair."

The soldier bit his lip and was murmuring some foolish excuse, when the meal was suddenly interrupted by the appearance of a pale, thin, poorly-clad woman. No one had noticed her approach, for she had come so noiselessly that at night she might have been taken for a ghost.

"Give this poor woman something to eat," cried the old women. "*Oy,* come here!"

Still the strange woman kept on her way to the table where the curate was seated. As he turned his face and recognized her, his knife dropped from his hand.

"Give this woman something to eat," ordered Ibarra.

"The night is dark and the boys disappear," murmured the wandering woman, but at sight of the alferez, who spoke to her, she became frightened and ran away among the trees.

"Who is she?" he asked.

"An unfortunate woman who has become insane from fear and sorrow," answered Don Filipo. "For four days now she has been so."

"Is her name Sisá?" asked Ibarra with interest.

"Your soldiers arrested her," continued the teniente-mayor, rather bitterly, to the alferez. "They marched her through the town on account of something about her sons which is n't very clearly known."

"What!" exclaimed the alferez, turning to the curate, "she is n't the mother of your two sacristans?"

The curate nodded in affirmation.

"They disappeared and nobody made any inquiries about them," added Don Filipo with a severe look at the gobernadorcillo, who dropped his eyes.

"Look for that woman," Crisostomo ordered the servants. "I promised to try to learn where her sons are."

"They disappeared, did you say?" asked the alferez. "Your sacristans disappeared, Padre?"

The friar emptied the glass of wine before him and again nodded.

"*Caramba,* Padre!" exclaimed the alferez with a sarcastic laugh, pleased at the thought of a little revenge. "A few pesos of your Reverence's disappear and my sergeant is routed out early to hunt for them — two sacristans disappear and your Reverence says nothing — and you, señor capitan — It's also true that you —"

Here he broke off with another laugh as he buried his spoon in the red meat of a wild papaya.

The curate, confused, and not over-intent upon what he was saying, replied, "That's because I have to answer for the money —"

"A good answer, reverend shepherd of souls!" interrupted the alferez with his mouth full of food. "A splendid answer, holy man!"

Ibarra wished to intervene, but Padre Salvi controlled himself by an effort and said with a forced smile, "Then you don't know, sir, what is said about the disappearance of those boys? No? Then ask your soldiers!"

"What!" exclaimed the alferez, all his mirth gone.

"It's said that on the night they disappeared several shots were heard."

"Several shots?" echoed the alferez, looking around at the other guests, who nodded their heads in corroboration of the padre's statement.

Padre Salvi then replied slowly and with cutting sarcasm: "Come now, I see that you don't catch the criminals nor do you know what is going on in your own house, yet you try to set yourself up as a preacher to point out their duties to others. You ought to keep in mind that proverb about the fool in his own house —"[1]

"Gentlemen!" interrupted Ibarra, seeing that the alferez had grown pale. "In this connection I should like to have your opinion about a project of mine. I'm think-

---

[1] "Más sabe el loco en su casa que el cuerdo en la ajena." The fool knows more in his own house than a wise man does in another's. — Tr.

ing of putting this crazy woman under the care of a skilful physician and, in the meantime, with your aid and advice, I'll search for her sons."

The return of the servants without the madwoman, whom they had been unable to find, brought peace by turning the conversation to other matters.

The meal ended, and while the tea and coffee were being served, both old and young scattered about in different groups. Some took the chessmen, others the cards, while the girls, curious about the future, chose to put questions to a *Wheel of Fortune*.

"Come, Señor Ibarra," called Capitan Basilio in merry mood, "we have a lawsuit fifteen years old, and there isn't a judge in the Audiencia who can settle it. Let's see if we can't end it on the chess-board."

"With the greatest pleasure," replied the youth. "Just wait a moment, the alferez is leaving."

Upon hearing about this match all the old men who understood chess gathered around the board, for it promised to be an interesting one, and attracted even spectators who were not familiar with the game. The old women, however, surrounded the curate in order to converse with him about spiritual matters, but Fray Salvi apparently did not consider the place and time appropriate, for he gave vague answers and his sad, rather bored, looks wandered in all directions except toward his questioners.

The chess-match began with great solemnity. "If this game ends in a draw, it's understood that the lawsuit is to be dropped," said Ibarra.

In the midst of the game Ibarra received a telegram which caused his eyes to shine and his face to become pale. He put it into his pocketbook, at the same time glancing toward the group of young people, who were still with laughter and shouts putting questions to Destiny.

"Check to the king!" called the youth.

Capitan Basilio had no other recourse than to hide the piece behind the queen.

IN THE WOOD

"Check to the queen!" called the youth as he threatened that piece with a rook which was defended by a pawn.

Being unable to protect the queen or to withdraw the piece on account of the king behind it, Capitan Basilio asked for time to reflect.

"Willingly," agreed Ibarra, "especially as I have something to say this very minute to those young people in that group over there." He arose with the agreement that his opponent should have a quarter of an hour.

Iday had the round card on which were written the forty-eight questions, while Albino held the book of answers.

"A lie! It's not so!" cried Sinang, half in tears.

"What's the matter?" asked Maria Clara.

"Just imagine, I asked, 'When shall I have some sense?' I threw the dice and that worn-out priest read from the book, 'When the frogs raise hair.' What do you think of that?" As she said this, Sinang made a grimace at the laughing ex-theological student.

"Who told you to ask that question?" her cousin Victoria asked her. "To ask it is enough to deserve such an answer."

"You ask a question," they said to Ibarra, offering him the wheel. "We've decided that whoever gets the best answer shall receive a present from the rest. Each of us has already had a question."

"Who got the best answer?"

"Maria Clara, Maria Clara!" replied Sinang. "We made her ask, willy-nilly, 'Is your sweetheart faithful and constant?' And the book answered—"

But here the blushing Maria Clara put her hands over Sinang's mouth so that she could not finish.

"Well, give me the wheel," said Crisostomo, smiling. "My question is, 'Shall I succeed in my present enterprise?'"

"What an ugly question!" exclaimed Sinang.

Ibarra threw the dice and in accordance with the resulting number the page and line were sought.

"Dreams are dreams," read Albino.

Ibarra drew out the telegram and opened it with trembling hands. "This time your book is wrong!" he exclaimed joyfully. "Read this: 'School project approved. Suit decided in your favor.'"

"What does it mean?" all asked.

"Didn't you say that a present is to be given to the one receiving the best answer?" he asked in a voice shaking with emotion as he tore the telegram carefully into two pieces.

"Yes, yes!"

"Well then, this is my present," he said as he gave one piece to Maria Clara. "A school for boys and girls is to be built in the town and this school is my present."

"And the other part, what does it mean?"

"It's to be given to the one who has received the worst answer."

"To me, then, to me!" cried Sinang.

Ibarra gave her the other piece of the telegram and hastily withdrew.

"What does it mean?" she asked, but the happy youth was already at a distance, returning to the game of chess.

Fray Salvi in abstracted mood approached the circle of young people. Maria Clara wiped away her tears of joy, the laughter ceased, and the talk died away. The curate stared at the young people without offering to say anything, while they silently waited for him to speak.

"What's this?" he at length asked, picking up the book and turning its leaves.

"*The Wheel of Fortune,* a book of games," replied Leon.

"Don't you know that it's a sin to believe in these things?" he scolded, tearing the leaves out angrily.

Cries of surprise and anger escaped from the lips of all.

"It's a greater sin to dispose of what isn't yours, against the wish of the owner," contradicted Albino, rising. "Padre, that's what is called stealing and it is forbidden by God and men!"

Maria Clara clasped her hands and gazed with tearful eyes at the remnants of the book which a few moments before had been the source of so much happiness for her.

Contrary to the general expectation, Fray Salvi did not reply to Albino, but stood staring at the torn leaves as they were whirled about, some falling in the wood, some in the water, then he staggered away with his hands over his head. He stopped for a few moments to speak with Ibarra, who accompanied him to one of the carriages, which were at the disposal of the guests.

"He's doing well to leave, that kill-joy," murmured Sinang. "He has a face that seems to say, 'Don't laugh, for I know about your sins!'"

After making the present to his fiancée, Ibarra was so happy that he began to play without reflection or a careful examination of the positions of the pieces. The result was that although Capitan Basilio was hard pressed the game became a stalemate, owing to many careless moves on the young man's part.

"It's settled, we're at peace!" exclaimed Capitan Basilio heartily.

"Yes, we're at peace," repeated the youth, "whatever the decision of the court may be." And the two shook hands cordially.

While all present were rejoicing over this happy termination of a quarrel of which both parties were tired, the sudden arrival of a sergeant and four soldiers of the Civil Guard, all armed and with bayonets fixed, disturbed the mirth and caused fright among the women.

"Keep still, everybody!" shouted the sergeant. "Shoot any one who moves!"

In spite of this blustering command, Ibarra arose and approached the sergeant. "What do you want?" he asked.

"That you deliver to us at once a criminal named Elias, who was your pilot this morning," was the threatening reply.

"A criminal — the pilot? You must be mistaken," answered Ibarra.

"No, sir, this Elias has just been accused of putting his hand on a priest —"

"Oh, was that the pilot?"

"The very same, according to reports. You admit persons of bad character into your fiestas, Señor Ibarra."

Ibarra looked him over from head to foot and replied with great disdain, "I don't have to give you an account of my actions! At our fiestas all are welcome. Had you yourself come, you would have found a place at our table, just as did your alferez, who was with us a couple of hours ago." With this he turned his back.

The sergeant gnawed at the ends of his mustache but, considering himself the weaker party, ordered the soldiers to institute a search, especially among the trees, for the pilot, a description of whom he carried on a piece of paper.

Don Filipo said to him, "Notice that this description fits nine tenths of the natives. Don't make any false move!"

After a time the soldiers returned with the report that they had been unable to see either banka or man that could be called suspicious-looking, so the sergeant muttered a few words and went away as he had come — in the manner of the Civil Guard!

The merriment was little by little restored, amid questions and comments.

"So that's the Elias who threw the alferez into the mudhole," said Leon thoughtfully.

"How did that happen? How was it?" asked some of the more curious.

"They say that on a very rainy day in September the alferez met a man who was carrying a bundle of firewood. The road was very muddy and there was only a narrow path at the side, wide enough for but one person. They say that the alferez, instead of reining in his pony, put spurs to it, at the same time calling to the man to get out

IN THE WOOD

of the way. It seemed that this man, on account of the heavy load he was carrying on his shoulder, had little relish for going back nor did he want to be swallowed up in the mud, so he continued on his way forward. The alferez in irritation tried to knock him down, but he snatched a piece of wood from his bundle and struck the pony on the head with such great force that it fell, throwing its rider into the mud. They also say that the man went on his way tranquilly without taking any notice of the five bullets that were fired after him by the alferez, who was blind with mud and rage. As the man was entirely unknown to him it was supposed that he might be the famous Elias who came to the province several months ago, having come from no one knows where. He has given the Civil Guard cause to know him in several towns for similar actions."

" Then he's a tulisan? " asked Victoria shuddering.

" I don't think so, for they say that he fought against some tulisanes one day when they were robbing a house."

" He has n't the look of a criminal," commented Sinang.

" No, but he looks very sad. I did n't see him smile the whole morning," added Maria Clara thoughtfully.

So the afternoon passed away and the hour for returning to the town came. Under the last rays of the setting sun they left the woods, passing in silence by the mysterious tomb of Ibarra's ancestors. Afterwards, the merry talk was resumed in a lively manner, full of warmth, beneath those branches so little accustomed to hear so many voices. The trees seemed sad, while the vines swung back and forth as if to say, " Farewell, youth! Farewell, dream of a day! "

Now in the light of the great red torches of bamboo and with the sound of the guitars let us leave them on the road to the town. The groups grow smaller, the lights are extinguished, the songs die away, and the guitar becomes silent as they approach the abodes of men. Put on the mask now that you are once more amongst your kind!

CHAPTER XXV

IN THE HOUSE OF THE SAGE

ON the morning of the following day, Ibarra, after visiting his lands, made his way to the home of old Tasio. Complete stillness reigned in the garden, for even the swallows circling about the eaves scarcely made any noise. Moss grew on the old wall, over which a kind of ivy clambered to form borders around the windows. The little house seemed to be the abode of silence.

Ibarra hitched his horse carefully to a post and walking almost on tiptoe crossed the clean and well-kept garden to the stairway, which he ascended, and as the door was open, he entered. The first sight that met his gaze was the old man bent over a book in which he seemed to be writing. On the walls were collections of insects and plants arranged among maps and stands filled with books and manuscripts. The old man was so absorbed in his work that he did not notice the presence of the youth until the latter, not wishing to disturb him, tried to retire.

"Ah, you here?" he asked, gazing at Ibarra with a strange expression.

"Excuse me," answered the youth, "I see that you're very busy —"

"True, I was writing a little, but it's not urgent, and I want to rest. Can I do anything for you?"

"A great deal," answered Ibarra, drawing nearer, "but —"

A glance at the book on the table caused him to exclaim in surprise, "What, are you given to deciphering hieroglyphics?"

"No," replied the old man, as he offered his visitor a chair. "I don't understand Egyptian or Coptic either,

IN THE HOUSE OF THE SAGE 189

but I know something about the system of writing, so I write in hieroglyphics."

"You write in hieroglyphics! Why?" exclaimed the youth, doubting what he saw and heard.

"So that I cannot be read now."

Ibarra gazed at him fixedly, wondering to himself if the old man were not indeed crazy. He examined the book rapidly to learn if he was telling the truth and saw neatly drawn figures of animals, circles, semicircles, flowers, feet, hands, arms, and such things.

"But why do you write if you don't want to be read?"

"Because I'm not writing for this generation, but for other ages. If this generation could read, it would burn my books, the labor of my whole life. But the generation that deciphers these characters will be an intelligent generation, it will understand and say, 'Not all were asleep in the night of our ancestors!' The mystery of these curious characters will save my work from the ignorance of men, just as the mystery of strange rites has saved many truths from the destructive priestly classes."

"In what language do you write?" asked Ibarra after a pause.

"In our own, Tagalog."

"Are the hieroglyphical signs suitable?"

"If it were not for the difficulty of drawing them, which takes time and patience, I would almost say that they are more suitable than the Latin alphabet. The ancient Egyptian had our vowels; our *o,* which is only final and is not like that of the Spanish, which is a vowel between *o* and *u.* Like us, the Egyptians lacked the true sound of *e,* and in their language are found our *ha* and *kha,* which we do not have in the Latin alphabet such as is used in Spanish. For example, in this word *mukha,*" he went on, pointing to the book, "I transcribe the syllable *ha* more correctly with the figure of a fish than with the Latin *h,* which in Europe is pronounced in different ways. For a weaker aspirate, as for example in this word *hain,* where the *h* has less force, I avail myself of this lion's head or of these three lotus flowers, according to the quantity of the vowel. Besides, I have the nasal sound which does not exist in the Latin-Spanish alphabet. I repeat that if it were not for the difficulty of drawing them exactly, these hieroglyphics could almost be adopted, but this same difficulty obliges me to be concise and not say more than what is exact and necessary. Moreover, this work keeps me company when my guests from China and Japan go away."

"Your guests from China and Japan?"

"Don't you hear them? My guests are the swallows. This year one of them is missing — some bad boy in China or Japan must have caught it."

"How do you know that they come from those countries?"

"Easily enough! Several years ago, before they left I tied to the foot of each one a slip of paper with the name 'Philippines' in English on it, supposing that they must not travel very far and because English is understood nearly everywhere. For years my slips brought no reply, so that at last I had it written in Chinese and here in the following November they have returned with other notes which I have had deciphered. One is written in Chinese and is a greeting from the banks of the Hoang-Ho and the other, as the Chinaman whom I consulted supposes, must be in Japanese. But I'm taking your time with these things and have n't asked you what I can do for you."

"I've come to speak to you about a matter of importance," said the youth. "Yesterday afternoon — "

"Have they caught that poor fellow?"

"You mean Elias? How did you know about him?"

"I saw the Muse of the Civil Guard!"

"The Muse of the Civil Guard? Who is she?"

"The alferez's woman, whom you did n't invite to your picnic. Yesterday morning the incident of the cayman became known through the town. The Muse of the Civil

IN THE HOUSE OF THE SAGE 191

Guard is as astute as she is malignant and she guessed that the pilot must be the bold person who threw her husband into the mudhole and who assaulted Padre Damaso. As she reads all the reports that her husband is to receive, scarcely had he got back home, drunk and not knowing what he was doing, when to revenge herself on you she sent the sergeant with the soldiers to disturb the merriment of your picnic. Be careful! Eve was a good woman, sprung from the hands of God — they say that Doña Consolacion is evil and it's not known whose hands she came from! In order to be good, a woman needs to have been, at least sometime, either a maid or a mother."

Ibarra smiled slightly and replied by taking some documents from his pocketbook. "My dead father used to consult you in some things and I recall that he had only to congratulate himself on following your advice. I have on hand a little enterprise, the success of which I must assure." Here he explained briefly his plan for the school, which he had offered to his fiancée, spreading out in view of the astonished Sage some plans which had been prepared in Manila.

"I would like to have you advise me as to what persons in the town I must first win over in order to assure the success of the undertaking. You know the inhabitants well, while I have just arrived and am almost a stranger in my own country."

Old Tasio examined the plans before him with tear-dimmed eyes. "What you are going to do has been my dream, the dream of a poor lunatic!" he exclaimed with emotion. "And now the first thing that I advise you to do is never to come to consult with me."

The youth gazed at him in surprise.

"Because the sensible people," he continued with bitter irony, "would take you for a madman also. The people consider madmen those who do not think as they do, so they hold me as such, which I appreciate, because the day in which they think me returned to sanity, they will deprive me of the little liberty that I've purchased at the expense of the reputation of being a sane individual. And who knows but they are right? I do not live according to their rules, my principles and ideals are different. The gobernadorcillo enjoys among them the reputation of being a wise man because he learned nothing more than to serve chocolate and to put up with Padre Damaso's bad humor, so now he is wealthy, he disturbs the petty destinies of his fellow-townsmen, and at times he even talks of justice. 'That's a man of talent,' think the vulgar, 'look how from nothing he has made himself great!' But I, I inherited fortune and position, I have studied, and now I am poor, I am not trusted with the most ridiculous office, and all say, 'He's a fool! He does n't know how to live!' The curate calls me 'philosopher' as a nickname and gives to understand that I am a charlatan who is making a show of what I learned in the higher schools, when that is exactly what benefits me the least. Perhaps I really am the fool and they the wise ones — who can say?"

The old man shook his head as if to drive away that thought, and continued· "The second thing I can advise is that you consult the curate, the gobernadorcillo, and all persons in authority. They will give you bad, stupid, or useless advice, but consultation does n't mean compliance, although you should make it appear that you are taking their advice and acting according to it."

Ibarra reflected a moment before he replied:. "The advice is good, but difficult to follow. Could n't I go ahead with my idea without a shadow being thrown upon it? Could n't a worthy enterprise make its way over everything, since truth does n't need to borrow garments from error?"

"Nobody loves the naked truth!" answered the old man. "That is good in theory and practicable in the world of which youth dreams. Here is the schoolmaster, who has struggled in a vacuum; with the enthusiasm of a child, he has sought the good, yet he has won only jests and

IN THE HOUSE OF THE SAGE

laughter. You have said that you are a stranger in your own country, and I believe it. The very first day you arrived you began by wounding the vanity of a priest who is regarded by the people as a saint, and as a sage among his fellows. God grant that such a misstep may not have already determined your future! Because the Dominicans and Augustinians look with disdain on the *guingón* habit, the rope girdle, and the immodest foot-wear, because a learned doctor in Santo Tomas [1] may have once recalled that Pope Innocent III described the statutes of that order as more fit for hogs than men, don't believe but that all of them work hand in hand to affirm what a preacher once said, 'The most insignificant lay brother can do more than the government with all its soldiers!' *Cave ne cadas!* [2] Gold is powerful — the golden calf has thrown God down from His altars many times, and that too since the days of Moses!"

"I'm not so pessimistic nor does life appear to me so perilous in my country," said Ibarra with a smile. "I believe that those fears are somewhat exaggerated and I hope to be able to carry out my plans without meeting any great opposition in that quarter."

"Yes, if they extend their hands to you; no, if they withhold them. All your efforts will be shattered against the walls of the rectory if the friar so much as waves his girdle or shakes his habit; tomorrow the alcalde will on some pretext deny you what today he has granted; no mother will allow her son to attend the school, and then all your labors will produce a counter-effect — they will dishearten those who afterwards may wish to attempt altruistic undertakings."

---

[1] The College of Santo Tomas was established in 1619 through a legacy of books and money left for that purpose by Fray Miguel de Benavides, O. P., second archbishop of Manila. By royal decree and papal bull, it became in 1645 the Royal and Pontifical University of Santo Tomas, and never, during the Spanish régime, got beyond the Thomistic theology in its courses of instruction. — TR.

[2] Take heed lest you fall!

"But, after all," replied the youth, "I can't believe in that power of which you speak, and even supposing it to exist and making allowance for it, I should still have on my side the sensible people and the government, which is animated by the best intentions, which has great hopes, and which frankly desires the welfare of the Philippines."

"The government! The government!" muttered the Sage, raising his eyes to stare at the ceiling. "However inspired it may be with the desire for fostering the greatness of the country for the benefit of the country itself and of the mother country, however some official or other may recall the generous spirit of the Catholic Kings [1] and may agree with it, too, the government sees nothing, hears nothing, nor does it decide anything, except what the curate or the Provincial causes it to see, hear, and decide. The government is convinced that it depends for its salvation wholly on them, that it is sustained because they uphold it, and that the day on which they cease to support it, it will fall like a manikin that has lost its prop. They intimidate the government with an uprising of the people and the people with the forces of the government, whence originates a simple game, very much like what happens to timid persons when they visit gloomy places, taking for ghosts their own shadows and for strange voices the echoes of their own. As long as the government does not deal directly with the country it will not get away from this tutelage, it will live like those imbecile youths who tremble at the voice of their tutor, whose kindness they are begging for. The government has no dream of a healthy future; it is the arm, while the head is the convento. By this inertia with which it allows itself to be dragged from depth to depth, it becomes changed into a shadow, its integrity is impaired, and in a weak and incapable way it trusts everything to mercenary hands. But compare our

[1] Ferdinand and Isabella, the builders of Spain's greatness, are known in Spanish history as "Los Reyes Católicos." — TR.

IN THE HOUSE OF THE SAGE

system of government with those of the countries you have visited —"

"Oh!" interrupted Ibarra, "that's asking too much! Let us content ourselves with observing that our people do not complain or suffer as do the people of other countries, thanks to Religion and the benignity of the governing powers."

"This people does not complain because it has no voice, it does not move because it is lethargic, and you say that it does not suffer because you have n't seen how its heart bleeds. But some day you will see this, you will hear its complaints, and then woe unto those who found their strength on ignorance and fanaticism! Woe unto those who rejoice in deceit and labor during the night, believing that all are asleep! When the light of day shows up the monsters of darkness, the frightful reaction will come. So many sighs suppressed, so much poison distilled drop by drop, so much force repressed for centuries, will come to light and burst! Who then will pay those accounts which oppressed peoples present from time to time and which History preserves for us on her bloody pages?"

"God, the government, and Religion will not allow that day to come!" replied Ibarra, impressed in spite of himself. "The Philippines is religious and loves Spain, the Philippines will realize how much the nation is doing for her. There are abuses, yes, there are defects, that cannot be denied, but Spain is laboring to introduce reforms that will correct these abuses and defects, she is formulating plans, she is not selfish!"

"I know it, and that is the worst of it! The reforms which emanate from the higher places are annulled in the lower circles, thanks to the vices of all, thanks, for instance, to the eager desire to get rich in a short time, and to the ignorance of the people, who consent to everything. A royal decree does not correct abuses when there is no zealous authority to watch over its execution, while freedom of speech against the insolence of petty tyrants is not conceded. Plans will remain plans, abuses will still be abuses, and the satisfied ministry will sleep in peace in spite of everything. Moreover, if perchance there does come into a high place a person with great and generous ideas, he will begin to hear, while behind his back he is considered a fool, 'Your Excellency does not know the country, your Excellency does not understand the character of the Indians, your Excellency is going to ruin them, your Excellency will do well to trust So-and-so,' and his Excellency in fact does not know the country, for he has been until now stationed in America, and besides that, he has all the shortcomings and weaknesses of other men, so he allows himself to be convinced. His Excellency also remembers that to secure the appointment he has had to sweat much and suffer more, that he holds it for only three years, that he is getting old and that it is necessary to think, not of quixotisms, but of the future: a modest mansion in Madrid, a cozy house in the country, and a good income in order to live in luxury at the capital — these are what he must look for in the Philippines. Let us not ask for miracles, let us not ask that he who comes as an outsider to make his fortune and go away afterwards should interest himself in the welfare of the country. What matters to him the gratitude or the curses of a people whom he does not know, in a country where he has no associations, where he has no affections? Fame to be sweet must resound in the ears of those we love, in the atmosphere of our home or of the land that will guard our ashes; we wish that fame should hover over our tomb to warm with its breath the chill of death, so that we may not be completely reduced to nothingness, that something of us may survive. Naught of this can we offer to those who come to watch over our destinies. And the worst of all this is that they go away just when they are beginning to get an understanding of their duties. But we are getting away from our subject."

"But before getting back to it I must make some

IN THE HOUSE OF THE SAGE

things plain," interrupted the youth eagerly. "I can admit that the government does not know the people, but I believe that the people know the government even less. There are useless officials, bad ones, if you wish, but there are also good ones, and if these are unable to do anything it is because they meet with an inert mass, the people, who take little part in the affairs that concern them. But I did n't come to hold a discussion with you on that point, I came to ask for advice and you tell me to lower my head before grotesque idols!"

"Yes, I repeat it, because here you must either lower your head or lose it."

"Either lower my head or lose it!" repeated Ibarra thoughtfully. "The dilemma is hard! But why? Is love for my country incompatible with love for Spain? Is it necessary to debase oneself to be a good Christian, to prostitute one's conscience in order to carry out a good purpose? I love my native land, the Philippines, because to it I owe my life and my happiness, because every man should love his country. I love Spain, the fatherland of my ancestors, because in spite of everything the Philippines owes to it, and will continue to owe, her happiness and her future. I am a Catholic, I preserve pure the faith of my fathers, and I do not see why I have to lower my head when I can raise it, to give it over to my enemies when I can humble them!"

"Because the field in which you wish to sow is in possession of your enemies and against them you are powerless. It is necessary that you first kiss the hand that —"

But the youth let him go no farther, exclaiming passionately, "Kiss their hands! You forget that among them they killed my father and threw his body from the tomb! I who am his son do not forget it, and that I do not avenge it is because I have regard for the good name of the Church!"

The old Sage bowed his head as he answered slowly: "Señor Ibarra, if you preserve those memories, which I cannot counsel you to forget, abandon the enterprise you are undertaking and seek in some other way the welfare of your countrymen. The enterprise needs another man, because to make it a success zeal and money alone are not sufficient; in our country are required also self-denial, tenacity of purpose, and faith, for the soil is not ready, it is only sown with discord."

Ibarra appreciated the value of these observations, but still would not be discouraged. The thought of Maria Clara was in his mind and his promise must be fulfilled.

"Does n't your experience suggest any other than this hard means?" he asked in a low voice.

The old man took him by the arm and led him to the window. A fresh breeze, the precursor of the north wind, was blowing, and before their eyes spread out the garden bounded by the wide forest that was a kind of park.

"Why can we not do as that weak stalk laden with flowers and buds does?" asked the Sage, pointing to a beautiful jasmine plant. "The wind blows and shakes it and it bows its head as if to hide its precious load. If the stalk should hold itself erect it would be broken, its flowers would be scattered by the wind, and its buds would be blighted. The wind passes by and the stalk raises itself erect, proud of its treasure, yet who will blame it for having bowed before necessity? There you see that gigantic *kupang,* which majestically waves its light foliage wherein the eagle builds his nest. I brought it from the forest as a weak sapling and braced its stem for months with slender pieces of bamboo. If I had transplanted it large and full of life, it is certain that it would not have lived here, for the wind would have thrown it down before its roots could have fixed themselves in the soil, before it could have become accustomed to its surroundings, and before it could have secured sufficient nourishment for its size and height. So you, transplanted from Europe to this stony soil, may end, if you do not seek support and do not humble yourself. You are among evil conditions, alone,

IN THE HOUSE OF THE SAGE

elevated, the ground shakes, the sky presages a storm, and the top of your family tree has shown that it draws the thunderbolt. It is not courage, but foolhardiness, to fight alone against all that exists. No one censures the pilot who makes for a port at the first gust of the whirlwind. To stoop as the bullet passes is not cowardly — it is worse to defy it only to fall, never to rise again."

"But could this sacrifice produce the fruit that I hope for?" asked Ibarra. "Would the priest believe in me and forget the affront? Would they aid me frankly in behalf of the education that contests with the conventos the wealth of the country? Can they not pretend friendship, make a show of protection, and yet underneath in the shadows fight it, undermine it, wound it in the heel, in order to weaken it quicker than by attacking it in front? Granted the previous actions which you surmise, anything may be expected!"

The old man remained silent from inability to answer these questions. After meditating for some time, he said: "If such should happen, if the enterprise should fail, you would be consoled by the thought that you had done what was expected of you and thus something would be gained. You would have placed the first stone, you would have sown the seed, and after the storm had spent itself perhaps some grain would have survived the catastrophe to grow and save the species from destruction and to serve afterwards as the seed for the sons of the dead sower. The example may encourage others who are only afraid to begin."

Weighing these reasons, Ibarra realized the situation and saw that with all the old man's pessimism there was a great deal of truth in what he said.

"I believe you!" he exclaimed, pressing the old man's hand. "Not in vain have I looked to you for advice. This very day I'll go and reach an understanding with the curate, who, after all is said, has done me no wrong and who must be good, since all of them are not like the persecutor of my father. I have, besides, to interest him in behalf of that unfortunate madwoman and her sons. I put my trust in God and men!"

After taking leave of the old man he mounted his horse and rode away. As the pessimistic Sage followed him with his gaze, he muttered: "Now let's watch how Destiny will unfold the drama that began in the cemetery." But for once he was greatly mistaken — the drama had begun long before!

CHAPTER XXVI

THE EVE OF THE FIESTA

IT is now the tenth of November, the eve of the fiesta. Emerging from its habitual monotony, the town has given itself over to unwonted activity in house, church, cockpit, and field. Windows are covered with banners and many-hued draperies. All space is filled with noise and music, and the air is saturated with rejoicings.

On little tables with embroidered covers the *dalagas* arrange in bright-hued glass dishes different kinds of sweetmeats made from native fruits. In the yard the hens cackle, the cocks crow, and the hogs grunt, all terrified by this merriment of man. Servants move in and out carrying fancy dishes and silver cutlery. Here there is a quarrel over a broken plate, there they laugh at the simple country girl. Everywhere there is ordering, whispering, shouting. Comments and conjectures are made, one hurries the other, — all is commotion, noise, and confusion. All this effort and all this toil are for the stranger as well as the acquaintance, to entertain every one, whether he has been seen before or not, or whether he is expected to be seen again, in order that the casual visitor, the foreigner, friend, enemy, Filipino, Spaniard, the poor and the rich, may go away happy and contented. No gratitude is even asked of them nor is it expected that they do no damage to the hospitable family either during or after digestion! The rich, those who have ever been to Manila and have seen a little more than their neighbors, have bought beer, champagne, liqueurs, wines, and food-stuffs from Europe, of which they will hardly taste a bite or drink a drop.

Their tables are luxuriously furnished. In the center

is a well-modeled artificial pineapple in which are arranged toothpicks elaborately carved by convicts in their rest-hours. Here they have designed a fan, there a bouquet of flowers, a bird, a rose, a palm leaf, or a chain, all wrought from a single piece of wood, the artisan being a forced laborer, the tool a dull knife, and the taskmaster's voice the inspiration. Around this toothpick-holder are placed glass fruit-trays from which rise pyramids of oranges, lansons, ates, chicos, and even mangos in spite of the fact that it is November. On wide platters upon bright-hued sheets of perforated paper are to be seen hams from Europe and China, stuffed turkeys, and a big pastry in the shape of an Agnus Dei or a dove, the Holy Ghost perhaps. Among all these are jars of appetizing *acharas* with fanciful decorations made from the flowers of the areca palm and other fruits and vegetables, all tastefully cut and fastened with sirup to the sides of the flasks.

Glass lamp globes that have been handed down from father to son are cleaned, the copper ornaments polished, the kerosene lamps taken out of the red wrappings which have protected them from the flies and mosquitoes during the year and which have made them unserviceable; the prismatic glass pendants shake to and fro, they clink together harmoniously in song, and even seem to take part in the fiesta as they flash back and break up the rays of light, reflecting them on the white walls in all the colors of the rainbow. The children play about amusing themselves by chasing the colors, they stumble and break the globes, but this does not interfere with the general merriment, although at other times in the year the tears in their round eyes would be taken account of in a different way.

Along with these venerated lamps there also come forth from their hiding-places the work of the girls: crocheted scarfs, rugs, artificial flowers. There appear old glass trays, on the bottoms of which are sketched miniature lakes with little fishes, caymans, shell-fish, seaweeds, coral, and glassy stones of brilliant hues. These are heaped

THE EVE OF THE FIESTA

with cigars, cigarettes, and diminutive buyos prepared by the delicate fingers of the maidens. The floor of the house shines like a mirror, curtains of piña and husi festoon the doorways, from the windows hang lanterns covered with glass or with paper, pink, blue, green, or red. The house itself is filled with plants and flower-pots on stands of Chinese porcelain. Even the saints bedeck themselves, the images and relics put on a festive air, the dust is brushed from them and on the freshly-washed glass of their cases are hung flowery garlands.

In the streets are raised at intervals fanciful bamboo arches, known as *sinkában,* constructed in various ways and adorned with *kaluskús,* the curling bunches of shavings scraped on their sides, at the sight of which alone the hearts of the children rejoice. About the front of the church, where the procession is to pass, is a large and costly canopy upheld on bamboo posts. Beneath this the children run and play, climbing, jumping, and tearing the new camisas in which they should shine on the principal day of the fiesta.

There on the plaza a platform has been erected, the scenery being of bamboo, nipa, and wood; there the Tondo comedians will perform wonders and compete with the gods in improbable miracles, there will sing and dance Marianito, Chananay, Balbino, Ratia, Carvajal, Yeyeng, Liceria, etc. The Filipino enjoys the theater and is a deeply interested spectator of dramatic representations, but he listens in silence to the song, he gazes delighted at the dancing and mimicry, he never hisses or applauds. If the show is not to his liking, he chews his buyo or withdraws without disturbing the others who perhaps find pleasure in it. Only at times the commoner sort will howl when the actors embrace or kiss the actresses, but they never go beyond that. Formerly, dramas only were played; the local poet composed a piece in which there must necessarily be a fight every second minute, a clown, and terrifying transformations. But since the Tondo artists have begun to fight every fifteen seconds, with two clowns, and even greater marvels than before, they have put to rout their provincial compeers. The gobernadorcillo was very fond of this sort of thing, so, with the approval of the curate, he chose a spectacle with magic and fireworks, entitled, "The Prince Villardo or the Captives Rescued from the Infamous Cave."[1]

From time to time the bells chime out merrily, those same bells that ten days ago were tolling so mournfully. Pin-wheels and mortars rend the air, for the Filipino pyrotechnist, who learned the art from no known instructor, displays his ability by preparing fire bulls, castles of Bengal lights, paper balloons inflated with hot air, bombs, rockets, and the like.

Now distant strains of music are heard and the small boys rush headlong toward the outskirts of the town to meet the bands of music, five of which have been engaged, as well as three orchestras. The band of Pagsanhan belonging to the escribano must not be lacking nor that of San Pedro de Tunasan, at that time famous because it was directed by the maestro Austria, the vagabond "Corporal Mariano" who, according to report, carried fame and harmony in the tip of his baton. Musicians praise his funeral march, "El Sauce,"[2] and deplore his lack of musical education, since with his genius he might have brought glory to his country. The bands enter the town playing lively airs, followed by ragged or half-naked urchins, one in the camisa of his brother, another in his father's pantaloons. As soon as the band ceases, the boys know the piece by heart, they hum and whistle it with rare skill, they pronounce their judgment upon it.

[1] These spectacular performances, known as "Moro-Moro," often continued for several days, consisting principally of noisy combats between Moros and Christians, in which the latter were, of course, invariably victorious. Typical sketches of them may be found in Foreman's *The Philippine Islands*, Chap. XXIII, and Stuntz's *The Philippines and the Far East*, Chap. III. — TR.
[2] "The Willow."

THE EVE OF THE FIESTA 205

Meanwhile, there are arriving in conveyances of all kinds relatives, friends, strangers, the gamblers with their best game-cocks and their bags of gold, ready to risk their fortune on the green cloth or within the arena of the cockpit.

"The alferez has fifty pesos for each night," murmurs a small, chubby individual into the ears of the latest arrivals. "Capitan Tiago's coming and will set up a bank; Capitan Joaquin's bringing eighteen thousand. There'll be *liam-pó:* Carlos the Chinaman will set it up with ten thousand. Big stakes are coming from Tanawan, Lipa, and Batangas, as well as from Santa Cruz.[1] It's going to be on a big scale, yes, sir, on a grand scale! But have some chocolate! This year Capitan Tiago won't break us as he did last, since he's paid for only three thanksgiving masses and I've got a cacao *mutyâ*. And how's your family?"

"Well, thank you," the visitors respond, "and Padre Damaso?"

"Padre Damaso will preach in the morning and sit in with us at night."

"Good enough! Then there's no danger."

"Sure, we're sure! Carlos the Chinaman will loosen up also." Here the chubby individual works his fingers as though counting out pieces of money.

Outside the town the hill-folk, the *kasamá*, are putting on their best clothes to carry to the houses of their landlords well-fattened chickens, wild pigs, deer, and birds. Some load firewood on the heavy carts, others fruits, ferns, and orchids, the rarest that grow in the forests, others bring broad-leafed caladiums and flame-colored *tikas-tikas* blossoms to decorate the doors of the houses.

But the place where the greatest activity reigns, where it is converted into a tumult, is there on a little plot of

---

[1] The capital of Laguna Province, not to be confused with the Santa Cruz mentioned before, which is a populous and important district in the city of Manila. Tanawan, Lipa, and Batangas are towns in Batangas Province, the latter being its capital. — TR.

raised ground, a few steps from Ibarra's house. Pulleys screech and yells are heard amid the metallic sound of iron striking upon stone, hammers upon nails, of axes chopping out posts. A crowd of laborers is digging in the earth to open a wide, deep trench, while others place in line the stones taken from the town quarries. Carts are unloaded, piles of sand are heaped up, windlasses and derricks are set in place.

"Hey, you there! Hurry up!" cries a little old man with lively and intelligent features, who has for a cane a copper-bound rule around which is wound the cord of a plumb-bob. This is the foreman of the work, Ñor Juan, architect, mason, carpenter, painter, locksmith, stonecutter, and, on occasions, sculptor. "It must be finished right now! Tomorrow there'll be no work and the day after tomorrow is the ceremony. Hurry!"

"Cut that hole so that this cylinder will fit it exactly," he says to some masons who are shaping a large square block of stone. "Within that our names will be preserved."

He repeats to every newcomer who approaches the place what he has already said a thousand times: "You know what we're going to build? Well, it's a schoolhouse, a model of its kind, like those in Germany, and even better. A great architect has drawn the plans, and I — I am bossing the job! Yes, sir, look at it, it's going to be a palace with two wings, one for the boys and the other for the girls. Here in the middle a big garden with three fountains, there on the sides shaded walks with little plots for the children to sow and cultivate plants in during their recess-time, that they may improve the hours and not waste them. Look how deep the foundations are, three meters and seventy-five centimeters! This building is going to have storerooms, cellars, and for those who are not diligent students dungeons near the playgrounds so that the culprits may hear how the studious children are enjoying themselves. Do you see that big space? That will be a lawn for running and exercising in the open air. The little girls will have a garden with benches, swings, walks where they can jump the rope, fountains, bird-cages, and so on. It's going to be magnificent!"

Then Ñor Juan would rub his hands together as he thought of the fame that he was going to acquire. Strangers would come to see it and would ask, "Who was the great artisan that built this?" and all would answer, "Don't you know? Can it be that you've never heard of Ñor Juan? Undoubtedly you've come from a great distance!" With these thoughts he moved from one part to the other, examining and reexamining everything.

"It seems to me that there's too much timber for one derrick," he remarked to a yellowish man who was overseeing some laborers. "I should have enough with three large beams for the tripod and three more for the braces."

"Never mind!" answered the yellowish man, smiling in a peculiar way. "The more apparatus we use in the work, so much the greater effect we'll get. The whole thing will look better and of more importance, so they'll say, 'How hard they've worked!' You'll see, you'll see what a derrick I'll put up! Then I'll decorate it with banners, and garlands of leaves and flowers. You'll say afterwards that you were right in hiring me as one of your laborers, and Señor Ibarra couldn't ask for more!" As he said this the man laughed and smiled. Ñor Juan also smiled, but shook his head.

Some distance away were seen two kiosks united by a kind of arbor covered with banana leaves. The schoolmaster and some thirty boys were weaving crowns and fastening banners upon the frail bamboo posts, which were wrapped in white cloth.

"Take care that the letters are well written," he admonished the boys who were preparing inscriptions. "The alcalde is coming, many curates will be present, perhaps even the Captain-General, who is now in the province. If they see that you draw well, maybe they'll praise you."

"And give us a blackboard?"

"Perhaps, but Señor Ibarra has already ordered one from Manila. Tomorrow some things will come to be distributed among you as prizes. Leave those flowers in the water and tomorrow we'll make the bouquets. Bring more flowers, for it's necessary that the table be covered with them — flowers please the eye."

"My father will bring some water-lilies and a basket of sampaguitas tomorrow."

"Mine has brought three cartloads of sand without pay."

"My uncle has promised to pay a teacher," added a nephew of Capitan Basilio.

Truly, the project was receiving help from all. The curate had asked to stand sponsor for it and himself bless the laying of the corner-stone, a ceremony to take place on the last day of the fiesta as one of its greatest solemnities. The very coadjutor had timidly approached Ibarra with an offer of all the fees for masses that the devout would pay until the building was finished. Even more, the rich and economical Sister Rufa had declared that if money should be lacking she would canvass other towns and beg for alms, with the mere condition that she be paid her expenses for travel and subsistence. Ibarra thanked them all, as he answered, "We aren't going to have anything very great, since I am not rich and this building is not a church. Besides, I didn't undertake to erect it at the expense of others."

The younger men, students from Manila, who had come to take part in the fiesta, gazed at him in admiration and took him for a model; but, as it nearly always happens, when we wish to imitate great men, that we copy only their foibles and even their defects, since we are capable of nothing else, so many of these admirers took note of the way in which he tied his cravat, others of the style of his collar, and not a few of the number of buttons on his coat and vest.

THE EVE OF THE FIESTA

The funereal presentiments of old Tasio seemed to have been dissipated forever. So Ibarra observed to him one day, but the old pessimist answered: "Remember what Baltazar says:

> Kung ang isalúbong sa iyong pagdating
> Ay masayang maukha't may pakitang giliw,
> Lalong pag-iñgata't kaaway na lihim [1]

Baltazar was no less a thinker than a poet."

Thus in the gathering shadows before the setting of the sun events were shaping themselves.

---

[1] "If on your return you are met with a smile, beware! for it means that you have a secret enemy." — From the *Florante*, being the advice given to the hero by his old teacher when he set out to return to his home.

Francisco Baltazar was a Tagalog poet, native of the province of Bulacan, born about 1788, and died in 1862. The greater part of his life was spent in Manila, — in Tondo and in Pandakan, a quaint little village on the south bank of the Pasig, now included in the city, — where he appears to have shared the fate largely of poets of other lands, from suffering "the pangs of disprized love" and persecution by the religious authorities, to seeing himself considered by the people about him as a crack-brained dreamer. He was educated in the Dominican school of San Juan de Letran, one of his teachers being Fray Mariano Pilapil, about whose services to humanity there may be some difference of opinion on the part of those who have ever resided in Philippine towns, since he was the author of the "Passion Song" which enlivens the Lenten evenings. This "Passion Song," however, seems to have furnished the model for Baltazar's *Florante*, with the pupil surpassing the master, for while it has the subject and characters of a medieval European romance, the spirit and settings are entirely Malay. It is written in the peculiar Tagalog verse, in the form of a *corrido* or metrical romance, and has been declared by Fray Toribio Menguella, Rizal himself, and others familiar with Tagalog, to be a work of no mean order, by far the finest and most characteristic composition in that, the richest of the Malay dialects. — TR.

CHAPTER XXVII

IN THE TWILIGHT

IN Capitan Tiago's house also great preparations had been made. We know its owner, whose love of ostentation and whose pride as a Manilan imposed the necessity of humiliating the provincials with his splendor. Another reason, too, made it his duty to eclipse all others: he had his daughter Maria Clara with him, and there was present his future son-in-law, who was attracting universal attention.

In fact one of the most serious newspapers in Manila had devoted to Ibarra an article on its front page, entitled, "Imitate him!" heaping him with praise and giving him some advice. It had called him, "The cultivated young gentleman and rich capitalist;" two lines further on, "The distinguished philanthropist;" in the following paragraph, "The disciple of Minerva who had gone to the mother country to pay his respects to the true home of the arts and sciences;" and a little further on, "The Filipino Spaniard." Capitan Tiago burned with generous zeal to imitate him and wondered whether he ought not to erect a convento at his own expense.

Some days before there had arrived at the house where Maria Clara and Aunt Isabel were staying a profusion of cases of European wines and food-stuffs, colossal mirrors, paintings, and Maria Clara's piano. Capitan Tiago had arrived on the day before the fiesta and as his daughter kissed his hand, had presented her with a beautiful locket set with diamonds and emeralds, containing a sliver from St. Peter's boat, in which Our Savior sat during the fishing.

His first interview with his future son-in-law could not

IN THE TWILIGHT

have been more cordial. Naturally, they talked about the school, and Capitan Tiago wanted it named "School of St. Francis." "Believe me," he said, "St. Francis is a good patron. If you call it 'School of Primary Instruction,' you will gain nothing. Who is Primary Instruction, anyhow?"

Some friends of Maria Clara came and asked her to go for a walk. "But come back quickly," said Capitan Tiago to his daughter, when she asked his permission, "for you know that Padre Damaso, who has just arrived, will dine with us."

Then turning to Ibarra, who had become thoughtful, he said, "You dine with us also, you'll be all alone in your house."

"I would with the greatest pleasure, but I have to be at home in case visitors come," stammered the youth, as he avoided the gaze of Maria Clara.

"Bring your friends along," replied Capitan Tiago heartily. "In my house there's always plenty to eat. Also, I want you and Padre Damaso to get on good terms."

"There'll be time enough for that," answered Ibarra with a forced smile, as he prepared to accompany the girls.

They went downstairs, Maria Clara in the center between Victoria and Iday, Aunt Isabel following. The people made way for them respectfully. Maria Clara was startling in her beauty; her pallor was all gone, and if her eyes were still pensive, her mouth on the contrary seemed to know only smiles. With maiden friendliness the happy young woman greeted the acquaintances of her childhood, now the admirers of her promising youth. In less than a fortnight she had succeeded in recovering that frank confidence, that childish prattle, which seemed to have been benumbed between the narrow walls of the nunnery. It might be said that on leaving the cocoon the butterfly recognized all the flowers, for it seemed to be enough for her to spread her wings for a moment and warm herself in the sun's rays to lose all the stiffness of the chrysalis. This new life manifested itself in her whole nature. Everything she found good and beautiful, and she showed her love with that maiden modesty which, having never been conscious of any but pure thoughts, knows not the meaning of false blushes. While she would cover her face when she was teased, still her eyes smiled, and a light thrill would course through her whole being.

The houses were beginning to show lights, and in the streets where the music was moving about there were lighted torches of bamboo and wood made in imitation of those in the church. From the streets the people in the houses might be seen through the windows in an atmosphere of music and flowers, moving about to the sounds of piano, harp, or orchestra. Swarming in the streets were Chinese, Spaniards, Filipinos, some dressed in European style, some in the costumes of the country. Crowding, elbowing, and pushing one another, walked servants carrying meat and chickens, students in white, men and women, all exposing themselves to be knocked down by the carriages which, in spite of the drivers' cries, made their way with difficulty.

In front of Capitan Basilio's house some young women called to our acquaintances and invited them to enter. The merry voice of Sinang as she ran down the stairs put an end to all excuses. "Come up a moment so that I may go with you," she said. "I'm bored staying here among so many strangers who talk only of game-cocks and cards."

They were ushered into a large room filled with people, some of whom came forward to greet Ibarra, for his name was now well known. All gazed in ecstasy at the beauty of Maria Clara and some old women murmured, as they chewed their buyo, "She looks like the Virgin!"

There they had to have chocolate, as Capitan Basilio had become a warm friend and defender of Ibarra since the day of the picnic. He had learned from the half of the telegram given to his daughter Sinang that Ibarra had known beforehand about the court's decision in the latter's favor, so, not wishing to be outdone in generosity, he had tried to set aside the decision of the chess-match. But when Ibarra would not consent to this, he had proposed that the money which would have been spent in court fees should be used to pay a teacher in the new school. In consequence, the orator employed all his eloquence to the end that other litigants should give up their extravagant claims, saying to them, " Believe me, in a lawsuit the winner is left without a camisa." But he had succeeded in convincing no one, even though he cited the Romans.

After drinking the chocolate our young people had to listen to piano-playing by the town organist. " When I listen to him in the church," exclaimed Sinang, pointing to the organist, " I want to dance, and now that he's playing here I feel like praying, so I 'm going out with you."

" Don't you want to join us tonight?" whispered Capitan Basilio into Ibarra's ear as they were leaving. " Padre Damaso is going to set up a little bank." Ibarra smiled and answered with an equivocal shake of his head.

" Who's that?" asked Maria Clara of Victoria, indicating with a rapid glance a youth who was following them.

" He's — he's a cousin of mine," she answered with some agitation.

" And the other?"

" He's no cousin of mine," put in Sinang merrily. " He's my uncle's son."

They passed in front of the parish rectory, which was not one of the least animated buildings. Sinang was unable to repress an exclamation of surprise on seeing the lamps burning, those lamps of antique pattern which Padre Salvi had never allowed to be lighted, in order not to waste kerosene. Loud talk and resounding bursts of laughter might be heard as the friars moved slowly about, nodding their heads in unison with the big cigars that adorned their lips. The laymen with them, who from their European garments appeared to be officials and employees of the province, were endeavoring to imitate whatever the good priests did. Maria Clara made out the rotund figure of Padre Damaso at the side of the trim silhouette of Padre Sibyla. Motionless in his place stood the silent and mysterious Fray Salvi.

"He's sad," observed Sinang, "for he's thinking about how much so many visitors are going to cost. But you'll see how he'll not pay it himself, but the sacristans will. His visitors always eat at other places."

"Sinang!" scolded Victoria.

"I haven't been able to endure him since he tore up the *Wheel of Fortune*. I don't go to confession to him any more."

Of all the houses one only was to be noticed without lights and with all the windows closed — that of the alferez. Maria Clara expressed surprise at this.

"The witch! The Muse of the Civil Guard, as the old man says," exclaimed the irrepressible Sinang. "What has she to do with our merrymakings? I imagine she's raging! But just let the cholera come and you'd see her give a banquet."

"But, Sinang!" again her cousin scolded.

"I never was able to endure her and especially since she disturbed our picnic with her civil-guards. If I were the Archbishop I'd marry her to Padre Salvi — then think what children! Look how she tried to arrest the poor pilot, who threw himself into the water simply to please —"

She was not allowed to finish, for in the corner of the plaza where a blind man was singing to the accompaniment of a guitar, a curious spectacle was presented. It was a man miserably dressed, wearing a broad salakot of palm leaves. His clothing consisted of a ragged coat and wide pantaloons, like those worn by the Chinese, torn in many places. Wretched sandals covered his feet. His countenance remained hidden in the shadow of his wide hat, but from this shadow there flashed intermittently two burning rays. Placing a flat basket on the ground, he would withdraw a few paces and utter strange, incomprehensible sounds, remaining the while standing entirely alone as if he and the crowd were mutually avoiding each other. Then some women would approach the basket and put into it fruit, fish, or rice. When no one any longer approached, from the shadows would issue sadder but less pitiful sounds, cries of gratitude perhaps. Then he would take up the basket and make his way to another place to repeat the same performance.

Maria Clara divined that there must be some misfortune there, and full of interest she asked concerning the strange creature.

"He's a leper," Iday told her. "Four years ago he contracted the disease, some say from taking care of his mother, others from lying in a damp prison. He lives in the fields near the Chinese cemetery, having intercourse with no one, because all flee from him for fear of contagion. If you might only see his home! It's a tumble-down shack, through which the wind and rain pass like a needle through cloth. He has been forbidden to touch anything belonging to the people. One day when a little child fell into a shallow ditch as he was passing, he helped to get it out. The child's father complained to the gobernadorcillo, who ordered that the leper be flogged through the streets and that the rattan be burned afterwards. It was horrible! The leper fled with his flogger in pursuit, while the gobernadorcillo cried, 'Catch him! Better be drowned than get the disease you have!'"

"Can it be true!" murmured Maria Clara, then, without saying what she was about to do, went up to the wretch's basket and dropped into it the locket her father had given her.

"What have you done?" her friends asked.

"I hadn't anything else," she answered, trying to conceal her tears with a smile.

"What is he going to do with your locket?" Victoria asked her. "One day they gave him some money, but he pushed it away with a stick; why should he want it when no one accepts anything that comes from him? As if the locket could be eaten!"

Maria Clara gazed enviously at the women who were selling food-stuffs and shrugged her shoulders. The leper approached the basket, picked up the jeweled locket, which glittered in his hands, then fell upon his knees, kissed it, and taking off his salakot buried his forehead in the dust where the maiden had stepped. Maria Clara hid her face behind her fan and raised her handkerchief to her eyes.

Meanwhile, a poor woman had approached the leper, who seemed to be praying. Her long hair was loose and unkempt, and in the light of the torches could be recognized the extremely emaciated features of the crazy Sisa. Feeling the touch of her hand, the leper jumped up with a cry, but to the horror of the onlookers Sisa caught him by the arm and said:

"Let us pray, let us pray! Today is All Souls' day! Those lights are the souls of men! Let us pray for my sons!"

"Separate them! Separate them! The madwoman will get the disease!" cried the crowd, but no one dared to go near them.

"Do you see that light in the tower? That is my son Basilio sliding down a rope! Do you see that light in the convento? That is my son Crispin! But I'm not going to see them because the curate is sick and had many gold pieces and the gold pieces are lost! Pray, let us pray for the soul of the curate! I took him the finest fruits, for my garden was full of flowers and I had two sons! I had a garden, I used to take care of my flowers, and I had two sons!"

Then releasing her hold of the leper, she ran away singing, "I had a garden and flowers, I had two sons, a garden, and flowers!"

"What have you been able to do for that poor woman?" Maria Clara asked Ibarra.

"Nothing! Lately she has been missing from the town and was n't to be found," answered the youth, rather confusedly. "Besides, I have been very busy. But don't let it trouble you. The curate has promised to help me, but advised that I proceed with great tact and caution, for the Civil Guard seems to be mixed up in it. The curate is greatly interested in her case."

"Did n't the alferez say that he would have search made for her sons?"

"Yes, but at the time he was somewhat — drunk.'

Scarcely had he said this when they saw the crazy woman being led, or rather dragged along, by a soldier. Sisa was offering resistance.

"Why are you arresting her? What has she done?" asked Ibarra.

"Why, have n't you seen how she's been raising a disturbance?" was the reply of the guardian of the public peace.

The leper caught up his basket hurriedly and ran away.

Maria Clara wanted to go home, as she had lost all her mirth and good humor. "So there are people who are not happy," she murmured. Arriving at her door, she felt her sadness increase when her fiancé declined to go in, excusing himself on the plea of necessity. Maria Clara went upstairs thinking what a bore are the fiesta days, when strangers make their visits.

CHAPTER XXVIII

CORRESPONDENCE

Cada uno habla de la feria como le va en ella.[1]

AS nothing of importance to our characters happened during the first two days, we should gladly pass on to the third and last, were it not that perhaps some foreign reader may wish to know how the Filipinos celebrate their fiestas. For this reason we shall faithfully reproduce in this chapter several letters, one of them being that of the correspondent of a noted Manila newspaper, respected for its grave tone and deep seriousness. Our readers will correct some natural and trifling slips of the pen. Thus the worthy correspondent of the respectable newspaper wrote:

"To the Editor, my distinguished Friend, — Never did I witness, nor had I ever expected to see in the provinces, a religious fiesta so solemn, so splendid, and so impressive as that now being celebrated in this town by the Most Reverend and virtuous Franciscan Fathers.

"Great crowds are in attendance. I have here had the pleasure of greeting nearly all the Spaniards who reside in this province, three Reverend Augustinian Fathers from the province of Batangas, and two Reverend Dominican Fathers. One of the latter is the Very Reverend Fray Hernando Sibyla, who has come to honor this town with his presence, a distinction which its worthy inhabitants should never forget. I have also seen a great number of the best people of Cavite and Pampanga, many wealthy persons from Manila, and many bands of music, — among these the very artistic one of Pagsanhan belonging to the escribano, Don Miguel Guevara, — swarms of Chinamen

---

[1] Every one talks of the fiesta according to the way he fared at it.

and Indians, who, with the curiosity of the former and the piety of the latter, awaited anxiously the day on which was to be celebrated the comic-mimic-lyric-lightning-change-dramatic spectacle, for which a large and spacious- theater had been erected in the middle of the plaza.

"At nine on the night of the 10th, the eve of the fiesta, after a succulent dinner set before us by the *hermano mayor*, the attention of all the Spaniards and friars in the convento was attracted by strains of music from a surging multitude which, with the noise of bombs and rockets, preceded by the leading citizens of the town, came to the convento to escort us to the place prepared and arranged for us that we might witness the spectacle. Such a courteous offer we had to accept, although I should have preferred to rest in the arms of Morpheus and repose my weary limbs, which were aching, thanks to the joltings of the vehicle furnished us by the gobernadorcillo of B——.

"Accordingly we joined them and proceeded to look for our companions, who were dining in the house owned here by the pious and wealthy Don Santiago de los Santos. The curate of the town, the Very Reverend Fray Bernardo Salvi, and the Very Reverend Fray Damaso Verdolagas, who is now by the special favor of Heaven recovered from the suffering caused him by an impious hand, in company with the Very Reverend Fray Hernando Sibyla and the virtuous curate of Tanawan, with other Spaniards, were guests in the house of the Filipino Croesus. There we had the good fortune of admiring not only the luxury and good taste of the host, which are not usual among the natives, but also the beauty of the charming and wealthy heiress, who showed herself to be a polished disciple of St. Cecelia by playing on her elegant piano, with a mastery that recalled Galvez to me, the best German and Italian compositions. It is a matter of regret that such a charming young lady should be so excessively modest as to hide her talents from a society which has only admiration for her. Nor should I leave unwritten that in the house of our host there were set before us champagne and fine liqueurs with the profusion and splendor that characterize the well-known capitalist.

"We attended the spectacle. You already know our artists, Ratia, Carvajal, and Fernandez, whose cleverness was comprehended by us alone, since the uncultured crowd did not understand a jot of it. Chananay and Balbino were very good, though a little hoarse; the latter made one break, but together, and as regards earnest effort, they were admirable. The Indians were greatly pleased with the Tagalog drama, especially the gobernadorcillo, who rubbed his hands and informed us that it was a pity that they had not made the princess join in combat with the giant who had stolen her away, which in his opinion would have been more marvelous, especially if the giant had been represented as vulnerable only in the navel, like a certain Ferragus of whom the stories of the Paladins tell. The Very Reverend Fray Damaso, in his customary goodness of heart, concurred in this opinion, and added that in such case the princess should be made to discover the giant's weak spot and give him the *coup de grâce*.

"Needless to tell you that during the show the affability of the Filipino Rothschild allowed nothing to be lacking: ice-cream, lemonade, wines, and refreshments of all kinds circulated profusely among us. A matter of reasonable and special note was the absence of the well-known and cultured youth, Don Juan Crisostomo Ibarra, who, as you know, will tomorrow preside at the laying of the corner-stone for the great edifice which he is so philanthropically erecting. This worthy descendant of the Pelayos and Elcanos (for I have learned that one of his paternal ancestors was from our heroic and noble northern provinces, perhaps one of the companions of Magellan or Legazpi) did not show himself during the entire day, owing to a slight indisposition. His name runs from mouth to mouth, being uttered with praises that can only reflect glory upon Spain and true Spaniards like ourselves, who never deny our blood, however mixed it may be.

"Today, at eleven o'clock in the morning, we attended a deeply-moving spectacle. Today, as is generally known, is the fiesta of the Virgin of Peace and is being observed by the Brethren of the Holy Rosary. Tomorrow will occur the fiesta of the patron, San Diego, and it will be observed principally by the Venerable Tertiary Order. Between these two societies there exists a pious rivalry in serving God, which piety has reached the extreme of holy quarrels among them, as has just happened in the dispute over the preacher of acknowledged fame, the oft-mentioned Very Reverend Fray Damaso, who tomorrow will occupy the pulpit of the Holy Ghost with a sermon, which, according to general expectation, will be a literary and religious event.

"So, *as we were saying,* we attended a highly edifying and moving spectacle. Six pious youths, three to recite the mass and three for acolytes, marched out of the sacristy and prostrated themselves before the altar, while the officiating priest, the Very Reverend Fray Hernando Sibyla, chanted the *Surge Domine* — the signal for commencing the procession around the church — with the magnificent voice and religious unction that all recognize and that make him so worthy of general admiration. When the *Surge Domine* was concluded, the gobernadorcillo, in a frock coat, carrying the standard and followed by four acolytes with incense-burners, headed the procession. Behind them came the tall silver candelabra, the municipal corporation, the precious images dressed in satin and gold, representing St. Dominic and the Virgin of Peace in a magnificent blue robe trimmed with gilded silver, the gift of the pious ex-gobernadorcillo, the so-worthy-of-being-imitated and never-sufficiently-praised Don Santiago de los Santos. All these images were borne on silver cars. Behind the Mother of God came the Spaniards and the rest of the clergy, while the officiating priest was protected by a canopy carried by the cabezas de barangay, and the procession was closed by a squad of the worthy Civil Guard. I believe it unnecessary to state that a multitude of Indians, carrying lighted candles with great devotion, formed the two lines of the procession. The musicians played religious marches, while bombs and pinwheels furnished repeated salutes. It causes admiration to see the modesty and the fervor which these ceremonies inspire in the hearts of the true believers, the grand, pure faith professed for the Virgin of Peace, the solemnity and fervent devotion with which such ceremonies are performed by those of us who have had the good fortune to be born under the sacrosanct and immaculate banner of Spain.

"The procession concluded, there began the mass rendered by the orchestra and the theatrical artists. After the reading of the Gospel, the Very Reverend Fray Manuel Martin, an Augustinian from the province of Batangas, ascended the pulpit and kept the whole audience enraptured and hanging on his words, especially the Spaniards, during the exordium in Castilian, as he spoke with vigor and in such flowing and well-rounded periods that our hearts were filled with fervor and enthusiasm. This indeed is the term that should be used for what is felt, or what we feel, when the Virgin of our beloved Spain is considered, and above all when there can be intercalated in the text, if the subject permits, the ideas of a prince of the Church, the *Señor Monescillo*,[1] which are surely those of all Spaniards.

"At the conclusion of the services all of us went up into the convento with the leading citizens of the town and other persons of note. There we were especially honored by the refinement, attention, and prodigality that characterize the Very Reverend Fray Salvi, there being set before us cigars and an abundant lunch which the *hermano mayor* had prepared under the convento for all who might feel the necessity for appeasing the cravings of their stomachs.

"During the day nothing has been lacking to make the fiesta joyous and to preserve the animation so characteristic of Spaniards, and which it is impossible to restrain on such occasions as this, showing itself sometimes in singing and dancing, at other times in simple and merry diversions of so strong and noble a nature that all sorrow is driven away, and it is enough for three Spaniards to be gathered together in one place in order that sadness and ill-humor be banished thence. Then homage was paid to Terpsichore in many homes, but especially in that of the cultured Filipino millionaire, where we were all invited to dine. Needless to say, the banquet, which was sumptuous and elegantly served, was a second edition of the wedding-feast in Cana, or of Camacho,[2] corrected and enlarged. While we were enjoying the meal, which was directed by a cook from "La Campana," an orchestra played harmonious melodies. The beautiful young lady of the house, in a mestiza

---

[1] A Spanish prelate, notable for his determined opposition in the Constituent Cortes of 1869 to the clause in the new Constitution providing for religious liberty. — TR.

[2] "Camacho's wedding" is an episode in *Don Quixote*, wherein a wealthy man named Camacho is cheated out of his bride after he has prepared a magnificent wedding-feast. — TR.

gown¹ and a cascade of diamonds, was as ever the queen of the feast. All of us deplored from the bottom of our hearts a light sprain in her shapely foot that deprived her of the pleasures of the dance, for if we have to judge by her other conspicuous perfections, the young lady must dance like a sylph.

"The alcalde of the province arrived this afternoon for the purpose of honoring with his presence the ceremony of tomorrow. He has expressed regret over the poor health of the distinguished landlord, Señor Ibarra, who in God's mercy is now, according to report, somewhat recovered.

"Tonight there was a solemn procession, but of that I will speak in my letter tomorrow, because in addition to the explosions that have bewildered me and made me somewhat deaf I am tired and falling over with sleep. While, therefore, I recover my strength in the arms of Morpheus — or rather on a cot in the convento — I desire for you, my distinguished friend, a pleasant night and take leave of you until tomorrow, which will be the great day.

Your affectionate friend,

THE CORRESPONDENT."

SAN DIEGO, November 11.

Thus wrote the worthy correspondent. Now let us see what Capitan Martin wrote to his friend, Luis Chiquito:

"DEAR CHOY, — Come a-running if you can, for there's something doing at the fiesta. Just imagine, Capitan Joaquin is almost broke. Capitan Tiago has doubled up on him three times and won at the first turn of the cards each time, so that Capitan Manuel, the owner of the house, is growing smaller every minute from sheer joy. Padre Damaso smashed a lamp with his fist because up to now he hasn't won on a single card. The Consul has lost on his cocks and in the bank all

---

¹ The full dress of the Filipino women, consisting of the *camisa*, *pañuelo*, and *saya suelta*, the latter a heavy skirt with a long train. The name *mestiza* is not inappropriate, as well from its composition as its use, since the first two are distinctly native, antedating the conquest, while the *saya suelta* was no doubt introduced by the Spaniards.

that he won from us at the fiesta of Biñan and at that of the Virgin of the Pillar in Santa Cruz.

"We expected Capitan Tiago to bring us his future son-in-law, the rich heir of Don Rafael, but it seems that he wishes to imitate his father, for he does not even show himself. It's a pity, for it seems he never will be any use to us.

"Carlos the Chinaman is making a big fortune with the *liam-pó*. I suspect that he carries something hidden, probably a charm, for he complains constantly of headaches and keeps his head bandaged, and when the wheel of the *liam-pó* is slowing down he leans over, almost touching it, as if he were looking at it closely. I am shocked, because I know more stories of the same kind.

"Good-by, Choy. My birds are well and my wife is happy and having a good time.

Your friend,

MARTIN ARISTORENAS."

Ibarra had received a perfumed note which Andeng, Maria Clara's foster-sister, delivered to him on the evening of the first day of the fiesta. This note said:

"CRISOSTOMO,—It has been over a day since you have shown yourself. I have heard that you are ill and have prayed for you and lighted two candles, although papa says that you are not seriously ill. Last night and today I've been bored by requests to play on the piano and by invitations to dance. I didn't know before that there are so many tiresome people in the world! If it were not for Padre Damaso, who tries to entertain me by talking to me and telling me many things, I would have shut myself up in my room and gone to sleep. Write me what the matter is with you and I'll tell papa to visit you. For the present I send Andeng to make you some tea, as she knows how to prepare it well, probably better than your servants do.

MARIA CLARA."

"P.S. If you don't come tomorrow, I won't go to the ceremony. *Vale!*"

CHAPTER XXIX

THE MORNING

AT the first flush of dawn bands of music awoke the tired people of the town with lively airs. Life and movement reawakened, the bells began to chime, and the explosions commenced. It was the last day of the fiesta, in fact the fiesta proper. Much was hoped for, even more than on the previous day. The Brethren of the Venerable Tertiary Order were more numerous than those of the Holy Rosary, so they smiled piously, secure that they would humiliate their rivals. They had purchased a greater number of tapers, wherefor the Chinese dealers had reaped a harvest and in gratitude were thinking of being baptized, although some remarked that this was not so much on account of their faith in Catholicism as from a desire to get a wife. To this the pious women answered, "Even so, the marriage of so many Chinamen at once would be little short of a miracle and their wives would convert them."

The people arrayed themselves in their best clothes and dragged out from their strong-boxes all their jewelry. The sharpers and gamblers all shone in embroidered camisas with large diamond studs, heavy gold chains, and white straw hats. Only the old Sage went his way as usual in his dark-striped sinamay camisa buttoned up to the neck, loose shoes, and wide gray felt hat.

"You look sadder than ever!" the teniente-mayor accosted him. "Don't you want us to be happy now and then, since we have so much to weep over?"

"To be happy does n't mean to act the fool," answered the old man. "It's the senseless orgy of every year!

And all for no end but to squander money, when there is so much misery and want. Yes, I understand it all, it's the same orgy, the revel to drown the woes of all."

"You know that I share your opinion, though," replied Don Filipo, half jestingly and half in earnest. "I have defended it, but what can one do against the gobernadorcillo and the curate?"

"Resign!" was the old man's curt answer as he moved away.

Don Filipo stood perplexed, staring after the old man. "Resign!" he muttered as he made his way toward the church. "Resign! Yes, if this office were an honor and not a burden, yes, I would resign."

The paved court in front of the church was filled with people; men and women, young and old, dressed in their best clothes, all crowded together, came and went through the wide doors. There was a smell of powder, of flowers, of incense, and of perfumes, while bombs, rockets, and serpent-crackers made the women run and scream, the children laugh. One band played in front of the convento, another escorted the town officials, and still others marched about the streets, where floated and waved a multitude of banners. Variegated colors and lights distracted the sight, melodies and explosions the hearing, while the bells kept up a ceaseless chime. Moving all about were carriages whose horses at times became frightened, frisked and reared — all of which, while not included in the program of the fiesta, formed a show in itself, free and by no means the least entertaining.

The *hermano mayor* for this day had sent servants to seek in the streets for whomsoever they might invite, as did he who gave the feast of which the Gospel tells us. Almost by force were urged invitations to partake of chocolate, coffee, tea, and sweetmeats, these invitations not seldom reaching the proportions of a demand.

There was to be celebrated the high mass, that known as the dalmatic, like the one of the day before, about which

THE MORNING

the worthy correspondent wrote, only that now the officiating priest was to be Padre Salvi, and that the alcalde of the province, with many other Spaniards and persons of note, was to attend it in order to hear Padre Damaso, who enjoyed a great reputation in the province. Even the alferez, smarting under the preachments of Padre Salvi, would also attend in order to give evidence of his good-will and to recompense himself, if possible, for the bad spells the curate had caused him.

Such was the reputation of Padre Damaso that the correspondent wrote beforehand to the editor of his newspaper:

"As was announced in my badly executed account of yesterday, so it has come to pass. We have had the especial pleasure of listening to the Very Reverend Fray Damaso Verdolagas, former curate of this town, recently transferred to a larger parish in recognition of his meritorious services. The illustrious and holy orator occupied the pulpit of the Holy Ghost and preached a most eloquent and profound sermon, which edified and left marveling all the faithful who had waited so anxiously to see spring from his fecund lips the restoring fountain of eternal life. Sublimity of conception, boldness of imagination, novelty of phraseology, gracefulness of style, naturalness of gestures, cleverness of speech, vigor of ideas — these are the traits of the Spanish Bossuet, who has justly earned such a high reputation not only among the enlightened Spaniards but even among the rude Indians and the cunning sons of the Celestial Empire."

But the confiding correspondent almost saw himself obliged to erase what he had written. Padre Damaso complained of a cold that he had contracted the night before, for after singing a few merry songs he had eaten three plates of ice-cream and attended the show for a short time. As a result of all this, he wished to renounce his part as the spokesman of God to men, but as no one else was to be found who was so well versed in the life and miracles of

San Diego, — the curate knew them, it is true, but it was his place to celebrate mass, — the other priests unanimously declared that the tone of Padre Damaso's voice could not be improved upon and that it would be a great pity for him to forego delivering such an eloquent sermon as he had written and memorized. Accordingly, his former housekeeper prepared for him lemonade, rubbed his chest and neck with liniment and olive-oil, massaged him, and wrapped him in warm cloths. He drank some raw eggs beaten up in wine and for the whole morning neither talked nor breakfasted, taking only a glass of milk and a cup of chocolate with a dozen or so of crackers, heroically renouncing his usual fried chicken and half of a Laguna cheese, because the housekeeper affirmed that cheese contained salt and grease, which would aggravate his cough.

"All for the sake of meriting heaven and of converting us!" exclaimed the Tertiary Sisters, much affected, upon being informed of these sacrifices.

"May Our Lady of Peace punish him!" muttered the Sisters of the Holy Rosary, unable to forgive him for leaning to the side of their rivals.

At half past eight the procession started from the shadow of the canvas canopy. It was the same as that of the previous day but for the introduction of one novelty: the older members of the Venerable Tertiary Order and some maidens dressed as old women displayed long gowns, the poor having them of coarse cloth and the rich of silk, or rather of Franciscan *guingón,* as it is called, since it is most used by the reverend Franciscan friars. All these sacred garments were genuine, having come from the convento in Manila, where the people may obtain them as alms at a fixed price, if a commercial term may be permitted; this fixed price was liable to increase but not to reduction. In the convento itself and in the nunnery of St. Clara [1] are

---

[1] The nunnery of St. Clara, situated on the Pasig River just east of Fort Santiago, was founded in 1621 by the Poor Clares, an order of nuns affiliated with the Franciscans, and was taken under the royal

sold these same garments which possess, besides the special
merit of gaining many indulgences for those who may be
shrouded in them, the very special merit of being dearer
in proportion as they are old, threadbare, and unserviceable. We write this in case any pious reader need such
sacred relics — or any cunning rag-picker of Europe wish
to make a fortune by taking to the Philippines a consignment of patched and grimy garments, since they are valued
at sixteen pesos or more, according to their more or less
tattered appearance.

San Diego de Alcala was borne on a float adorned with
plates of repoussé silver. The saint, though rather thin,
had an ivory bust which gave him a severe and majestic
mien, in spite of abundant kingly bangs like those of the
Negrito. His mantle was of satin embroidered with gold.

Our venerable father, St. Francis, followed the Virgin
as on yesterday, except that the priest under the canopy
this time was Padre Salvi and not the graceful Padre
Sibyla, so refined in manner. But if the former lacked a
beautiful carriage he had more than enough unction, walking half bent over with lowered eyes and hands crossed
in mystic attitude. The bearers of the canopy were the
same cabezas de barangay, sweating with satisfaction at
seeing themselves at the same time semi-sacristans, collectors of the tribute, redeemers of poor erring humanity,
and consequently Christs who were giving their blood for
the sins of others. The surpliced coadjutor went from float
to float carrying the censer, with the smoke from which he
from time to time regaled the nostrils of the curate, who
then became even more serious and grave.

So the procession moved forward slowly and deliberately
to the sound of bombs, songs, and religious melodies let
loose into the air by bands of musicians that followed the
floats. Meanwhile, the *hermano mayor* distributed candles

---

patronage as the "Real Monasterio de Santa Clara" in 1662. It is
still in existence and is perhaps the most curious of all the curious
relics of the Middle Ages in old Manila. — TR.

with such zeal that many of the participants returned to their homes with light enough for four nights of card-playing. Devoutly the curious spectators knelt at the passage of the float of the Mother of God, reciting Credos and Salves fervently. In front of a house in whose gaily decorated windows were to be seen the alcalde, Capitan Tiago, Maria Clara, and Ibarra, with various Spaniards and young ladies, the float was detained. Padre Salvi happened to raise his eyes, but made not the slightest movement that might have been taken for a salute or a recognition of them. He merely stood erect, so that his cope fell over his shoulders more gracefully and elegantly.

In the street under the window was a young woman of pleasing countenance, dressed in deep mourning, carrying in her arms a young baby. She must have been a nursemaid only, for the child was white and ruddy while she was brown and had hair blacker than jet. Upon seeing the curate the tender infant held out its arms, laughed with the laugh that neither causes nor is caused by sorrow, and cried out stammeringly in the midst of a brief silence, "Pa-pa! Papa! Papa!" The young woman shuddered, slapped her hand hurriedly over the baby's mouth and ran away in dismay, with the baby crying.

Malicious ones winked at each other, and the Spaniards who had witnessed the short scene smiled, while the natural pallor of Padre Salvi changed to the hue of poppies. Yet the people were wrong, for the curate was not acquainted with the woman at all, she being a stranger in the town.

CHAPTER XXX

IN THE CHURCH

FROM end to end the huge barn that men dedicate as a home to the Creator of all existing things was filled with people. Pushing, crowding, and crushing one another, the few who were leaving and the many who were entering filled the air with exclamations of distress. Even from afar an arm would be stretched out to dip the fingers in the holy water, but at the critical moment the surging crowd would force the hand away. Then would be heard a complaint, a trampled woman would upbraid some one, but the pushing would continue. Some old people might succeed in dipping their fingers in the water, now the color of slime, where the population of a whole town, with transients besides, had washed. With it they would anoint themselves devoutly, although with difficulty, on the neck, on the crown of the head, on the forehead, on the chin, on the chest, and on the abdomen, in the assurance that thus they were sanctifying those parts and that they would suffer neither stiff neck, headache, consumption, nor indigestion. The young people, whether they were not so ailing or did not believe in that holy prophylactic, hardly more than moistened the tip of a finger — and this only in order that the devout might have no cause to talk — and pretended to make the sign of the cross on their foreheads, of course without touching them. "It may be blessed and everything you may wish," some young woman doubtless thought, "but it has such a color!"

It was difficult to breathe in the heat amid the smells of the human animal, but the preacher was worth all these inconveniences, as the sermon was costing the town two hundred and fifty pesos. Old Tasio had said: "Two hundred and fifty pesos for a sermon! One man on one occasion! Only a third of what comedians cost, who will work for three nights! Surely you must be very rich!"

"What has that to do with the drama?" testily inquired the nervous leader of the Tertiary Brethren. "With the drama souls go to hell but with the sermon to heaven! If he had asked a thousand, we would have paid him and should still owe him gratitude."

"After all, you're right," replied the Sage, "for the sermon is more amusing to me at least than the drama."

"But I am not amused even by the drama!" yelled the other furiously.

"I believe it, since you understand one about as well as you do the other!" And the impious old man moved away without paying any attention to the insults and the direful prophecies that the irritated leader offered concerning his future existence.

While they were waiting for the alcalde, the people sweated and yawned, agitating the air with fans, hats, and handkerchiefs. Children shouted and cried, which kept the sacristans busy putting them out of the sacred edifice. Such action brought to the dull and conscientious leader of the Brotherhood of the Holy Rosary this thought: "'Suffer little children to come unto me,' said Our Savior, it is true, but here must be understood, children who do not cry."

An old woman in a *guingón* habit, Sister Puté, chid her granddaughter, a child of six years, who was kneeling at her side, "O lost one, give heed, for you're going to hear a sermon like that of Good Friday!" Here the old lady gave her a pinch to awaken the piety of the child, who made a grimace, stuck out her nose, and wrinkled up her eyebrows.

Some men squatted on their heels and dozed beside the confessional. One old man nodding caused our old woman to believe that he was mumbling prayers, so, running her fingers rapidly over the beads of her rosary — as that was the most reverent way of respecting the designs of Heaven — little by little she set herself to imitating him.

Ibarra stood in one corner while Maria Clara knelt near the high altar in a space which the curate had had the courtesy to order the sacristans to clear for her. Capitan Tiago, in a frock coat, sat on one of the benches provided for the authorities, which caused the children who did not know him to take him for another gobernadorcillo and to be wary about getting near him.

At last the alcalde with his staff arrived, proceeding from the sacristy and taking their seats in magnificent chairs placed on strips of carpet. The alcalde wore a full-dress uniform and displayed the cordon of Carlos III, with four or five other decorations. The people did not recognize him.

"*Abá!*" exclaimed a rustic. "A civil-guard dressed as a comedian!"

"Fool!" rejoined a bystander, nudging him with his elbow. "It's the Prince Villardo that we saw at the show last night!"

So the alcalde went up several degrees in the popular estimation by becoming an enchanted prince, a vanquisher of giants.

When the mass began, those who were seated arose and those who had been asleep were awakened by the ringing of the bells and the sonorous voices of the singers. Padre Salvi, in spite of his gravity, wore a look of deep satisfaction, since there were serving him as deacon and subdeacon none less than two Augustinians. Each one, as it came his turn, sang well, in a more or less nasal tone and with unintelligible articulation, except the officiating priest himself, whose voice trembled somewhat, even getting out of tune at times, to the great wonder of those who knew him. Still he moved about with precision and elegance while he recited the *Dominus vobiscum* unctuously, dropping his head a little to the side and gazing toward heaven. Seeing him receive the smoke from the incense one would have said that Galen was right in averring the passage of smoke in the nasal canals to the head through a screen of ethmoids, since he straightened himself, threw his head back, and moved toward the middle of the altar with such pompousness and gravity that Capitan Tiago found him more majestic than the Chinese comedian of the night before, even though the latter had been dressed as an emperor, paint-bedaubed, with beribboned sword, stiff beard like a horse's mane, and high-soled slippers. "Undoubtedly," so his thoughts ran, "a single curate of ours has more majesty than all the emperors."

At length came the expected moment, that of hearing Padre Damaso. The three priests seated themselves in their chairs in an edifying attitude, as the worthy correspondent would say, the alcalde and other persons of place and position following their example. The music ceased.

The sudden transition from noise to silence awoke our aged Sister Puté, who was already snoring under cover of the music. Like Segismundo,[1] or like the cook in the story of the Sleeping Beauty, the first thing that she did upon awaking was to whack her granddaughter on the neck, as the child had also fallen asleep. The latter screamed, but soon consoled herself at the sight of a woman who was beating her breast with contrition and enthusiasm. All tried to place themselves comfortably, those who had no benches squatting down on the floor or on their heels.

Padre Damaso passed through the congregation preceded by two sacristans and followed by another friar carrying a massive volume. He disappeared as he went up the winding staircase, but his round head soon reappeared, then his fat neck, followed immediately by his body. Coughing slightly, he looked about him with assurance. He noticed Ibarra and with a special wink gave to understand that he would not overlook that youth in

[1] The principal character in Calderon de la Barca's *La Vida es Sueño*. There is also a Tagalog *corrido*, or metrical romance, with this title. — TR.

IN THE CHURCH 235

his prayers. Then he turned a look of satisfaction upon Padre Sibyla and another of disdain upon Padre Martin, the preacher of the previous day. This inspection concluded, he turned cautiously and said, "Attention, brother!" to his companion, who opened the massive volume.

But the sermon deserves a separate chapter. A young man who was then learning stenography and who idolizes great orators, took it down; thanks to this fact, we can here present a selection from the sacred oratory of those regions.

CHAPTER XXXI

THE SERMON

FRAY DAMASO began slowly in a low voice: "'*Et spiritum bonum dedisti, qui doceret eos, et manna tuum non prohibuisti ab ore eorum, et aquam dedisti eis in siti.* And thou gavest thy good Spirit to teach them, and thy manna thou didst not withhold from their mouth, and thou gavest them water for their thirst!' Words which the Lord spoke through the mouth of Esdras, in the second book, the ninth chapter, and the twentieth verse."[1]

Padre Sibyla glanced in surprise at the preacher. Padre Manuel Martin turned pale and swallowed hard — that was better than his! Whether Padre Damaso noticed this or whether he was still hoarse, the fact is that he coughed several times as he placed both hands on the rail of the pulpit. The Holy Ghost was above his head, freshly painted, clean and white, with rose-colored beak and feet. "Most honorable sir" (to the alcalde), "most holy priests, Christians, brethren in Jesus Christ!"

Here he made a solemn pause as again he swept his gaze over the congregation, with whose attention and concentration he seemed satisfied.

"The first part of the sermon is to be in Spanish and the other in Tagalog; *loquebantur omnes linguas.*"

After the salutations and the pause he extended his right hand majestically toward the altar, at the same time fixing his gaze on the alcalde. He slowly crossed his arms without uttering a word, then suddenly passing from calmness to action, threw back his head and made a sign toward the main door, sawing the air with his open hand so forcibly that the sacristans interpreted the gesture as a com-

[1] The Douay version. — TR.

THE SERMON

mand and closed the doors. The alferez became uneasy, doubting whether he should go or stay, when the preacher began in a strong voice, full and sonorous; truly his old housekeeper was skilled in medicine.

"Radiant and resplendent is the altar, wide is the great door, the air is the vehicle of the holy and divine words that will spring from my mouth! Hear ye then with the ears of your souls and hearts that the words of the Lord may not fall on the stony soil where the birds of Hell may consume them, but that ye may grow and flourish as holy seed in the field of our venerable and seraphic father, St. Francis! O ye great sinners, captives of the Moros of the soul that infest the sea of eternal life in the powerful craft of the flesh and the world, ye who are laden with the fetters of lust and avarice, and who toil in the galleys of the infernal Satan, look ye here with reverent repentance upon him who saved souls from the captivity of the devil, upon the intrepid Gideon, upon the valiant David, upon the triumphant Roland of Christianity, upon the celestial Civil Guard, more powerful than all the Civil Guards together, now existing or to exist!" (The alferez frowned.) "Yes, señor alferez, more valiant and powerful, he who with no other weapon than a wooden cross boldly vanquishes the eternal tulisan of the shades and all the hosts of Lucifer, and who would have exterminated them forever, were not the spirits immortal! This marvel of divine creation, this wonderful prodigy, is the blessed Diego of Alcala, who, if I may avail myself of a comparison, since comparisons aid in the comprehension of incomprehensible things, as another has said, I say then that this great saint is merely a private soldier, a steward in the powerful company which our seraphic father, St. Francis, sends from Heaven, and to which I have the honor to belong as a corporal or sergeant, by the grace of God!"

The "rude Indians," as the correspondent would say, caught nothing more from this paragraph than the words "Civil Guard," "tulisan," "San Diego," and "St. Francis," so, observing the wry face of the alferez and the bellicose gestures of the preacher, they deduced that the latter was reprehending him for not running down the tulisanes. San Diego and St. Francis would be commissioned in this duty and justly so, as is proved by a picture existing in the convento at Manila, representing St. Francis, by means of his girdle only, holding back the Chinese invasion in the first years after the discovery. The devout were accordingly not a little rejoiced and thanked God for this aid, not doubting that once the tulisanes had disappeared, St. Francis would also destroy the Civil Guard. With redoubled attention, therefore, they listened to Padre Damaso, as he continued:

"Most honorable sir: Great affairs are great affairs even by the side of the small and the small are always small even by the side of the great. So History says, but since History hits the nail on the head only once in a hundred times, being a thing made by men, and men make mistakes — *errarle es hominum*,[1] as Cicero said — he who opens his mouth makes mistakes, as they say in my country — then the result is that there are profound truths which History does not record. These truths, most honorable sir, the divine Spirit spoke with that supreme wisdom which human intelligence has not comprehended since the times of Seneca and Aristotle, those wise priests of antiquity, even to our sinful days, and these truths are that not always are small affairs small, but that they are great, not by the side of the little things, but by the side of the grandest of the earth and of the heavens and of the air and of the clouds and of the waters and of space and of life and of death!"

"Amen!" exclaimed the leader of the Tertiaries, crossing himself.

With this figure of rhetoric, which he had learned from a famous preacher in Manila, Padre Damaso wished to startle his audience, and in fact his holy ghost was so

[1] "Errare humanum est": "To err is human."

fascinated with such great truths that it was necessary to kick him to remind him of his business.

"Patent to your eyes —" prompted the holy ghost below.

"Patent to your eyes is the conclusive and impressive proof of this eternal philosophical truth! Patent is that sun of virtue, and I say sun and not moon, for there is no great merit in the fact that the moon shines during the night, — in the land of the blind the one-eyed man is king; by night may shine a light, a tiny star, — so the greatest merit is to be able to shine even in the middle of the day, as the sun does; so shines our brother Diego even in the midst of the greatest saints! Here you have patent to your eyes, in your impious disbelief, the masterpiece of the Highest for the confusion of the great of the earth, yes, my brethren, patent, *patent* to all, PATENT!"

A man rose pale and trembling and hid himself in a confessional. He was a liquor dealer who had been dozing and dreaming that the carbineers were demanding the patent, or license, that he did not have. It may safely be affirmed that he did not come out from his hiding-place while the sermon lasted.

"Humble and lowly saint, thy wooden cross" (the one that the image held was of silver), "thy modest gown, honors the great Francis whose sons and imitators we are. We propagate thy holy race in the whole world, in the remote places, in the cities, in the towns, without distinction between black and white" (the alcalde held his breath), "suffering hardships and martyrdoms, thy holy race of faith and religion militant" ("Ah!" breathed the alcalde) "which holds the world in balance and prevents it from falling into the depths of perdition."

His hearers, including even Capitan Tiago, yawned little by little. Maria Clara was not listening to the sermon, for she knew that Ibarra was near and was thinking about him while she fanned herself and gazed at an evangelical bull that had all the outlines of a small carabao.

"All should know by heart the Holy Scriptures and the lives of the saints and then I should not have to preach to you, O sinners! You should know such important and necessary things as the Lord's Prayer, although many of you have forgotten it, living now as do the Protestants or heretics, who, like the Chinese, respect not the ministers of God. But the worse for you, O ye accursed, moving as you are toward damnation!"

"*Abá*, Pale Lamaso, what!"[1] muttered Carlos, the Chinese, looking angrily at the preacher, who continued to extemporize, emitting a series of apostrophes and imprecations.

"You will die in final unrepentance, O race of heretics! God punishes you even on this earth with jails and prisons! Women should flee from you, the rulers should hang all of you so that the seed of Satan be not multiplied in the vineyard of the Lord! Jesus Christ said: 'If you have an evil member that leads you to sin, cut it off, and cast it into the fire —'"

Having forgotten both his sermon and his rhetoric, Fray Damaso began to be nervous. Ibarra became uneasy and looked about for a quiet corner, but the church was crowded. Maria Clara neither heard nor saw anything as she was analyzing a picture of the blessed souls in purgatory, souls in the shape of men and women dressed in hides, with miters, hoods, and cowls, all roasting in the fire and clutching St. Francis' girdle, which did not break even with such great weight. With that improvisation on the preacher's part, the holy-ghost friar lost the thread of the sermon and skipped over three long paragraphs, giving the wrong cue to the now laboriously-panting Fray Damaso.

"Who of you, O sinners, would lick the sores of a poor and ragged beggar? Who? Let him answer by raising his hand! None! That I knew, for only a saint like Diego de Alcala would do it. He licked all the sores, saying to

---

[1] To the Philippine Chinese "d" and "l" look and sound about the same. — TR.

THE SERMON

an astonished brother, 'Thus is this sick one cured!' O Christian charity! O matchless example! O virtue of virtues! O inimitable pattern! O spotless talisman!" Here he continued a long series of exclamations, the while crossing his arms and raising and lowering them as though he wished to fly or to frighten the birds away.

"Before dying he spoke in Latin, without knowing Latin! Marvel, O sinners! You, in spite of what you study, for which blows are given to you, you do not speak Latin, and you will die without speaking it! To speak Latin is a gift of God and therefore the Church uses Latin! I, too, speak Latin! Was God going to deny this consolation to His beloved Diego? Could he die, could he be permitted to die, without speaking Latin? Impossible! God wouldn't be just, He wouldn't be God! So he talked in Latin, and of that fact the writers of his time bear witness!"

He ended this exordium with the passage which had cost him the most toil and which he had plagiarized from a great writer, Sinibaldo de Mas. "Therefore, I salute thee, illustrious Diego, the glory of our Order! Thou art the pattern of virtue, meek with honor, humble with nobility, compliant with fortitude, temperate with ambition, hostile with loyalty, compassionate with pardon, holy with conscientiousness, full of faith with devotion, credulous with sincerity, chaste with love, reserved with secrecy; long-suffering with patience, brave with timidity, moderate with desire, bold with resolution, obedient with subjection, modest with pride, zealous with disinterestedness, skilful with capability, ceremonious with politeness, astute with sagacity, merciful with piety, secretive with modesty, revengeful with valor, poor on account of thy labors with true conformity, prodigal with economy, active with ease, economical with liberality, innocent with sagacity, reformer with consistency, indifferent with zeal for learning: God created thee to feel the raptures of Platonic love! Aid me in singing thy greatness and thy name higher than the stars and clearer than the sun itself that circles about thy feet! Aid me, all of you, as you appeal to God for sufficient inspiration by reciting the Ave Maria!"

All fell upon their knees and raised a murmur like the humming of a thousand bees. The alcalde laboriously bent one knee and wagged his head in a disgusted manner, while the alferez looked pale and penitent.

"To the devil with the curate!" muttered one of two youths who had come from Manila.

"Keep still!" admonished his companion. "His woman might hear us."

Meanwhile, Padre Damaso, instead of reciting the Ave Maria, was scolding his holy ghost for having skipped three of his best paragraphs; at the same time he consumed a couple of cakes and a glass of Malaga, secure of encountering therein greater inspiration than in all the holy ghosts, whether of wood in the form of a dove or of flesh in the shape of an inattentive friar.

Then he began the sermon in Tagalog. The devout old woman again gave her granddaughter a hearty slap. The child awoke ill-naturedly and asked, "Is it time to cry now?"

"Not yet, O lost one, but don't go to sleep again!" answered the good grandmother.

Of the second part of the sermon — that in Tagalog — we have only a few rough notes, for Padre Damaso extemporized in this language, not because he knew it better, but because, holding the provincial Filipinos ignorant of rhetoric, he was not afraid of making blunders before them. With Spaniards the case was different; he had heard rules of oratory spoken of, and it was possible that among his hearers some one had been in college-halls, perhaps the alcalde, so he wrote out his sermons, corrected and polished them, and then memorized and rehearsed them for several days beforehand.

It is common knowledge that none of those present understood the drift of the sermon. They were so dull of

THE SERMON

understanding and the preacher was so profound, as Sister Rufa said, that the audience waited in vain for an opportunity to weep, and the lost grandchild of the blessed old woman went to sleep again. Nevertheless, this part had greater consequences than the first, at least for certain hearers, as we shall see later.

He began with a "*Mana capatir con cristiano*,"[1] followed by an avalanche of untranslatable phrases. He talked of the soul, of Hell, of "*mahal na santo pintacasi*,"[2] of the Indian sinners and of the virtuous Franciscan Fathers.

"The devil!" exclaimed one of the two irreverent Manilans to his companion. "That's all Greek to me. I'm going." Seeing the doors closed, he went out through the sacristy, to the great scandal of the people and especially of the preacher, who turned pale and paused in the midst of his sentence. Some looked for a violent apostrophe, but Padre Damaso contented himself with watching the delinquent, and then he went on with his sermon.

Then were let loose curses upon the age, against the lack of reverence, against the growing indifference to Religion. This matter seemed to be his forte, for he appeared to be inspired and expressed himself with force and clearness. He talked of the sinners who did not attend confession, who died in prisons without the sacraments, of families accursed, of proud and puffed-up little half-breeds, of young sages and little philosophers, of pettifoggers, of picayunish students, and so on. Well known is this habit that many have when they wish to ridicule their enemies; they apply to them belittling epithets because their brains do not appear to furnish them any other means, and thus they are happy.

Ibarra heard it all and understood the allusions. Preserving an outward calm, he turned his eyes to God and the authorities, but saw nothing more than the images of saints, and the alcalde was sleeping.

---

[1] "Brothers in Christ."
[2] "Venerable patron saint."

Meanwhile, the preacher's enthusiasm was rising by degrees. He spoke of the times when every Filipino upon meeting a priest took off his hat, knelt on the ground, and kissed the priest's hand. "But now," he added, "you only take off your salakot or your felt hat, which you have placed on the side of your head in order not to ruffle your nicely combed hair! You content yourself with saying, 'good day, *among*,' and there are proud dabblers in a little Latin who, from having studied in Manila or in Europe, believe that they have the right to shake a priest's hand instead of kissing it. Ah, the day of judgment will quickly come, the world will end, as many saints have foretold; it will rain fire, stones, and ashes to chastise your pride!" The people were exhorted not to imitate such "savages" but to hate and shun them, since they were beyond the religious pale.

"Hear what the holy decrees say! When an Indian meets a curate in the street he should bow his head and offer his neck for his master to step upon. If the curate and the Indian are both on horseback, then the Indian should stop and take off his hat or salakot reverently; and finally, if the Indian is on horseback and the curate on foot, the Indian should alight and not mount again until the curate has told him to go on, or is far away. This is what the holy decrees say and he who does not obey will be excommunicated."

"And when one is riding a carabao?" asked a scrupulous countryman of his neighbor.

"Then — keep on going!" answered the latter, who was a casuist.

But in spite of the cries and gestures of the preacher many fell asleep or wandered in their attention, since these sermons were ever the same. In vain some devout women tried to sigh and sob over the sins of the wicked; they had to desist in the attempt from lack of supporters. Even Sister Puté was thinking of something quite different. A man beside her had dropped off to sleep in such a way that

THE SERMON

he had fallen over and crushed her habit, so the good woman caught up one of her clogs and with blows began to wake him, crying out, "Get away, savage, brute, devil, carabao, cur, accursed!"

Naturally, this caused somewhat of a stir. The preacher paused and arched his eyebrows, surprised at so great a scandal. Indignation choked the words in his throat and he was able only to bellow, while he pounded the pulpit with his fists. This had the desired effect, however, for the old woman, though still grumbling, dropped her clog and, crossing herself repeatedly, fell devoutly upon her knees.

"Aaah! Aaah!" the indignant priest was at last able to roar out as he crossed his arms and shook his head. "For this do I preach to you the whole morning, savages! Here in the house of God you quarrel and curse, shameless ones! Aaaah! You respect nothing! This is the result of the luxury and the looseness of the age! That's just what I've told you, aah!"

Upon this theme he continued to preach for half an hour. The alcalde snored, and Maria Clara nodded, for the poor child could no longer keep from sleeping, since she had no more paintings or images to study, nor anything else to amuse her. On Ibarra the words and allusions made no more impression, for he was thinking of a cottage on the top of a mountain and saw Maria Clara in the garden; let men crawl about in their miserable towns in the depths of the valley!

Padre Salvi had caused the altar bell to be rung twice, but this was only adding fuel to the flame, for Padre Damaso became stubborn and prolonged the sermon. Fray Sibyla gnawed at his lips and repeatedly adjusted his gold-mounted eye-glasses. Fray Manuel Martin was the only one who appeared to listen with pleasure, for he was smiling.

But at last God said "Enough"; the orator became weary and descended from the pulpit. All knelt to render thanks to God. The alcalde rubbed his eyes, stretched out one arm as if to waken himself, and yawned with a deep *aah*. The mass continued.

When all were kneeling and the priests had lowered their heads while the *Incarnatus est* was being sung, a man murmured in Ibarra's ear, " At the laying of the cornerstone, don't move away from the curate, don't go down into the trench, don't go near the stone — your life depends upon it! "

Ibarra turned to see Elias, who, as soon as he had said this, disappeared in the crowd.

CHAPTER XXXII

THE DERRICK

THE yellowish individual had kept his word, for it was no simple derrick that he had erected above the open trench to let the heavy block of granite down into its place. It was not the simple tripod that Ñor Juan had wanted for suspending a pulley from its top, but was much more, being at once a machine and an ornament, a grand and imposing ornament. Over eight meters in height rose the confused and complicated scaffolding. Four thick posts sunk in the ground served as a frame, fastened to each other by huge timbers crossing diagonally and joined by large nails driven in only half-way, perhaps for the reason that the apparatus was simply for temporary use and thus might easily be taken down again. Huge cables stretched from all sides gave an appearance of solidity and grandeur to the whole. At the top it was crowned with many-colored banners, streaming pennants, and enormous garlands of flowers and leaves artistically interwoven.

There at the top in the shadow made by the posts, the garlands, and the banners, hung fastened with cords and iron hooks an unusually large three-wheeled pulley over the polished sides of which passed in a crotch three cables even larger than the others. These held suspended the smooth, massive stone hollowed out in the center to form with a similar hole in the lower stone, already in place, the little space intended to contain the records of contemporaneous history, such as newspapers, manuscripts, money, medals, and the like, and perhaps to transmit them to very remote generations. The cables extended downward and connected with another equally large pulley at the bottom of the apparatus, whence they passed to the drum of a windlass held in place by means of heavy timbers. This windlass, which could be turned with two cranks, increased the strength of a man a hundredfold by the movement of notched wheels, although it is true that what was gained in force was lost in velocity.

"Look," said the yellowish individual, turning the crank, "look, Ñor Juan, how with merely my own strength I can raise and lower the great stone. It's so well arranged that at will I can regulate the rise or fall inch by inch, so that a man in the trench can easily fit the stones together while I manage it from here."

Ñor Juan could not but gaze in admiration at the speaker, who was smiling in his peculiar way. Curious bystanders made remarks praising the yellowish individual.

"Who taught you mechanics?" asked Ñor Juan.

"My father, my dead father," was the answer, accompanied by his peculiar smile.

"Who taught your father?"

"Don Saturnino, the grandfather of Don Crisostomo."

"I did n't know that Don Saturnino —"

"Oh, he knew a lot of things! He not only beat his laborers well and exposed them out in the sun, but he also knew how to wake the sleepers and put the waking to sleep. You'll see in time what my father taught me, you'll see!"

Here the yellowish individual smiled again, but in a strange way.

On a table covered with a piece of Persian tapestry rested a leaden cylinder containing the objects that were to be kept in the tomb-like receptacle and a glass case with thick sides, which would hold that mummy of an epoch and preserve for the future the records of a past.

Tasio, the Sage, who was walking about there thoughtfully, murmured: "Perchance some day when this edifice, which is today begun, has grown old and after many vicissitudes has fallen into ruins, either from the visitations of Nature or the destructive hand of man, and above

THE DERRICK 249

the ruins grow the ivy and the moss, — then when Time has destroyed the moss and ivy, and scattered the ashes of the ruins themselves to the winds, wiping from the pages of History the recollection of it and of those who destroyed it, long since lost from the memory of man: perchance when the races have been buried in their mantle of earth or have disappeared, only by accident the pick of some miner striking a spark from this rock will dig up mysteries and enigmas from the depths of the soil. Perchance the learned men of the nation that dwells in these regions will labor, as do the present Egyptologists, with the remains of a great civilization which occupied itself with eternity, little dreaming that upon it was descending so long a night. Perchance some learned professor will say to his students of five or six years of age, in a language spoken by all mankind, 'Gentlemen, after studying and examining carefully the objects found in the depths of our soil, after deciphering some symbols and translating a few words, we can without the shadow of a doubt conclude that these objects belonged to the barbaric age of man, to that obscure era which we are accustomed to speak of as fabulous. In short, gentlemen, in order that you may form an approximate idea of the backwardness of our ancestors, it will be sufficient that I point out to you the fact that those who lived here not only recognized kings, but also for the purpose of settling questions of local government they had to go to the other side of the earth, just as if we should say that a body in order to move itself would need to consult a head existing in another part of the globe, perhaps in regions now sunk under the waves. This incredible defect, however improbable it may seem to us now, must have existed, if we take into consideration the circumstances surrounding those beings, whom I scarcely dare to call human! In those primitive times men were still (or at least so they believed) in direct communication with their Creator, since they had ministers from Him, beings different from the rest, designated always with the mysterious letters "M. R. P.",[1] concerning the meaning of which our learned men do not agree. According to the professor of languages whom we have here, rather mediocre, since he does not speak more than a hundred of the imperfect languages of the past, "M. R. P." may signify "*Muy Rico Propietario.*"[2] These ministers were a species of demigods, very virtuous and enlightened, and were very eloquent orators, who, in spite of their great power and prestige, never committed the slightest fault, which fact strengthens my belief in supposing that they were of a nature distinct from the rest. If this were not sufficient to sustain my belief, there yet remains the argument, disputed by no one and day by day confirmed, that these mysterious beings could make God descend to earth merely by saying a few words, that God could speak only through their mouths, that they ate His flesh and drank His blood, and even at times allowed the common folk to do the same.'"

These and other opinions the skeptical Sage put into the mouths of all the corrupt men of the future. Perhaps, as may easily be the case, old Tasio was mistaken, but we must return to our story.

In the kiosks which we saw two days ago occupied by the schoolmaster and his pupils, there was now spread out a toothsome and abundant meal. Noteworthy is the fact that on the table prepared for the school children there was not a single bottle of wine but an abundance of fruits. In the arbors joining the two kiosks were the seats for the musicians and a table covered with sweetmeats and confections, with bottles of water for the thirsty public, all decorated with leaves and flowers. The schoolmaster had erected near by a greased pole and hurdles, and had hung up pots and pans for a number of games.

[1] *Muy Reverendo Padre:* Very Reverend Father.
[2] Very rich landlord. The United States Philippine Commission, constituting the government of the Archipelago, paid to the religious orders "a lump sum of $7,239,000, more or less," for the bulk of the lands claimed by them. See the *Annual Report of the Philippine Commission to the Secretary of War*, December 23, 1903. — TR.

The crowd, resplendent in bright-colored garments, gathered as people fled from the burning sun, some into the shade of the trees, others under the arbor. The boys climbed up into the branches or on the stones in order to see the ceremony better, making up in this way for their short stature. They looked with envy at the clean and well-dressed school children, who occupied a place especially assigned to them and whose parents were overjoyed, as they, poor country folk, would see their children eat from a white tablecloth, almost the same as the curate or the alcalde. Thinking of this alone was enough to drive away hunger, and such an event would be recounted from father to son.

Soon were heard the distant strains of the band, which was preceded by a motley throng made up of persons of all ages, in clothing of all colors. The yellowish individual became uneasy and with a glance examined his whole apparatus. A curious countryman followed his glance and watched all his movements; this was Elias, who had also come to witness the ceremony, but in his salakot and rough attire he was almost unrecognizable. He had secured a very good position almost at the side of the windlass, on the edge of the excavation. With the music came the alcalde, the municipal officials, the friars, with the exception of Padre Damaso, and the Spanish employees. Ibarra was conversing with the alcalde, of whom he had made quite a friend since he had addressed to him some well-turned compliments over his decorations and ribbons, for aristocratic pretensions were the weakness of his Honor. Capitan Tiago, the alferez, and some other wealthy personages came in the gilded cluster of maidens displaying their silken parasols. Padre Salvi followed, silent and thoughtful as ever.

"Count upon my support always in any worthy enterprise," the alcalde was saying to Ibarra. "I will give you whatever appropriation you need or else see that it is furnished by others."

As they drew nearer the youth felt his heart beat faster. Instinctively he glanced at the strange scaffolding raised there. He saw the yellowish individual salute him respectfully and gaze at him fixedly for a moment. With surprise he noticed Elias, who with a significant wink gave him to understand that he should remember the warning in the church.

The curate put on his sacerdotal robes and commenced the ceremony, while the one-eyed sacristan held the book and an acolyte the hyssop and jar of holy water. The rest stood about him uncovered, and maintained such a profound silence that, in spite of his reading in a low tone, it was apparent that Padre Salvi's voice was trembling.

Meanwhile, there had been placed in the glass case the manuscripts, newspapers, medals, coins, and the like, and the whole enclosed in the leaden cylinder, which was then hermetically sealed.

"Señor Ibarra, will you put the box in its place? The curate is waiting," murmured the alcalde into the young man's ear.

"I would with great pleasure," answered the latter, "but that would be usurping the honorable duty of the escribano. The escribano must make affidavit of the act."

So the escribano gravely took the box, descended the carpeted stairway leading to the bottom of the excavation and with due solemnity placed it in the hole in the stone. The curate then took the hyssop and sprinkled the stones with holy water.

Now the moment had arrived for each one to place his trowelful of mortar on the face of the large stone lying in the trench, in order that the other might be fitted and fastened to it. Ibarra handed the alcalde a mason's trowel, on the wide silver blade of which was engraved the date. But the alcalde first gave a harangue in Spanish:

"People of San Diego! We have the honor to preside over a ceremony whose importance you will not understand unless we tell you of it. A school is being founded, and the school is the basis of society, the school is the book in which is written the future of the nations! Show us the schools of a people and We will show you what that people is.

"People of San Diego! Thank God, who has given you holy priests, and the government of the mother country, which untiringly spreads civilization through these fertile isles, protected beneath her glorious mantle! Thank God, who has taken pity on you and sent you these humble priests who enlighten you and teach you the divine word! Thank the government, which has made, is making, and will continue to make, so many sacrifices for you and your children!

"And now that the first stone of this important edifice is consecrated, We, alcalde-mayor of this province, in the name of his Majesty the King, whom God preserve, King of the Spains, in the name of the illustrious Spanish government and under the protection of its spotless and ever-victorious banner, We consecrate this act and begin the construction of this schoolhouse! People of San Diego, long live the King! Long live Spain! Long live the friars! Long live the Catholic Religion!"

Many voices were raised in answer, adding, "Long live the Señor Alcalde!"

He then majestically descended to the strains of the band, which began to play, deposited several trowelfuls of mortar on the stone, and with equal majesty reascended. The employees applauded.

Ibarra offered another trowel to the curate, who, after fixing his eyes on him for a moment, descended slowly. Half-way down the steps he raised his eyes to look at the stone, which hung fastened by the stout cables, but this was only for a second, and he then went on down. He did the same as the alcalde, but this time more applause was heard, for to the employees were added some friars and Capitan Tiago.

Padre Salvi then seemed to seek for some one to whom

he might give the trowel. He looked doubtfully at Maria Clara, but changing his mind, offered it to the escribano. The latter in gallantry offered it to Maria Clara, who smilingly refused it. The friars, the employees, and the alferez went down one after another, nor was Capitan Tiago forgotten. Ibarra only was left, and the order was about to be given for the yellowish individual to lower the stone when the curate remembered the youth and said to him in a joking tone, with affected familiarity:

"Aren't you going to put on your trowelful, Señor Ibarra?"

"I should be a Juan Palomo, to prepare the meal and eat it myself," answered the latter in the same tone.

"Go on!" said the alcalde, shoving him forward gently. "Otherwise, I'll order that the stone be not lowered at all and we'll be here until doomsday."

Before such a terrible threat Ibarra had to obey. He exchanged the small silver trowel for a large iron one, an act which caused some of the spectators to smile, and went forward tranquilly. Elias gazed at him with such an indefinable expression that on seeing it one might have said that his whole life was concentrated in his eyes. The yellowish individual stared into the trench, which opened at his feet. After directing a rapid glance at the heavy stone hanging over his head and another at Elias and the yellowish individual, Ibarra said to Ñor Juan in a somewhat unsteady voice, "Give me the mortar and get me another trowel up there."

The youth remained alone. Elias no longer looked at him, for his eyes were fastened on the hand of the yellowish individual, who, leaning over the trench, was anxiously following the movements of Ibarra. There was heard the noise of the trowel scraping on the stone in the midst of a feeble murmur among the employees, who were congratulating the alcalde on his speech.

Suddenly a crash was heard. The pulley tied at the base

THE DERRICK

of the derrick jumped up and after it the windlass, which struck the heavy posts like a battering-ram. The timbers shook, the fastenings flew apart, and the whole apparatus fell in a second with a frightful crash. A cloud of dust arose, while a cry of horror from a thousand voices filled the air. Nearly all fled; only a few dashed toward the trench. Maria Clara and Padre Salvi remained in their places, pale, motionless, and speechless.

When the dust had cleared away a little, they saw Ibarra standing among beams, posts, and cables, between the windlass and the heavy stone, which in its rapid descent had shaken and crushed everything. The youth still held the trowel in his hand and was staring with frightened eyes at the body of a man which lay at his feet half-buried among the timbers.

"You're not killed! You're still alive! For God's sake, speak!" cried several employees, full of terror and solicitude.

"A miracle! A miracle!" shouted some.

"Come and extricate the body of this poor devil!" exclaimed Ibarra like one arousing himself from sleep.

On hearing his voice Maria Clara felt her strength leave her and fell half-fainting into the arms of her friends.

Great confusion prevailed. All were talking, gesticulating, running about, descending into the trench, coming up again, all amazed and terrified.

"Who is the dead man? Is he still alive?" asked the **alferez.**

The corpse was identified as that of the yellowish individual who had been operating the windlass.

"Arrest the foreman on the work!" was the first thing that the alcalde was able to say.

They examined the corpse, placing their hands on the chest, but the heart had ceased to beat. The blow had struck him on the head, and blood was flowing from his nose, mouth, and ears. On his neck were to be noticed some peculiar marks, four deep depressions toward the back and one more somewhat larger on the other side, which induced the belief that a hand of steel had caught him as in a pair of pincers.

The priests felicitated the youth warmly and shook his hand. The Franciscan of humble aspect who had served as holy ghost for Padre Damaso exclaimed with tearful eyes, "God is just, God is good!"

"When I think that a few moments before I was down there!" said one of the employees to Ibarra. "What if I had happened to be the last!"

"It makes my hair stand on end!" remarked another partly bald individual.

"I'm glad that it happened to you and not to me," murmured an old man tremblingly.

"Don Pascual!" exclaimed some of the Spaniards.

"I say that because the young man is not dead. If I had not been crushed, I should have died afterwards merely from thinking about it."

But Ibarra was already at a distance informing himself as to Maria Clara's condition.

"Don't let this stop the fiesta, Señor Ibarra," said the alcalde. "Praise God, the dead man is neither a priest nor a Spaniard! We must rejoice over your escape! Think if the stone had caught you!"

"There are presentiments, there are presentiments!" exclaimed the escribano. "I've said so before! Señor Ibarra did n't go down willingly. I saw it!"

"The dead man is only an Indian!"

"Let the fiesta go on! Music! Sadness will never resuscitate the dead!"

"An investigation shall be made right here!"

"Send for the directorcillo!"

"Arrest the foreman on the work! To the stocks with him!"

"To the stocks! Music! To the stocks with the foreman!"

"Señor Alcalde," said Ibarra gravely, "if mourning

will not resuscitate the dead, much less will arresting this man about whose guilt we know nothing. I will be security for his person and so I ask his liberty for these days at least."

"Very well! But don't let him do it again!"

All kinds of rumors began to circulate. The idea of a miracle was soon an accepted fact, although Fray Salvi seemed to rejoice but little over a miracle attributed to a saint of his Order and in his parish. There were not lacking those who added that they had seen descending into the trench, when everything was tumbling down, a figure in a dark robe like that of the Franciscans. There was no doubt about it; it was San Diego himself! It was also noted that Ibarra had attended mass and that the yellowish individual had not — it was all as clear as the sun!

"You see! You didn't want to go to mass!" said a mother to her son. "If I hadn't whipped you to make you go you would now be on your way to the town hall, like him, in a cart!"

The yellowish individual, or rather his corpse, wrapped up in a mat, was in fact being carried to the town hall.

Ibarra hurried home to change his clothes.

"A bad beginning, huh!" commented old Tasio, as he moved away.

CHAPTER XXXIII

FREE THOUGHT

IBARRA was just putting the finishing touches to a change of clothing when a servant informed him that a countryman was asking for him. Supposing it to be one of his laborers, he ordered that he be brought into his office, or study, which was at the same time a library and a chemical laboratory. Greatly to his surprise he found himself face to face with the severe and mysterious figure of Elias.

"You saved my life," said the pilot in Tagalog, noticing Ibarra's start of surprise. "I have partly paid the debt and you have nothing to thank me for, but quite the opposite. I've come to ask a favor of you."

"Speak!" answered the youth in the same language, puzzled by the pilot's gravity.

Elias stared into Ibarra's eyes for some seconds before he replied, "When human courts try to clear up this mystery, I beg of you not to speak to any one of the warning that I gave you in the church."

"Don't worry," answered the youth in a rather disgusted tone. "I know that you're wanted, but I'm no informer."

"Oh, it's not on my account, not on my account!" exclaimed Elias with some vigor and haughtiness. "It's on your own account. I fear nothing from men."

Ibarra's surprise increased. The tone in which this rustic — formerly a pilot — spoke was new and did not seem to harmonize with either his condition or his fortune. "What do you mean?" he asked, interrogating that mysterious individual with his looks.

"I do not talk in enigmas but try to express myself clearly; for your greater security, it is better that your enemies think you unsuspecting and unprepared."

Ibarra recoiled. "My enemies? Have I enemies?"

"All of us have them, sir, from the smallest insect up to man, from the poorest and humblest to the richest and most powerful! Enmity is the law of life!"

Ibarra gazed at him in silence for a while, then murmured, "You are neither a pilot nor a rustic!"

"You have enemies in high and low places," continued Elias, without heeding the young man's words. "You are planning a great undertaking, you have a past. Your father and your grandfather had enemies because they had passions, and in life it is not the criminal who provokes the most hate but the honest man."

"Do you know who my enemies are?"

Elias meditated for a moment. "I knew one — him who is dead," he finally answered. "Last night I learned that a plot against you was being hatched, from some words exchanged with an unknown person who lost himself in the crowd. 'The fish will not eat him, as they did his father; you'll see tomorrow,' the unknown said. These words caught my attention not only by their meaning but also on account of the person who uttered them, for he had some days before presented himself to the foreman on the work with the express request that he be allowed to superintend the placing of the stone. He didn't ask for much pay but made a show of great knowledge. I hadn't sufficient reason for believing in his bad intentions, but something within told me that my conjectures were true and therefore I chose as the suitable occasion to warn you a moment when you could not ask me any questions. The rest you have seen for yourself."

For a long time after Elias had become silent Ibarra remained thoughtful, not answering him or saying a word. "I'm sorry that that man is dead!" he exclaimed at length. "From him something more might have been learned."

"If he had lived, he would have escaped from the trembling hand of blind human justice. God has judged him, God has killed him, let God be the only Judge!"

Crisostomo gazed for a moment at the man, who, while he spoke thus, exposed his muscular arms covered with lumps and bruises. "Do you also believe in the miracle?" he asked with a smile. "You know what a miracle the people are talking about."

"Were I to believe in miracles, I should not believe in God. I should believe in a deified man, I should believe that man had really created a god in his own image and likeness," the mysterious pilot answered solemnly. "But I believe in Him, I have felt His hand more than once. When the whole apparatus was falling down and threatening destruction to all who happened to be near it, I, I myself, caught the criminal, I placed myself at his side. He was struck and I am safe and sound."

"You! So it was you—"

"Yes! I caught him when he tried to escape, once his deadly work had begun. I saw his crime, and I say this to you: let God be the sole judge among men, let Him be the only one to have the right over life, let no man ever think to take His place!"

"But you in this instance—"

"No!" interrupted Elias, guessing the objection. "It's not the same. When a man condemns others to death or destroys their future forever he does it with impunity and uses the strength of others to execute his judgments, which after all may be mistaken or erroneous. But I, in exposing the criminal to the same peril that he had prepared for others, incurred the same risk as he did. I did not kill him, but let the hand of God smite him."

"Then you don't believe in accidents?"

"Believing in accidents is like believing in miracles; both presuppose that God does not know the future. What

FREE THOUGHT

is an accident? An event that no one has at all foreseen. What is a miracle? A contradiction, an overturning of natural laws. Lack of foresight and contradiction in the Intelligence that rules the machinery of the world indicate two great defects."

"Who are you?" Ibarra again asked with some awe. "Have you ever studied?"

"I have had to believe greatly in God, because I have lost faith in men," answered the pilot, avoiding the question.

Ibarra thought he understood this hunted youth; he rejected human justice, he refused to recognize the right of man to judge his fellows, he protested against force and the superiority of some classes over others.

"But nevertheless you must admit the necessity of human justice, however imperfect it may be," he answered. "God, in spite of the many ministers He may have on earth, cannot, or rather does not, pronounce His judgments clearly to settle the million conflicts that our passions excite. It is proper, it is necessary, it is just, that man sometimes judge his fellows."

"Yes, to do good, but not to do ill, to correct and to better, but not to destroy, for if his judgments are wrong he has n't the power to remedy the evil he has done. But," he added with a change of tone, "this discussion is beyond my powers and I 'm detaining you, who are being waited for. Don't forget what I 've just told you — you have enemies. Take care of yourself for the good of our country." Saying this, he turned to go.

"When shall I see you again?" asked Ibarra.

"Whenever you wish and always when I can be of service to you. I am still your debtor."

CHAPTER XXXIV

THE DINNER

THERE in the decorated kiosk the great men of the province were dining. The alcalde occupied one end of the table and Ibarra the other. At the young man's right sat Maria Clara and at his left the escribano. Capitan Tiago, the alferez, the gobernadorcillo, the friars, the employees, and the few young ladies who had remained sat, not according to rank, but according to their inclinations. The meal was quite animated and happy.

When the dinner was half over, a messenger came in search of Capitan Tiago with a telegram, to open which he naturally requested the permission of the others, who very naturally begged him to do so. The worthy capitan at first knitted his eyebrows, then raised them; his face became pale, then lighted up as he hastily folded the paper and arose.

"Gentlemen," he announced in confusion, "his Excellency the Captain-General is coming this evening to honor my house." Thereupon he set off at a run, hatless, taking with him the message and his napkin.

He was followed by exclamations and questions, for a cry of "Tulisanes!" would not have produced greater effect. "But, listen!" "When is he coming?" "Tell us about it!" "His Excellency!" But Capitan Tiago was already far away.

"His Excellency is coming and will stay at Capitan Tiago's!" exclaimed some without taking into consideration the fact that his daughter and future son-in-law were present.

"The choice couldn't be better," answered the latter.

THE DINNER

The friars gazed at one another with looks that seemed to say: "The Captain-General is playing another one of his tricks, he is slighting us, for he ought to stay at the convento," but since this was the thought of all they remained silent, none of them giving expression to it.

"I was told of this yesterday," said the alcalde, "but at that time his Excellency had not yet fully decided."

"Do you know, Señor Alcalde, how long the Captain-General thinks of staying here?" asked the alferez uneasily.

"With certainty, no. His Excellency likes to give surprises."

"Here come some more messages." These were for the alcalde, the alferez, and the gobernadorcillo, and contained the same announcement. The friars noted well that none came directed to the curate.

"His Excellency will arrive at four this afternoon, gentlemen!" announced the alcalde solemnly. "So we can finish our meal in peace." Leonidas at Thermopylae could not have said more cheerfully, "Tonight we shall sup with Pluto!"

The conversation again resumed its ordinary course.

"I note the absence of our great preacher," timidly remarked an employee of inoffensive aspect who had not opened his mouth up to the time of eating, and who spoke now for the first time in the whole morning.

All who knew the history of Crisostomo's father made a movement and winked, as if to say, "Get out! Fools rush in — " But some one more charitably disposed answered, "He must be rather tired."

"Rather?" exclaimed the alferez. "He must be exhansted, and as they say here, all fagged out. What a sermon it was!"

"A splendid sermon — wonderful!" said the escribano.

"Magnificent — profound!" added the correspondent.

"To be able to talk so much, it's necessary to have the lungs that he has," observed Padre Manuel Martin. The

Augustinian did not concede him anything more than lungs.

"And his fertility of expression!" added Padre Salvi.

"Do you know that Señor Ibarra has the best cook in the province?" remarked the alcalde, to cut short such talk.

"You may well say that, but his beautiful neighbor does n't wish to honor the table, for she is scarcely eating a bite," observed one of the employees.

Maria Clara blushed. "I thank the gentleman, he troubles himself too much on my account," she stammered timidly, "but—"

"But you honor it enough merely by being present," concluded the gallant alcalde as he turned to Padre Salvi.

"Padre," he said in a loud voice, "I've observed that during the whole day your Reverence has been silent and thoughtful."

"The alcalde is a great observer," remarked Fray Sibyla in a meaning tone.

"It's a habit of mine," stammered the Franciscan. "It pleases me more to listen than to talk."

"Your Reverence always takes care to win and not to lose," said the alferez in a jesting tone.

Padre Salvi, however, did not take this as a joke, for his gaze brightened a moment as he replied, "The alferez knows very well these days that I'm not the one who is winning or losing most."

The alferez turned the hit aside with a forced laugh, pretending not to take it to himself.

"But, gentlemen, I don't understand how it is possible to talk of winnings and losses," interposed the alcalde. "What will these amiable and discreet young ladies who honor us with their company think of us? For me the young women are like the Æolian harps in the middle of the night—it is necessary to listen with close attention in order that their ineffable harmonies may elevate the soul to the celestial spheres of the infinite and the ideal!"

THE DINNER 265

"Your Honor is becoming poetical!" exclaimed the escribano gleefully, and both emptied their wine-glasses.

"I can't help it," said the alcalde as he wiped his lips. "Opportunity, while it does n't always make the thief, makes the poet. In my youth I composed verses which were really not bad."

"So your Excellency has been unfaithful to the Muses to follow Themis," emphatically declared our mythical or mythological correspondent.

"Pshaw, what would you have? To run through the entire social scale was always my dream. Yesterday I was gathering flowers and singing songs, today I wield the rod of justice and serve Humanity, tomorrow—"

"Tomorrow your Honor will throw the rod into the fire to warm yourself by it in the winter of life, and take an appointment in the cabinet," added Padre Sibyla.

"Pshaw! Yes—no—to be a cabinet official is n't exactly my beau-ideal: any upstart may become one. A villa in the North in which to spend the summer, a mansion in Madrid, and some property in Andalusia for the winter—there we shall live remembering our beloved Philippines. Of me Voltaire would not say, 'We have lived among these people only to enrich ourselves and to calumniate them.'"

The alcalde quoted this in French, so the employees, thinking that his Honor had cracked a joke, began to laugh in appreciation of it. Some of the friars did likewise, since they did not know that the Voltaire mentioned was the same Voltaire whom they had so often cursed and consigned to hell. But Padre Sibyla was aware of it and became serious from the belief that the alcalde had said something heretical or impious.

In the other kiosk the children were eating under the direction of their teacher. For Filipino children they were rather noisy, since at the table and in the presence of other persons their sins are generally more of omission than of commission. Perhaps one who was using the tableware improperly would be corrected by his neighbor and from this there would arise a noisy discussion in which each would have his partisans. Some would say the spoon, others the knife or the fork, and as no one was considered an authority there would arise the contention that God is Christ or, more clearly, a dispute of theologians. Their fathers and mothers winked, made signs, nudged one another, and showed their happiness by their smiles.

"Ya!" exclaimed a countrywoman to an old man who was mashing buyo in his *kalikut,* "in spite of the fact that my husband is opposed to it, my Andoy shall be a priest. It's true that we're poor, but we'll work, and if necessary we'll beg alms. There are not lacking those who will give money so that the poor may take holy orders. Does not Brother Mateo, a man who does not lie, say that Pope Sextus was a herder of carabaos in Batangas? Well then, look at my Andoy, see if he hasn't already the face of a St. Vincent!" The good mother watered at the mouth to see her son take hold of a fork with both hands.

"God help us!" added the old man, rolling his quid of buyo. "If Andoy gets to be Pope we'll go to Rome — he, he! I can still walk well, and if I die — he, he!"

"Don't worry, granddad! Andoy won't forget that you taught him how to weave baskets."

"You're right, Petra. I also believe that your son will be great, at least a patriarch. I have never seen any one who learned the business in a shorter time. Yes, he'll remember me when as Pope or bishop he entertains himself in making baskets for his cook. He'll then say masses for my soul — he, he!" With this hope the good old man again filled his *kalikut* with buyo.

"If God hears my prayers and my hopes are fulfilled, I'll say to Andoy, 'Son, take away all our sins and send us to Heaven!' Then we shan't need to pray and fast and buy indulgences. One whose son is a blessed Pope can commit sins!"

"Send him to my house tomorrow, Petra," cried the old

THE DINNER

man enthusiastically, "and I'll teach him to weave the *nito!*"

"Huh! Get out! What are you dreaming about, granddad? Do you still think that the Popes even move their hands? The curate, being nothing more than a curate, only works in the mass — when he turns around! The Archbishop does n't even turn around, for he says mass sitting down. So the Pope — the Pope says it in bed with a fan! What are you thinking about?"

"Of nothing more, Petra, than that he know how to weave the *nito*. It would be well for him to be able to sell hats and cigar-cases so that he would n't have to beg alms, as the curate does here every year in the name of the Pope. It always fills me with compassion to see a saint poor, so I give all my savings."

Another countryman here joined in the conversation, saying, "It's all settled, cumare,[1] my son has got to be a doctor, there's nothing like being a doctor!"

"Doctor! What are you talking about, cumpare?" retorted Petra "There's nothing like being a curate!"

"A curate, pish! A curate? The doctor makes lots of money, the sick people worship him, cumare!"

"Excuse me! The curate, by making three or four turns and saying *deminos pabiscum*,[2] eats God and makes money. All, even the women, tell him their secrets."

"And the doctor? What do you think a doctor is? The doctor sees all that the women have, he feels the pulses of the *dalagas!* I'd just like to be a doctor for a week!"

"And the curate, perhaps the curate does n't see what your doctor sees? Better still, you know the saying, 'the fattest chicken and the roundest leg for the curate!'"

[1] *Cumare* and *cumpare* are corruptions of the Spanish *comadre* and *compadre*, which have an origin analogous to the English "gossip" in its original meaning of "sponsor in baptism." In the Philippines these words are used among the simpler folk as familiar forms of address, "friend," "neighbor." — TR.

[2] Dominus vobiscum.

"What of that? Do the doctors eat dried fish? Do they soil their fingers eating salt?"

"Does the curate dirty his hands as your doctors do? He has great estates and when he works he works with music and has sacristans to help him."

"But the confessing, cumare? Is n't that work?"

"No work about that! I 'd just like to be confessing everybody! While we work and sweat to find out what our own neighbors are doing, the curate does nothing more than take a seat and they tell him everything. Sometimes he falls asleep, but he lets out two or three blessings and we are again the children of God! I 'd just like to be a curate for one evening in Lent!"

"But the preaching? You can't tell me that it 's not work. Just look how the fat curate was sweating this morning," objected the rustic, who felt himself being beaten into retreat.

"Preaching! Work to preach! Where 's your judgment? I 'd just like to be talking half a day from the pulpit, scolding and quarreling with everybody, without any one daring to reply, and be getting paid for it besides. I 'd just like to be the curate for one morning when those who are in debt to me are attending mass! Look there now, how Padre Damaso gets fat with so much scolding and beating."

Padre Damaso was, indeed, approaching with the gait of a heavy man. He was half smiling, but in such a malignant way that Ibarra, upon seeing him, lost the thread of his talk. The padre was greeted with some surprise but with signs of pleasure on the part of all except Ibarra. They were then at the dessert and the champagne was foaming in the glasses.

Padre Damaso's smile became nervous when he saw Maria Clara seated at Crisostomo's right. He took a seat beside the alcalde and said in the midst of a significant silence, "Were you discussing something, gentlemen? Go ahead!"

"We were at the toasts," answered the alcalde. "Señor Ibarra was mentioning all who have helped him in his philanthropic enterprise and was speaking of the architect when your Reverence —"

"Well, I don't know anything about architecture," interrupted Padre Damaso, "but I laugh at architects and the fools who employ them. Here you have it — I drew the plan of this church and it's perfectly constructed, so an English jeweler who stopped in the convento one day assured me. To draw a plan one needs only to have two fingers' breadth of forehead."

"Nevertheless," answered the alcalde, seeing that Ibarra was silent, "when we consider certain buildings, as, for example, this schoolhouse, we need an expert."

"Get out with your experts!" exclaimed the priest with a sneer. "Only a fool needs experts! One must be more of a brute than the Indians, who build their own houses, not to know how to construct four walls and put a roof on top of them. That's all a schoolhouse is!"

The guests gazed at Ibarra, who had turned pale, but he continued as if in conversation with Maria Clara.

"But your Reverence should consider —"

"See now," went on the Franciscan, not allowing the alcalde to continue, "look how one of our lay brothers, the most stupid that we have, has constructed a hospital, good, pretty, and cheap. He made them work hard and paid only eight cuartos a day even to those who had to come from other towns. He knew how to handle them, not like a lot of cranks and little mestizos who are spoiling them by paying three or four reals."

"Does your Reverence say that he paid only eight cuartos? Impossible!" The alcalde was trying to change the course of the conversation.

"Yes, sir, and those who pride themselves on being good Spaniards ought to imitate him. You see now, since the Suez Canal was opened, the corruption that has come in here. Formerly, when we had to double the Cape, neither so many vagabonds came here nor so many others went from here to become vagabonds."

"But, Padre Damaso —"

"You know well enough what the Indian is — just as soon as he gets a little learning he sets himself up as a doctor! All these little fellows that go to Europe —"

"But, listen, your Reverence!" interrupted the alcalde, who was becoming nervous over the aggressiveness of such talk.

"Every one ends up as he deserves," the friar continued. "The hand of God is manifest in the midst of it all, and one must be blind not to see it. Even in this life the fathers of such vipers receive their punishment, they die in jail — ha, ha! As we might say, they have nowhere —"

But he did not finish the sentence. Ibarra, livid, had been following him with his gaze and upon hearing this allusion to his father jumped up and dropped a heavy hand on the priest's head, so that he fell back stunned. The company was so filled with surprise and fright that no one made any movement to interfere.

"Keep off!" cried the youth in a terrible voice, as he caught up a sharp knife and placed his foot on the neck of the friar, who was recovering from the shock of his fall. "Let him who values his life keep away!"

The youth was beside himself. His whole body trembled and his eyes rolled threateningly in their sockets. Fray Damaso arose with an effort, but the youth caught him by the neck and shook him until he again fell doubled over on his knees.

"Señor Ibarra! Señor Ibarra!" stammered some.

But no one, not even the alferez himself, dared to approach the gleaming knife, when they considered the youth's strength and the condition of his mind. All seemed to be paralyzed.

"You, here! You have been silent, now it is my turn! I have tried to avoid this, but God brings me to it — let God be the judge!" The youth was breathing laboriously, but with a hand of iron he held down the Franciscan, who was struggling vainly to free himself.

"My heart beats tranquilly, my hand is sure," he began, looking around him. "First, is there one among you, one who has not loved his father, who was born in such shame and humiliation that he hates his memory? You see? You understand this silence? Priest of a God of peace, with your mouth full of sanctity and religion and your heart full of evil, you cannot know what a father is, or you might have thought of your own! In all this crowd which you despise there is not one like you! You are condemned!"

The persons surrounding him, thinking that he was about to commit murder, made a movement.

"Away!" he cried again in a threatening voice. "What, do you fear that I shall stain my hands with impure blood? Have I not told you that my heart beats tranquilly? Away from us! Listen, priests and judges, you who think yourselves other men and attribute to yourselves other rights: my father was an honorable man, — ask these people here, who venerate his memory. My father was a good citizen and he sacrificed himself for me and for the good of his country. His house was open and his table was set for the stranger and the outcast who came to him in distress! He was a Christian who always did good and who never oppressed the unprotected or afflicted those in trouble. To this man here he opened his doors, he made him sit at his table and called him his friend. And how has this man repaid him? He calumniated him, persecuted him, raised up against him all the ignorant by availing himself of the sanctity of his position; he outraged his tomb, dishonored his memory, and persecuted him even in the sleep of death! Not satisfied with this, he persecutes the son now! I have fled from him, I have avoided his presence. You this morning heard him profane the pulpit, pointing me out to popular fanaticism, and I held my peace! Now he comes here to seek a quarrel with me. To your surprise, I have suffered in silence, but he again insults the most sacred memory that there is for a son. You who are here, priests and judges, have you seen your aged father wear himself out working for you, separating himself from you for your welfare, have you seen him die of sorrow in a prison sighing for your embrace, seeking some one to comfort him, alone, sick, when you were in a foreign land? Have you afterwards heard his name dishonored, have you found his tomb empty when you went to pray beside it? No? You are silent, you condemn him!"

He raised his hand, but with the swiftness of light a girlish form put itself between them and delicate fingers restrained the avenging arm. It was Maria Clara. Ibarra stared at her with a look that seemed to reflect madness. Slowly his clenched fingers relaxed, letting fall the body of the Franciscan and the knife. Covering his face, he fled through the crowd.

CHAPTER XXXV

COMMENTS

NEWS of the incident soon spread throughout the town. At first all were incredulous, but, having to yield to the fact, they broke out into exclamations of surprise. Each one, according to his moral lights, made his comments.

"Padre Damaso is dead," said some. "When they picked him up his face was covered with blood and he was n't breathing."

"May he rest in peace! But he has n't any more than settled his debts!" exclaimed a young man. "Look what he did this morning in the convento — there is n't any name for it."

"What did he do? Did he beat up the coadjutor again?"

"What did he do? Tell us about it!"

"You saw that Spanish mestizo go out through the sacristy in the midst of the sermon?"

"Yes, we saw him. Padre Damaso took note of him."

"Well, after the sermon he sent for the young man and asked him why he had gone out. 'I don't understand Tagalog, Padre,' was the reply. 'And why did you joke about it, saying that it was Greek?' yelled Padre Damaso, slapping the young man in the face. The latter retorted and the two came to blows until they were separated."

"If that had happened to me —" hissed a student between his teeth.

"I don't approve of the action of the Franciscan," said another, "since Religion ought not to be imposed on any one as a punishment or a penance. But I am almost glad of it, for I know that young man, I know that he's from

San Pedro Makati and that he talks Tagalog well. Now he wants to be taken for a recent arrival from Russia and prides himself on appearing not to know the language of his fathers."

"Then God makes them and they rush together!"[1]

"Still we must protest against such actions," exclaimed another student. "To remain silent would be to assent to the abuse, and what has happened may be repeated with any one of us. We're going back to the times of Nero!"

You're wrong," replied another. "Nero was a great artist, while Padre Damaso is only a tiresome preacher."

The comments of the older persons were of a different kind. While they were waiting for the arrival of the Captain-General in a hut outside the town, the gobernadorcillo was saying, "To tell who was right and who was wrong, is not an easy matter. Yet if Señor Ibarra had used more prudence —"

"If Padre Damaso had used half the prudence of Señor Ibarra, you mean to say, perhaps!" interrupted Don Filipo. "The bad thing about it is that they exchanged parts — the youth conducted himself like an old man and the old man like a youth."

"Did you say that no one moved, no one went near to separate them, except Capitan Tiago's daughter?" asked Capitan Martin. "None of the friars, nor the alcalde? Ahem! Worse and worse! I shouldn't like to be in that young man's skin. No one will forgive him for having been afraid of him. Worse and worse, ahem!"

"Do you think so?" asked Capitan Basilio curiously.

"I hope," said Don Filipo, exchanging a look with the latter, "that the people won't desert him. We must keep in mind what his family has done and what he is trying to do now. And if, as may happen, the people, being intimidated, are silent, his friends —"

"But, gentlemen," interrupted the gobernadorcillo,

[1] The Spanish proverb equivalent to the English "Birds of a feather flock together."— Tr.

"what can we do? What can the people do? Happen what will, the friars are always right!"

"They are *always* right because we *always* allow them to be," answered Don Filipo impatiently, putting double stress on the italicized word. "Let us be right once and then we'll talk."

The gobernadorcillo scratched his head and stared at the roof while he replied in a sour tone, "Ay! the heat of the blood! You don't seem to realize yet what country we're in, you don't know your countrymen. The friars are rich and united, while we are divided and poor. Yes, try to defend yourself and you'll see how the people will leave you in the lurch."

"Yes!" exclaimed Don Filipo bitterly. "That will happen as long as you think that way, as long as fear and prudence are synonyms. More attention is paid to a possible evil than to a necessary good. At once fear, and not confidence, presents itself; each one thinks only of himself, no one thinks of the rest, and therefore we are all weak!"

"Well then, think of others before yourself and you'll see how they'll leave you in the lurch. Don't you know the proverb, 'Charity begins at home'?"

"You had better say," replied the exasperated teniente-mayor, "that cowardice begins in selfishness and ends in shame! This very day I'm going to hand in my resignation to the alcalde. I'm tired of passing for a joke without being useful to anybody. Good-by!"

The women had opinions of still another kind.

"Ay!" sighed one woman of kindly expression. "The young men are always so! If his good mother were alive, what would she say? When I think that the like may happen to my son, who has a violent temper, I almost envy his dead mother. I should die of grief!"

"Well, I should n't," replied another. "It would n't cause me any shame if such a thing should happen to my two sons."

"What are you saying, Capitana Maria!" exclaimed the first, clasping her hands.

"It pleases me to see a son defend the memory of his parents, Capitana Tinay. What would you say if some day when you were a widow you heard your husband spoken ill of and your son Antonio should hang his head and remain silent?"

"I would deny him my blessing!" exclaimed a third, Sister Rufa, "but—"

"Deny him my blessing, never!" interrupted the kind Capitana Tinay. "A mother ought not to say that! But I don't know what I should do — I don't know — I believe I'd die — but I shouldn't want to see him again. But what do you think about it, Capitana Maria?"

"After all," added Sister Rufa, "it must not be forgotten that it's a great sin to place your hand on a sacred person."

"A father's memory is more sacred!" replied Capitana Maria. "No one, not even the Pope himself, much less Padre Damaso, may profane such a holy memory."

"That's true!" murmured Capitana Tinay, admiring the wisdom of both. "Where did you get such good ideas?"

"But the excommunication and the condemnation?" exclaimed Sister Rufa. "What are honor and a good name in this life if in the other we are damned? Everything passes away quickly — but the excommunication — to outrage a minister of Christ! No one less than the Pope can pardon that!"

"God, who commands honor for father and mother, will pardon it, God will not excommunicate him! And I tell you that if that young man comes to my house I will receive him and talk with him, and if I had a daughter I would want him for a son-in-law; he who is a good son will be a good husband and a good father — believe it, Sister Rufa!"

"Well, I don't think so. Say what you like, and even

though you may appear to be right, I'll always rather believe the curate. Before everything else, I'll save my soul. What do you say, Capitana Tinay?"

"Oh, what do you want me to say? You're both right — the curate is right, but God must also be right. I don't know, I'm only a foolish woman. What I'm going to do is to tell my son not to study any more, for they say that persons who know anything die on the gallows. *Maria Santisima,* my son wants to go to Europe!"

"What are you thinking of doing?"

"Tell him to stay with me — why should he know more? Tomorrow or the next day we shall die, the learned and the ignorant alike must die, and the only question is to live in peace." The good old woman sighed and raised her eyes toward the sky.

"For my part," said Capitana Maria gravely, "if I were rich like you I would let my sons travel; they are young and will some day be men. I have only a little while to live, we should see one another in the other life, so sons should aspire to be more than their fathers, but at our sides we only teach them to be children."

"Ay, what rare thoughts you have!" exclaimed the astonished Capitana Tinay, clasping her hands. "It must be that you did n't suffer in bearing your twin boys."

"For the very reason that I did bear them with suffering, that I have nurtured and reared them in spite of our poverty, I do not wish that, after the trouble they've cost me, they be only half-men."

"It seems to me that you don't love your children as God commands," said Sister Rufa in a rather severe tone.

"Pardon me, every mother loves her sons in her own way. One mother loves them for her own sake and another loves them for their sake. I am one of the latter, for my husband has so taught me."

"All your ideas, Capitana Maria," said Sister Rufa, as if preaching, "are but little religious. Become a sister **of** the Holy Rosary or of St. Francis or of St. Rita or of St. Clara."

"Sister Rufa, when I am a worthy sister of men then I'll try to be a sister of the saints," she answered with a smile.

To put an end to this chapter of comments and that the reader may learn in passing what the simple country folk thought of the incident, we will now go to the plaza, where under the large awning some rustics are conversing, one of them — he who dreamed about doctors of medicine — being an acquaintance of ours.

"What I regret most," said he, "is that the schoolhouse won't be finished."

"What's that?" asked the bystanders with interest.

"My son won't be a doctor but a carter, nothing more! Now there won't be any school!"

"Who says there won't be any school?" asked a rough and robust countryman with wide cheeks and a narrow head.

"I do! The white padres have called Don Crisostomo *plibastiero*.[1] Now there won't be any school."

All stood looking questioningly at each other; that was a new term to them.

"And is that a bad name?" the rough countryman made bold to ask.

"The worst thing that one Christian can say to another!"

"Worse than *tarantado* and *saragate*?"[2]

"If it were only that! I've been called those names several times and they didn't even give me a bellyache."

"Well, it can't be worse than '*indio*,' as the alferez says."

The man who was to have a carter for a son became gloomier, while the other scratched his head in thought.

---

[1] For "filibustero."

[2] *Tarantado* is a Spanish vulgarism meaning "blunderhead," "bungler." *Saragate* (or *zaragate*) is a Mexican provincialism meaning "disturber," "mischief-maker." — TR.

"Then it must be like the *betelapora* ¹ that the alferez's old woman says. Worse than that is to spit on the Host."

"Well, it's worse than to spit on the Host on Good Friday," was the grave reply. "You remember the word *ispichoso* ² which when applied to a man is enough to have the civil-guards take him into exile or put him in jail — well, *plibustiero* is much worse. According to what the telegrapher and the directorcillo said, *plibustiero*, said by a Christian, a curate, or a Spaniard to another Christian like us is a *santusdeus with requimiternam*,³ for if they ever call you a *plibustiero* then you'd better get yourself shriven and pay your debts, since nothing remains for you but to be hanged. You know whether the telegrapher and the directorcillo ought to be informed; one talks with wires and the other knows Spanish and works only with a pen."

All were appalled.

"May they force me to wear shoes and in all my life to drink nothing but that vile stuff they call beer, if I ever let myself be called *pelbistero!*" swore the countryman, clenching his fists. "What, rich as Don Crisostomo is, knowing Spanish as he does, and able to eat fast with a knife and spoon, I'd laugh at five curates!"

"The next civil-guard I catch stealing my chickens I'm going to call *palabistiero*, then I'll go to confession at once," murmured one of the rustics in a low voice as he withdrew from the group.

---

¹ *Vete á la porra* is a vulgarism almost the same in meaning and use as the English slang, "Tell it to the policeman," *porra* being the Spanish term for the policeman's "billy." — TR.

² For *sospechoso*, "a suspicious character." — TR.

³ *Sanctus Deus* and *Requiem aeternam* (so called from their first words) are prayers for the dead. — TR.

CHAPTER XXXVI

THE FIRST CLOUD

IN Capitan Tiago's house reigned no less disorder than in the people's imagination. Maria Clara did nothing but weep and would not listen to the consoling words of her aunt and of Andeng, her foster-sister. Her father had forbidden her to speak to Ibarra until the priests should absolve him from the excommunication. Capitan Tiago himself, in the midst of his preparations for receiving the Captain-General properly, had been summoned to the convento.

"Don't cry, daughter," said Aunt Isabel, as she polished the bright plates of the mirrors with a piece of chamois. "They'll withdraw the excommunication, they'll write now to the Pope, and we'll make a big poor-offering. Padre Damaso only fainted, he's not dead."

"Don't cry," whispered Andeng. "I'll manage it so that you may talk with him. What are confessionals for if not that we may sin? Everything is forgiven by telling it to the curate."

At length Capitan Tiago returned. They sought in his face the answer to many questions, and it announced discouragement. The poor fellow was perspiring; he rubbed his hand across his forehead, but was unable to say a single word.

"What has happened, Santiago?" asked Aunt Isabel anxiously.

He answered by sighing and wiping away a tear.

"For God's sake, speak! What has happened?"

"Just what I feared," he broke out at last, half in tears.

THE FIRST CLOUD

"All is lost! Padre Damaso has ordered me to break the engagement, otherwise he will damn me in this life and in the next. All of them told me the same, even Padre Sibyla. I must close the doors of my house against him, and I owe him over fifty thousand pesos! I told the padres this, but they refused to take any notice of it. 'Which do you prefer to lose,' they asked me, ' fifty thousand pesos or your life and your soul?' Ay, St. Anthony, if I had only known, if I had only known! Don't cry, daughter," he went on, turning to the sobbing girl. "You're not like your mother, who never cried except just before you were born. Padre Damaso told me that a relative of his has just arrived from Spain and you are to marry him."

Maria Clara covered her ears, while Aunt Isabel screamed, "Santiago, are you crazy? To talk to her of another sweetheart now! Do you think that your daughter changes sweethearts as she does her camisa?"

"That's just the way I felt, Isabel. Don Crisostomo is rich, while the Spaniards marry only for love of money. But what do you want me to do? They've threatened me with another excommunication. They say that not only my soul but also my body is in great danger — my body, do you hear, my body!"

"But you're only making your daughter more disconsolate! Isn't the Archbishop your friend? Why don't you write to him?"

"The Archbishop is also a friar, the Archbishop does only what the friars tell him to do. But, Maria, don't cry. The Captain-General is coming, he'll want to see you, and your eyes are all red. Ay, I was thinking to spend a happy evening! Without this misfortune I should be the happiest of men — every one would envy me! Be calm, my child, I'm more unfortunate than you and I'm not crying. You can have another and better husband, while I — I've lost fifty thousand pesos! Ay, Virgin of Antipolo, if tonight I may only have luck!"

Salvos, the sound of carriage wheels, the galloping of

horses, and a band playing the royal march, announced the arrival of his Excellency, the Captain-General of the Philippines. Maria Clara ran to hide herself in her chamber. Poor child, rough hands that knew not its delicate chords were playing with her heart! While the house became filled with people and heavy steps, commanding voices, and the clank of sabers and spurs resounded on all sides, the afflicted maiden reclined half-kneeling before a picture of the Virgin represented in that sorrowful loneliness perceived only by Delaroche, as if he had surprised her returning from the sepulcher of her Son. But Maria Clara was not thinking of that mother's sorrow, she was thinking of her own. With her head hanging down over her breast and her hands resting on the floor she made the picture of a lily bent by the storm. A future dreamed of and cherished for years, whose illusions, born in infancy and grown strong throughout youth, had given form to the very fibers of her being, to be wiped away now from her mind and heart by a single word! It was enough to stop the beating of one and to deprive the other of reason.

Maria Clara was a loving daughter as well as a good and pious Christian, so it was not the excommunication alone that terrified her, but the command and the ominous calmness of her father demanding the sacrifice of her love. Now she felt the whole force of that affection which until this moment she had hardly suspected. It had been like a river gliding along peacefully with its banks carpeted by fragrant flowers and its bed covered with fine sand, so that the wind hardly ruffled its current as it moved along, seeming hardly to flow at all; but suddenly its bed becomes narrower, sharp stones block the way, hoary logs fall across it forming a barrier — then the stream rises and roars with its waves boiling and scattering clouds of foam, it beats against the rocks and rushes into the abyss!

She wanted to pray, but who in despair can pray? Prayers are for the hours of hope, and when in the absence of this we turn to God it is only with complaints. "My

THE FIRST CLOUD

God," cried her heart, "why dost Thou thus cut a man off, why dost Thou deny him the love of others? Thou dost not deny him thy sunlight and thy air nor hide from him the sight of thy heaven! Why then deny him love, for without a sight of the sky, without air or sunlight, one can live, but without love — never!"

Would these cries unheard by men reach the throne of God or be heard by the Mother of the distressed? The poor maiden who had never known a mother dared to confide these sorrows of an earthly love to that pure heart that knew only the love of daughter and of mother. In her despair she turned to that deified image of womanhood, the most beautiful idealization of the most ideal of all creatures, to that poetical creation of Christianity who unites in herself the two most beautiful phases of womanhood without its sorrows: those of virgin and mother, — to her whom we call Mary!

"Mother, mother!" she moaned.

Aunt Isabel came to tear her away from her sorrow since she was being asked for by some friends and by the Captain-General, who wished to talk with her.

"Aunt, tell them that I'm ill," begged the frightened girl. "They're going to make me play on the piano and sing."

"Your father has promised. Are you going to put your father in a bad light?"

Maria Clara rose, looked at her aunt, and threw back her shapely arms, murmuring, "Oh, if I only had —"

But without concluding the phrase she began to make herself ready for presentation.

CHAPTER XXXVII

HIS EXCELLENCY

"I WANT to talk with that young man," said his Excellency to an aide. "He has aroused all my interest."

"They have already gone to look for him, General. But here is a young man from Manila who insists on being introduced. We told him that your Excellency had no time for interviews, that you had not come to give audiences, but to see the town and the procession, and he answered that your Excellency always has time to dispense justice—"

His Excellency turned to the alcalde in wonder. "If I am not mistaken," said the latter with a slight bow, "he is the young man who this morning had a quarrel with Padre Damaso over the sermon."

"Still another? Has this friar set himself to stir up the whole province or does he think that he governs here? Show the young man in." His Excellency paced nervously from one end of the sala to the other.

In the hall were gathered various Spaniards mingled with soldiers and officials of San Diego and neighboring towns, standing in groups conversing or disputing. There were also to be seen all the friars, with the exception of Padre Damaso, and they wanted to go in to pay their respects to his Excellency.

"His Excellency the Captain-General begs your Reverences to wait a moment," said the aide. "Come in, young man!" The Manilan who had confounded Greek with Tagalog entered the room pale and trembling.

All were filled with surprise; surely his Excellency must

be greatly irritated to dare to make the friars wait! Padre Sibyla remarked, "I have n't anything to say to him, I 'm wasting my time here."

"I say the same," added an Augustinian. "Shall we go?"

"Would n't it be better that we find out how he stands?" asked Padre Salvi. "We should avoid a scandal, and should be able to remind him of his duties toward — religion."

"Your Reverences may enter, if you so desire," said the aide as he ushered out the youth who did not understand Greek and whose countenance was now beaming with satisfaction.

Fray Sibyla entered first, Padre Salvi, Padre Martin, and the other priests following. They all made respectful bows with the exception of Padre Sibyla, who even in bending preserved a certain air of superiority. Padre Salvi on the other hand almost doubled himself over the girdle.

"Which of your Reverences is Padre Damaso?" asked the Captain-General without any preliminary greeting, neither asking them to be seated nor inquiring about their health nor addressing them with the flattering speeches to which such important personages are accustomed.

"Padre Damaso is not here among us, sir," replied Fray Sibyla in the same dry tone as that used by his Excellency.

"Your Excellency's servant is in bed sick," added Padre Salvi humbly. "After having the pleasure of welcoming you and of informing ourselves concerning your Excellency's health, as is the duty of all good subjects of the King and of every person of culture, we have come in the name of the respected servant of your Excellency who has had the misfortune —"

"Oh!" interrupted the Captain-General, twirling a chair about on one leg and smiling nervously, "if all the servants of my Excellency were like his Reverence, Padre Damaso, I should prefer myself to serve my Excellency!"

The reverend gentlemen, who were standing up physically, did so mentally at this interruption.

"Won't your Reverences be seated?" he added after a brief pause, moderating his tone a little.

Capitan Tiago here appeared in full dress, walking on tiptoe and leading by the hand Maria Clara, who entered timidly and with hesitation. Still she bowed gracefully and ceremoniously.

"Is this young lady your daughter?" asked the Captain-General in surprise.

"And your Excellency's, General," answered Capitan Tiago seriously.[1]

The alcalde and the aides opened their eyes wide, but his Excellency lost none of his gravity as he took the girl's hand and said affably, "Happy are the fathers who have daughters like you, señorita! I have heard you spoken of with respect and admiration and have wanted to see you and thank you for your beautiful action of this afternoon. I am informed of *everything* and when I make my report to his Majesty's government I shall not forget your noble conduct. Meanwhile, permit me to thank you in the name of his Majesty, the King, whom I represent here and who loves *peace and tranquillity* in his loyal subjects, and for myself, a father who has daughters of your age, and to propose a reward for you."

"Sir—" answered the trembling Maria Clara.

His Excellency guessed what she wanted to say, and so continued: "It is well, señorita, that you are at peace with your conscience and content with the good opinion of your fellow-countrymen, with the faith which is its own best reward and beyond which we should not aspire. But you must not deprive me of an opportunity to show that if Justice knows how to punish she also knows how to reward

---

[1] Spanish etiquette requires that the possessor of an object immediately offer it to any person who asks about it with the conventional phrase, "It is yours." Capitan Tiago is rather overdoing his Latin refinement. — TR.

and that she is not always *blind!*" The italicized words were all spoken in a loud and significant tone.

"Señor Don Juan Crisostomo Ibarra awaits the orders of your Excellency!" announced the aide in a loud voice.

Maria Clara shuddered.

"Ah!" exclaimed the Captain-General. "Allow me, señorita, to express my desire to see you again before leaving the town, as I still have some very important things to say to you. Señor Alcalde, you will accompany me during the walk which I wish to take after the conference that I will hold alone with Señor Ibarra."

"Your Excellency will permit us to inform you," began Padre Salvi humbly, "that Señor Ibarra is excommunicated."

His Excellency cut short this speech, saying, "I am happy that I have only to regret the condition of Padre Damaso, for whom I *sincerely* desire a *complete* recovery, since at his age *a voyage to Spain* on account of his health may not be very agreeable. But that depends on him! Meanwhile, may God preserve the health of your Reverences!"

"And so much depends on him," murmured Padre Salvi as they retired.

"We'll see who makes that voyage soonest!" remarked another Franciscan.

"I shall leave at once," declared the indignant Padre Sibyla.

"And we shall go back to our province," said the Augustinians. Neither the Dominican nor the Augustinians could endure the thought that they had been so coldly received on a Franciscan's account.

In the hall they met Ibarra, their amphitryon of a few hours before, but no greetings were exchanged, only looks that said many things. But when the friars had withdrawn the alcalde greeted him familiarly, although the entrance of the aide looking for the young man left no time for conversation. In the doorway he met Maria Clara; their looks also said many things but quite different from what the friars' eyes had expressed.

Ibarra was dressed in deep mourning, but presented himself serenely and made a profound bow, even though the visit of the friars had not appeared to him to be a good augury. The Captain-General advanced toward him several steps.

"I take pleasure, Señor Ibarra, in shaking your hand. Permit me to receive you in all confidence." His Excellency examined the youth with marked satisfaction.

"Sir, such kindness — '

"Your surprise offends me, signifying as it does that you had not expected to be well received. That is casting a doubt on my sense of justice!"

"A cordial reception, sir, for an insignificant subject of his Majesty like myself is not justice but a favor."

"Good, good," exclaimed his Excellency, seating himself and waving Ibarra to a chair. "Let us enjoy a brief period of frankness. I am very well satisfied with your conduct and have already recommended you to his Majesty for a decoration on account of your philanthropic idea of erecting a schoolhouse. If you had let me know, I would have attended the ceremony with pleasure, and perhaps might have prevented a disagreeable incident."

"It seemed to me such a small matter," answered the youth, "that I did not think it worth while troubling your Excellency with it in the midst of your numerous cares. Besides, my duty was to apply first to the chief authority of my province."

His Excellency nodded with a satisfied air and went on in an even more familiar tone: "In regard to the trouble you've had with Padre Damaso, don't hold any fear or rancor, for they won't touch a hair of your head while I govern the islands. As for the excommunication, I'll speak to the Archbishop, since it is necessary for us to adjust ourselves to circumstances. Here we can't laugh at such things in public as we can in the Peninsula and in enlightened Europe. Nevertheless, be more prudent in the future. You have placed yourself in opposition to the religious orders, who must be respected on account of their influence and their wealth. But I will protect you, for I like good sons, I like to see them honor the memory of their fathers. I loved mine, and, as God lives, I don't know what I would have done in your place!"

Then, changing the subject of conversation quickly, he asked, " I 'm told that you have just returned from Europe; were you in Madrid?"

" Yes, sir, several months."

" Perhaps you heard my family spoken of?"

" Your Excellency had just left when I had the honor of being introduced to your family."

" How is it, then, that you came without bringing any recommendations to me?"

" Sir," replied Ibarra with a bow, "because I did not come direct from Spain and because I have heard your Excellency so well spoken of that I thought a letter of recommendation might not only be valueless but even offensive; all Filipinos are recommended to you."

A smile played about the old soldier's lips and he replied slowly, as though measuring and weighing his words, " You flatter me by thinking so, and — so it ought to be. Nevertheless, young man, you must know what burdens weigh upon our shoulders here in the Philippines. Here we, old soldiers, have to do and to be everything: King, Minister of State, of War, of Justice, of Finance, of Agriculture, and of all the rest. The worst part of it too is that in every matter we have to consult the distant mother country, which accepts or rejects our proposals according to circumstances there — and at times blindly. As we Spaniards say, ' He who attempts many things succeeds in none.' Besides, we generally come here knowing little about the country and leave it when we begin to get acquainted with it. With you I can be frank, for it would be useless to try to be otherwise. Even in Spain, where each department has its own minister, born and reared in the locality, where there are a press and a public opinion, where the opposition frankly opens the eyes of the government and keeps it informed, everything moves along imperfectly and defectively; thus it is a miracle that here things are not completely topsyturvy in the lack of these safeguards, and having to live and work under the shadow of a most powerful opposition. Good intentions are not lacking to us, the governing powers, but we find ourselves obliged to avail ourselves of the eyes and arms of others whom ordinarily we do not know and who perhaps, instead of serving their country, serve only their own private interests. This is not our fault but the fault of circumstances — the friars aid us not a little in getting along, but they are not sufficient. You have aroused my interest and it is my desire that the imperfections of our present system of government be of no hindrance to you. I cannot look after everybody nor can everybody come to me. Can I be of service to you in any way? Have you no request to make?"

Ibarra reflected a moment before he answered. "Sir, my dearest wish is the happiness of my country, a happiness which I desire to see owed to the mother country and to the efforts of my fellow-citizens, the two united by the eternal bonds of common aspirations and common interests. What I would request can only be given by the government after years of unceasing toil and after the introduction of definite reforms."

His Excellency gazed at him for a few seconds with a searching look, which Ibarra sustained with naturalness. "You are the first man that I've talked to in this country!" he finally exclaimed, extending his hand.

"Your Excellency has seen only those who drag themselves about in the city; you have not visited the slandered huts of our towns or your Excellency would have been able to see real men, if to be a man it is sufficient to have a generous heart and simple customs."

The Captain-General rose and began to walk back and forth in the room. "Señor Ibarra," he exclaimed, pausing suddenly, and the young man also rose, "perhaps within a month I shall leave. Your education and your mode of thinking are not for this country. Sell what you have, pack your trunk, and come with me to Europe; the climate there will be more agreeable to you."

"I shall always while I live preserve the memory of your Excellency's kindness," replied Ibarra with emotion, "but I must remain in this country where my fathers have lived."

"Where they have died you might say with more exactness! Believe me, perhaps I know your country better than you yourself do. Ah, now I remember," he exclaimed with a change of tone, "you are going to marry an adorable young woman and I'm detaining you here! Go, go to her, and that you may have greater freedom send her father to me," this with a smile. "Don't forget, though, that I want you to accompany me in my walk."

Ibarra bowed and withdrew. His Excellency then called to his aide. "I'm satisfied," he said, slapping the latter lightly on the shoulder. "Today I've seen for the first time how it is possible for one to be a good Spaniard without ceasing to be a good Filipino and to love his country. Today I showed their Reverences that we are not all puppets of theirs. This young man gave me the opportunity and I shall soon have settled all my accounts with the friars. It's a pity that some day or other this young man — But call the alcalde."

The alcalde presented himself immediately. As he entered, the Captain-General said to him, "Señor Alcalde, in order to avoid any repetition of *scenes* such as you *witnessed* this afternoon, scenes that I regret, as they *hurt the prestige* of the government and of all good Spaniards, allow me to recommend to your *especial* care Señor Ibarra, so that you may afford him means for carrying out his patriotic intentions and also that in the future you prevent his being molested by persons of any class whatsoever, under any pretext at all."

The alcalde understood the reprimand and bowed to conceal his confusion.

"Have the same order communicated to the alferez who commands in the district here. Also, investigate whether that gentleman has affairs of his own that are not sanctioned by the regulations. I've heard more than one complaint in regard to that."

Capitan Tiago presented himself stiff and formal. "Don Santiago," said his Excellency in an affable tone, "a little while ago I felicitated you on the happiness of having a daughter such as the Señorita de los Santos; now let me congratulate you on your future son-in-law. The most virtuous of daughters is certainly worthy of the best citizen of the Philippines. Is it permitted to know when the wedding will occur?"

"Sir!" stammered Capitan Tiago, wiping the perspiration from his forehead.

"Come now, I see that there is nothing definitely arranged. If persons are lacking to stand up with them, I shall take the greatest pleasure in being one of them. That's for the purpose of ridding myself of the feeling of disgust which the many weddings I've heretofore taken part in have given me," he added, turning to the alcalde.

"Yes, sir," answered Capitan Tiago with a smile that would move to pity.

Ibarra almost ran in search of Maria Clara — he had so many things to tell her. Hearing merry voices in one of the rooms, he knocked lightly on the door.

"Who's there?" asked the voice of Maria Clara.

"I!"

The voices became hushed and the door — did not open.

"It's I, may I come in?" called the young man, his heart beating violently.

The silence continued. Then light footsteps approached the door and the merry voice of Sinang murmured through the keyhole, " Crisostomo, we're going to the theater tonight. Write what you have to say to Maria."

The footsteps retreated again as rapidly as they approached.

"What does this mean?" murmured Ibarra thoughtfully as he retired slowly from the door.

CHAPTER XXXVIII

THE PROCESSION

AT nightfall, when all the lanterns in the windows had been lighted, for the fourth time the procession started amid the ringing of bells and the usual explosions of bombs. The Captain-General, who had gone out on foot in company with his two aides, Capitan Tiago, the alcalde, the alferez, and Ibarra, preceded by civil-guards and officials who opened the way and cleared the street, was invited to review the procession from the house of the gobernadorcillo, in front of which a platform had been erected where a *loa* [1] would be recited in honor of the Blessed Patron.

[1] A metrical discourse for a special occasion or in honor of some distinguished personage. Padre Zuñiga (*Estadismo*, Chap. III) thus describes one heard by him in Lipa, Batangas, in 1800, on the occasion of General Alava's visit to that place: "He who is to recite the *loa* is seen in the center of the stage dressed as a Spanish cavalier, reclining in a chair as if asleep, while behind the scenes musicians sing a lugubrious chant in the vernacular. The sleeper awakes and shows by signs that he thinks he has heard, or dreamed of hearing, some voice. He again disposes himself to sleep and the chant is repeated in the same lugubrious tone. Again he awakes, rises, and shows that he has heard a voice. This scene is repeated several times, until at length he is persuaded that the voice is announcing the arrival of the hero who is to be eulogized. He then commences to recite his *loa*, carrying himself like a clown in a circus, while he sings the praises of the person in whose honor the fiesta has been arranged. This *loa*, which was in rhetorical verse in a diffuse style suited to the Asiatic taste, set forth the general's naval expeditions and the honors he had received from the King, concluding with thanks and acknowledgment of the favor that he had conferred in passing through their town and visiting such poor wretches as they. There were not lacking in it the wanderings of Ulysses, the journeys of Aristotle, the unfortunate death of Pliny, and other passages from ancient history, which they delight in introducing into their stories. All these passages are usually filled with fables touching upon the marvelous, such as the following, which merit special

Ibarra would gladly have renounced the pleasure of hearing this poetical composition, preferring to watch the procession from Capitan Tiago's house, where Maria Clara had remained with some of her friends, but his Excellency wished to hear the *loa*, so he had no recourse but to console himself with the prospect of seeing her at the theater.

The procession was headed by the silver candelabra borne by three begloved sacristans, behind whom came the school children in charge of their teacher, then boys with paper lanterns of varied shapes and colors placed on the ends of bamboo poles of greater or less length and decorated according to the caprice of each boy, since this illumination was furnished by the children of the barrios, who gladly performed this service, imposed by the *matanda sa nayon*,[1] each one designing and fashioning his own lantern, adorning it as his fancy prompted and his finances permitted with a greater or less number of frills and little streamers, and lighting it with a piece of candle if he had a friend or relative who was a sacristan, or if he could buy one of the small red tapers such as the Chinese burn before their altars.

In the midst of the crowd came and went alguazils, guardians of justice to take care that the lines were not broken and the people did not crowd together. For this purpose they availed themselves of their rods, with blows from which, administered opportunely and with sufficient force, they endeavored to add to the glory and brilliance of the procession — all for the edification of souls and the

notice: of Aristotle it was said that being unable to learn the depth of the sea he threw himself into its waves and was drowned, and of Pliny that he leaped into Vesuvius to investigate the fire within the volcano. In the same way other historical accounts are confused. I believe that these *loas* were introduced by the priests in former times, although the fables with which they abound would seem to offer an objection to this opinion, as nothing is ever told in them that can be found in the writings of any European author; still they appear to me to have been suited to the less critical taste of past centuries. The verses are written by the natives, among whom there are many poets, this art being less difficult in Tagalog than in any other language." — TR.

[1] "The old man of the village," patriarch. — TR.

splendor of religious show. At the same time that the alguazils were thus distributing free their sanctifying blows, other persons, to console the recipients, distributed candles and tapers of different sizes, also free.

"Señor Alcalde," said Ibarra in a low voice, "do they administer those blows as a punishment for sin or simply because they like to do so?"

"You're right, Señor Ibarra," answered the Captain-General, overhearing the question. "This barbarous sight is a wonder to all who come here from other countries. It ought to be forbidden."

Without any apparent reason, the first saint that appeared was St. John the Baptist. On looking at him it might have been said that the fame of Our Savior's cousin did not amount to much among the people, for while it is true that he had the feet and legs of a maiden and the face of an anchorite, yet he was placed on an old wooden *andas*, and was hidden by a crowd of children who, armed with candles and unlighted lanterns, were engaging in mock fights.

"Unfortunate saint!" muttered the Sage Tasio, who was watching the procession from the street, "it avails you nothing to have been the forerunner of the Good Tidings or that Jesus bowed before you! Your great faith and your austerity avail you nothing, nor the fact that you died for the truth and your convictions, all of which men forget when they consider nothing more than their own merits. It avails more to preach badly in the churches than to be the eloquent voice crying in the desert, this is what the Philippines teaches you! If you had eaten turkey instead of locusts and had worn garments of silk rather than hides, if you had joined a Corporation —"

But the old man suspended his apostrophe at the approach of St. Francis. "Didn't I say so?" he then went on, smiling sarcastically. "This one rides on a car, and, good Heavens, what a car! How many lights and how many glass lanterns! Never did I see you surrounded by so many luminaries, Giovanni Bernardone![1] And what music! Other tunes were heard by your followers after your death! But, venerable and humble founder, if you were to come back to life now you would see only degencrate Eliases of Cortona, and if your followers should recognize you, they would put you in jail, and perhaps you would share the fate of Cesareus of Spyre."

After the music came a banner on which was pictured the same saint, but with seven wings, carried by the Tertiary Brethren dressed in *guingón* habits and praying in high, plaintive voices. Rather inexplicably, next came St. Mary Magdalene, a beautiful image with abundant hair, wearing a pañuelo of embroidered piña held by fingers covered with rings, and a silk gown decorated with gilt spangles. Lights and incense surrounded her while her glass tears reflected the colors of the Bengal lights, which, while giving a fantastic appearance to the procession, also made the saintly sinner weep now green, now red, now blue tears. The houses did not begin to light up until St. Francis was passing; St. John the Baptist did not enjoy this honor and passed hastily by as if ashamed to be the only one dressed in hides in such a crowd of folk covered with gold and jewels.

"There goes our saint!" exclaimed the daughter of the gobernadorcillo to her visitors. "I've lent him all my rings, but that's in order to get to heaven."

The candle-bearers stopped around the platform to listen to the *loa* and the blessed saints did the same; either they or their bearers wished to hear the verses. Those who were carrying St. John, tired of waiting, squatted down on their heels and agreed to set him on the ground.

"The alguazil may scold!" objected one of them.

"Huh, in the sacristy they leave him in a corner among the cobwebs!"

---

[1] The secular name of St. Francis of Assisi, founder of the Franciscan order. — TR.

So St. John, once on the ground, became one of the townsfolk.

As the Magdalene set out the women joined the procession, only that instead of beginning with the children, as among the men, the old women came first and the girls filled up the lines to the car of the Virgin, behind which came the curate under his canopy. This practise they had from Padre Damaso, who said: "To the Virgin the maidens and not the old women are pleasing!" This statement had caused wry faces on the part of many saintly old ladies, but the Virgin did not change her tastes.

San Diego followed the Magdalene but did not seem to be rejoicing over this fact, since he moved along as repentantly as he had in the morning when he followed St. Francis. His float was drawn by six Tertiary Sisters — whether because of some vow or on account of some sickness, the fact is that they dragged him along, and with zeal. San Diego stopped in front of the platform and waited to be saluted.

But it was necessary to wait for the float of the Virgin, which was preceded by persons dressed like phantoms, who frightened the little children so that there were heard the cries and screams of terrified babies. Yet in the midst of that dark mass of gowns, hoods, girdles, and nuns' veils, from which arose a monotonous and snuffling prayer, there were to be seen, like white jasmines or fresh sampaguitas among old rags, twelve girls dressed in white, crowned with flowers, their hair curled, and flashing from their eyes glances as bright as their necklaces. Like little genii of light who were prisoners of specters they moved along holding to the wide blue ribbons tied to the Virgin's car and suggesting the doves that draw the car of Spring.

Now all the images were in attitudes of attention, crowded one against the other to listen to the verses. Everybody kept his eyes fixed on the half-drawn curtain until at length a sigh of admiration escaped from the lips of all. Deservedly so, too, for it was a boy with wings, riding-boots, sash, belt, and plumed hat.

"It's the alcalde!" cried some one, but this prodigy of creation began to recite a poem like himself and took no offense at the comparison.

But why record here what he said in Latin, Tagalog, and Spanish, all in verse — this poor victim of the gobernadorcillo? Our readers have enjoyed Padre Damaso's sermon of the morning and we do not wish to spoil them by too many wonders. Besides, the Franciscan might feel hard toward us if we were to put forward a competitor, and this is far from being the desire of such peaceful folk as we have the good fortune to be.

Afterwards, the procession moved on, St. John proceeding along his vale of tears. When the Virgin passed the house of Capitan Tiago a heavenly song greeted her with the words of the archangel. It was a voice tender, melodious, pleading, sighing out the *Ave Maria* of Gounod to the accompaniment of a piano that prayed with it. The music of the procession became hushed, the praying ceased, and even Padre Salvi himself paused. The voice trembled and became plaintive, expressing more than a salutation — rather a prayer and a protest.

Terror and melancholy settled down upon Ibarra's heart as he listened to the voice from the window where he stood. He comprehended what that suffering soul was expressing in a song and yet feared to ask himself the cause of such sorrow. Gloomy and thoughtful, he turned to the Captain-General.

"You will join me at the table," the latter said to him. "There we'll talk about those boys who disappeared."

"Could I be the cause?" murmured the young man, staring without seeing the Captain-General, whom he was following mechanically.

CHAPTER XXXIX

DOÑA CONSOLACION

WHY were the windows closed in the house of the alferez? Where were the masculine features and the flannel camisa of the Medusa or Muse of the Civil Guard while the procession was passing? Had Doña Consolacion realized how disagreeable were her forehead seamed with thick veins that appeared to conduct not blood but vinegar and gall, and the thick cigar that made a fit ornament for her purple lips, and her envious leer, and yielding to a generous impulse had she wished not to disturb the pleasure of the populace by her sinister appearance? Ah, for her generous impulses existed in the Golden Age! The house showed neither lanterns nor banners and was gloomy precisely because the town was making merry, as Sinang said, and but for the sentinel walking before the door appeared to be uninhabited.

A dim light shone in the disordered sala, rendering transparent the dirty concha-panes on which the cobwebs had fastened and the dust had become incrusted. The lady of the house, according to her indolent custom, was dozing on a wide sofa. She was dressed as usual, that is, badly and horribly: tied round her head a pañuelo, from beneath which escaped thin locks of tangled hair, a camisa of blue flannel over another which must once have been white, and a faded skirt which showed the outlines of her thin, flat thighs, placed one over the other and shaking feverishly. From her mouth issued little clouds of smoke which she puffed wearily in whatever direction she happened to be looking when she opened her eyes. If at that moment Don

DOÑA CONSOLACION

Francisco de Cañamaque[1] could have seen her, he would have taken her for a cacique of the town or the *mankukúlam*, and then decorated his discovery with commentaries in the vernacular of the markets, invented by him for her particular use.

That morning she had not attended mass, not because she had not so desired, for on the contrary she had wished to show herself to the multitude and to hear the sermon, but her spouse had not permitted her to do so, his refusal being accompanied as usual by two or three insults, oaths, and threats of kicking. The alferez knew that his mate dressed ridiculously and had the appearance of what is known as a "*querida* of the soldiers," so he did not care to expose her to the gaze of strangers and persons from the capital. But she did not so understand it. She knew that she was beautiful and attractive, that she had the airs of a queen and dressed much better and with more splendor than Maria Clara herself, who wore a tapis while she went in a flowing skirt. It was therefore necessary for the alferez to threaten her, "Either shut up, or I'll kick you back to your damned town!" Doña Consolacion did not care to return to her town at the toe of a boot, but she meditated revenge.

Never had the dark face of this lady been such as to inspire confidence in any one, not even when she painted, but that morning it greatly worried the servants, especially when they saw her move about the house from one part to another, silently, as if meditating something terrible or malign. Her glance reflected the look that springs from the eyes of a serpent when caught and about to be crushed; it was cold, luminous, and penetrating, with something fascinat-

---

[1] A Spanish official, author of several works relating to the Philippines, one of which, *Recuerdos de Filipinas* (Madrid, 1877 and 1880), — a loose series of sketches and impressions giving anything but a complimentary picture of the character and conduct of the Spaniards in the Islands, and in a rather naïve and perhaps unintentional way throwing some lurid side-lights on the governmental administration and the friar régime, — enjoyed the distinction of being officially prohibited from circulation in the archipelago. -- TR.

ing, loathsome, and cruel in it. The most insignificant error, the least unusual noise, drew from her a vile insult that struck into the soul, but no one answered her, for to excuse oneself would have been an additional fault.

So the day passed. Not encountering any obstacle that would block her way, — her husband had been invited out, — she became saturated with bile, the cells of her whole organism seemed to become charged with electricity which threatened to burst in a storm of hate. Everything about her folded up as do the flowers at the first breath of the hurricane, so she met with no resistance nor found any point or high place to discharge her evil humor. The soldiers and servants kept away from her. That she might not hear the sounds of rejoicing outside she had ordered the windows closed and charged the sentinel to let no one enter. She tied a handkerchief around her head as if to keep it from bursting and, in spite of the fact that the sun was still shining, ordered the lamps to be lighted.

Sisa, as we saw, had been arrested as a disturber of the peace and taken to the barracks. The alferez was not then present, so the unfortunate woman had had to spend the night there seated on a bench in an abandoned attitude. The next day the alferez saw her, and fearing for her in those days of confusion nor caring to risk a disagreeable scene, he had charged the soldiers to look after her, to treat her kindly, and to give her something to eat. Thus the madwoman spent two days.

Tonight, whether the nearness to the house of Capitan Tiago had brought to her Maria Clara's sad song or whether other recollections awoke in her old melodies, whatever the cause, Sisa also began to sing in a sweet and melancholy voice the *kundiman* of her youth. The soldiers heard her and fell silent; those airs awoke old memories of the days before they had been corrupted. Doña Consolacion also heard them in her tedium, and on learning who it was that sang, after a few moments of meditation, ordered that Sisa be brought to her instantly. Something like a smile wandered over her dry lips.

When Sisa was brought in she came calmly, showing neither wonder nor fear. She seemed to see no lady or mistress, and this wounded the vanity of the Muse, who endeavored to inspire respect and fear. She coughed, made a sign to the soldiers to leave her, and taking down her husband's whip, said to the crazy woman in a sinister tone, "Come on, *magcantar icau!*"[1]

Naturally, Sisa did not understand such Tagalog, and this ignorance calmed the Medusa's wrath, for one of the beautiful qualities of this lady was to try not to know Tagalog, or at least to appear not to know it. Speaking it the worst possible, she would thus give herself the air of a genuine *orofea,*[2] as she was accustomed to say. But she did well, for if she martyrized Tagalog, Spanish fared no better with her, either in regard to grammar or pronunciation, in spite of her husband, the chairs and the shoes, all of which had done what they could to teach her.

One of the words that had cost her more effort than the hieroglyphics cost Champollion was the name *Filipinas.* The story goes that on the day after her wedding, when she was talking with her husband, who was then a corporal, she had said *Pilipinas.* The corporal thought it his duty to correct her, so he said, slapping her on the head, "Say *Felipinas,* woman! Don't be stupid! Don't you know that's what your damned country is called, from *Felipe?*"

The woman, dreaming through her honeymoon, wished to obey and said *Felepinas.* To the corporal it seemed that she was getting nearer to it, so he increased the slaps and reprimanded her thus: "But, woman, can't you pronounce *Felipe?* Don't forget it; you know the king, Don Felipe — the fifth —. Say *Felipe,* and add to it *nas,* which in Latin means 'islands of Indians,' and you have the name of your damned country!"

[1] "Magcanta-ca!" "(You) sing!" — Tr.
[2] Europea: European woman. — Tr.

Consolacion, at that time a washerwoman, patted her bruises and repeated with symptoms of losing her patience, "Fe-li-pe, Felipe—nas, Fe-li-pe-nas, Felipinas, so?"

The corporal saw visions. How could it be *Felipenas* instead of *Felipinas?* One of two things: either it was *Felipenas* or it was necessary to say *Felipi!* So that day he very prudently dropped the subject. Leaving his wife, he went to consult the books. Here his astonishment reached a climax: he rubbed his eyes — let's see — slowly, now! *F-i-l-i-p-i-n-a-s,* Filipinas! So all the well-printed books gave it — neither he nor his wife was right!

"How's this?" he murmured. "Can history lie? Does n't this book say that Alonso Saavedra gave the country that name in honor of the prince, Don Felipe? How was that name corrupted? Can it be that this Alonso Saavedra was an Indian?"[1]

With these doubts he went to consult the sergeant Gomez, who, as a youth, had wanted to be a curate. Without deigning to look at the corporal the sergeant blew out a mouthful of smoke and answered with great pompousness, "In ancient times it was pronounced *Filipi* instead of *Felipe.* But since we moderns have become Frenchified we can't endure two *i*'s in succession, so cultured people, especially in Madrid — you 've never been in Madrid? — cultured people, as I say, have begun to change the first *i* to *e* in many words. This is called modernizing yourself."

The poor corporal had never been in Madrid — here was the cause of his failure to understand the riddle: what things are learned in Madrid! "So now it's proper to say —"

"In the ancient style, man! This country's not yet cul-

---

[1] In 1527–29 *Alvaro* de Saavedra led an unsuccessful expedition to take possession of the "Western Isles." The name "Filipina," in honor of the Prince of the Asturias, afterwards Felipe II (Philip II), was first applied to what is probably the present island of Leyte by Ruy Lopez de Villalobos, who led another unsuccessful expedition thither in 1542–43, this name being later extended to the whole group. — TR.

tured! In the ancient style, *Filipinas!*" exclaimed Gomez disdainfully.

The corporal, even if he was a bad philologist, was yet a good husband. What he had just learned his spouse must also know, so he proceeded with her education: "Consola, what do you call your damned country?"

"What should I call it? Just what you taught me: *Felifinas!*"

"I'll throw a chair at you, you ——! Yesterday you pronounced it even better in the modern style, but now it's proper to pronounce it like an ancient: *Feli*, I mean, *Filipinas!*"

"Remember that I'm no ancient! What are you thinking about?"

"Never mind! Say *Filipinas!*"

"I don't want to. I'm no ancient baggage, scarcely thirty years old!" she replied, rolling up her sleeves and preparing herself for the fray.

"Say it, you ——, or I'll throw this chair at you!"

Consolacion saw the movement, reflected, then began to stammer with heavy breaths, "*Feli-, Fele-, File* —"

Pum! Crack! The chair finished the word. So the lesson ended in fisticuffs, scratchings, slaps. The corporal caught her by the hair; she grabbed his goatee, but was unable to bite because of her loose teeth. He let out a yell, released her and begged her pardon. Blood began to flow, one eye got redder than the other, a camisa was torn into shreds, many things came to light, but not *Filipinas*.

Similar incidents occurred every time the question of language came up. The corporal, watching her linguistic progress, sorrowfully calculated that in ten years his mate would have completely forgotten how to talk, and this was about what really came to pass. When they were married she still knew Tagalog and could make herself understood in Spanish, but now, at the time of our story, she no longer spoke any language. She had become so addicted to expressing herself by means of signs — and of these she chose the loudest and most impressive — that she could have given odds to the inventor of Volapuk.

Sisa, therefore, had the good fortune not to understand her, so the Medusa smoothed out her eyebrows a little, while a smile of satisfaction lighted up her face; undoubtedly she did not know Tagalog, she was an *orofea!*

"Boy, tell her in Tagalog to sing! She does n't understand me, she does n't understand Spanish!"

The madwoman understood the boy and began to sing the *Song of the Night.* Doña Consolacion listened at first with a sneer, which disappeared little by little from her lips. She became attentive, then serious, and even somewhat thoughtful. The voice, the sentiment in the lines, and the song itself affected her — that dry and withered heart was perhaps thirsting for rain. She understood it well: "The sadness, the cold, and the moisture that descend from the sky when wrapped in the mantle of night," so ran the *kundíman,* seemed to be descending also on her heart. "The withered and faded flower which during the day flaunted her finery, seeking applause and full of vanity, at eventide, repentant and disenchanted, makes an effort to raise her drooping petals to the sky, seeking a little shade to hide herself and die without the mocking of the light that saw her in her splendor, without seeing the vanity of her pride, begging also that a little dew should weep upon her. The nightbird leaves his solitary retreat, the hollow of an ancient trunk, and disturbs the sad loneliness of the open places —"

"No, don't sing!" she exclaimed in perfect Tagalog, as she rose with agitation. "Don't sing! Those verses hurt me."

The crazy woman became silent. The boy ejaculated, "*Abá!* She talks Tagalog!" and stood staring with admiration at his mistress, who, realizing that she had given herself away, was ashamed of it, and as her nature was not that of a woman, the shame took the aspect of rage and

hate; so she showed the door to the imprudent boy and
closed it behind him with a kick.

Twisting the whip in her nervous hands, she took a few
turns around the room, then stopping suddenly in front of
the crazy woman, said to her in Spanish, "Dance!" But
Sisa did not move.

"Dance, dance!" she repeated in a sinister tone.

The madwoman looked at her with wandering, expressionless eyes, while the alfereza lifted one of her arms, then
the other, and shook them, but to no purpose, for Sisa did
not understand. Then she began to jump about and shake
herself, encouraging Sisa to imitate her. In the distance
was to be heard the music of the procession playing a grave
and majestic march, but Doña Consolacion danced furiously,
keeping other time to other music resounding within her.
Sisa gazed at her without moving, while her eyes expressed
curiosity and something like a weak smile hovered around
her pallid lips: the lady's dancing amused her. The latter
stopped as if ashamed, raised the whip, — that terrible
whip known to thieves and soldiers, made in Ulango [1] and
perfected by the alferez with twisted wires, — and said,
"Now it's your turn to dance — dance!"

She began to strike the madwoman's bare feet gently
with the whip. Sisa's face drew up with pain and she
was forced to protect herself with her hands.

"Aha, now you're starting!" she exclaimed with savage
joy, passing from *lento* to *allegro vivace*.

The afflicted Sisa gave a cry of pain and quickly raised
her foot.

"You've got to dance, you Indian —!" The whip
swung and whistled.

Sisa let herself fall to the floor and placed both hands
on her knees while she gazed at her tormentor with wildly-
staring eyes. Two sharp cuts of the whip on her shoulder
made her stand up, and it was not merely a cry but a howl

---

[1] A barrio of Tanawan, Batangas, noted for the manufacture of
horsewhips. — TR.

that the unfortunate woman uttered. Her thin camisa was torn, her skin broken, and the blood was flowing.

The sight of blood arouses the tiger; the blood of her victim aroused Doña Consolacion. "Dance, damn you, dance! Evil to the mother who bore you!" she cried. "Dance, or I'll flog you to death!" She then caught Sisa with one hand and, whipping her with the other, began to dance about.

The crazy woman at last understood and followed the example by swinging her arms about awkwardly. A smile of satisfaction curled the lips of her teacher, the smile of a female Mephistopheles who succeeds in getting a great pupil. There were in it hate, disdain, jest, and cruelty; with a burst of demoniacal laughter she could not have expressed more.

Thus, absorbed in the joy of the sight, she was not aware of the arrival of her husband until he opened the door with a loud kick. The alferez appeared pale and gloomy, and when he saw what was going on he threw a terrible glance at his wife, who did not move from her place but stood smiling at him cynically.

The alferez put his hand as gently as he could on the shoulder of the strange dancer and made her stop. The crazy woman sighed and sank slowly to the floor covered with her own blood.

The silence continued. The alferez breathed heavily, while his wife watched him with questioning eyes. She picked up the whip and asked in a smooth, soft voice, "What's the matter with you? You haven't even wished me good evening."

The alferez did not answer, but instead called the boy and said to him, "Take this woman away and tell Marta to get her some other clothes and attend to her. You give her something to eat and a good bed. Take care that she isn't ill-treated! Tomorrow she'll be taken to Señor Ibarra's house."

Then he closed the door carefully, bolted it, and approached his wife. "You're tempting me to kill you!" he exclaimed, doubling up his fists.

"What's the matter with you?" she asked, rising and drawing away from him.

"What's the matter with me!" he yelled in a voice of thunder, letting out an oath and holding up before her a sheet of paper covered with scrawls. "Didn't you write this letter to the alcalde saying that I'm bribed to permit gambling, huh? I don't know why I don't beat you to death."

"Let's see you! Let's see you try it if you dare!" she replied with a jeering laugh. "The one who beats me to death has got to be more of a man than you are!"

He heard the insult, but saw the whip. Catching up a plate from the table, he threw it at her head, but she, accustomed to such fights, dodged quickly and the plate was shattered against the wall. A cup and saucer met with a similar fate.

"Coward!" she yelled; "you're afraid to come near me!" And to exasperate him the more, she spat upon him.

The alferez went blind from rage and with a roar attempted to throw himself upon her, but she, with astonishing quickness, hit him across the face with the whip and ran hurriedly into an inner room, shutting and bolting the door violently behind her. Bellowing with rage and pain, he followed, but was only able to run against the door, which made him vomit oaths.

"Accursed be your offspring, you sow! Open, open, or I'll break your head!" he howled, beating the door with his hands and feet.

No answer was heard, but instead the scraping of chairs and trunks as if she was building a barricade with the furniture. The house shook under the kicks and curses of the alferez.

"Don't come in, don't come in!" called the sour voice inside. "If you show yourself, I'll shoot you."

By degrees he appeared to become calm and contented himself with walking up and down the room like a wild beast in its cage.

"Go out into the street and cool off your head!" the woman continued to jeer at him, as she now seemed to have completed her preparations for defense.

"I swear that if I catch you, even God won't save you, you old sow!"

"Yes, now you can say what you like. You did n't want me to go to mass! You did n't let me attend to my religious duties!" she answered with such sarcasm as only she knew how to use.

The alferez put on his helmet, arranged his clothing a little, and went out with heavy steps, but returned after a few minutes without making the least noise, having taken off his shoes. The servants, accustomed to these brawls, were usually bored, but this novelty of the shoes attracted their attention, so they winked to one another. The alferez sat down quietly in a chair at the side of the Sublime Port and had the patience to wait for more than half an hour.

"Have you really gone out or are you still there, old goat?" asked the voice from time to time, changing the epithets and raising the tone. At last she began to take away the furniture piece by piece. He heard the noise and smiled.

"Boy, has your master gone out?" cried Doña Consolacion.

At a sign from the alferez the boy answered, "Yes, señora, he's gone out."

A gleeful laugh was heard from her as she pulled back the bolt. Slowly her husband arose, the door opened a little way —

A yell, the sound of a falling body, oaths, howls, curses, blows, hoarse voices — who can tell what took place in the darkness of that room?

As the boy went out into the kitchen he made a significant sign to the cook, who said to him, "You'll pay for that."

"I? In any case the whole town will! She asked me if he had gone out, not if he had come back!"

CHAPTER XL

RIGHT AND MIGHT

TEN o'clock at night: the last rockets rose lazily in the dark sky where a few paper balloons recently inflated with smoke and hot air still glimmered like new stars. Some of those adorned with fireworks took fire, threatening all the houses, so there might be seen on the ridges of the roofs men armed with pails of water and long poles with pieces of cloth on the ends. Their black silhouettes stood out in the vague clearness of the air like phantoms that had descended from space to witness the rejoicings of men. Many pieces of fireworks of fantastic shapes — wheels, castles, bulls, carabaos — had been set off, surpassing in beauty and grandeur anything ever before seen by the inhabitants of San Diego.

Now the people were moving in crowds toward the plaza to attend the theater for the last time. Here and there might be seen Bengal lights fantastically illuminating the merry groups while the boys were availing themselves of torches to hunt in the grass for unexploded bombs and other remnants that could still be used. But soon the music gave the signal and all abandoned the open places.

The great stage was brilliantly illuminated. Thousands of lights surrounded the posts, hung from the roof, or sowed the floor with pyramidal clusters. An alguazil was looking after these, and when he came forward to attend to them the crowd shouted at him and whistled, "There he is! there he is!"

In front of the curtain the orchestra players were tuning their instruments and playing preludes of airs. Behind them was the space spoken of by the correspondent in his letter, where the leading citizens of the town, the Spaniards, and the rich visitors occupied rows of chairs. The general public, the nameless rabble, filled up the rest of the place, some of them bringing benches on their shoulders not so much for seats as to make up for their lack of stature. This provoked noisy protests on the part of the benchless, so the offenders got down at once; but before long they were up again as if nothing had happened.

Goings and comings, cries, exclamations, bursts of laughter, a serpent-cracker turned loose, a firecracker set off — all contributed to swell the uproar. Here a bench had a leg broken off and the people fell to the ground amid the laughter of the crowd. They were visitors who had come from afar to observe and now found themselves the observed. Over there they quarreled and disputed over a seat, a little farther on was heard the noise of breaking glass; it was Andeng carrying refreshments and drinks, holding the wide tray carefully with both hands, but by chance she had met her sweetheart, who tried to take advantage of the situation.

The teniente-mayor, Don Filipo, presided over the show, as the gobernadorcillo was fond of monte. He was talking with old Tasio. "What can I do? The alcalde was unwilling to accept my resignation. 'Don't you feel strong enough to attend to your duties?' he asked me."

"How did you answer him?"

"'Señor Alcalde,' I answered, 'the strength of a teniente-mayor, however insignificant it may be, is like all other authority — it emanates from higher spheres. The King himself receives his strength from the people and the people theirs from God. That is exactly what I lack, Señor Alcalde.' But he did not care to listen to me, telling me that we would talk about it after the fiesta."

"Then may God help you!" said the old man, starting away.

"Don't you want to see the show?"

"Thanks, no! For dreams and nonsense I am sufficient

unto myself," the Sage answered with a sarcastic smile. "But now I think of it, has your attention never been drawn to the character of our people? Peaceful, yet fond of warlike shows and bloody fights; democratic, yet adoring emperors, kings, and princes; irreligious, yet impoverishing itself by costly religious pageants. Our women have gentle natures yet go wild with joy when a princess flourishes a lance. Do you know to what it is due? Well —"

The arrival of Maria Clara and her friends put an end to this conversation. Don Filipo met them and ushered them to their seats. Behind them came the curate with another Franciscan and some Spaniards. Following the priests were a number of the townsmen who make it their business to escort the friars. "May God reward them also in the next life," muttered old Tasio as he went away.

The play began with Chananay and Marianito in *Crispino é la comare*. All now had their eyes and ears turned to the stage, all but one: Padre Salvi, who seemed to have gone there for no other purpose than that of watching Maria Clara, whose sadness gave to her beauty an air so ideal and interesting that it was easy to understand how she might be looked upon with rapture. But the eyes of the Franciscan, deeply hidden in their sunken sockets, spoke nothing of rapture. In that gloomy gaze was to be read something desperately sad — with such eyes Cain might have gazed from afar on the Paradise whose delights his mother pictured to him!

The first scene was over when Ibarra entered. His appearance caused a murmur, and attention was fixed on him and the curate. But the young man seemed not to notice anything as he greeted Maria Clara and her friends in a natural way and took a seat beside them.

The only one who spoke to him was Sinang. "Did you see the fireworks?" she asked.

"No, little friend, I had to go with the Captain-General."

"Well, that's a shame! The curate was with us and

told us stories of the damned — can you imagine it! — to fill us with fear so that we might not enjoy ourselves — can you imagine it!"

The curate arose and approached Don Filipo, with whom he began an animated conversation. The former spoke in a nervous manner, the latter in a low, measured voice.

"I'm sorry that I can't please your Reverence," said Don Filipo, "but Señor Ibarra is one of the heaviest contributors and has a right to be here as long as he does n't disturb the peace."

"But is n't it disturbing the peace to scandalize good Christians? It's letting a wolf enter the fold. You will answer for this to God and the authorities!"

"I always answer for the actions that spring from my own will, Padre," replied Don Filipo with a slight bow. "But my little authority does not empower me to mix in religious affairs. Those who wish to avoid contact with him need not talk to him. Señor Ibarra forces himself on no one."

"But it's giving opportunity for danger, and he who loves danger perishes in it."

"I don't see any danger, Padre. The alcalde and the Captain-General, my superior officers, have been talking with him all the afternoon and it's not for me to teach them a lesson."

"If you don't put him out of here, we'll leave."

"I'm very sorry, but I can't put any one out of here."

The curate repented of his threat, but it was too late to retract, so he made a sign to his companion, who arose with regret, and the two went out together. The persons attached to them followed their example, casting looks of hatred at Ibarra.

The murmurs and whispers increased. A number of people approached the young man and said to him, "We're with you, don't take any notice of them."

"Whom do you mean by *them?*" Ibarra asked in surprise.

"Those who 've just left to avoid contact with you."

"Left to avoid contact with me?"

"Yes, they say that you 're excommunicated."

"Excommunicated?" The astonished youth did not know what to say. He looked about him and saw that Maria Clara was hiding her face behind her fan. "But is it possible?" he exclaimed finally. "Are we still in the Dark Ages? So —"

He approached the young women and said with a change of tone, "Excuse me, I 've forgotten an engagement. I 'll be back to see you home."

"Stay!" Sinang said to him. "Yeyeng is going to dance *La Calandria*. She dances divinely."

"I can't, little friend, but I 'll be back."

The uproar increased.

Yeyeng appeared fancifully dressed, with the "*Da usté su permiso?*" and Carvajal was answering her, "*Pase usté adelante,*" when two soldiers of the Civil Guard went up to Don Filipo and ordered him to stop the performance.

"Why?" asked the teniente-mayor in surprise.

"Because the alferez and his wife have been fighting and can't sleep."

"Tell the alferez that we have permission from the alcalde and that against such permission *no one* in the town has any authority, not even the gobernadorcillo himself, and *he* is my *only superior.*"

"Well, the show must stop!" repeated the soldiers.

Don Filipo turned his back and they went away. In order not to disturb the merriment he told no one about the incident.

After the selection of vaudeville, which was loudly applauded, the Prince Villardo presented himself, challenging to mortal combat the Moros who held his father prisoner. The hero threatened to cut off all their heads at a single stroke and send them to the moon, but fortunately for the Moros, who were disposing themselves for the combat, a tumult arose. The orchestra suddenly ceased playing, threw their instruments away, and jumped up on the stage. The valiant Villardo, not expecting them and taking them for allies of the Moros, dropped his sword and shield, and started to run. The Moros, seeing that such a doughty Christian was fleeing, did not consider it improper to imitate him. Cries, groans, prayers, oaths were heard, while the people ran and pushed one another about. The lights were extinguished, blazing lamps were thrown into the air. "Tulisanes! Tulisanes!" cried some. "Fire, fire! Robbers!" shouted others. Women and children wept, benches and spectators were rolled together on the ground amid the general pandemonium.

The cause of all this uproar was two civil-guards, clubs in hand, chasing the musicians in order to break up the performance. The teniente-mayor, with the aid of the cuadrilleros, who were armed with old sabers, managed at length to arrest them, in spite of their resistance.

"Take them to the town hall!" cried Don Filipo. "Take care that they don't get away!"

Ibarra had returned to look for Maria Clara. The frightened girls clung to him pale and trembling while Aunt Isabel recited the Latin litany.

When the people were somewhat calmed down from their fright and had learned the cause of the disturbance, they were beside themselves with indignation. Stones rained on the squad of cuadrilleros who were conducting the two offenders from the scene, and there were even those who proposed to set fire to the barracks of the Civil Guard so as to roast Doña Consolacion along with the alferez.

"That's what they're good for!" cried a woman, doubling up her fists and stretching out her arms. "To disturb the town! They don't chase any but honest folks! Out yonder are the tulisanes and the gamblers. Let's set fire to the barracks!"

One man was beating himself on the arm and begging for confession. Plaintive sounds issued from under the overturned benches — it was a poor musician. The stage was crowded with actors and spectators, all talking at the same time. There was Chananay dressed as Leonor in *Il Trovatore*, talking in the language of the markets to Ratia in the costume of a schoolmaster; Yeyeng, wrapped in a silk shawl, was clinging to the Prince Villardo; while Balbino and the Moros were exerting themselves to console the more or less injured musicians.[1] Several Spaniards went from group to group haranguing every one they met.

A large crowd was forming, whose intention Don Filipo seemed to be aware of, for he ran to stop them. "Don't disturb the peace!" he cried. "Tomorrow we'll ask for an accounting and we'll get justice. I'll answer for it that we get justice!"

"No!" was the reply of several. "They did the same thing in Kalamba,[2] the same promise was made, but the alcalde did nothing. We'll take the law into our own hands! To the barracks!"

In vain the teniente-mayor pleaded with them. The crowd maintained its hostile attitude, so he looked about him for help and noticed Ibarra.

"Señor Ibarra, as a favor! Restrain them while I get some cuadrilleros."

"What can I do?" asked the perplexed youth, but the teniente-mayor was already at a distance. He gazed about him seeking he knew not whom, when accidentally he discerned Elias, who stood impassively watching the disturbance.

Ibarra ran to him, caught him by the arm, and said to him in Spanish: "For God's sake, do something, if you can! I can't do anything." The pilot must have understood him, for he disappeared in the crowd. Lively dis-

---

[1] The actors named were real persons. Ratia was a Spanish-Filipino who acquired quite a reputation not only in Manila but also in Spain. He died in Manila in 1910. — TR.

[2] In the year 1879. — *Author's note*.

putes and sharp exclamations were heard. Gradually the crowd began to break up, its members each taking a less hostile attitude. It was high time, indeed, for the soldiers were already rushing out armed and with fixed bayonets.

Meanwhile, what had the curate been doing? Padre Salvi had not gone to bed but had stood motionless, resting his forehead against the curtains and gazing toward the plaza. From time to time a suppressed sigh escaped him, and if the light of the lamp had not been so dim, perhaps it would have been possible to see his eyes fill with tears. Thus nearly an hour passed.

The tumult in the plaza awoke him from his reverie. With startled eyes he saw the confused movements of the people, while their voices came up to him faintly. A breathless servant informed him of what was happening. A thought shot across his mind: in the midst of confusion and tumult is the time when libertines take advantage of the consternation and weakness of woman. Every one seeks to save himself, no one thinks of any one else; a cry is not heard or heeded, women faint, are struck and fall, terror and fright heed not shame, under the cover of night — and when they are in love! He imagined that he saw Crisostomo snatch the fainting Maria Clara up in his arms and disappear into the darkness. So he went down the stairway by leaps and bounds, and without hat or cane made for the plaza like a madman. There he met some Spaniards who were reprimanding the soldiers, but on looking toward the seats that the girls had occupied he saw that they were vacant.

"Padre! Padre!" cried the Spaniards, but he paid no attention to them as he ran in the direction of Capitan Tiago's. There he breathed more freely, for he saw in the open hallway the adorable silhouette, full of grace and soft in outline, of Maria Clara, and that of the aunt carrying cups and glasses.

"Ah!" he murmured, "it seems that she has been taken sick only."

Aunt Isabel at that moment closed the windows and the graceful shadow was no longer to be seen. The curate moved away without heeding the crowd. He had before his eyes the beautiful form of a maiden sleeping and breathing sweetly. Her eyelids were shaded by long lashes which formed graceful curves like those of the Virgins of Raphael, the little mouth was smiling, all the features breathed forth virginity, purity, and innocence. That countenance formed a sweet vision in the midst of the white coverings of her bed like the head of a cherub among the clouds. His imagination went still further — but who can write what a burning brain can imagine?

Perhaps only the newspaper correspondent, who concluded his account of the fiesta and its accompanying incidents in the following manner·

"A thousand thanks, infinite thanks, to the opportune and active intervention of the Very Reverend Padre Fray Bernardo Salvi, who, defying every danger in the midst of the unbridled mob, without hat or cane, calmed the wrath of the crowd, using only his persuasive word with the majesty and authority that are never lacking to a minister of a Religion of Peace. With unparalleled self-abnegation this virtuous priest tore himself from sweet repose, such as every good conscience like his enjoys, and rushed to protect his flock from the least harm. The people of San Diego will hardly forget this sublime deed of their heroic Pastor, remembering to hold themselves grateful to him for all eternity!"

CHAPTER XLI

TWO VISITS

IBARRA was in such a state of mind that he found it impossible to sleep, so to distract his attention from the sad thoughts which are so exaggerated during the night-hours he set to work in his lonely cabinet. Day found him still making mixtures and combinations, to the action of which he subjected pieces of bamboo and other substances, placing them afterwards in numbered and sealed jars.

A servant entered to announce the arrival of a man who had the appearance of being from the country. "Show him in," said Ibarra without looking around.

Elias entered and remained standing in silence.

"Ah, it's you!" exclaimed Ibarra in Tagalog when he recognized him. "Excuse me for making you wait, I didn't notice that it was you. I'm making an important experiment."

"I don't want to disturb you," answered the youthful pilot. "I've come first to ask you if there is anything I can do for you in the province of Batangas, for which I am leaving immediately, and also to bring you some bad news."

Ibarra questioned him with a look.

"Capitan Tiago's daughter is ill," continued Elias quietly, "but not seriously."

"That's what I feared," murmured Ibarra in a weak voice. "Do you know what is the matter with her?"

"A fever. Now, if you have nothing to command—"

"Thank you, my friend, no. I wish you a pleasant journey. But first let me ask you a question — if it is indiscreet, do not answer."

Elias bowed.

"How were you able to quiet the disturbance last night?" asked Ibarra, looking steadily at him.

"Very easily," answered Elias in the most natural manner. "The leaders of the commotion were two brothers whose father died from a beating given him by the Civil Guard. One day I had the good fortune to save them from the same hands into which their father had fallen, and both are accordingly grateful to me. I appealed to them last night and they undertook to dissuade the rest."

"And those two brothers whose father died from the beating —"

"Will end as their father did," replied Elias in a low voice. "When misfortune has once singled out a family all its members must perish, — when the lightning strikes a tree the whole is reduced to ashes."

Ibarra fell silent on hearing this, so Elias took his leave. When the youth found himself alone he lost the serene self-possession he had maintained in the pilot's presence. His sorrow pictured itself on his countenance. "I, I have made her suffer," he murmured.

He dressed himself quickly and descended the stairs. A small man, dressed in mourning, with a large scar on his left cheek, saluted him humbly, and detained him on his way.

"What do you want?" asked Ibarra.

"Sir, my name is Lucas, and I'm the brother of the man who was killed yesterday."

"Ah, you have my sympathy. Well?"

"Sir, I want to know how much you're going to pay my brother's family."

"Pay?" repeated the young man, unable to conceal his disgust. "We'll talk of that later. Come back this afternoon, I'm in a hurry now."

"Only tell me how much you're willing to pay," insisted Lucas.

"I've told you that we'll talk about that some other time. I have n't time now," repeated Ibarra impatiently.

"You have n't time now, sir?" asked Lucas bitterly, placing himself in front of the young man. "You have n't time to consider the dead?"

"Come this afternoon, my good man," replied Ibarra, restraining himself. "I 'm on my way now to visit a sick person."

"Ah, for the sick you forget the dead? Do you think that because we are poor —"

Ibarra looked at him and interrupted, "Don't try my patience!" then went on his way.

Lucas stood looking after him with a smile full of hate.

"It 's easy to see that you 're the grandson of the man who tied my father out in the sun," he muttered between his teeth. "You still have the same blood."

Then with a change of tone he added, "But, if you pay well — friends!"

CHAPTER XLII

THE ESPADAÑAS

THE fiesta is over. The people of the town have again found, as in every other year, that their treasury is poorer, that they have worked, sweated, and stayed awake much without really amusing themselves, without gaining any new friends, and, in a word, that they have dearly bought their dissipation and their headaches. But this matters nothing, for the same will be done next year, the same the coming century, since it has always been the custom.

In Capitan Tiago's house sadness reigns. All the windows are closed, the inmates move about noiselessly, and only in the kitchen do they dare to speak in natural tones. Maria Clara, the soul of the house, lies sick in bed and her condition is reflected in all the faces, as the sorrows of the mind may be read in the countenance of an individual.

"Which seems best to you, Isabel, shall I make a poor-offering to the cross of Tunasan or to the cross of Matahong?" asks the afflicted father in a low voice. "The Tunasan cross grows while the Matahong cross sweats — which do you think is more miraculous?"

Aunt Isabel reflects, shakes her head, and murmurs, "To grow, to grow is a greater miracle than to sweat. All of us sweat, but not all of us grow."

"That's right, Isabel; but remember that to sweat — for the wood of which bench-legs are made to sweat — is not a small miracle. Come, the best thing will be to make poor-offerings to both crosses, so neither will resent it, and Maria will get better sooner. Are the rooms ready? You know that with the doctors is coming a new gentleman, a distant relative of Padre Damaso's. Nothing should be lacking."

At the other end of the dining-room are the two cousins, Sinang and Victoria, who have come to keep the sick girl company. Andeng is helping them clean a silver tea-set.

"Do you know Dr. Espadaña?" the foster-sister of Maria Clara asks Victoria curiously.

"No," replies the latter, "the only thing that I know about him is that he charges high, according to Capitan Tiago."

"Then he must be good!" exclaims Andeng. "The one who performed an operation on Doña Maria charged high; so he was learned."

"Silly!" retorts Sinang. "Every one who charges high is not learned. Look at Dr. Guevara; after performing a bungling operation that cost the life of both mother and child, he charged the widower fifty pesos. The thing to know is how to charge!"

"What do you know about it?" asks her cousin, nudging her.

"Don't I know? The husband, who is a poor sawyer, after losing his wife had to lose his home also, for the alcalde, being a friend of the doctor's, made him pay. Don't I know about it, when my father lent him the money to make the journey to Santa Cruz?"[1]

The sound of a carriage stopping in front of the house put an end to these conversations. Capitan Tiago, followed by Aunt Isabel, ran down the steps to welcome the new arrivals: the Doctor Don Tiburcio de Espadaña, his señora the *Doctora* Doña Victorina de los Reyes *de* De Espadaña, and a young Spaniard of pleasant countenance and agreeable aspect.

Doña Victorina was attired in a loose silk gown embroidered with flowers and a hat with a huge parrot half-crushed between blue and red ribbons. The dust of the

---

[1] A similar incident occurred in Kalamba. — *Author's note*.

road mingled with the rice-powder on her cheeks seemed to accentuate her wrinkles. As at the time we saw her in Manila, she now supported her lame husband on her arm.

"I have the pleasure of introducing to you our cousin, Don Alfonso Linares de Espadaña," said Doña Victorina, indicating their young companion. "The gentleman is a godson of a relative of Padre Damaso's and has been private secretary to all the ministers."

The young man bowed politely and Capitan Tiago came very near to kissing his hand.

While their numerous trunks and traveling-bags are being carried in and Capitan Tiago is conducting them to their rooms, let us talk a little of this couple whose acquaintance we made slightly in the first chapters.

Doña Victorina was a lady of forty and five winters, which were equivalent to thirty and two summers according to her arithmetical calculations. She had been beautiful in her youth, having had, as she used to say, 'good flesh,' but in the ecstasies of contemplating herself she had looked with disdain on her many Filipino admirers, since her aspirations were toward another race. She had refused to bestow on any one her little white hand, not indeed from distrust, for not a few times had she given jewelry and gems of great value to various foreign and Spanish adventurers. Six months before the time of our story she had seen realized her most beautiful dream, — the dream of her whole life, — for which she might scorn the fond illusions of her youth and even the promises of love that Capitan Tiago had in other days whispered in her ear or sung in some serenade. Late, it is true, had the dream been realized, but Doña Victorina, who, although she spoke the language badly, was more Spanish than Augustina of Saragossa,[1] understood the proverb, "Better late than never," and found consolation in repeating it to herself. "Absolute happiness does not exist on earth,"

---

[1] "The Maid of Saragossa," noted for her heroic exploits during the siege of that city by the French in 1808–09. — Tr.

THE ESPADAÑAS

was another favorite proverb of hers, but she never used both together before other persons.

Having passed her first, second, third, and fourth youth in casting her nets in the sea of the world for the object of her vigils, she had been compelled at last to content herself with what fate was willing to apportion her. Had the poor woman been only thirty and one instead of thirty and two summers — the difference according to her mode of reckoning was great — she would have restored to Destiny the award it offered her to wait for another more suited to her taste, but since man proposes and necessity disposes, she saw herself obliged in her great need for a husband to content herself with a poor fellow who had been cast out from Estremadura [1] and who, after wandering about the world for six or seven years like a modern Ulysses, had at last found on the island of Luzon hospitality and a withered Calypso for his better half. This unhappy mortal, by name Tiburcio Espadaña, was only thirty-five years of age and looked like an old man, yet he was, nevertheless, younger than Doña Victorina, who was only thirty-two. The reason for this is easy to understand but dangerous to state.

Don Tiburcio had come to the Philippines as a petty official in the Customs, but such had been his bad luck that, besides suffering severely from seasickness and breaking a leg during the voyage, he had been dismissed within a fortnight, just at the time when he found himself without a cuarto. After his rough experience on the sea he did not care to return to Spain without having made his fortune, so he decided to devote himself to something. Spanish pride forbade him to engage in manual labor, although the poor fellow would gladly have done any kind of work in order to earn an honest living. But the prestige of the Spaniards would not have allowed it, even though this prestige did not protect him from want.

[1] A region in southwestern Spain, including the provinces of Badajoz and Caceres. — TR.

At first he had lived at the expense of some of his countrymen, but in his honesty the bread tasted bitter, so instead of getting fat he grew thin. Since he had neither learning nor money nor recommendations he was advised by his countrymen, who wished to get rid of him, to go to the provinces and pass himself off as a doctor of medicine. He refused at first, for he had learned nothing during the short period that he had spent as an attendant in a hospital, his duties there having been to dust off the benches and light the fires. But as his wants were pressing and as his scruples were soon laid to rest by his friends he finally listened to them and went to the provinces. He began by visiting some sick persons, and at first made only moderate charges, as his conscience dictated, but later, like the young philosopher of whom Samaniego[1] tells, he ended by putting a higher price on his visits. Thus he soon passed for a great physician and would probably have made his fortune if the medical authorities in Manila had not heard of his exorbitant fees and the competition that he was causing others. Both private parties and professionals interceded for him. "Man," they said to the zealous medical official, "let him make his stake and as soon as he has six or seven thousand pesos he can go back home and live there in peace. After all, what does it matter to you if he does deceive the unwary Indians? They should be more careful! He's a poor devil — don't take the bread from his mouth — be a good Spaniard!" This official was a good Spaniard and agreed to wink at the matter, but the news soon reached the ears of the people and they began to distrust him, so in a little while he lost his practise and again saw himself obliged almost to

---

[1] Author of a little book of fables in Castilian verse for the use of schools. The fable of the young philosopher illustrates the thought in Pope's well-known lines:

> "Vice is a monster of so frightful mien,
> As to be hated needs but to be seen;
> Yet seen too oft, familiar with her face,
> We first endure, then pity, then embrace." — TR.

beg his daily bread. It was then that he learned through a friend, who was an intimate acquaintance of Doña Victorina's, of the dire straits in which that lady was placed and also of her patriotism and her kind heart. Don Tiburcio then saw a patch of blue sky and asked to be introduced to her.

Doña Victorina and Don Tiburcio met: *tarde venientibus ossa*,[1] he would have exclaimed had he known Latin! She was no longer passable, she was passée. Her abundant hair had been reduced to a knot about the size of an onion, according to her maid, while her face was furrowed with wrinkles and her teeth were falling loose. Her eyes, too, had suffered considerably, so that she squinted frequently in looking any distance. Her disposition was the only part of her that remained intact.

At the end of a half-hour's conversation they understood and accepted each other. She would have preferred a Spaniard who was less lame, less stuttering, less bald, less toothless, who slobbered less when he talked, and who had more " spirit " and " quality," as she used to say, but that class of Spaniards no longer came to seek her hand. She had more than once heard it said that opportunity is pictured as being bald, and firmly believed that Don Tiburcio was opportunity itself, for as a result of his misfortunes he suffered from premature baldness. And what woman is not prudent at thirty-two years of age?

Don Tiburcio, for his part, felt a vague melancholy when he thought of his honeymoon, but smiled with resignation and called to his support the specter of hunger. Never had he been ambitious or pretentious; his tastes were simple and his desires limited; but his heart, untouched till then, had dreamed of a very different divinity. Back there in his youth when, worn out with work, he lay down on his rough bed after a frugal meal, he used to fall asleep dreaming of an image, smiling and tender. Afterwards, when troubles and privations increased and with the

[1] Bones for those who come late.

passing of years the poetical image failed to materialize, he thought modestly of a good woman, diligent and industrious, who would bring him a small dowry, to console him for the fatigues of his toil and to quarrel with him now and then — yes, he had thought of quarrels as a kind of happiness! But when obliged to wander from land to land in search not so much of fortune as of some simple means of livelihood for the remainder of his days; when, deluded by the stories of his countrymen from overseas, he had set out for the Philippines, realism gave place to an arrogant mestiza or a beautiful Indian with big black eyes, gowned in silks and transparent draperies, loaded down with gold and diamonds, offering him her love, her carriages, her all. When he reached Manila he thought for a time that his dream was to be realized, for the young women whom he saw driving on the Luneta and the Malecon in silver-mounted carriages had gazed at him with some curiosity. Then after his position was gone, the mestiza and the Indian disappeared and with great effort he forced before himself the image of a widow, of course an agreeable widow! So when he saw his dream take shape in part he became sad, but with a certain touch of native philosophy said to himself, " Those were all dreams and in this world one does not live on dreams!" Thus he dispelled his doubts: she used rice-powder, but after their marriage he would break her of the habit; her face had many wrinkles, but his coat was torn and patched; she was a pretentious old woman, domineering and mannish, but hunger was more terrible, more domineering and pretentious still, and anyway, he had been blessed with a mild disposition for that very end, and love softens the character. She spoke Spanish badly, but he himself did not talk it well, as he had been told when notified of his dismissal. Moreover, what did it matter to him if she was an ugly and ridiculous old woman? He was lame, toothless, and bald! Don Tiburcio preferred to take charge of her rather than to become a public charge from hunger. When some

THE ESPADAÑAS

friends joked with him about it, he answered, "Give me bread and call me a fool."

Don Tiburcio was one of those men who are popularly spoken of as unwilling to harm a fly. Modest, incapable of harboring an unkind thought, in bygone days he would have been made a missionary. His stay in the country had not given him the conviction of grand superiority, of great valor, and of elevated importance that the greater part of his countrymen acquire in a few weeks. His heart had never been capable of entertaining hate nor had he been able to find a single filibuster; he saw only unhappy wretches whom he must despoil if he did not wish to be more unhappy than they were. When he was threatened with prosecution for passing himself off as a physician he was not resentful nor did he complain. Recognizing the justness of the charge against him, he merely answered, "But it's necessary to live!"

So they married, or rather, bagged each other, and went to Santa Ana to spend their honeymoon. But on their wedding-night Doña Victorina was attacked by a horrible indigestion and Don Tiburcio thanked God and showed himself solicitous and attentive. A few days afterward, however, he looked into a mirror and smiled a sad smile as he gazed at his naked gums, for he had aged ten years at least.

Very well satisfied with her husband, Doña Victorina had a fine set of false teeth made for him and called in the best tailors of the city to attend to his clothing. She ordered carriages, sent to Batangas and Albay for the best ponies, and even obliged him to keep a pair for the races. Nor did she neglect her own person while she was transforming him. She laid aside the native costume for the European and substituted false frizzes for the simple Filipino coiffure, while her gowns, which fitted her marvelously ill, disturbed the peace of all the quiet neighborhood.

Her husband, who never went out on foot, — she did not care to have his lameness noticed, — took her on lonely drives in unfrequented places to her great sorrow, for she wanted to show him off in public, but she kept quiet out of respect for their honeymoon. The last quarter was coming on when he took up the subject of the rice-powder, telling her that the use of it was false and unnatural. Doña Victorina wrinkled up her eyebrows and stared at his false teeth. He became silent, and she understood his weakness.

She placed a *de* before her husband's surname, since the *de* cost nothing and gave "quality" to the name, signing herself "Victorina de los Reyes *de* De Espadaña." This *de* was such a mania with her that neither the stationer nor her husband could get it out of her head. "If I write only one *de* it may be thought that you don't have it, you fool!" she said to her husband.[1]

Soon she believed that she was about to become a mother, so she announced to all her acquaintances, "Next month De Espadaña and I are going to the *Penyinsula*. I don't want our son to be born here and be called a revolutionist." She talked incessantly of the journey, having memorized the names of the different ports of call, so that it was a treat to hear her talk: "I'm going to see the isthmus in the Suez Canal — De Espadaña thinks it very beautiful and De Espadaña has traveled over the whole world." "I'll probably not return to this land of savages." "I wasn't born to live here — Aden or Port Said would suit me better — I've thought so ever since I was a girl." In her geography Doña Victorina divided the world into the Philippines and Spain; rather differently from the clever people who divide it into Spain and America or China for another name.

Her husband realized that these things were barbarisms, but held his peace to escape a scolding or reminders of his stuttering. To increase the illusion of approaching maternity she became whimsical, dressed herself in colors with

---

[1] According to Spanish custom, a matron is known by prefixing her maiden name with *de* (possessive *of*) to her husband's name. — TR.

a profusion of flowers and ribbons, and appeared on the Escolta in a wrapper. But oh, the disenchantment! Three months went by and the dream faded, and now, having no reason for fearing that her son would be a revolutionist, she gave up the trip. She consulted doctors, midwives, old women, but all in vain. Having to the great displeasure of Capitan Tiago jested about St. Pascual Bailon, she was unwilling to appeal to any saint. For this reason a friend of her husband's remarked to her:

"Believe me, señora, you are the only *strong-spirited* person in this tiresome country."

She had smiled, without knowing what *strong-spirited* meant, but that night she asked her husband.

"My dear," he answered, "the s-strongest s-spirit that I know of is ammonia. My f-friend must have s-spoken f-figuratively."

After that she would say on every possible occasion, "I'm the only ammonia in this tiresome country, speaking figuratively. So Señor N. de N., a Peninsular gentleman of quality, told me."

Whatever she said had to be done, for she had succeeded in dominating her husband completely. He on his part did not put up any great resistance and so was converted into a kind of lap-dog of hers. If she was displeased with him she would not let him go out, and when she was really angry she tore out his false teeth, thus leaving him a horrible sight for several days.

It soon occurred to her that her husband ought to be a doctor of medicine and surgery, and she so informed him.

"My dear, do you w-want me to be arrested?" he asked fearfully.

"Don't be a fool! Leave me to arrange it," she answered. "You're not going to treat any one, but I want people to call you *Doctor* and me *Doctora*, see?"

So on the following day Rodoreda [1] received an order

[1] The marble-shop of Rodoreda is still in existence on Calle Carriedo, Santa Cruz. — TR.

to engrave on a slab of black marble: DR. DE ESPADAÑA, SPECIALIST IN ALL KINDS OF DISEASES. All the servants had to address them by their new titles, and as a result she increased the number of frizzes, the layers of rice-powder, the ribbons and laces, and gazed with more disdain than ever on her poor and unfortunate countrywomen whose husbands belonged to a lower grade of society than hers did. Day by day she felt more dignified and exalted and, by continuing in this way, at the end of a year she would have believed herself to be of divine origin.

These sublime thoughts, however, did not keep her from becoming older and more ridiculous every day. Every time Capitan Tiago saw her and recalled having made love to her in vain he forthwith sent a peso to the church for a mass of thanksgiving. Still, he greatly respected her husband on account of his title of specialist in all kinds of diseases and listened attentively to the few phrases that he was able to stutter out. For this reason and because this doctor was more exclusive than others, Capitan Tiago had selected him to treat his daughter.

In regard to young Linares, that is another matter. When arranging for the trip to Spain, Doña Victorina had thought of having a Peninsular administrator, as she did not trust the Filipinos. Her husband bethought himself of a nephew of his in Madrid who was studying law and who was considered the brightest of the family. So they wrote to him, paying his passage in advance, and when the dream disappeared he was already on his way.

Such were the three persons who had just arrived. While they were partaking of a late breakfast, Padre Salvi came in. The Espadañas were already acquainted with him, and they introduced the blushing young Linares with all his titles.

As was natural, they talked of Maria Clara, who was resting and sleeping. They talked of their journey, and Doña Victorina exhibited all her verbosity in criticising the customs of the provincials, — their nipa houses, their bamboo bridges; without forgetting to mention to the curate her intimacy with this and that high official and other persons of "quality" who were very fond of her.

"If you had come two days ago, Doña Victorina," put in Capitan Tiago during a slight pause, "you would have met his Excellency, the Captain-General. He sat right there."

"What! How's that? His Excellency here! In your house? No!"

"I tell you that he sat right there. If you had only come two days ago —"

"Ah, what a pity that Clarita did not get sick sooner!" she exclaimed with real feeling. Then turning to Linares, "Do you hear, cousin? His Excellency was here! Don't you see now that De Espadaña was right when he told you that you were n't going to the house of a miserable Indian? Because, you know, Don Santiago, in Madrid our cousin was the friend of ministers and dukes and dined in the house of Count El Campanario."

"The Duke of La Torre, Victorina," corrected her husband.[1]

"It's the same thing. If you will tell me —"

"Shall I find Padre Damaso in his town?" interrupted Linares, addressing Padre Salvi. "I've been told that it's near here."

"He's right here and will be over in a little while," replied the curate.

"How glad I am of that! I have a letter to him," exclaimed the youth, "and if it were not for the happy chance that brings me here, I would have come expressly to visit him."

In the meantime the *happy* chance had awakened.

"De Espadaña," said Doña Victorina, when the meal was over, "shall we go in to see Clarita?" Then to Capitan Tiago, "Only for you, Don Santiago, only for

---

[1] There is a play on words here, *Campanario* meaning belfry and *Torre* tower. — TR.

you! My husband only attends persons of quality, and yet, and yet —! He's not like those here. In Madrid he only visited persons of quality."

They adjourned to the sick girl's chamber. The windows were closed from fear of a draught, so the room was almost dark, being only dimly illuminated by two tapers which burned before an image of the Virgin of Antipolo. Her head covered with a handkerchief saturated in cologne, her body wrapped carefully in white sheets which swathed her youthful form with many folds, under curtains of jusi and piña, the girl lay on her kamagon bed. Her hair formed a frame around her oval countenance and accentuated her transparent paleness, which was enlivened only by her large, sad eyes. At her side were her two friends and Andeng with a bouquet of tuberoses.

De Espadaña felt her pulse, examined her tongue, asked a few questions, and said, as he wagged his head from side to side, "S-she's s-sick, but s-she c-can be c-cured."

Doña Victorina looked proudly at the bystanders.

"Lichen with milk in the morning, syrup of marshmallow, two cynoglossum pills!" ordered De Espadaña.

"Cheer up, Clarita!" said Doña Victorina, going up to her. "We've come to cure you. I want to introduce our cousin."

Linares was so absorbed in the contemplation of those eloquent eyes, which seemed to be searching for some one, that he did not hear Doña Victorina name him.

"Señor Linares," said the curate, calling him out of his abstraction, "here comes Padre Damaso."

It was indeed Padre Damaso, but pale and rather sad. On leaving his bed his first visit was for Maria Clara. Nor was it the Padre Damaso of former times, hearty and self-confident; now he moved silently and with some hesitation.

CHAPTER XLIII

PLANS

WITHOUT heeding any of the bystanders, Padre Damaso went directly to the bed of the sick girl and taking her hand said to her with ineffable tenderness, while tears sprang into his eyes, "Maria, my daughter, you must n't die!"

The sick girl opened her eyes and stared at him with a strange expression. No one who knew the Franciscan had suspected in him such tender feelings, no one had believed that under his rude and rough exterior there might beat a heart. Unable to go on, he withdrew from the girl's side, weeping like a child, and went outside under the favorite vines of Maria Clara's balcony to give free rein to his grief.

"How he loves his goddaughter!" thought all present, while Fray Salvi gazed at him motionlessly and in silence, lightly gnawing his lips the while.

When he had become somewhat calm again Doña Victorina introduced Linares, who approached him respectfully. Fray Damaso silently looked him over from head to foot, took the letter offered and read it, but apparently without understanding, for he asked, "And who are you?"

"Alfonso Linares, the godson of your brother-in-law," stammered the young man.

Padre Damaso threw back his body and looked the youth over again carefully. Then his features lighted up and he arose. "So you are the godson of Carlicos!" he exclaimed. "Come and let me embrace you! I got your letter several days ago. So it's you! I did n't recognize you, — which is easily explained, for you were n't born when I left the country, — I did n't recognize you!" Padre Damaso squeezed his robust arms about the young man, who became very red, whether from modesty or lack of breath is not known.

After the first moments of effusion had passed and inquiries about Carlicos and his wife had been made and answered, Padre Damaso asked, " Come now, what does Carlicos want me to do for you?"

" I believe he says something about that in the letter," Linares again stammered.

" In the letter? Let's see! That's right! He wants me to get you a job and a wife. Ahem! A job, a job — that's easy! Can you read and write?"

" I received my degree of law from the University."

" *Carambas!* So you 're a pettifogger! You don't show it; you look more like a shy maiden. So much the better! But to get you a wife — "

" Padre, I'm not in such a great hurry," interrupted Linares in confusion.

But Padre Damaso was already pacing from one end of the hallway to the other, muttering, " A wife, a wife!" His countenance was no longer sad or merry but now wore an expression of great seriousness, while he seemed to be thinking deeply. Padre Salvi gazed on the scene from a distance.

" I did n't think that the matter would trouble me so much," murmured Padre Damaso in a tearful voice. " But of two evils, the lesser!" Then raising his voice he approached Linares and said to him, " Come, boy, let's talk to Santiago."

Linares turned pale and allowed himself to be dragged along by the priest, who moved thoughtfully. Then it was Padre Salvi's turn to pace back and forth, pensive as ever.

A voice wishing him good morning drew him from his monotonous walk. He raised his head and saw Lucas, who saluted him humbly.

"What do you want?" questioned the curate's eyes.

"Padre, I'm the brother of the man who was killed on the day of the fiesta," began Lucas in tearful accents.

The curate recoiled and murmured in a scarcely audible voice, "Well?"

Lucas made an effort to weep and wiped his eyes with a handkerchief. "Padre," he went on tearfully, "I've been to Don Crisostomo to ask for an indemnity. First he received me with kicks, saying that he wouldn't pay anything since he himself had run the risk of getting killed through the fault of my dear, unfortunate brother. I went to talk to him yesterday, but he had gone to Manila. He left me five hundred pesos for charity's sake and charged me not to come back again. Ah, Padre, five hundred pesos for my poor brother — five hundred pesos! Ah, Padre —"

At first the curate had listened with surprise and attention while his lips curled slightly with a smile of such disdain and sarcasm at the sight of this farce that, had Lucas noticed it, he would have run away at top speed.

"Now what do you want?" he asked, turning away.

"Ah, Padre, tell me for the love of God what I ought to do. The padre has always given good advice."

"Who told you so? You don't belong in these parts."

"The padre is known all over the province."

With irritated looks Padre Salvi approached him and pointing to the street said to the now startled Lucas, "Go home and be thankful that Don Crisostomo didn't have you sent to jail! Get out of here!"

Lucas forgot the part he was playing and murmured, "But I thought —"

"Get out of here!" cried Padre Salvi nervously.

"I would like to see Padre Damaso."

"Padre Damaso is busy. Get out of here!" again ordered the curate imperiously.

Lucas went down the stairway muttering, "He's another of them — as he doesn't pay well — the one who pays best!"

At the sound of the curate's voice all had hurried to the spot, including Padre Damaso, Capitan Tiago, and Linares.

"An insolent vagabond who came to beg and who does n't want to work," explained Padre Salvi, picking up his hat and cane to return to the convento.

CHAPTER XLIV

AN EXAMINATION OF CONSCIENCE

LONG days and weary nights passed at the sick girl's bed. After having confessed herself, Maria Clara had suffered a relapse, and in her delirium she uttered only the name of the mother whom she had never known. But her girl friends, her father, and her aunt kept watch at her side. Offerings and alms were sent to all the miraculous images, Capitan Tiago vowed a gold cane to the Virgin of Antipolo, and at length the fever began to subside slowly and regularly.

Doctor De Espadaña was astonished at the virtues of the syrup of marshmallow and the infusion of lichen, prescriptions that he had not varied. Doña Victorina was so pleased with her husband that one day when he stepped on the train of her gown she did not apply her penal code to the extent of taking his set of false teeth away from him, but contented herself with merely exclaiming, "If you were n't lame you'd even step on my corset!" — an article of apparel she did not wear.

One afternoon while Sinang and Victoria were visiting their friend, the curate, Capitan Tiago, and Doña Vietorina's family were conversing over their lunch in the dining-room.

"Well, I feel very sorry about it," said the doctor; "Padre Damaso also will regret it very much."

"Where do you say they're transferring him to?" Linares asked the curate.

"To the province of Tayabas," replied the curate negligently.

"One who will be greatly affected by it is Maria Clara,

when she learns of it," said Capitan Tiago. " She loves him like a father."

Fray Salvi looked at him askance.

" I believe, Padre," continued Capitan Tiago, " that all her illness is the result of the trouble on the last day of the fiesta."

" I 'm of the same opinion, and think that you 've done well not to let Señor Ibarra see her. She would have got worse."

" If it was n't for us," put in Doña Victorina, " Clarita would already be in heaven singing praises to God."

" Amen ! " Capitan Tiago thought it his duty to exclaim.

" It 's lucky for you that my husband did n't have any patient of greater quality, for then you 'd have had to call in another, and all those here are ignoramuses. My husband — "

" Just as I was saying," the curate in turn interrupted, " I think that the confession that Maria Clara made brought on the favorable crisis which has saved her life. A clean conscience is worth more than a lot of medicine. Don't think that I deny the power of science, above all, that of surgery, but a clean conscience! Read the pious books and you 'll see how many cures are effected merely by a clean confession."

" Pardon me," objected the piqued Doña Victorina, " this power of the confessional — cure the alferez's woman with a confession ! "

" A wound, madam, is not a form of illness which the conscience can affect," replied Padre Salvi severely. " Nevertheless, a clean confession will preserve her from receiving in the future such blows as she got this morning."

" She deserves them ! " went on Doña Victorina as if she had not heard what Padre Salvi said. " That woman is so insolent! In the church she did nothing but stare at me. You can see that she 's a nobody. Sunday I was going to ask her if she saw anything funny about my face

AN EXAMINATION OF CONSCIENCE

but who would lower oneself to speak to people that are not of rank?"

The curate, on his part, continued just as though he had not heard this tirade. "Believe me, Don Santiago, to complete your daughter's recovery it's necessary that she take communion tomorrow. I'll bring the viaticum over here. I don't think she has anything to confess, but yet, if she wants to confess herself tonight —"

"I don't know," Doña Victorina instantly took advantage of a slight hesitation on Padre Salvi's part to add, "I don't understand how there can be men capable of marrying such a fright as that woman is. It's easily seen where she comes from. She's just dying of envy, you can see it! How much does an alferez get?"

"Accordingly, Don Santiago, tell your cousin to prepare the sick girl for the communion tomorrow. I'll come over tonight to absolve her of her peccadillos."

Seeing Aunt Isabel come from the sick-room, he said to her in Tagalog, "Prepare your niece for confession tonight. Tomorrow I'll bring over the viaticum. With that she'll improve faster."

"But, Padre," Linares gathered up enough courage to ask faintly, "you don't think that she's in any danger of dying?"

"Don't you worry," answered the padre without looking at him. "I know what I'm doing; I've helped take care of plenty of sick people before. Besides, she'll decide herself whether or not she wishes to receive the holy communion and you'll see that she says yes."

Capitan Tiago immediately agreed to everything, while Aunt Isabel returned to the sick girl's chamber. Maria Clara was still in bed, pale, very pale, and at her side were **her two friends.**

"Take one more grain," Sinang whispered, as she offered her a white tablet that she took from a small glass tube. "He says that when you feel a rumbling or buzzing **in** your ears you are to stop the medicine."

"Hasn't he written to you again?" asked the sick girl in a low voice.

"No, he must be very busy."

"Hasn't he sent any message?"

"He says nothing more than that he's going to try to get the Archbishop to absolve him from the excommunication, so that—"

This conversation was suspended at the aunt's approach.

"The padre says for you to get ready for confession, daughter," said the latter. "You girls must leave her so that she can make her examination of conscience."

"But it hasn't been a week since she confessed!" protested Sinang. "I'm not sick and I don't sin as often as that."

"*Abá!* Don't you know what the curate says: the righteous sin seven times a day? Come, what book shall I bring you, the *Ancora,* the *Ramillete,* or the *Camino Recto para ir al Cielo?*"

Maria Clara did not answer.

"Well, you mustn't tire yourself," added the good aunt to console her. "I'll read the examination myself and you'll have only to recall your sins."

"Write to him not to think of me any more," murmured Maria Clara in Sinang's ear as the latter said good-by to her.

"What?"

But the aunt again approached, and Sinang had to go away without understanding what her friend had meant. The good old aunt drew a chair up to the light, put her spectacles on the end of her nose, and opened a booklet. "Pay close attention, daughter. I'm going to begin with the Ten Commandments. I'll go slow so that you can meditate. If you don't hear well tell me so that I can repeat. You know that in looking after your welfare I'm never weary."

She began to read in a monotonous and snuffling voice the considerations of cases of sinfulness. At the end of each paragraph she made a long pause in order to give the girl time to recall her sins and to repent of them.

Maria Clara stared vaguely into space. After finishing the first commandment, *to love God above all things*, Aunt Isabel looked at her over her spectacles and was satisfied with her sad and thoughtful mien. She coughed piously and after a long pause began to read the second commandment. The good old woman read with unction and when she had finished the commentaries looked again at her niece, who turned her head slowly to the other side.

"Bah!" said Aunt Isabel to herself. "With taking His holy name in vain the poor child has nothing to do. Let's pass on to the third." [1]

The third commandment was analyzed and commented upon. After citing all the cases in which one can break it she again looked toward the bed. But now she lifted up her glasses and rubbed her eyes, for she had seen her niece raise a handkerchief to her face as if to wipe away tears.

"Hum, ahem! The poor child once went to sleep during the sermon." Then replacing her glasses on the end of her nose, she said, "Now let's see if, just as you've failed to keep holy the Sabbath, you've failed to honor your father and mother."

So she read the fourth commandment in an even slower and more snuffling voice, thinking thus to give solemnity to the act, just as she had seen many friars do. Aunt Isabel had never heard a Quaker preach or she would also have trembled.

The sick girl, in the meantime, raised the handkerchief to her eyes several times and her breathing became more noticeable.

"What a good soul!" thought the old woman. "She who is so obedient and submissive to every one! I've committed more sins and yet I've never been able really to cry."

---

[1] The Roman Catholic decalogue does not contain the commandment forbidding the worship of "graven images," its second being the prohibition against "taking His holy name in vain." To make up the ten, the commandment against covetousness is divided into two. — Tr.

She then began the fifth commandment with greater pauses and even more pronounced snuffling, if that were possible, and with such great enthusiasm that she did not hear the stifled sobs of her niece. Only in a pause which she made after the comments on homicide by violence did she notice the groans of the sinner. Then her tone passed into the sublime as she read the rest of the commandment in accents that she tried to render threatening, seeing that her niece was still weeping.

"Weep, daughter, weep!" she said, approaching the bed. "The more you weep the sooner God will pardon you. Hold the sorrow of repentance as better than that of mere penitence. Weep, daughter, weep! You don't know how much I enjoy seeing you weep. Beat yourself on the breast also, but not hard, for you're still sick."

But, as if her sorrow needed mystery and solitude to make it increase, Maria Clara, on seeing herself observed, little by little stopped sighing and dried her eyes without saying anything or answering her aunt, who continued the reading. Since the wails of her audience had ceased, however, she lost her enthusiasm, and the last commandments made her so sleepy that she began to yawn, with great detriment to her snuffling, which was thus interrupted.

"If I hadn't seen it with my own eyes, I wouldn't have believed it," thought the good old lady afterwards. "This girl sins like a soldier against the first five and from the sixth to the tenth not a venial sin, just the opposite to us! How the world does move now!"

So she lighted a large candle to the Virgin of Antipolo and two other smaller ones to Our Lady of the Rosary and Our Lady of the Pillar,[1] taking care to put away in a corner a marble crucifix to make it understand that the candles were not lighted for it. Nor did the Virgin of Delaroche have any share; she was an unknown foreigner, and Aunt Isabel had never heard of any miracle of hers.

---

[1] The famous Virgin of Saragossa, Spain, and patroness of Santa Cruz, Manila. — TR.

We do not know what occurred during the confession that night and we respect such secrets. But the confession was a long one and the aunt, who stood watch over her niece at a distance, could note that the curate, instead of turning his ear to hear the words of the sick girl, rather had his face turned toward hers, and seemed only to be trying to read, or divine, her thoughts by gazing into her beautiful eyes.

Pale and with contracted lips Padre Salvi left the chamber. Looking at his forehead, which was gloomy and covered with perspiration, one would have said that it was he who had confessed and had not obtained absolution.

"*Jesús, María, y José!*" exclaimed Aunt Isabel, crossing herself to dispel an evil thought, "who understands the girls nowadays?"

CHAPTER XLV

THE HUNTED

IN the dim light shed by the moonbeams sifting through the thick foliage a man wandered through the forest with slow and cautious steps. From time to time, as if to find his way, he whistled a peculiar melody, which was answered in the distance by some one whistling the same air. The man would listen attentively and then make his way in the direction of the distant sound, until at length, after overcoming the thousand obstacles offered by the virgin forest in the night-time, he reached a small open space, which was bathed in the light of the moon in its first quarter. The high, tree-crowned rocks that rose about formed a kind of ruined amphitheater, in the center of which were scattered recently felled trees and charred logs among boulders covered with nature's mantle of verdure.

Scarcely had the unknown arrived when another figure started suddenly from behind a large rock and advanced with drawn revolver. "Who are you?" he asked in Tagalog in an imperious tone, cocking the weapon.

"Is old Pablo among you?" inquired the unknown in an even tone, without answering the question or showing any signs of fear.

"You mean the capitan? Yes, he's here."

"Then tell him that Elias is here looking for him," was the answer of the unknown, who was no other than the mysterious pilot.

"Are you Elias?" asked the other respectfully, as he approached him, not, however, ceasing to cover him with the revolver. "Then come!"

Elias followed him, and they penetrated into a kind of

cave sunk down in the depths of the earth. The guide, who seemed to be familiar with the way, warned the pilot when he should descend or turn aside or stoop down, so they were not long in reaching a kind of hall which was poorly lighted by pitch torches and occupied by twelve to fifteen armed men with dirty faces and soiled clothing, some seated and some lying down as they talked fitfully to one another. Resting his arms on a stone that served for a table and gazing thoughtfully at the torches, which gave out so little light for so much smoke, was seen an old, sad-featured man with his head wrapped in a bloody bandage. Did we not know that it was a den of tulisanes we might have said, on reading the look of desperation in the old man's face, that it was the Tower of Hunger on the eve before Ugolino devoured his sons.

Upon the arrival of Elias and his guide the figures partly rose, but at a signal from the latter they settled back again, satisfying themselves with the observation that the newcomer was unarmed. The old man turned his head slowly and saw the quiet figure of Elias, who stood uncovered, gazing at him with sad interest.

"It's you at last," murmured the old man, his gaze lighting up somewhat as he recognized the youth.

"In what condition do I find you!" exclaimed the youth in a suppressed tone, shaking his head.

The old man dropped his head in silence and made a sign to the others, who arose and withdrew, first taking the measure of the pilot's muscles and stature with a glance.

"Yes!" said the old man to Elias as soon as they were alone. "Six months ago when I sheltered you in my house, it was I who pitied you. Now we have changed parts and it is you who pity me. But sit down and tell me how you got here."

"It's fifteen days now since I was told of your misfortune," began the young man slowly in a low voice as he stared at the light. "I started at once and have been seeking you from mountain to mountain. I've traveled over nearly the whole of two provinces."

"In order not to shed innocent blood," continued the old man, "I have had to flee. My enemies were afraid to show themselves. I was confronted merely with some unfortunates who have never done me the least harm."

After a brief pause during which he seemed to be occupied in trying to read the thoughts in the dark countenance of the old man, Elias replied: "I've come to make a proposition to you. Having sought in vain for some survivor of the family that caused the misfortunes of mine, I've decided to leave the province where I live and move toward the North among the independent pagan tribes. Don't you want to abandon the life you have entered upon and come with me? I will be your son, since you have lost your own; I have no family, and in you will find a father."

The old man shook his head in negation, saying, "When one at my age makes a desperate resolution, it's because there is no other recourse. A man who, like myself, has spent his youth and his mature years toiling for the future of himself and his sons; a man who has been submissive to every wish of his superiors, who has conscientiously performed difficult tasks, enduring all that he might live in peace and quiet — when that man, whose blood time has chilled, renounces all his past and foregoes all his future, even on the very brink of the grave, it is because he has with mature judgment decided that peace does not exist and that it is not the highest good. Why drag out miserable days on foreign soil? I had two sons, a daughter, a home, a fortune, I was esteemed and respected; now I am as a tree shorn of its branches, a wanderer, a fugitive, hunted like a wild beast through the forest, and all for what? Because a man dishonored my daughter, because her brothers called that man's infamy to account, and because that man is set above his fellows with the title of minister of God! In spite of everything, I, her father,

I, dishonored in my old age, forgave the injury, for I was indulgent with the passions of youth and the weakness of the flesh, and in the face of irreparable wrong what could I do but hold my peace and save what remained to me? But the culprit, fearful of vengeance sooner or later, sought the destruction of my sons. Do you know what he did? No? You don't know, then, that he pretended that there had been a robbery committed in the convento and that one of my sons figured among the accused? The other could not be included because he was in another place at the time. Do you know what tortures they were subjected to? You know of them, for they are the same in all the towns! I, I saw my son hanging by the hair, I heard his cries, I heard him call upon me, and I, coward and lover of peace, had n't the courage either to kill or to die! Do you know that the theft was not proved, that it was shown to be a false charge, and that in punishment the curate was transferred to another town, but that my son died as a result of his tortures? The other, the one who was left to me, was not a coward like his father, so our persecutor was still fearful that he would wreak vengeance on him, and, under the pretext of his not having his cedula,[1] which he had not carried with him just at that time, had him arrested by the Civil Guard, mistreated him, enraged and harassed him with insults until he was driven to suicide! And I, I have outlived so much shame; but if I had not the courage of a father to defend my sons, there yet remains to me a heart burning for revenge, and I will have it! The discontented are gathering under my command, my enemies increase my forces, and on the day that I feel myself strong enough I will descend to the lowlands

[1] In 1883 the old system of "tribute" was abolished and in its place a graduated personal tax imposed. The certificate that this tax had been paid, known as the *cédula personal*, which also served for personal identification, could be required at any time or place, and failure to produce it was cause for summary arrest. It therefore became, in unscrupulous hands, a fruitful source of abuse, since any "undesirable" against whom no specific charge could be brought might be put out of the way by this means. — TR.

and in flames sate my vengeance and end my own existence. And that day will come or there is no God!"[1]

The old man arose trembling. With fiery look and hollow voice, he added, tearing his long hair, "Curses, curses upon me that I restrained the avenging hands of my sons — I have murdered them! Had I let the guilty perish, had I confided less in the justice of God and men, I should now have my sons — fugitives, perhaps, but I should have them; they would not have died under torture! I was not born to be a father, so I have them not! Curses upon me that I had not learned with my years to know the conditions under which I lived! But in fire and blood by my own death I will avenge them!"

In his paroxysm of grief the unfortunate father tore away the bandage, reopening a wound in his forehead from which gushed a stream of blood.

"I respect your sorrow," said Elias, "and I understand your desire for revenge. I, too, am like you, and yet from fear of injuring the innocent I prefer to forget my misfortunes."

"You can forget because you are young and because you haven't lost a son, your last hope! But I assure you that I shall injure no innocent one. Do you see this wound? Rather than kill a poor cuadrillero, who was doing his duty, I let him inflict it."

"But look," urged Elias, after a moment's silence, "look what a frightful catastrophe you are going to bring down upon our unfortunate people. If you accomplish your revenge by your own hand, your enemies will make terrible reprisals, not against you, not against those who are armed, but against the peaceful, who as usual will be accused — and then the cases of injustice!"

"Let the people learn to defend themselves, let each one defend himself!"

---

[1] Tanawan or Pateros? — *Author's note.* The former is a town in Batangas Province, the latter a village on the northern shore of the Lake of Bay, in what is now Rizal Province. — TR.

"You know that that is impossible. Sir, I knew you in other days when you were happy; then you gave me good advice, will you now permit me — "

The old man folded his arms in an attitude of attention.

"Sir," continued Elias, weighing his words well, "I have had the good fortune to render a service to a young man who is rich, generous, noble, and who desires the welfare of his country. They say that this young man has friends in Madrid — I don't know myself — but I can assure you that he is a friend of the Captain-General's. What do you say that we make him the bearer of the people's complaints, if we interest him in the cause of the unhappy?"

The old man shook his head. "You say that he is rich? The rich think only of increasing their wealth, pride and show blind them, and as they are generally safe, above all when they have powerful friends, none of them troubles himself about the woes of the unfortunate. I know all, because I was rich!"

"But the man of whom I speak is not like the others. He is a son who has been insulted over the memory of his father, and a young man who, as he is soon to have a family, thinks of the future, of a happy future for his children."

"Then he is a man who is going to be happy — our cause is not for happy men."

"But it is for men who have feelings!"

"Perhaps!" replied the old man, seating himself. "Suppose that he agrees to carry our cry even to the Captain-General, suppose that he finds in the Cortes [1] delegates who will plead for us; do you think that we shall get justice?"

"Let us try it before we resort to violent measures," answered Elias. "You must be surprised that I, another unfortunate, young and strong, should propose to you, old and weak, peaceful measures, but it's because I've seen

---

[1] The Spanish Parliament. — TR.

as much misery caused by us as by the tyrants. The defenseless are the ones who pay."

"And if we accomplish nothing?"

"Something we shall accomplish, believe me, for all those who are in power are not unjust. But if we accomplish nothing, if they disregard our entreaties, if man has become deaf to the cry of sorrow from his kind, then I will put myself under your orders!"

The old man embraced the youth enthusiastically. "I accept your proposition, Elias. I know that you will keep your word. You will come to me, and I shall help you to revenge your ancestors, you will help me to revenge my sons, my sons that were like you!"

"In the meantime, sir, you will refrain from violent measures?"

"You will present the complaints of the people, you know them. When shall I know your answer?"

"In four days send a man to the beach at San Diego and I will tell him what I shall have learned from the person in whom I place so much hope. If he accepts, they will give us justice; and if not, I'll be the first to fall in the struggle that we will begin."

"Elias will not die, Elias will be the leader when Capitan Pablo falls, satisfied in his revenge," concluded the old man, as he accompanied the youth out of the cave into the open air.

CHAPTER XLVI

THE COCKPIT

TO keep holy the afternoon of the Sabbath one generally goes to the cockpit in the Philippines, just as to the bull-fights in Spain. Cockfighting, a passion introduced into the country and exploited for a century past, is one of the vices of the people, more widely spread than opium-smoking among the Chinese. There the poor man goes to risk all that he has, desirous of getting rich without work. There the rich man goes to amuse himself, using the money that remains to him from his feasts and his masses of thanksgiving. The fortune that he gambles is his own, the cock is raised with much more care perhaps than his son and successor in the cockpit, so we have nothing to say against it. Since the government permits it and even in a way recommends it, by providing that the spectacle may take place only in the *public plazas*, on *holidays* (in order that all may see it and be encouraged by the example?), *from the high mass until nightfall* (eight hours), let us proceed thither to seek out some of our acquaintances.

The cockpit of San Diego does not differ from those to be found in other towns, except in some details. It consists of three parts, the first of which, the entrance, is a large rectangle some twenty meters long by fourteen wide. On one side is the gateway, generally tended by an old woman whose business it is to collect the *sa pintu,* or admission fee. Of this contribution, which every one pays, the government receives a part, amounting to some hundreds of thousands of pesos a year. It is said that with this money, with which vice pays its license, magnificent schoolhouses are erected, bridges and roads are constructed, prizes for encouraging agriculture and commerce are distributed: blessed be the vice that produces such good results! In this first enclosure are the vendors of buyos, cigars, sweetmeats, and foodstuffs. There swarm the boys in company with their fathers or uncles, who carefully initiate them into the secrets of life.

This enclosure communicates with another of somewhat larger dimensions, — a kind of foyer where the public gathers while waiting for the combats. There are the greater part of the fighting-cocks tied with cords which are fastened to the ground by means of a piece of bone or hard wood; there are assembled the gamblers, the devotees, those skilled in tying on the gaffs; there they make agreements, they deliberate, they beg for loans, they curse, they swear, they laugh boisterously. That one fondles his chicken, rubbing his hand over its brilliant plumage, this one examines and counts the scales on its legs, they recount the exploits of the champions.

There you will see many with mournful faces carrying by the feet corpses picked of their feathers; the creature that was the favorite for months, petted and cared for day and night, on which were founded such flattering hopes, is now nothing more than a carcass to be sold for a peseta or to be stewed with ginger and eaten that very night. *Sic transit gloria mundi!* The loser returns to the home where his anxious wife and ragged children await him, without his money or his chicken. Of all that golden dream, of all those vigils during months from the dawn of day to the setting of the sun, of all those fatigues and labors, there results only a peseta, the ashes left from so much smoke.   . .   . .

In this foyer even the least intelligent takes part in the discussion, while the man of most hasty judgment conscientiously investigates the matter, weighs, examines, extends the wings, feels the muscles of the cocks. Some go very well-dressed, surrounded and followed by the partisans of their champions; others who are dirty and bear the imprint of vice on their squalid features anxiously follow the movements of the rich to note the bets, since the purse may become empty but the passion never satiated. No countenance here but is animated — not here is to be found the indolent, apathetic, silent Filipino — all is movement, passion, eagerness. It may be, one would say, that they have that thirst which is quickened by the water of the swamp.

From this place one passes into the arena, which is known as the *Rueda*, the wheel. The ground here, surrounded by bamboo-stakes, is usually higher than that in the two other divisions. In the back part, reaching almost to the roof, are tiers of seats for the spectators, or gamblers, since these are the same. During the fights these seats are filled with men and boys who shout, clamor, sweat, quarrel, and blaspheme — fortunately, hardly any women get in this far. In the *Rueda* are the men of importance, the rich, the famous bettors, the contractor, the referee. On the perfectly leveled ground the cocks fight, and from there Destiny apportions to the families smiles or tears, feast or famine.

At the time of entering we see the gobernadorcillo, Capitan Pablo, Capitan Basilio, and Lucas, the man with the scar on his face who felt so deeply the death of his brother.

Capitan Basilio approaches one of the townsmen and asks, "Do you know which cock Capitan Tiago is going to bring?"

"I don't know, sir. This morning two came, one of them the *lásak* that whipped the Consul's *talisain*." [1]

"Do you think that my *bulik* is a match for it?"

"I should say so! I'll bet my house and my camisa on it!"

At that moment Capitan Tiago arrives, dressed like the heavy gamblers, in a camisa of Canton linen, woolen panta-

---

[1] *Lásak, talisain,* and *bulik* are some of the numerous terms used in the vernacular to describe fighting-cocks. — TR.

loons, and a wide straw hat. Behind him come two servants carrying the *lásak* and a white cock of enormous size.

"Sinang tells me that Maria is improving all the time," says Capitan Basilio.

"She has no more fever but is still very weak."

"Did you lose last night?"

"A little. I hear that you won. I'm going to see if I can't get even here."

"Do you want to fight the *lásak?*" asks Capitan Basilio, looking at the cock and taking it from the servant.

"That depends — if there's a bet."

"How much will you put up?"

"I won't gamble for less than two."

"Have you seen my *bulik?*" inquires Capitan Basilio, calling to a man who is carrying a small game-cock.

Capitan Tiago examines it and after feeling its weight and studying its scales returns it with the question, "How much will you put up?"

"Whatever you will."

"Two, and five hundred?"

"Three?"

"Three!"

"For the next fight after this!"

The chorus of curious bystanders and the gamblers spread the news that two celebrated cocks will fight, each of which has a history and a well-earned reputation. All wish to see and examine the two celebrities, opinions are offered, prophecies are made.

Meanwhile, the murmur of the voices grows, the confusion increases, the *Rueda* is broken into, the seats are filled. The skilled attendants carry the two cocks into the arena, a white and a red, already armed but with the gaffs still sheathed. Cries are heard, "On the white!" "On the white!" while some other voice answers, "On the red!" The odds are on the white, he is the favorite; the red is the "outsider," the *dejado*.

THE COCKPIT

Members of the Civil Guard move about in the crowd. They are not dressed in the uniform of that meritorious corps, but neither are they in civilian costume. Trousers of *guingón* with a red stripe, a camisa stained blue from the faded blouse, and a service-cap, make up their costume, in keeping with their deportment; they make bets and keep watch, they raise disturbances and talk of keeping the peace.

While the spectators are yelling, waving their hands, flourishing and clinking pieces of silver; while they search in their pockets for the last coin, or, in the lack of such, try to pledge their word, promising to sell the carabao or the next crop, two boys, brothers apparently, follow the bettors with wistful eyes, loiter about, murmur timid words to which no one listens, become more and more gloomy and gaze at one another ill-humoredly and dejectedly. Lucas watches them covertly, smiles malignantly, jingles his silver, passes close to them, and gazing into the *Rueda*, cries out:

"Fifty, fifty to twenty on the white!"

The two brothers exchange glances.

"I told you," muttered the elder, "that you shouldn't have put up all the money. If you had listened to me we should now have something to bet on the red."

The younger timidly approached Lucas and touched him on the arm.

"Oh, it's you!" exclaimed the latter, turning around with feigned surprise. "Does your brother accept my proposition or do you want to bet?"

"How can we bet when we've lost everything?"

"Then you accept?"

"He doesn't want to! If you would lend us something, now that you say you know us—"

Lucas scratched his head, pulled at his camisa, and replied, "Yes, I know you. You are Tarsilo and Bruno, both young and strong. I know that your brave father died as a result of the hundred lashes a day those soldiers gave him. I know that you don't think of revenging him."

"Don't meddle in our affairs!" broke in Tarsilo, the elder. "That might lead to trouble. If it were not that we have a sister, we should have been hanged long ago."

"Hanged? They only hang a coward, one who has no money or influence. And at all events the mountains are near."

"A hundred to twenty on the white!" cried a passer-by.

"Lend us four pesos, three, two," begged the younger. "We'll soon pay them back double. The fight is going to commence."

Lucas again scratched his head "Tush! This money is n't mine. Don Crisostomo has given it to me for those who are willing to serve him. But I see that you're not like your father — he was really brave — let him who is not so not seek amusement!" So saying, he drew away from them a little.

"Let's take him up, what's the difference?" said Bruno. "It's the same to be shot as to be hanged. We poor folks are good for nothing else."

"You're right — but think of our sister!"

Meanwhile, the ring has been cleared and the combat is about to begin. The voices die away as the two starters, with the expert who fastens the gaffs, are left alone in the center. At a signal from the referee, the expert unsheathes the gaffs and the fine blades glitter threateningly.

Sadly and silently the two brothers draw nearer to the ring until their foreheads are pressed against the railing. A man approaches them and calls into their ears, "*Pare*,[1] a hundred to ten on the white!"

Tarsilo stares at him in a foolish way and responds to Bruno's nudge with a grunt.

The starters hold the cocks with skilful delicacy, taking care not to wound themselves. A solemn silence reigns;

---

[1] Another form of the corruption of *compadre*, "friend," "neighbor." — Tr.

the spectators seem to be changed into hideous wax figures. They present one cock to the other, holding his head down so that the other may peck at it and thus irritate him. Then the other is given a like opportunity, for in every duel there must be fair play, whether it is a question of Parisian cocks or Filipino cocks. Afterwards, they hold them up in sight of each other, close together, so that each of the enraged little creatures may see who it is that has pulled out a feather, and with whom he must fight. Their neck-feathers bristle up as they gaze at each other fixedly with flashes of anger darting from their little round eyes. Now the moment has come; the attendants place them on the ground a short distance apart and leave them a clear field.

Slowly they advance, their footfalls are audible on the hard ground. No one in the crowd speaks, no one breathes. Raising and lowering their heads as if to gauge one another with a look, the two cocks utter sounds of defiance and contempt. Each sees the bright blade throwing out its cold, bluish reflections. The danger animates them and they rush directly toward each other, but a pace apart they check themselves with fixed gaze and bristling plumage. At that moment their little heads are filled with a rush of blood, their anger flashes forth, and they hurl themselves together with instinctive valor. They strike beak to beak, breast to breast, gaff to gaff, wing to wing, but the blows are skilfully parried, only a few feathers fall. Again they size each other up: suddenly the white rises on his wings, brandishing the deadly knife, but the red has bent his legs and lowered his head, so the white smites only the empty air. Then on touching the ground the white, fearing a blow from behind, turns quickly to face his adversary. The red attacks him furiously, but he defends himself calmly — not undeservedly is he the favorite of the spectators, all of whom tremulously and anxiously follow the fortunes of the fight, only here and there an involuntary cry being heard.

The ground becomes strewn with red and white feathers dyed in blood, but the contest is not for the first blood; the Filipino, carrying out the laws dictated by his government, wishes it to be to the death or until one or the other turns tail and runs. Blood covers the ground, the blows are more numerous, but victory still hangs in the balance. At last, with a supreme effort, the white throws himself forward for a final stroke, fastens his gaff in the wing of the red and catches it between the bones. But the white himself has been wounded in the breast and both are weak and feeble from loss of blood. Breathless, their strength spent, caught one against the other, they remain motionless until the white, with blood pouring from his beak, falls, kicking his death-throes. The red remains at his side with his wing caught, then slowly doubles up his legs and gently closes his eyes.

Then the referee, in accordance with the rule prescribed by the government, declares the red the winner. A savage yell greets the decision, a yell that is heard over the whole town, even and prolonged. He who hears this from afar then knows that the winner is the one against which the odds were placed, or the joy would not be so lasting. The same happens with the nations: when a small one gains a victory over a large one, it is sung and recounted from age to age.

"You see now!" said Bruno dejectedly to his brother, "if you had listened to me we should now have a hundred pesos. You're the cause of our being penniless."

Tarsilo did not answer, but gazed about him as if looking for some one.

"There he is, talking to Pedro," added Bruno. "He's giving him money, lots of money!"

True it was that Lucas was counting silver coins into the hand of Sisa's husband. The two then exchanged some words in secret and separated, apparently satisfied.

"Pedro must have agreed. That's what it is to be decided," sighed Bruno.

Tarsilo remained gloomy and thoughtful, wiping away with the cuff of his camisa the perspiration that ran down his forehead.

"Brother," said Bruno, "I'm going to accept, if you don't decide. The *law*[1] continues, the *lásak* must win and we ought not to lose any chance. I want to bet on the next fight. What's the difference? We'll revenge our father."

"Wait!" said Tarsilo, as he gazed at him fixedly, eye to eye, while both turned pale. "I'll go with you, you're right. We'll revenge our father." Still, he hesitated, and again wiped away the perspiration.

"What's stopping you?" asked Bruno impatiently.

"Do you know what fight comes next? Is it worth while?"

"If you think that way, no! Haven't you heard? The *bulik* of Capitan Basilio's against Capitan Tiago's *lásak*. According to the *law* the *lásak* must win."

"Ah, the *lásak!* I'd bet on it, too. But let's be sure first."

Bruno made a sign of impatience, but followed his brother, who examined the cock, studied it, meditated and reflected, asked some questions. The poor fellow was in doubt. Bruno gazed at him with nervous anger.

"But don't you see that wide scale he has by the side of his spur? Don't you see those feet? What more do you want? Look at those legs, spread out his wings! And this split scale above this wide one, and this double one?"

Tarsilo did not hear him, but went on examining the cock. The clinking of gold and silver came to his ears. "Now let's look at the *bulik*," he said in a thick voice.

Bruno stamped on the ground and gnashed his teeth, but obeyed. They approached another group where a cock was being prepared for the ring. A gaff was selected, red

---

[1] It is a superstition of the cockpit that the color of the victor in the first bout decides the winners for that session: thus, the red having won, the *lásak*, in whose plumage a red color predominates, should be the victor in the succeeding bout. — TR.

silk thread for tying it on was waxed and rubbed thoroughly. Tarsilo took in the creature with a gloomily impressive gaze, as if he were not looking at the bird so much as at something in the future. He rubbed his hand across his forehead and said to his brother in a stifled voice, "Are you ready?"

"I? Long ago! Without looking at them!"

"But, our poor sister —"

"*Abá!* Haven't they told you that Don Crisostomo is the leader? Didn't you see him walking with the Captain-General? What risk do we run?"

"And if we get killed?"

"What's the difference? Our father was flogged to death!"

"You're right!"

The brothers now sought for Lucas in the different groups. As soon as they saw him Tarsilo stopped. "No! Let's get out of here! We're going to ruin ourselves!" he exclaimed.

"Go on if you want to! I'm going to accept!"

"Bruno!"

Unfortunately, a man approached them, saying, "Are you betting? I'm for the *bulik!*"

The brothers did not answer.

"I'll give odds!"

"How much?" asked Bruno.

The man began to count out his pesos. Bruno watched him breathlessly.

"I have two hundred. Fifty to forty!"

"No," said Bruno resolutely. "Put —"

"All right! Fifty to thirty!"

"Double it if you want to."

"All right. The *bulik* belongs to my protector and I've just won. A hundred to sixty!'

"Taken! Wait till I get the money."

"But I'll hold the stakes," said the other, not confiding much in Bruno's looks.

"It's all the same to me," answered the latter, trusting to his fists. Then turning to his brother he added, "Even if you do keep out, I'm going in."

Tarsilo reflected: he loved his brother and liked the sport, and, unable to desert him, he murmured, "Let it go."

They made their way to Lucas, who, on seeing them approach, smiled.

"Sir!" called Tarsilo.

"What's up?"

"How much will you give us?" asked the two brothers together.

"I've already told you. If you will undertake to get others for the purpose of making a surprise-attack on the barracks, I'll give each of you thirty pesos and ten pesos for each companion you bring. If all goes well, each one will receive a hundred pesos and you double that amount. Don Crisostomo is rich."

"Accepted!" exclaimed Bruno. "Let's have the money."

"I knew you were brave, as your father was! Come, so that those fellows who killed him may not overhear us," said Lucas, indicating the civil-guards.

Taking them into a corner, he explained to them while he was counting out the money, "Tomorrow Don Crisostomo will get back with the arms. Day after tomorrow, about eight o'clock at night, go to the cemetery and I'll let you know the final arrangements. You have time to look for companions."

After they had left him the two brothers seemed to have changed parts — Tarsilo was calm, while Bruno was uneasy.

CHAPTER XLVII

THE TWO SEÑORAS

WHILE Capitan Tiago was gambling on his *lásak*, Doña Victorina was taking a walk through the town for the purpose of observing how the indolent Indians kept their houses and fields. She was dressed as elegantly as possible with all her ribbons and flowers over her silk gown, in order to impress the provincials and make them realize what a distance intervened between them and her sacred person. Giving her arm to her lame husband, she strutted along the streets amid the wonder and stupefaction of the natives. Her cousin Linares had remained in the house.

"What ugly shacks these Indians have!" she began with a grimace. "I don't see how they can live in them — one must have to be an Indian! And how rude they are and how proud! They don't take off their hats when they meet us! Hit them over the head as the curates and the officers of the Civil Guard do — teach them politeness!"

"And if they hit me back?" asked Dr. De Espadaña.

"That's what you're a man for!"

"B-but, I'm l-lame!"

Doña Victorina was falling into a bad humor. The streets were unpaved and the train of her gown was covered with dust. Besides, they had met a number of young women, who, in passing them, had dropped their eyes and had not admired her rich costume as they should have done. Sinang's cochero, who was driving Sinang and her cousin in an elegant carriage, had the impudence to yell "*Tabi!*" in such a commanding tone that she had to jump out of the way, and could only protest: "Look at that brute of a cochero! I'm going to tell his master to train his servants better."

"Let's go back to the house," she commanded to her husband, who, fearing a storm, wheeled on his crutch in obedience to her mandate.

They met and exchanged greetings with the alferez. This increased Doña Victorina's ill humor, for the officer not only did not proffer any compliment on her costume, but even seemed to stare at it in a mocking way.

"You ought not to shake hands with a mere alferez," she said to her husband as the soldier left them. "He scarcely touched his helmet while you took off your hat. You don't know how to maintain your rank!"

"He's the b-boss here!"

"What do we care for that? We are Indians, perhaps?"

"You're right," he assented, not caring to quarrel.

They passed in front of the officer's dwelling. Doña Consolacion was at the window, as usual, dressed in flannel and smoking her cigar. As the house was low, the two señoras measured one another with looks; Doña Victorina stared while the Muse of the Civil Guard examined her from head to foot, and then, sticking out her lower lip, turned her head away and spat on the ground. This used up the last of Doña Victorina's patience. Leaving her husband without support, she planted herself in front of the alfereza, trembling with anger from head to foot and unable to speak. Doña Consolacion slowly turned her head, calmly looked her over again, and once more spat, this time with greater disdain.

"What's the matter with you, Doña?" she asked.

"Can you tell me, señora, why you look at me so? Are you envious?" Doña Victorina was at length able to articulate.

"I, envious of you, I, of you?" drawled the Muse. "Yes, I envy you those frizzes!"

"Come, woman!" pleaded the doctor. "D-don't t-take any n-notice!"

"Let me teach this shameless slattern a lesson," replied his wife, giving him such a shove that he nearly kissed the ground. Then she again turned to Doña Consolacion.

"Remember who you're dealing with!" she exclaimed. "Don't think that I'm a provincial or a soldier's *querida!* In my house in Manila the alfereces don't enter, they wait at the door."

"Oho, *Excelentísima Señora!* Alfereces don't enter, but cripples do — like that one — ha, ha, ha!"

Had it not been for the rouge, Doña Victorina would have been seen to blush. She tried to get to her antagonist, but the sentinel stopped her. In the meantime the street was filling up with a curious crowd.

"Listen, I lower myself talking to you — people of quality — Don't you want to wash my clothes? I'll pay you well! Do you think that I don't know that you were a washerwoman?"

Doña Consolacion straightened up furiously; the remark about washing hurt her. "Do you think that we don't know who you are and what class of people you belong with? Get out, my husband has already told me! Señora, I at least have never belonged to more than one, but you? One must be dying of hunger to take the leavings, the mop of the whole world!"

This shot found its mark with Doña Victorina. She rolled up her sleeves, clenched her fists, and gritted her teeth. "Come down, old sow!" she cried. "I'm going to smash that dirty mouth of yours! *Querida* of a battalion, filthy hag!"

The Muse immediately disappeared from the window and was soon seen running down the stairs flourishing her husband's whip.

Don Tiburcio interposed himself supplicatingly, but they would have come to blows had not the alferez arrived on the scene.

"Ladies! Don Tiburcio!"

"Train your woman better, buy her some decent clothes,

and if you have n't any money left, rob the people — that's what you 've got soldiers for!" yelled Doña Victorina.

"Here I am, señora! Why does n't your Excellency smash my mouth? You 've only tongue and spittle, Doña Excelencia!"

"Señora!" cried the alferez furiously to Doña Victorina, "be thankful that I remember that you 're a woman or else I 'd kick you to pieces — frizzes, ribbons, and all!"

"S-señor Alferez!"

"Get out, you quack! You don't wear the pants!"

The women brought into play words and gestures, insults and abuse, dragging out all the evil that was stored in the recesses of their minds. Since all four talked at once and said so many things that might hurt the prestige of certain classes by the truths that were brought to light, we forbear from recording what they said. The curious spectators, while they may not have understood all that was said, got not a little entertainment out of the scene and hoped that the affair would come to blows. Unfortunately for them, the curate came along and restored order.

"Señores! Señoras! What a shame! Señor Alferez!"

"What are you doing here, you hypocrite, Carlist!"

"Don Tiburcio, take your wife away! Señora, hold your tongue!"

"Say that to these robbers of the poor!"

Little by little the lexicon of epithets was exhausted, the review of shamelessness of the two couples completed, and with threats and insults they gradually drew away from one another. Fray Salvi moved from one group to the other, giving animation to the scene. Would that our friend the correspondent had been present!

"This very day we 'll go to Manila and see the Captain-General!" declared the raging Doña Victorina to her husband. "You 're not a man! It 's a waste of money to buy trousers for you!"

"B-but, woman, the g-guards? I 'm l-lame!"

"You must challenge him for pistol or sword, or — or — " Doña Victorina stared fixedly at his false teeth.

"My d-dear, I've never had hold of a — "

But she did not let him finish. With a majestic sweep of her hand she snatched out his false teeth and trampled them in the street.

Thus, he half-crying and she breathing fire, they reached the house. Linares was talking with Maria Clara, Sinang, and Victoria, and as he had heard nothing of the quarrel, became rather uneasy at sight of his cousins. Maria Clara, lying in an easy-chair among pillows and wraps, was greatly surprised to see the new physiognomy of her doctor.

"Cousin," began Doña Victorina, "you must challenge the alferez right away, or — "

"Why?" asked the startled Linares.

"You challenge him right now or else I'll tell everybody here who you are."

"But, Doña Victorina!"

The three girls exchanged glances.

"You'll see! The alferez has insulted us and said that you are what you are! His old hag came down with a whip and he, this thing here, permitted the insult — a man!"

"*Abá!*" exclaimed Sinang, "they've had a fight and we didn't see it!"

"The alferez smashed the doctor's teeth," observed Victoria.

"This very day we go to Manila. You, you stay here to challenge him or else I'll tell Don Santiago that all we've told him is a lie, I'll tell him — "

"But, Doña Victorina, Doña Victorina," interrupted the now pallid Linares, going up to her, "be calm, don't call up — " Then he added in a whisper, "Don't be imprudent, especially just now."

At that moment Capitan Tiago came in from the cockpit, sad and sighing; he had lost his *lásak*. But Doña Victorina left him no time to grieve. In a few words but with no lack of strong language she related what had happened, trying of course to put herself in the best light possible.

"Linares is going to challenge him, do you hear? If he does n't, don't let him marry your daughter, don't you permit it! If he has n't any courage, he does n't deserve Clarita!"

"So you 're going to marry this gentleman?" asked Sinang, but her merry eyes filled with tears. "I knew that you were prudent but not that you were fickle."

Pale as wax, Maria Clara partly rose and stared with frightened eyes at her father, at Doña Victorina, at Linares. The latter blushed, Capitan Tiago dropped his eyes, while the señora went on:

"Clarita, bear this in mind: never marry a man that does n't wear trousers. You expose yourself to insults, even from the dogs!"

The girl did not answer her, but turned to her friends and said, "Help me to my room, I can't walk alone."

By their aid she rose, and with her waist encircled by the round arms of her friends, resting her marble-like head on the shoulder of the beautiful Victoria, she went to her chamber.

That same night the married couple gathered their effects together and presented Capitan Tiago with a bill which amounted to several thousand pesos. Very early the following day they left for Manila in his carriage, committing to the bashful Linares the office of avenger.

CHAPTER XLVIII

THE ENIGMA

Volverán las oscuras golondrinas.[1]

BECQUER.

AS Lucas had foretold, Ibarra arrived on the following day. His first visit was to the family of Capitan Tiago for the purpose of seeing Maria Clara and informing her that his Grace had reconciled him with religion, and that he brought to the curate a letter of recommendation in the handwriting of the Archbishop himself. Aunt Isabel was not a little rejoiced at this, for she liked the young man and did not look favorably on the marriage of her niece with Linares. Capitan Tiago was not at home.

"Come in," said the aunt in her broken Spanish. "Maria, Don Crisostomo is once more in the favor of God. The Archbishop has *discommunicated* him."

But the youth was unable to advance, the smile froze on his lips, words failed him. Standing on the balcony at the side of Maria Clara was Linares, arranging bouquets of flowers and leaves. Roses and sampaguitas were scattered about on the floor. Reclining in a big chair, pale, with a sad and pensive air, Maria Clara toyed with an ivory fan which was not whiter than her shapely fingers.

At the appearance of Ibarra, Linares turned pale and Maria Clara's cheeks flushed crimson. She tried to rise, but strength failed her, so she dropped her eyes and let the fan fall. An embarrassed silence prevailed for a few moments. Ibarra was then able to move forward and murmur tremblingly, "I've just got back and have come im-

[1] The dark swallows will return.

mediately to see you. I find you better than I had thought I should."

The girl seemed to have been stricken dumb; she neither said anything nor raised her eyes.

Ibarra looked Linares over from head to foot with a stare which the bashful youth bore haughtily.

"Well, I see that my arrival was unexpected," said Ibarra slowly "Maria, pardon me that I did n't have myself announced. At some other time I 'll be able to make explanations to you about my conduct. We 'll still see one another — surely."

These last words were accompanied by a look at Linares. The girl raised toward him her lovely eyes, full of purity and sadness. They were so beseeching and eloquent that Ibarra stopped in confusion.

"May I come tomorrow?"

"You know that for my part you are always welcome," she answered faintly.

Ibarra withdrew in apparent calm, but with a tempest in his head and ice in his heart. What he had just seen and felt was incomprehensible to him: was it doubt, dislike, or faithlessness?

"Oh, only a woman after all!" he murmured.

Taking no note of where he was going, he reached the spot where the schoolhouse was under construction. The work was well advanced, Ñor Juan with his rule and plumb-bob coming and going among the numerous laborers. Upon catching sight of Ibarra he ran to meet him.

"Don Crisostomo, at last you 've come! We 've all been waiting for you. Look at the walls, they 're already more than a meter high and within two days they 'll be up to the height of a man. I 've put in only the strongest and most durable woods — molave, dungon, ipil, langil — and sent for the finest — tindalo, malatapay, pino, and narra — for the finishings. Do you want to look at the foundations?"

The workmen saluted Ibarra respectfully, while Ñor

Juan made voluble explanations. "Here is the piping that I have taken the liberty to add," he said. "These subterranean conduits lead to a sort of cesspool, thirty yards away. It will help fertilize the garden. There was nothing of that in the plan. Does it displease you?"

"Quite the contrary, I approve what you've done and congratulate you. You are a real architect. From whom did you learn the business?"

"From myself, sir," replied the old man modestly.

"Oh, before I forget about it — tell those who may have scruples, if perhaps there is any one who fears to speak to me, that I'm no longer excommunicated. The Archbishop invited me to dinner."

"*Abá*, sir, we don't pay any attention to excommunications! All of us are excommunicated. Padre Damaso himself is and yet he stays fat."

"How's that?"

"It's true, sir, for a year ago he caned the coadjutor, who is just as much a sacred person as he is. Who pays any attention to excommunications, sir?"

Among the laborers Ibarra caught sight of Elias, who, as he saluted him along with the others, gave him to understand by a look that he had something to say to him.

"Ñor Juan," said Ibarra, "will you bring me your list of the laborers?"

Ñor Juan disappeared, and Ibarra approached Elias, who was by himself, lifting a heavy stone into a cart.

"If you can grant me a few hours' conversation, sir, walk down to the shore of the lake this evening and get into my banka." The youth nodded, and Elias moved away.

Ñor Juan now brought the list, but Ibarra scanned it in vain; the name of Elias did not appear on it!

CHAPTER XLIX

THE VOICE OF THE HUNTED

AS the sun was sinking below the horizon Ibarra stepped into Elias's banka at the shore of the lake. The youth looked out of humor.

"Pardon me, sir," said Elias sadly, on seeing him, "that I have been so bold as to make this appointment. I wanted to talk to you freely and so I chose this means, for here we won't have any listeners. We can return within an hour."

"You're wrong, friend," answered Ibarra with a forced smile. "You'll have to take me to that town whose belfry we see from here. A mischance forces me to this."

"A mischance?"

"Yes. On my way here I met the alferez and he forced his company on me. I thought of you and remembered that he knows you, so to get away from him I told him that I was going to that town. I'll have to stay there all day, since he will look for me tomorrow afternoon."

"I appreciate your thoughtfulness, but you might simply have invited him to accompany you," answered Elias naturally.

"What about you?"

"He wouldn't have recognized me, since the only time he ever saw me he wasn't in a position to take careful note of my appearance."

"I'm in bad luck," sighed Ibarra, thinking of Maria Clara. "What did you have to tell me?"

Elias looked about him. They were already at a distance from the shore, the sun had set, and as in these latitudes there is scarcely any twilight, the shades were lengthening, bringing into view the bright disk of the full moon.

"Sir," replied Elias gravely, "I am the bearer of the wishes of many unfortunates."

"Unfortunates? What do you mean?"

In a few words Elias recounted his conversation with the leader of the tulisanes, omitting the latter's doubts and threats. Ibarra listened attentively and was the first to break the long silence that reigned after he had finished his story.

"So they want —"

"Radical reforms in the armed forces, in the priesthood, and in the administration of justice; that is to say, they ask for paternal treatment from the government."

"Reforms? In what sense?"

"For example, more respect for a man's dignity, more security for the individual, less force in the armed forces, fewer privileges for that corps which so easily abuses what it has."

"Elias," answered the youth, "I don't know who you are, but I suspect that you are not a man of the people; you think and act so differently from others. You will understand me if I tell you that, however imperfect the condition of affairs may be now, it would be more so if it were changed. I might be able to get the friends that I have in Madrid to talk, *by paying them;* I might even be able to see the Captain-General; but neither would the former accomplish anything nor has the latter sufficient power to introduce so many novelties. Nor would I ever take a single step in that direction, for the reason that, while I fully understand that it is true that these corporations have their faults, they are necessary at this time. They are what is known as a necessary evil."

Greatly surprised, Elias raised his head and looked at him in astonishment. "Do you, then, also believe in a necessary evil, sir?" he asked in a voice that trembled

THE VOICE OF THE HUNTED

slightly. "Do you believe that in order to do good it is necessary to do evil?"

"No, I believe in it as in a violent remedy that we make use of when we wish to cure a disease. Now then, the country is an organism suffering from a chronic malady, and in order to cure it, the government sees the necessity of employing such means, harsh and violent if you wish, but useful and necessary."

"He is a bad doctor, sir, who seeks only to destroy or stifle the symptoms without an effort to examine into the origin of the malady, or, when knowing it, fears to attack it. The Civil Guard has only this purpose: the repression of crime by means of terror and force, a purpose that it does not fulfil or accomplishes only incidentally. You must take into account the truth that society can be severe with individuals only when it has provided them with the means necessary for their moral perfection. In our country, where there is no society, since there is no unity between the people and the government, the latter should be indulgent, not only because indulgence is necessary but also because the individual, abandoned and uncared for by it, has less responsibility, for the very reason that he has received less guidance. Besides, following out your comparison, the treatment that is applied to the ills of the country is so destructive that it is felt only in the sound parts of the organism, whose vitality is thus weakened and made receptive of evil. Would it not be more rational to strengthen the diseased parts of the organism and lessen the violence of the remedy a little?"

"To weaken the Civil Guard would be to endanger the security of the towns."

"The security of the towns!" exclaimed Elias bitterly. "It will soon be fifteen years since the towns have had their Civil Guard, and look: still we have tulisanes, still we hear that they sack towns, that they infest the highways. Robberies continue and the perpetrators are not hunted down; crime flourishes, and the real criminal goes scot-free, but not so the peaceful inhabitant of the town. Ask any honorable citizen if he looks upon this institution as a benefit, a protection on the part of the government, and not as an imposition, a despotism whose outrageous acts do more damage than the violent deeds of criminals. These latter are indeed serious, but they are rare, and against them one has the right to defend himself, but against the molestations of legal force he is not even allowed a protest, and if they are not serious they are nevertheless continued and sanctioned. What effect does this institution produce among our people? It paralyzes communication because all are afraid of being abused on trifling pretexts. It pays more attention to formalities than to the real nature of things, which is the first symptom of incapacity. Because one has forgotten his cedula he must be manacled and knocked about, regardless of the fact that he may be a decent and respectable citizen. The superiors hold it their first duty to make people salute them, either willingly or forcibly, even in the darkness of the night, and their inferiors imitate them by mistreating and robbing the country folk, nor are pretexts lacking to this end. Sanctity of the home does not exist; not long ago in Kalamba they entered, by forcing their way through the windows, the house of a peaceful inhabitant to whom their chief owed money and favors. There is no personal security; when they need to have their barracks or houses cleaned they go out and arrest any one who does not resist them, in order to make him work the whole day. Do you care to hear more? During these holidays gambling, which is prohibited by law, has gone on while they forcibly broke up the celebrations permitted by the authorities. You saw what the people thought about these things; what have they got by repressing their anger and hoping for human justice? Ah, sir, if that is what you call keeping the peace — "

" I agree with you that there are evils," replied Ibarra, " but let us bear with those evils on account of the benefits,

THE VOICE OF THE HUNTED

that accompany them. This institution may be imperfect, but, believe me, by the fear that it inspires it keeps the number of criminals from increasing."

"Say rather that by this fear the number is increased," corrected Elias. "Before the creation of this corps almost all the evil-doers, with the exception of a very few, were criminals from hunger. They plundered and robbed in order to live, but when their time of want was passed, they again left the highways clear. Sufficient to put them to flight were the poor, but brave cuadrilleros, they who have been so calumniated by the writers about our country, who have for a right, death, for duty, fighting, and for reward, jests. Now there are tulisanes who are such for life. A single fault, a crime inhumanly punished, resistance against the outrages of this power, fear of atrocious tortures, cast them out forever from society and condemn them to slay or be slain. The terrorism of the Civil Guard closes against them the doors of repentance, and as outlaws they fight to defend themselves in the mountains better than the soldiers at whom they laugh. The result is that we are unable to put an end to the evil that we have created. Remember what the prudence of the Captain-General de la Torre[1] accomplished. The amnesty granted by him to those unhappy people has proved that in those mountains there still beat the hearts of men and that they only wait for pardon. Terrorism is useful when the people are slaves, when the mountains afford no hiding-places, when power places a sentinel behind every tree, and when the body of the slave contains nothing more than a stomach and intestines. But when in desperation he fights for his life, feeling his arm strong, his heart throb, his whole being fill with hate, how can terrorism hope to extinguish the flame to which it is only adding fuel?"

[1] General Carlos Maria de la Torre y Nava Carrada, the first "liberal" governor of the Philippines, was Captain-General from 1869 to 1871. He issued an amnesty to the outlaws and created the Civil Guard, largely from among those who surrendered themselves in response to it. — TR.

"I am perplexed, Elias, to hear you talk thus, and I should almost believe that you were right had I not my own convictions. But note this fact — and don't be offended, for I consider you an exception — look who the men are that ask for these reforms: nearly all criminals or on the way to be such!"

"Criminals now, or future criminals; but why are they such? Because their peace has been disturbed, their happiness destroyed, their dearest affections wounded, and when they have asked justice for protection, they have become convinced that they can expect it only from themselves. But you are mistaken, sir, if you think that only the criminals ask for justice. Go from town to town, from house to house, listen to the secret sighings in the bosoms of the families, and you will be convinced that the evils which the Civil Guard corrects are the same as, if not less than, those it causes all the time. Should we decide from this that all the people are criminals? If so, then why defend some from the others, why not destroy them all?"

"Some error exists here which I do not see just now, some fallacy in the theory to invalidate the practise, for in Spain, the mother country, this corps is displaying, and has ever displayed, great usefulness."

"I don't doubt it. Perhaps there it is better organized, the men of better grade, perhaps also Spain needs it while the Philippines does not. Our customs, our mode of life, which are always invoked when there is a desire to deny us some right, are entirely overlooked when the desire is to impose something upon us. And tell me, sir, why have not the other nations, which from their nearness to Spain must be more like her than the Philippines is, adopted this institution? Is it because of this that they still have fewer robberies on their railway trains, fewer riots, fewer murders, and fewer assassinations in their great capitals?"

Ibarra bowed his head in deep thought, raising it after a few moments to reply: "This question, my friend, calls for serious study. If my inquiries convince me that these complaints are well founded I will write to my friends in Madrid, since we have no representatives. Meanwhile, believe me that the government needs a corps with strength enough to make itself respected and to enforce its authority."

"Yes, sir, when the government is at war with the country. But for the welfare of the government itself we must not have the people think that they are in opposition to authority. Rather, if such were true, if we prefer force to prestige, we ought to take care to whom we grant this unlimited power, this authority. So much power in the hands of men, ignorant men filled with passions, without moral training, of untried principles, is a weapon in the hands of a madman in a defenseless multitude. I concede and wish to believe with you that the government needs this weapon, but then let it choose this weapon carefully, let it select the most worthy instruments, and since it prefers to take upon itself authority, rather than have the people grant it, at least let it be seen that it knows how to exercise it."

Elias spoke passionately, enthusiastically, in vibrating tones; his eyes flashed. A solemn pause followed. The banka, unimpelled by the paddle, seemed to stand still on the water. The moon shone majestically in a sapphire sky and a few lights glimmered on the distant shore.

"What more do they ask for?" inquired Ibarra.

"Reform in the priesthood," answered Elias in a sad and discouraged tone. "These unfortunates ask for more protection against —"

"Against the religious orders?"

"Against their oppressors, sir."

"Has the Philippines forgotten what she owes to those orders? Has she forgotten the immense debt of gratitude that is due from her to those who snatched her from error to give her the true faith, to those who have protected her against the tyrannical acts of the civil power? This is the evil result of not knowing the history of our native land!"

The surprised Elias could hardly credit what he heard. "Sir," he replied in a grave tone, "you accuse these people of ingratitude; let me, one of the people who suffer, defend them. Favors rendered, in order to have any claims to recognition, must be disinterested. Let us pass over its missionary work, the much-invoked Christian charity; let us brush history aside and not ask what Spain has done with the Jewish people, who gave all Europe a Book, a Religion, and a God; what she has done with the Arabic people, who gave her culture, who were tolerant with her religious beliefs, and who awoke her lethargic national spirit, so nearly destroyed during the Roman and Gothic dominations. You say that she snatched us from error and gave us the true faith: do you call faith these outward forms, do you call religion this traffic in girdles and scapularies, truth these miracles and wonderful tales that we hear daily? Is this the law of Jesus Christ? For this it was hardly necessary that a God should allow Himself to be crucified or that we should be obliged to show eternal gratitude. Superstition existed long before — it was only necessary to systematize it and raise the price of its merchandise!

"You will tell me that however imperfect our religion may be at present, it is preferable to what we had before. I believe that, too, and would agree with you in saying so, but the cost is too great, since for it we have given up our nationality, our independence. For it we have given over to its priests our best towns, our fields, and still give up our savings by the purchase of religious objects. An article of foreign manufacture has been introduced among us, we have paid well for it, and we are even.

"If you mean the protection that they afforded us against the *encomenderos*,[1] I might answer that through them we

---

[1] After the conquest (officially designated as the "pacification"), the Spanish soldiers who had rendered faithful service were allotted districts known as *encomiendas*, generally of about a thousand natives each. The *encomendero* was entitled to the tribute from the people in his district and was in return supposed to protect them and provide religious instruction. The early friars alleged extortionate greed and

fell under the power of the *encomenderos*. But no, I realize that a true faith and a sincere love for humanity guided the first missionaries to our shores; I realize the debt of gratitude we owe to those noble hearts; I know that at that time Spain abounded in heroes of all kinds, in religious as well as in political affairs, in civil and in military life. But because the forefathers were virtuous, should we consent to the abuses of their degenerate descendants? Because they have rendered us great service, should we be to blame for preventing them from doing us wrong? The country does not ask for their expulsion but only for reforms required by the changed circumstances and new needs."

"I love our native land as well as you can, Elias; I understand something of what it desires, and I have listened with attention to all you have said. But, after all, my friend, I believe that we are looking at things through rather impassioned eyes. Here, less than in other parts, do I see the necessity for reforms."

"Is it possible, sir," asked Elias, extending his arms in a gesture of despair, "that you do not see the necessity for reforms, you, after the misfortunes of your family?"

"Ah, I forget myself and my own troubles in the presence of the security of the Philippines, in the presence of the interests of Spain!" interrupted Ibarra warmly. "To preserve the Philippines it is meet that the friars continue as they are. On the union with Spain depends the welfare of our country."

When Ibarra had ceased Elias still sat in an attitude of attention with a sad countenance and eyes that had lost their luster. "The missionaries conquered the country, it is true," he replied, "but do you believe that by the friars the Philippines will be preserved?"

"Yes, by them alone. Such is the belief of all who have written about the country."

---

brutal conduct on the part of the *encomenderos* and made vigorous protests in the natives' behalf. — TR.

"Oh!" exclaimed Elias dejectedly, throwing the paddle down in the banka, "I did not believe that you would have so poor an idea of the government and of the country. Why don't you condemn both? What would you say of the members of a family that dwells in peace only through the intervention of an outsider: a country that is obedient because it is deceived; a government that commands because it avails itself of fraud, a government that does not know how to make itself loved or respected for its own sake? Pardon me, sir, but I believe that our government is stupid and is working its own ruin when it rejoices that such is the belief. I thank you for your kindness, where do you wish me to take you now?"

"No," replied Ibarra, "let us talk; it is necessary to see who is right on such an important subject."

"Pardon me, sir," replied Elias, shaking his head, "but I have n't the eloquence to convince you. Even though I have had some education I am still an Indian, my way of life seems to you a precarious one, and my words will always seem to you suspicious. Those who have given voice to the opposite opinion are Spaniards, and as such, even though they may speak idly and foolishly, their tones, their titles, and their origin make their words sacred and give them such authority that I have desisted forever from arguing against them. Moreover, when I see that you, who love your country, you, whose father sleeps beneath these quiet waters, you, who have seen yourself attacked, insulted, and persecuted, hold such opinions in spite of all these things, and in spite of your knowledge, I begin to doubt my own convictions and to admit the possibility that the people may be mistaken. I'll have to tell those unfortunates who have put their trust in men that they must place it in God and their own strength. Again I thank you — tell me where I shall take you."

"Elias, your bitter words touch my heart and make me also doubt. What do you want? I was not brought up among the people, so I am perhaps ignorant of their needs.

THE VOICE OF THE HUNTED

I spent my childhood in the Jesuit college, I grew up in Europe, I have been molded by books, learning only what men have been able to bring to light. What remains among the shadows, what the writers do not tell, that I am ignorant of. Yet I love our country as you do, not only because it is the duty of every man to love the country to which he owes his existence and to which he will no doubt owe his final rest, not only because my father so taught me, but also because my mother was an Indian, because my fondest recollections cluster around my country, and I love it also because to it I owe and shall ever owe my happiness!"

"And I, because to it I owe my misfortunes," muttered Elias.

"Yes, my friend, I know that you suffer, that you are unfortunate, and that those facts make you look into the future darkly and influence your way of thinking, so I am somewhat forearmed against your complaints. If I could understand your motives, something of your past —"

"My misfortunes had another source. If I thought that the story of them would be of any use, I would relate it to you, since, apart from the fact that I make no secret of it, it is quite well known to many."

"Perhaps on hearing it I might correct my opinions. You know that I do not trust much to theories, preferring rather to be guided by facts."

Elias remained thoughtful for a few moments. "If that is the case, sir, I will tell you my story briefly."

CHAPTER L

ELIAS'S STORY

"SOME sixty years ago my grandfather dwelt in Manila, being employed as a bookkeeper in a Spanish commercial house. He was then very young, was married, and had a son. One night from some unknown cause the warehouse burned down. The fire was communicated to the dwelling of his employer and from there to many other buildings. The losses were great, a scapegoat was sought, and the merchant accused my grandfather. In vain he protested his innocence, but he was poor and unable to pay the great lawyers, so he was condemned to be flogged publicly and paraded through the streets of Manila. Not so very long since they still used the infamous method of punishment which the people call the " *caballo y vaca*," [1] and which is a thousand times more dreadful than death itself. Abandoned by all except his young wife, my grandfather saw himself tied to a horse, followed by an unfeeling crowd, and whipped on every street-corner in the sight of men, his brothers, and in the neighborhood of numerous temples of a God of peace. When the wretch, now forever disgraced, had satisfied the vengeance of man with his blood, his tortures, and his cries, he had to be taken off the horse, for he had become unconscious. Would to God that he had died! But by one of those refinements of cruelty he was given his liberty. His wife, pregnant at the time, vainly begged from door to door for work or alms in order to care for her sick husband and their poor son, but who would trust the wife of an incendiary and a disgraced man? The wife, then, had to become a prostitute!"

[1] Horse and cow.

ELIAS'S STORY

Ibarra rose in his seat.

"Oh, don't get excited! Prostitution was not now a dishonor for her or a disgrace to her husband; for them honor and shame no longer existed. The husband recovered from his wounds and came with his wife and child to hide himself in the mountains of this province. Here they lived several months, miserable, alone, hated and shunned by all. The wife gave birth to a sickly child, which fortunately died. Unable to endure such misery and being less courageous than his wife, my grandfather, in despair at seeing his sick wife deprived of all care and assistance, hanged himself. His corpse rotted in sight of the son, who was scarcely able to care for his sick mother, and the stench from it led to their discovery. Her husband's death was attributed to her, for of what is the wife of a wretch, a woman who has been a prostitute besides, not believed to be capable? If she swears, they call her a perjurer; if she weeps, they say that she is acting; and that she blasphemes when she calls on God. Nevertheless, they had pity on her condition and waited for the birth of another child before they flogged her. You know how the friars spread the belief that the Indians can only be managed by blows: read what Padre Gaspar de San Agustin says![1]

---

[1] Fray Gaspar de San Agustin, O.S.A., who came to the Philippines in 1668 and died in Manila in 1724, was the author of a history of the conquest, but his chief claim to immortality comes from a letter written in 1720 on the character and habits of "the Indian inhabitants of these islands," a letter which was widely circulated and which has been extensively used by other writers. In it the writer with senile querulousness harped up and down the whole gamut of abuse in describing and commenting upon the vices of the natives, very artlessly revealing the fact in many places, however, that his observations were drawn principally from the conduct of the servants in the conventos and homes of Spaniards. To him in this letter is due the credit of giving its wide popularity to the specious couplet:

> El bejuco crece   (The rattan thrives
> Donde el indio nace, Where the Indian lives,)

which the holy men who delighted in quoting it took as an additional evidence of the wise dispensation of the God of Nature, rather incon-

"A woman thus condemned will curse the day on which her child is born, and this, besides prolonging her torture, violates every maternal sentiment. Unfortunately, she brought forth a healthy child. Two months afterwards, the sentence was executed to the great satisfaction of the men who thought that thus they were performing their duty. Not being at peace in these mountains, she then fled with her two sons to a neighboring province, where they lived like wild beasts, hating and hated. The elder of the two boys still remembered, even amid so much misery, the happiness of his infancy, so he became a tulisan as soon as he found himself strong enough. Before long the bloody name of Balat spread from province to province, a terror to the people, because in his revenge he did everything with blood and fire. The younger, who was by nature kind-hearted, resigned himself to his shameful fate along with his mother, and they lived on what the woods afforded, clothing themselves in the cast-off rags of travelers. She had lost her name, being known only as *the convict, the prostitute, the scourged.* He was known as the son of his mother only, because the gentleness of his disposition led every one to believe that he was not the son of the incendiary and because any doubt as to the morality of the Indians can be held reasonable.

"At last, one day the notorious Balat fell into the clutches of the authorities, who exacted of him a strict accounting for his crimes, and of his mother for having done nothing to rear him properly. One morning the

---

sistently overlooking its incongruity with the teachings of Him in whose name they assumed their holy office.

It seems somewhat strange that a spiritual father should have written in such terms about his charges until the fact appears that the letter was addressed to an influential friend in Spain for use in opposition to a proposal to carry out the provisions of the Council of Trent by turning the parishes in the islands over to the secular, and hence, native, clergy. A translation of this bilious tirade, with copious annotations showing to what a great extent it has been used by other writers, appears in Volume XL of Blair and Robertson's *The Philippine Islands.* — TR.

younger brother went to look for his mother, who had gone into the woods to gather mushrooms and had not returned. He found her stretched out on the ground under a cotton-tree beside the highway, her face turned toward the sky, her eyes fixed and staring, her clenched hands buried in the blood-stained earth. Some impulse moved him to look up in the direction toward which the eyes of the dead woman were staring, and he saw hanging from a branch a basket and in the basket the gory head of his brother!"

'My God!" ejaculated Ibarra.

"That might have been the exclamation of my father," continued Elias coldly. "The body of the brigand had been cut up and the trunk buried, but his limbs were distributed and hung up in different towns. If ever you go from Kalamba to Santo Tomas you will still see a withered lomboy-tree where one of my uncle's legs hung rotting — nature has blasted the tree so that it no longer grows or bears fruit. The same was done with the other limbs, but the head, as the best part of the person and the portion most easily recognizable, was hung up in front of his mother's hut!"

Ibarra bowed his head.

"The boy fled like one accursed," Elias went on. "He fled from town to town by mountain and valley. When he thought that he had reached a place where he was not known, he hired himself out as a laborer in the house of a rich man in the province of Tayabas. His activity and the gentleness of his character gained him the good-will of all who did not know his past, and by his thrift and economy he succeeded in accumulating a little capital. He was still young, he thought his sorrows buried in the past, and he dreamed of a happy future. His pleasant appearance, his youth, and his somewhat unfortunate condition won him the love of a young woman of the town, but he dared not ask for her hand from fear that his past might become known. But love is stronger than anything else and they wandered from the straight path, so, to save the woman's honor, he risked everything by asking for her in marriage. The records were sought and his whole past became known. The girl's father was rich and succeeded in having him prosecuted. He did not try to defend himself but admitted everything, and so was sent to prison. The woman gave birth to twins, a boy and a girl, who were nurtured in secret and made to believe that their father was dead — no difficult matter, since at a tender age they saw their mother die, and they gave little thought to tracing genealogies. As our maternal grandfather was rich our childhood passed happily. My sister and I were brought up together, loving one another as only twins can love when they have no other affections. When quite young I was sent to study in the Jesuit College, and my sister, in order that we might not be completely separated, entered the Concordia College.[1] After our brief education was finished, since we desired only to be farmers, we returned to the town to take possession of the inheritance left us by our grandfather. We lived happily for a time, the future smiled on us, we had many servants, our fields produced abundant harvests, and my sister was about to be married to a young man whom she adored and who responded equally to her affection.

"But in a dispute over money and by reason of my haughty disposition at that time, I alienated the good will of a distant relative, and one day he cast in my face my doubtful birth and shameful descent. I thought it all a slander and demanded satisfaction. The tomb which covered so much rottenness was again opened and to my consternation the whole truth came out to overwhelm me. To add to our sorrow, we had had for many years an old servant who had endured all my whims without ever leav-

---

[1] The Colegio de la Inmaculada Concepcion Concordia, situated near Santa Ana in the suburbs of Manila, was founded in 1868 for the education of native girls, by a pious Spanish-Filipino lady, who donated a building and grounds, besides bearing the expense of bringing out seven Sisters of Charity to take charge of it. — TR.

ing us, contenting himself merely with weeping and groaning at the rough jests of the other servants. I don't know how my relative had found it out, but the fact is that he had this old man summoned into court and made him tell the truth: that old servant, who had clung to his beloved children, and whom I had abused many times, was my father! Our happiness faded away, I gave up our fortune, my sister lost her betrothed, and with our father we left the town to seek refuge elsewhere. The thought that he had contributed to our misfortunes shortened the old man's days, but before he died I learned from his lips the whole story of the sorrowful past.

"My sister and I were left alone. She wept a great deal, but even in the midst of such great sorrows as heaped themselves upon us, she could not forget her love. Without complaining, without uttering a word, she saw her former sweetheart married to another girl, but I watched her gradually sicken without being able to console her. One day she disappeared, and it was in vain that I sought everywhere, in vain I made inquiries about her. About six months afterwards I learned that about that time, after a flood on the lake, there had been found in some rice fields bordering on the beach at Kalamba, the corpse of a young woman who had been either drowned or murdered, for she had had, so they said, a knife sticking in her breast. The officials of that town published the fact in the country round about, but no one came to claim the body, no young woman apparently had disappeared. From the description they gave me afterward of her dress, her ornaments, the beauty of her countenance, and her abundant hair, I recognized in her my poor sister.

"Since then I have wandered from province to province. My reputation and my history are in the mouths of many. They attribute great deeds to me, sometimes calumniating me, but I pay little attention to men, keeping ever on my way. Such in brief is my story, a story of one of the judgments of men."

Elias fell silent as he rowed along.

"I still believe that you are not wrong," murmured Crisostomo in a low voice, "when you say that justice should seek to do good by rewarding virtue and educating the criminals. Only, it's impossible, Utopian! And where could be secured so much money, so many new employees?"

"For what, then, are the priests who proclaim their mission of peace and charity? Is it more meritorious to moisten the head of a child with water, to give it salt to eat, than to awake in the benighted conscience of a criminal that spark which God has granted to every man to light him to his welfare? Is it more humane to accompany a criminal to the scaffold than to lead him along the difficult path from vice to virtue? Don't they also pay spies, executioners, civil-guards? These things, besides being dirty, also cost money."

"My friend, neither you nor I, although we may wish it, can accomplish this."

"Alone, it is true, we are nothing, but take up the cause of the people, unite yourself with the people, be not heedless of their cries, set an example to the rest, spread the idea of what is called a fatherland!"

"What the people ask for is impossible. We must wait."

"Wait! To wait means to suffer!"

"If I should ask for it, the powers that be would laugh at me."

"But if the people supported you?"

"Never! I will never be the one to lead the multitude to get by force what the government does not think proper to grant, no! If I should ever see that multitude armed I would place myself on the side of the government, for in such a mob I should not see my countrymen. I desire the country's welfare, therefore I would build a schoolhouse. I seek it by means of instruction, by progressive advancement; without light there is no road."

"Neither is there liberty without strife!" answered Elias.

"The fact is that I don't want that liberty!"

"The fact is that without liberty there is no light," replied the pilot with warmth. "You say that you are only slightly acquainted with your country, and I believe you. You don't see the struggle that is preparing, you don't see the cloud on the horizon. The fight is beginning in the sphere of ideas, to descend later into the arena, which will be dyed with blood. I hear the voice of God — woe unto them who would oppose it! For them History has not been written!"

Elias was transfigured; standing uncovered, with his manly face illuminated by the moon, there was something extraordinary about him. He shook his long hair, and went on:

"Don't you see how everything is awakening? The sleep has lasted for centuries, but one day the thunderbolt[1] struck, and in striking, infused life. Since then new tendencies are stirring our spirits, and these tendencies, today scattered, will some day be united, guided by the God who has not failed other peoples and who will not fail us, for His cause is the cause of liberty!"

A solemn silence followed these words, while the banka, carried along insensibly by the waves, neared the shore.

Elias was the first to break the silence. "What shall I tell those who sent me?" he asked with a change from his former tone.

"I've already told you: I greatly deplore their condition, but they should wait. Evils are not remedied by other evils, and in our misfortunes each of us has his share of blame."

Elias did not again reply, but dropped his head and rowed along until they reached the shore, where he took leave of Ibarra: "I thank you, sir, for the condescension you have shown me. Now, for your own good, I beg of you that in the future you forget me and that you do not

---

[1] The execution of the Filipino priests Burgos, Gomez, and Zamora, in 1872. — Tr.

recognize me again, no matter in what situation you may find me."

So saying, he drew away in the banka, rowing toward a thicket on the shore. As he covered the long distance he remained silent, apparently intent upon nothing but the thousands of phosphorescent diamonds that the oar caught up and dropped back into the lake, where they disappeared mysteriously into the blue waves.

When he had reached the shadow of the thicket a man came out of it and approached the banka. "What shall I tell the capitan?" he asked.

"Tell him that Elias, if he lives, will keep his word," was the sad answer.

"When will you join us, then?"

"When your capitan thinks that the hour of danger has come."

"Very well. Good-by!"

"If I don't die first," added Elias in a low voice.

CHAPTER LI

EXCHANGES

THE bashful Linares was anxious and ill at ease. He had just received from Doña Victorina a letter which ran thus:

DEER COZIN within 3 days i expec to here from you if the alferes has killed you or you him i dont want anuther day to pass befour that broot has his punishment if that tim passes an you havent challenjed him ill tel don santiago you was never segretary nor joked with canobas nor went on a spree with the general don arseño martinez ill tel clarita its all a humbug an ill not give you a sent more if you challenje him i promis all you want so lets see you challenje him i warn you there must be no excuses nor delays yore cozin who loves you

VICTORINA DE LOS REYES DE DE ESPADAÑA

sampaloc monday 7 in the evening

The affair was serious. He was well enough acquainted with the character of Doña Victorina to know what she was capable of. To talk to her of reason was to talk of honesty and courtesy to a revenue carbineer when he proposes to find contraband where there is none, to plead with her would be useless, to deceive her worse — there was no way out of the difficulty but to send the challenge.

"But how? Suppose he receives me with violence?" he soliloquized, as he paced to and fro. "Suppose I find him with his señora? Who will be willing to be my second? The curate? Capitan Tiago? Damn the hour in which I listened to her advice! The old toady! To oblige me to get myself tangled up, to tell lies, to make a blustering fool of myself! What will the young lady say about me? Now I'm sorry that I've been secretary to all the ministers!"

While the good Linares was in the midst of his soliloquy, Padre Salvi came in. The Franciscan was even thinner and paler than usual, but his eyes gleamed with a strange light and his lips wore a peculiar smile.

"Señor Linares, all alone?" was his greeting as he made his way to the sala, through the half-opened door of which floated the notes from a piano. Linares tried to smile.

"Where is Don Santiago?" continued the curate.

Capitan Tiago at that moment appeared, kissed the curate's hand, and relieved him of his hat and cane, smiling all the while like one of the blessed.

"Come, come!" exclaimed the curate, entering the sala, followed by Linares and Capitan Tiago, "I have good news for you all. I've just received letters from Manila which confirm the one Señor Ibarra brought me yesterday. So, Don Santiago, the objection is removed."

Maria Clara, who was seated at the piano between her two friends, partly rose, but her strength failed her, and she fell back again. Linares turned pale and looked at Capitan Tiago, who dropped his eyes.

"That young man seems to me to be very agreeable," continued the curate. "At first I misjudged him — he's a little quick-tempered — but he knows so well how to atone for his faults afterwards that one can't hold anything against him. If it were not for Padre Damaso —"

Here the curate shot a quick glance at Maria Clara, who was listening without taking her eyes off the sheet of music, in spite of the sly pinches of Sinang, who was thus expressing her joy — had she been alone she would have danced.

"Padre Damaso?" queried Linares.

"Yes, Padre Damaso has said," the curate went on, without taking his gaze from Maria Clara, "that as — being her sponsor in baptism, he can't permit — but, after all, I believe that if Señor Ibarra begs his pardon, which I don't doubt he'll do, everything will be settled."

Maria Clara rose, made some excuse, and retired to her chamber, accompanied by Victoria.

"But if Padre Damaso does n't pardon him?" asked Capitan Tiago in a low voice.

"Then Maria Clara will decide. Padre Damaso is her father — spiritually. But I think they'll reach an understanding."

At that moment footsteps were heard and Ibarra appeared, followed by Aunt Isabel. His appearance produced varied impressions. To his affable greeting Capitan Tiago did not know whether to laugh or to cry. He acknowledged the presence of Linares with a profound bow. Fray Salvi arose and extended his hand so cordially that the youth could not restrain a look of astonishment.

"Don't be surprised," said Fray Salvi, "for I was just now praising you."

Ibarra thanked him and went up to Sinang, who began with her childish garrulity, "Where have you been all day? We were all asking, where can that soul redeemed from purgatory have gone? And we all said the same thing."

"May I know what you said?"

"No, that's a secret, but I'll tell you soon alone. Now tell me where you've been, so we can see who guessed right."

"No, that's also a secret, but I'll tell you alone, if these gentlemen will excuse us."

"Certainly, certainly, by all means!" exclaimed Padre Salvi.

Rejoicing over the prospect of learning a secret, Sinang led Crisostomo to one end of the sala.

"Tell me, little friend," he asked, "is Maria angry with me?"

"I don't know, but she says that it's better for you to forget her, then she begins to cry. Capitan Tiago wants her to marry that man. So does Padre Damaso, but she does n't say either yes or no. This morning when we were talking about you and I said, 'Suppose he has gone to make love to some other girl?' she answered, 'Would that he had!' and began to cry."

Ibarra became grave. "Tell Maria that I want to talk with her alone."

"Alone?" asked Sinang, wrinkling her eyebrows and staring at him.

"Entirely alone, no, but not with that fellow present."

"It's rather difficult, but don't worry, I'll tell her."

"When shall I have an answer?"

"Tomorrow come to my house early. Maria does n't want to be left alone at all, so we stay with her. Victoria sleeps with her one night and I the other, and tonight it's my turn. But listen, your secret? Are you going away without telling me?"

"That's right! I was in the town of Los Baños. I'm going to develop some coconut-groves and I'm thinking of putting up an oil-mill. Your father will be my partner."

"Nothing more than that? What a secret!" exclaimed Sinang aloud, in the tone of a cheated usurer. "I thought —"

"Be careful! I don't want you to make it known!"

"Nor do I want to do it," replied Sinang, turning up her nose. "If it were something more important, I would tell my friends. But to buy coconuts! Coconuts! Who's interested in coconuts?" And with extraordinary haste she ran to join her friends.

A few minutes later Ibarra, seeing that the interest of the party could only languish, took his leave. Capitan Tiago wore a bitter-sweet look, Linares was silent and watchful, while the curate with assumed cheerfulness talked of indifferent matters. None of the girls had reappeared.

CHAPTER LII

THE CARDS OF THE DEAD AND THE SHADOWS

THE moon was hidden in a cloudy sky while a cold wind, precursor of the approaching December, swept the dry leaves and dust about in the narrow pathway leading to the cemetery. Three shadowy forms were conversing in low tones under the arch of the gateway.

"Have you spoken to Elias?" asked a voice.

"No, you know how reserved and circumspect he is. But he ought to be one of us. Don Crisostomo saved his life."

"That's why I joined," said the first voice. "Don Crisostomo had my wife cured in the house of a doctor in Manila. I'll look after the convento to settle some old scores with the curate."

"And we'll take care of the barracks to show the civil-guards that our father had sons."

"How many of us will there be?"

"Five, and five will be enough. Don Crisostomo's servant, though, says there'll be twenty of us."

"What if you don't succeed?"

"Hist!" exclaimed one of the shadows, and all fell silent.

In the semi-obscurity a shadowy figure was seen to approach, sneaking along by the fence. From time to time it stopped as if to look back. Nor was reason for this movement lacking, since some twenty paces behind it came another figure, larger and apparently darker than the first, but so lightly did it touch the ground that it vanished as rapidly as though the earth had swallowed it every time the first shadow paused and turned.

"They're following me," muttered the first figure. "Can it be the civil-guards? Did the senior sacristan lie?"

"They said that they would meet here," thought the second shadow. "Some mischief must be on foot when the two brothers conceal it from me."

At length the first shadow reached the gateway of the cemetery. The three who were already there stepped forward.

"Is that you?"

"Is that you?"

"We must scatter, for they've followed me. Tomorrow you'll get the arms and tomorrow night is the time. The cry is, 'Viva Don Crisostomo!' Go!"

The three shadows disappeared behind the stone walls. The later arrival hid in the hollow of the gateway and waited silently. "Let's see who's following me," he thought.

The second shadow came up very cautiously and paused as if to look about him. "I'm late," he muttered, "but perhaps they will return."

A thin fine rain, which threatened to last, began to fall, so it occurred to him to take refuge under the gateway. Naturally, he ran against the other.

"Ah! Who are you?" asked the latest arrival in a rough tone.

"Who are you?" returned the other calmly, after which there followed a moment's pause as each tried to recognize the other's voice and to make out his features.

"What are you waiting here for?" asked he of the rough voice.

"For the clock to strike eight so that I can play cards with the dead. I want to win something tonight," answered the other in a natural tone. "And you, what have you come for?"

"For — for the same purpose."

"*Abá!* I'm glad of that, I'll not be alone. I've

brought cards. At the first stroke of the bell I'll make the lay, at the second I'll deal. The cards that move are the cards of the dead and we'll have to cut for them. Have you brought cards?"

"No."

"Then how —"

"It's simple enough — just as you're going to deal for them, so I expect them to play for me."

"But what if the dead don't play?"

"What can we do? Gambling hasn't yet been made compulsory among the dead."

A short silence ensued.

"Are you armed? How are you going to fight with the dead?"

"With my fists," answered the larger of the two.

"Oh, the devil! Now I remember — the dead won't bet when there's more than one living person, and there are two of us."

"Is that right? Well, I don't want to leave."

"Nor I. I'm short of money," answered the smaller. "But let's do this: let's play for it, the one who loses to leave."

"All right," agreed the other, rather ungraciously.

"Then let's get inside. Have you any matches?"

They went in to seek in the semi-obscurity for a suitable place and soon found a niche in which they could sit. The shorter took some cards from his salakot, while the other struck a match, in the light from which they stared at each other, but, from the expressions on their faces, apparently without recognition. Nevertheless, we can recognize in the taller and deep-voiced one Elias and in the shorter one, from the scar on his cheek, Lucas.

"Cut!" called Lucas, still staring at the other. He pushed aside some bones that were in the niche and dealt an ace and a jack.

Elias lighted match after match. "On the jack!" he

said, and to indicate the card placed a vertebra on top of it.

"Play!" called Lucas, as he dealt an ace with the fourth or fifth card. "You've lost," he added. "Now leave me alone so that I can try to make a raise."

Elias moved away without a word and was soon swallowed up in the darkness.

Several minutes later the church-clock struck eight and the bell announced the hour of the souls, but Lucas invited no one to play nor did he call on the dead, as the superstition directs; instead, he took off his hat and muttered a few prayers, crossing and recrossing himself with the same fervor with which, at that same moment, the leader of the Brotherhood of the Holy Rosary was going through a similar performance.

Throughout the night a drizzling rain continued to fall. By nine o'clock the streets were dark and solitary. The coconut-oil lanterns, which the inhabitants were required to hang out, scarcely illuminated a small circle around each, seeming to be lighted only to render the darkness more apparent. Two civil-guards paced back and forth in the street near the church.

"It's cold!" said one in Tagalog with a Visayan accent. "We haven't caught any sacristan, so there is no one to repair the alferez's chicken-coop. They're all scared out by the death of that other one. This makes me tired."

"Me, too," answered the other. "No one commits robbery, no one raises a disturbance, but, thank God, they say that Elias is in town. The alferez says that whoever catches him will be exempt from floggings for three months."

"Aha! Do you remember his description?" asked the Visayan.

"I should say so! Height: tall, according to the alferez, medium, according to Padre Damaso; color, brown; eyes, black; nose, ordinary; beard, none; hair, black."

"Aha! But special marks?"

"Black shirt, black pantaloons, wood-cutter."

"Aha, he won't get away from me! I think I see him now."

"I wouldn't mistake him for any one else, even though he might look like him."

Thus the two soldiers continued on their round.

By the light of the lanterns we may again see two shadowy figures moving cautiously along, one behind the other. An energetic "*Quién vive?*" stops both, and the first answers, "*España!*" in a trembling voice.

The soldiers seize him and hustle him toward a lantern to examine him. It is Lucas, but the soldiers seem to be in doubt, questioning each other with their eyes.

"The alferez didn't say that he had a scar," whispered the Visayan. "Where you going?"

"To order a mass for tomorrow."

"Haven't you seen Elias?"

"I don't know him, sir," answered Lucas.

"I didn't ask you if you know him, you fool! Neither do we know him. I'm asking you if you've seen him."

"No, sir."

"Listen, I'll describe him: Height, sometimes tall, sometimes medium; hair and eyes, black; all the other features, ordinary," recited the Visayan. "Now do you know him?"

"No, sir," replied Lucas stupidly.

"Then get away from here! Brute! Dolt!" And they gave him a shove.

"Do you know why Elias is tall to the alferez and of medium height to the curate?" asked the Tagalog thoughtfully.

"No," answered the Visayan.

"Because the alferez was down in the mudhole when he saw him and the curate was on foot."

"That's right!" exclaimed the Visayan. "You're talented — how is it that you're a civil-guard?"

"I wasn't always one; I was a smuggler," answered the Tagalog with a touch of pride.

But another shadowy figure diverted their attention. They challenged this one also and took the man to the light. This time it was the real Elias.

"Where you going?"

"To look for a man, sir, who beat and threatened my brother. He has a scar on his face and is called Elias."

"Aha!" exclaimed the two guards, gazing at each other in astonishment, as they started on the run toward the church, where Lucas had disappeared a few moments before.

CHAPTER LIII

IL BUON DÍ SI CONOSCE DA MATTINA [1]

EARLY the next morning the report spread through the town that many lights had been seen in the cemetery on the previous night. The leader of the Venerable Tertiary Order spoke of lighted candles, of their shape and size, and, although he could not fix the exact number, had counted more than twenty. Sister Sipa, of the Brotherhood of the Holy Rosary, could not bear the thought that a member of a rival order should alone boast of having seen this divine marvel, so she, even though she did not live near the place, had heard cries and groans, and even thought she recognized by their voices certain persons with whom she, in other times, — but out of Christian charity she not only forgave them but prayed for them and would keep their names secret, for all of which she was declared on the spot to be a saint. Sister Rufa was not so keen of hearing, but she could not suffer that Sister Sipa had heard so much and she nothing, so she related a dream in which there had appeared before her many souls — not only of the dead but even of the living — souls in torment who begged for a part of those indulgences of hers which were so carefully recorded and treasured. She could furnish names to the families interested and only asked for a few alms to succor the Pope in his needs. A little fellow, a herder, who dared to assert that he had seen nothing more than one light and two men in salakots had difficulty in escaping with mere slaps and scoldings. Vainly he swore to it; there were his carabaos with him and could verify his statement. "Do you pretend to know more than the

[1] The fair day is foretold by the morn.

Warden and the Sisters, *paracmason*,[1] heretic?" he was asked amid angry looks. The curate went up into the pulpit and preached about purgatory so fervently that the pesos again flowed forth from their hiding-places to pay for masses.

But let us leave the suffering souls and listen to the conversation between Don Filipo and old Tasio in the lonely home of the latter. The Sage, or Lunatic, was sick, having been for days unable to leave his bed, prostrated by a malady that was rapidly growing worse.

"Really, I don't know whether to congratulate you or not that your resignation has been accepted. Formerly, when the gobernadorcillo so shamelessly disregarded the will of the majority, it was right for you to tender it, but now that you are engaged in a contest with the Civil Guard it's not quite proper. In time of war you ought to remain at your post."

"Yes, but not when the general sells himself," answered Don Filipo. "You know that on the following morning the gobernadorcillo liberated the soldiers that I had succeeded in arresting and refused to take any further action. Without the consent of my superior officer I could do nothing."

"You alone, nothing; but with the rest, much. You should have taken advantage of this opportunity to set an example to the other towns. Above the ridiculous authority of the gobernadorcillo are the rights of the people. It was the beginning of a good lesson and you have neglected it."

"But what could I have done against the representative of the interests? Here you have Señor Ibarra, he has bowed before the beliefs of the crowd. Do you think that he believes in excommunications?"

"You are not in the same fix. Señor Ibarra is trying to sow the good seed, and to do so he must bend himself and make what use he can of the material at hand. Your

[1] *Paracmason*, i. e. freemason.

mission was to stir things up, and for that purpose initiative and force are required. Besides, the fight should not be considered as merely against the gobernadorcillo. The principle ought to be, against him who makes wrong use of his authority, against him who disturbs the public peace, against him who fails in his duty. You would not have been alone, for the country is not the same now that it was twenty years ago."

"Do you think so?" asked Don Filipo.

"Don't you feel it?" rejoined the old man, sitting up in his bed. "Ah, that is because you haven't seen the past, you haven't studied the effect of European immigration, of the coming of new books, and of the movement of our youth to Europe. Examine and compare these facts. It is true that the Royal and Pontifical University of Santo Tomas, with its most sapient faculty, still exists and that some intelligences are yet exercised in formulating distinctions and in penetrating the subtleties of scholasticism; but where will you now find the metaphysical youth of our days, with their archaic education, who tortured their brains and died in full pursuit of sophistries in some corner of the provinces, without ever having succeeded in understanding the attributes of *being*, or solving the problem of *essence* and *existence*, those lofty concepts that made us forget what was essential, — our own existence and our own individuality? Look at the youth of today! Full of enthusiasm at the view of a wider horizon, they study history, mathematics, geography, literature, physical sciences, languages — all subjects that in our times we heard mentioned with horror, as though they were heresies. The greatest free-thinker of my day declared them inferior to the classifications of Aristotle and the laws of the syllogism. Man has at last comprehended that he is man; he has given up analyzing his God and searching into the imperceptible. into what he has not seen; he has given up framing laws for the phantasms of his brain; he comprehends that his heritage is the vast world, dominion over which is within his reach; weary of his useless and presumptuous toil, he lowers his head and examines what surrounds him. See how poets are now springing up among us! The Muses of Nature are gradually opening up their treasures to us and begin to smile in encouragement on our efforts; the experimental sciences have already borne their first-fruits; time only is lacking for their development. The lawyers of today are being trained in the new forms of the philosophy of law, some of them begin to shine in the midst of the shadows which surround our courts of justice, indicating a change in the course of affairs. Hear how the youth talk, visit the centers of learning! Other names resound within the walls of the schools, there where we heard only those of St. Thomas, Suarez, Amat, Sanchez,[1] and others who were the idols of our times. In vain do the friars cry out from the pulpits against our demoralization, as the fish-venders cry out against the cupidity of their customers, disregarding the fact that their wares are stale and unserviceable! In vain do the conventos extend their ramifications to check the new current. The gods are going! The roots of the tree may weaken the plants that support themselves under it, but they canot take away life from those other beings, which, like birds, are soaring toward the sky."

The Sage spoke with animation, his eyes gleamed.

"Still, the new seed is small," objected Don Filipo incredulously. "If all enter upon the progress we purchase so dearly, it may be stifled."

"Stifled! Who will stifle it? Man, that weak dwarf, stifle progress, the powerful child of time and action? When has he been able to do so? Bigotry, the gibbet, the stake, by endeavoring to stifle it, have hurried it along. *E pur si muove,*[2] said Galileo, when the Dominicans forced him to declare that the earth does not move, and the same statement might be applied to human progress. Some wills

---

[1] Scholastic theologians. — TR.
[2] And yet it does move!

are broken down, some individuals sacrificed, but that is of little import; progress continues on its way, and from the blood of those who fall new and vigorous offspring is born. See, the press itself, however backward it may wish to be, is taking a step forward. The Dominicans themselves do not escape the operation of this law, but are imitating the Jesuits, their irreconcilable enemies. They hold fiestas in their cloisters, they erect little theaters, they compose poems, because, as they are not devoid of intelligence in spite of believing in the fifteenth century, they realize that the Jesuits are right, and they will still take part in the future of the younger peoples that they have reared."

"So, according to you, the Jesuits keep up with progress?" asked Don Filipo in wonder. "Why, then, are they opposed in Europe?"

"I will answer you like an old scholastic," replied the Sage, lying down again and resuming his jesting expression. "There are three ways in which one may accompany the course of progress: in front of, beside, or behind it. The first guide it, the second suffer themselves to be carried along with it, and the last are dragged after it — and to these last the Jesuits belong. They would like to direct it, but as they see that it is strong and has other tendencies, they capitulate, preferring to follow rather than to be crushed or left alone among the shadows by the wayside. Well now, we in the Philippines are moving along at least three centuries behind the car of progress; we are barely beginning to emerge from the Middle Ages. Hence the Jesuits, who are reactionary in Europe, when seen from our point of view, represent progress. To them the Philippines owes her dawning system of instruction in the natural sciences, the soul of the nineteenth century, as she owed to the Dominicans scholasticism, already dead in spite of Leo XIII, for there is no Pope who can revive what common sense has judged and condemned.

"But where are we getting to?" he asked with a change

of tone. "Ah, we were speaking of the present condition of the Philippines. Yes, we are now entering upon a period of strife, or rather, I should say that you are, for my generation belongs to the night, we are passing away. This strife is between the past, which seizes and strives with curses to cling to the tottering feudal castle, and the future, whose song of triumph may be heard from afar amid the splendors of the coming dawn, bringing the message of Good-News from other lands. Who will fall and be buried in the moldering ruins?"

The old man paused. Noticing that Don Filipo was gazing at him thoughtfully, he said with a smile, "I can almost guess what you are thinking."

"Really?"

"You are thinking of how easily I may be mistaken," was the answer with a sad smile. "Today I am feverish, and I am not infallible: *homo sum et nihil humani a me alienum puto*,[1] said Terence, and if at any time one is allowed to dream, why not dream pleasantly in the last hours of life? And after all, I have lived only in dreams! You are right, it is a dream! Our youths think only of love affairs and dissipations; they expend more time and work harder to deceive and dishonor a maiden than in thinking about the welfare of their country; our women, in order to care for the house and family of God, neglect their own: our men are active only in vice and heroic only in shame; childhood develops amid ignorance and routine, youth lives its best years without ideals, and a sterile manhood serves only as an example for corrupting youth. Gladly do I die! *Claudite iam rivos, pueri!*"[2]

"Don't you want some medicine?" asked Don Filipo in order to change the course of the conversation, which had darkened the old man's face.

[1] I am a man and nothing that concerns humanity do I consider foreign to me.
[2] A portion of the closing words of Virgil's third eclogue, equivalent here to "Let the curtain drop." — Tr.

"The dying need no medicines; you who remain need them. Tell Don Crisostomo to come and see me tomorrow, for I have some important things to say to him. In a few days I am going away. The Philippines is in darkness!"

After a few moments more of talk, Don Filipo left the sick man's house, grave and thoughtful.

CHAPTER LIV

REVELATIONS

Quidquid latet, adparebit,
Nil inultum remanebit.¹

THE vesper bells are ringing, and at the holy sound all pause, drop their tasks, and uncover. The laborer returning from the fields ceases the song with which he was pacing his carabao and murmurs a prayer, the women in the street cross themselves and move their lips affectedly so that none may doubt their piety, a man stops caressing his game-cock and recites the angelus to bring better luck, while inside the houses they pray aloud. Every sound but that of the Ave Maria dies away, becomes hushed.

Nevertheless, the curate, without his hat, rushes across the street, to the scandalizing of many old women, and, greater scandal still, directs his steps toward the house of the alferez. The devout women then think it time to cease the movement of their lips in order to kiss the curate's hand, but Padre Salvi takes no notice of them. This evening he finds no pleasure in placing his bony hand on his Christian nose that he may slip it down dissemblingly (as Doña Consolacion has observed) over the bosom of the attractive young woman who may have bent over to receive his blessing. Some important matter must be engaging his attention when he thus forgets his own interests and those of the Church!

¹ "Whatever is hidden will be revealed, nothing will remain unaccounted for." From D*ies Irae*, the hymn in the mass for the dead, best known to English readers from the paraphrase of it in Scott's *Lay of the Last Minstrel*. The lines here quoted were thus metrically translated by Macaulay:
 "What was distant shall be near,
 What was hidden shall be clear." — TR.

REVELATIONS

In fact, he rushes headlong up the stairway and knocks impatiently at the alferez's door. The latter puts in his appearance, scowling, followed by his better half, who smiles like one of the damned.

"Ah, Padre, I was just going over to see you. That old goat of yours —"

"I have a very important matter —"

"I can't stand for his running about and breaking down the fence. I'll shoot him if he comes back!"

"That is, if you are alive tomorrow!" exclaimed the panting curate as he made his way toward the sala.

"What, do you think that puny doll will kill me? I'll bust him with a kick!"

Padre Salvi stepped backward with an involuntary glance toward the alferez's feet. "Whom are you talking about?" he asked tremblingly.

"About whom would I talk but that simpleton who has challenged me to a duel with revolvers at a hundred paces?"

"Ah!" sighed the curate, then he added, "I've come to talk to you about a very urgent matter."

"Enough of urgent matters! It'll be like that affair of the two boys."

Had the light been other than from coconut oil and the lamp globe not so dirty, the alferez would have noticed the curate's pallor.

"Now this is a serious matter, which concerns the lives of all of us," declared Padre Salvi in a low voice.

"A serious matter?" echoed the alferez, turning pale. "Can that boy shoot straight?"

"I'm not talking about him."

"Then, what?"

The friar made a sign toward the door, which the alferez closed in his own way — with a kick, for he had found his hands superfluous and had lost nothing by ceasing to be bimanous.

A curse and a roar sounded outside. "Brute, you've split my forehead open!" yelled his wife.

"Now, unburden yourself," he said calmly to the curate.

The latter stared at him for a space, then asked in the nasal, droning voice of the preacher, "Did n't you see me come — running?"

"Sure! I thought you 'd lost something."

"Well, now," continued the curate, without heeding the alferez's rudeness, "when I fail thus in my duty, it 's because there are grave reasons."

"Well, what else?" asked the other, tapping the floor with his foot.

"Be calm!"

"Then why did you come in such a hurry?"

The curate drew nearer to him and asked mysteriously, "Have n't — you — heard — anything?"

The alferez shrugged his shoulders.

"You admit that you know absolutely nothing?"

"Do you want to talk about Elias, who put away your senior sacristan last night?" was the retort.

"No, I 'm not talking about those matters," answered the curate ill-naturedly. "I 'm talking about a great danger."

"Well, damn it, out with it!"

"Come," said the friar slowly and disdainfully, "you see once more how important we ecclesiastics are. The meanest lay brother is worth as much as a regiment, while a curate —"

Then he added in a low and mysterious tone, "I 've discovered a big conspiracy!"

The alferez started up and gazed in astonishment at the friar.

"A terrible and well-organized plot, which will be carried out this very night."

"This very night!" exclaimed the alferez, pushing the curate aside and running to his revolver and sword hanging on the wall.

"Who 'll I arrest? Who 'll I arrest?" he cried.

"Calm yourself! There is still time, thanks to the promptness with which I have acted. We have till eight o'clock."

"I 'll shoot all of them!"

"Listen! This afternoon a woman whose name I can't reveal (it 's a secret of the confessional) came to me and told everything. At eight o'clock they will seize the barracks by surprise, plunder the convento, capture the police boat, and murder all of us Spaniards."

The alferez was stupefied.

"The woman did not tell me any more than this," added the curate.

"She did n't tell any more? Then I 'll arrest her!"

"I can't consent to that. The bar of penitence is the throne of the God of mercies."

"There 's neither God nor mercies that amount to anything! I 'll arrest her!"

"You 're losing your head! What you must do is to get yourself ready. Muster your soldiers quietly and put them in ambush, send me four guards for the convento, and notify the men in charge of the boat."

"The boat is n't here. I 'll ask for help from the other sections."

"No, for then the plotters would be warned and would not carry out their plans. What we must do is to catch them alive and make them talk — I mean, you 'll make them talk, since I, as a priest, must not meddle in such matters. Listen, here 's where you win crosses and stars. I ask only that you make due acknowledgment that it was I who warned you."

"It 'll be acknowledged, Padre, it 'll be acknowledged — and perhaps you 'll get a miter!" answered the glowing alferez, glancing at the cuffs of his uniform.

"So, you send me four guards in plain clothes, eh? Be discreet, and tonight at eight o'clock it 'll rain stars and crosses."

While all this was taking place, a man ran along the road leading to Ibarra's house and rushed up the stairway.

"Is your master here?" the voice of Elias called to a servant.

"He's in his study at work."

Ibarra, to divert the impatience that he felt while waiting for the time when he could make his explanations to Maria Clara, had set himself to work in his laboratory.

"Ah, that you, Elias?" he exclaimed. "I was thinking about you. Yesterday I forgot to ask you the name of that Spaniard in whose house your grandfather lived."

"Let's not talk about me, sir —"

"Look," continued Ibarra, not noticing the youth's agitation, while he placed a piece of bamboo over a flame, "I've made a great discovery. This bamboo is incombustible."

"It's not a question of bamboo now, sir, it's a question of your collecting your papers and fleeing at this very moment."

Ibarra glanced at him in surprise and, on seeing the gravity of his countenance, dropped the object that he held in his hands.

"Burn everything that may compromise you and within an hour put yourself in a place of safety."

"Why?" Ibarra was at length able to ask.

"Put all your valuables in a safe place —"

"Why?"

"Burn every letter written by you or to you — the most innocent thing may be wrongly construed —"

"But why all this?"

"Why! Because I've just discovered a plot that is to be attributed to you in order to ruin you."

"A plot? Who is forming it?"

"I haven't been able to discover the author of it, but just a moment ago I talked with one of the poor dupes who are paid to carry it out, and I wasn't able to dissuade him."

REVELATIONS

"But he — did n't he tell you who is paying him?"

"Yes! Under a pledge of secrecy he said that it was you."

"My God!" exclaimed the terrified Ibarra.

"There's no doubt of it, sir. Don't lose any time, for the plot will probably be carried out this very night."

Ibarra, with his hands on his head and his eyes staring unnaturally, seemed not to hear him.

"The blow cannot be averted," continued Elias. "I've come late, I don't know who the leaders are. Save yourself, sir, save yourself for your country's sake!"

"Whither shall I flee? She expects me tonight!" exclaimed Ibarra, thinking of Maria Clara.

"To any town whatsoever, to Manila, to the house of some official, but anywhere so that they may not say that you are directing this movement."

"Suppose that I myself report the plot?"

"You an informer!" exclaimed Elias, stepping back and staring at him. "You would appear as a traitor and coward in the eyes of the plotters and faint-hearted in the eyes of others. They would say that you planned the whole thing to curry favor. They would say—"

"But what's to be done?"

"I've already told you. Destroy every document that relates to your affairs, flee, and await the outcome."

"And Maria Clara?" exclaimed the young man. "No, I'll die first!"

Elias wrung his hands, saying, "Well then, at least parry the blow. Prepare for the time when they accuse you."

Ibarra gazed about him in bewilderment. "Then help me. There in that writing-desk are all the letters of my family. Select those of my father, which are perhaps the ones that may compromise me. Read the signatures."

So the bewildered and stupefied young man opened and shut boxes, collected papers, read letters hurriedly, tearing up some and laying others aside. He took down some books and began to turn their leaves.

Elias did the same, if not so excitedly, yet with equal eagerness. But suddenly he paused, his eyes bulged, he turned the paper in his hand over and over, then asked in a trembling voice:

"Was your family acquainted with Don Pedro Eibarramendia?"

"I should say so!" answered Ibarra, as he opened a chest and took out a bundle of papers. "He was my great-grandfather."

"Your great-grandfather Don Pedro Eibarramendia?" again asked Elias with changed and livid features.

"Yes," replied Ibarra absently, "we shortened the surname; it was too long."

"Was he a Basque?" demanded Elias, approaching him.

"Yes, a Basque — but what's the matter?" asked Ibarra in surprise.

Clenching his fists and pressing them to his forehead, Elias glared at Crisostomo, who recoiled when he saw the expression on the other's face. "Do you know who Don Pedro Eibarramendia was?" he asked between his teeth. "Don Pedro Eibarramendia was the villain who falsely accused my grandfather and caused all our misfortunes. I have sought for that name and God has revealed it to me! Render me now an accounting for our misfortunes!"

Elias caught and shook the arm of Crisostomo, who gazed at him in terror. In a voice that was bitter and trembling with hate, he said, "Look at me well, look at one who has suffered — and you live, you live, you have wealth, a home, reputation — you live, you live!"

Beside himself, he ran to a small collection of arms and snatched up a dagger. But scarcely had he done so when he let it fall again and stared like a madman at the motionless Ibarra.

"What was I about to do?" he muttered, fleeing from the house.

CHAPTER LV

THE CATASTROPHE

THERE in the dining-room Capitan Tiago, Linares, and Aunt Isabel were at supper, so that even in the sala the rattling of plates and dishes was plainly heard. Maria Clara had said that she was not hungry and had seated herself at the piano in company with the merry Sinang, who was murmuring mysterious words into her ear. Meanwhile Padre Salvi paced nervously back and forth in the room.

It was not, indeed, that the convalescent was not hungry, no; but she was expecting the arrival of a certain person and was taking advantage of this moment when her Argus was not present, Linares' supper-hour.

"You'll see how that specter will stay till eight," murmured Sinang, indicating the curate. "And at eight *he* will come. The curate's in love with Linares."

Maria Clara gazed in consternation at her friend, who went on heedlessly with her terrible chatter: "Oh, I know why he does n't go, in spite of my hints — he does n't want to burn up oil in the convento! Don't you know that since you 've been sick the two lamps that he used to keep lighted he has had put out? But look how he stares, and what a face!"

At that moment a clock in the house struck eight. The curate shuddered and sat down in a corner.

"Here he comes!" exclaimed Sinang, pinching Maria Clara. "Don't you hear him?"

The church bell boomed out the hour of eight and all rose to pray. Padre Salvi offered up a prayer in a weak and trembling voice, but as each was busy with his own thoughts no one paid any attention to the priest's agitation.

Scarcely had the prayer ceased when Ibarra appeared. The youth was in mourning not only in his attire but also in his face, to such an extent that, on seeing him, Maria Clara arose and took a step toward him to ask what the matter was. But at that instant the report of firearms was heard. Ibarra stopped, his eyes rolled, he lost the power of speech. The curate had concealed himself behind a post. More shots, more reports were heard from the direction of the convento, followed by cries and the sound of persons running. Capitan Tiago, Aunt Isabel, and Linares rushed in pell-mell, crying, "Tulisan! Tulisan!" Andeng followed, flourishing the gridiron as she ran toward her foster-sister.

Aunt Isabel fell on her knees weeping and reciting the *Kyrie eleyson;* Capitan Tiago, pale and trembling, carried on his fork a chicken-liver which he offered tearfully to the Virgin of Antipolo; Linares with his mouth full of food was armed with a case-knife; Sinang and Maria Clara were in each other's arms; while the only one that remained motionless, as if petrified, was Crisostomo, whose paleness was indescribable.

The cries and sound of blows continued, windows were closed noisily, the report of a gun was heard from time to time.

"*Christie eleyson!* Santiago, let the prophecy be fulfilled! Shut the windows!" groaned Aunt Isabel.

"Fifty big bombs and two thanksgiving masses!" responded Capitan Tiago. "*Ora pro nobis!*"

Gradually there prevailed a heavy silence which was soon broken by the voice of the alferez, calling as he ran: "Padre, Padre Salvi, come here!"

"*Miserere!* The alferez is calling for confession," cried Aunt Isabel.

"The alferez is wounded?" asked Linares hastily.

THE CATASTROPHE

"Ah!!!" Only then did he notice that he had not yet swallowed what he had in his mouth.

"Padre, come here! There's nothing more to fear!" the alferez continued to call out.

The pallid Fray Salvi at last concluded to venture out from his hiding-place, and went down the stairs.

"The outlaws have killed the alferez! Maria, Sinang, go into your room and fasten the door! *Kyrie eleyson!*"

Ibarra also turned toward the stairway, in spite of Aunt Isabel's cries: "Don't go out, you haven't been shriven, don't go out!" The good old lady had been a particular friend of his mother's.

But Ibarra left the house. Everything seemed to reel around him, the ground was unstable. His ears buzzed, his legs moved heavily and irregularly. Waves of blood, lights and shadows chased one another before his eyes, and in spite of the bright moonlight he stumbled over the stones and blocks of wood in the vacant and deserted street.

Near the barracks he saw soldiers, with bayonets fixed, who were talking among themselves so excitedly that he passed them unnoticed. In the town hall were to be heard blows, cries, and curses, with the voice of the alferez dominating everything: "To the stocks! Handcuff them! Shoot any one who moves! Sergeant, mount the guard! Today no one shall walk about, not even God! Captain, this is no time to go to sleep!"

Ibarra hastened his steps toward home, where his servants were anxiously awaiting him. "Saddle the best horse and go to bed!" he ordered them.

Going into his study, he hastily packed a traveling-bag, opened an iron safe, took out what money he found there and put it into some sacks. Then he collected his jewels, took down a portrait of Maria Clara, armed himself with a dagger and two revolvers, and turned toward a closet where he kept his instruments.

At that moment three heavy knocks sounded on the door.

"Who's there?" asked Ibarra in a gloomy tone.

"Open, in the King's name, open at once, or we'll break the door down," answered an imperious voice in Spanish.

Ibarra looked toward the window, his eyes gleamed, and he cocked his revolver. Then changing his mind, he put the weapons down and went to open the door just as the servant appeared. Three guards instantly seized him.

"Consider yourself a prisoner in the King's name," said the sergeant.

"For what?"

"They'll tell you over there. We're forbidden to say."

The youth reflected a moment and then, perhaps not wishing that the soldiers should discover his preparations for flight, picked up his hat, saying, "I'm at your service. I suppose that it will only be for a few hours."

"If you promise not to try to escape, we won't tie you — the alferez grants this favor — but if you run —"

Ibarra went with them, leaving his servants in consternation.

Meanwhile, what had become of Elias? Leaving the house of Crisostomo, he had run like one crazed, without heeding where he was going. He crossed the fields in violent agitation, he reached the woods; he fled from the town, from the light — even the moon so troubled him that he plunged into the mysterious shadows of the trees. There, sometimes pausing, sometimes moving along unfrequented paths, supporting himself on the hoary trunks or being entangled in the undergrowth, he gazed toward the town, which, bathed in the light of the moon, spread out before him on the plain along the shore of the lake. Birds awakened from their sleep flew about, huge bats and owls moved from branch to branch with strident cries and gazed at him with their round eyes, but Elias neither heard nor heeded them. In his fancy he was followed by the offended shades of his family, he saw on every branch the gruesome basket containing Balat's gory head, as his father had described it to him; at every tree he seemed to stumble over the corpse of his grandmother; he imagined that he saw the rotting skeleton of his dishonored grandfather swinging among the shadows — and the skeleton and the corpse and the gory head cried after him, "Coward! Coward!"

Leaving the hill, Elias descended to the lake and ran along the shore excitedly. There at a distance in the midst of the waters, where the moonlight seemed to form a cloud, he thought he could see a specter rise and soar — the shade of his sister with her breast bloody and her loose hair streaming about. He fell to his knees on the sand and extending his arms cried out, "You, too!"

Then with his gaze fixed on the cloud he arose slowly and went forward into the water as if he were following some one. He passed over the gentle slope that forms the bar and was soon far from the shore. The water rose to his waist, but he plunged on like one fascinated, following, ever following, the ghostly charmer. Now the water covered his chest — a volley of rifle-shots sounded, the vision disappeared, the youth returned to his senses. In the stillness of the night and the greater density of the air the reports reached him clearly and distinctly. He stopped to reflect and found himself in the water — over the peaceful ripples of the lake he could still make out the lights in the fishermen's huts.

He returned to the shore and started toward the town, but for what purpose he himself knew not. The streets appeared to be deserted, the houses were closed, and even the dogs that were wont to bark through the night had hidden themselves in fear. The silvery light of the moon added to the sadness and loneliness.

Fearful of meeting the civil-guards, he made his way along through yards and gardens, in one of which he thought he could discern two human figures, but he kept on his way, leaping over fences and walls, until after great labor he reached the other end of the town and went toward Crisostomo's house. In the doorway were the servants, lamenting their master's arrest.

After learning about what had occurred Elias pretended to go away, but really went around behind the house, jumped over the wall, and crawled through a window into the study where the candle that Ibarra had lighted was still burning. He saw the books and papers and found the arms, the jewels, and the sacks of money. Reconstructing in his imagination the scene that had taken place there and seeing so many papers that might be of a compromising nature, he decided to gather them up, throw them from the window, and bury them.

But, on glancing toward the street, he saw two guards approaching, their bayonets and caps gleaming in the moonlight. With them was the directorcillo. He made a sudden resolution: throwing the papers and some clothing into a heap in the center of the room, he poured over them the oil from a lamp and set fire to the whole. He was hurriedly placing the arms in his belt when he caught sight of the portrait of Maria Clara and hesitated a moment, then thrust it into one of the sacks and with them in his hands leaped from the window into the garden.

It was time that he did so, too, for the guards were forcing an entrance. "Let us in to get your master's papers!" cried the directorcillo.

"Have you permission? If you haven't, you won't get in," answered an old man.

But the soldiers pushed him aside with the butts of their rifles and ran up the stairway, just as a thick cloud of smoke rolled through the house and long tongues of flame shot out from the study, enveloping the doors and windows.

"Fire! Fire!" was the cry, as each rushed to save what he could. But the blaze had reached the little laboratory and caught the inflammable materials there, so the guards had to retire. The flames roared about, licking up everything in their way and cutting off the passages. Vainly was water brought from the well and cries for help raised, for the house was set apart from the rest. The fire swept through all the rooms and sent toward the sky thick spirals of smoke. Soon the whole structure was at the mercy of the flames, fanned now by the wind, which in the heat grew stronger. Some few rustics came up, but only to gaze on this great bonfire, the end of that old building which had been so long respected by the elements.

CHAPTER LVI

RUMORS AND BELIEFS

DAY dawned at last for the terrified town. The streets near the barracks and the town hall were still deserted and solitary, the houses showed no signs of life. Nevertheless, the wooden panel of a window was pushed back noisily and a child's head was stretched out and turned from side to side, gazing about in all directions. At once, however, a smack indicated the contact of tanned hide with the soft human article, so the child made a wry face, closed its eyes, and disappeared. The window slammed shut.

But an example had been set. That opening and shutting of the window had no doubt been heard on all sides, for soon another window opened slowly and there appeared cautiously the head of a wrinkled and toothless old woman: it was the same Sister Puté who had raised such a disturbance while Padre Damaso was preaching. Children and old women are the representatives of curiosity in this world: the former from a wish to know things and the latter from a desire to recollect them.

Apparently there was no one to apply a slipper to Sister Puté, for she remained gazing out into the distance with wrinkled eyebrows. Then she rinsed out her mouth, spat noisily, and crossed herself. In the house opposite, another window was now timidly opened to reveal Sister Rufa, she who did not wish to cheat or be cheated. They stared at each other for a moment, smiled, made some signs, and again crossed themselves.

"*Jesús*, it seemed like a thanksgiving mass, regular fireworks!" commented Sister Rufa.

"Since the town was sacked by Balat, I've never seen another night equal to it," responded Sister Puté.

"What a lot of shots! They say that it was old Pablo's band."

"Tulisanes? That can't be! They say that it was the cuadrilleros against the civil-guards. That's why Don Filipo has been arrested."

"*Sanctus Deus!* They say that at least fourteen were killed."

Other windows were now opened and more faces appeared to exchange greetings and make comments. In the clear light, which promised a bright day, soldiers could be seen in the distance, coming and going confusedly like gray silhouettes.

"There goes one more corpse!" was the exclamation from a window.

"One? I see two."

"And I — but really, can it be you don't know what it was?" asked a sly-featured individual.

"Oh, the cuadrilleros!"

"No, sir, it was a mutiny in the barracks!"

"What kind of mutiny? The curate against the alferez?"

"No, it was nothing of the kind," answered the man who had asked the first question. "It was the Chinamen who have rebelled." With this he shut his window.

"The Chinamen!" echoed all in great astonishment.

"That's why not one of them is to be seen!"

"They've probably killed them all!"

"I thought they were going to do something bad. Yesterday —"

"I saw it myself. Last night —"

"What a pity!" exclaimed Sister Rufa. "To get killed just before Christmas when they bring around their presents! They should have waited until New Year's."

Little by little the street awoke to life. Dogs, chickens, pigs, and doves began the movement, and these animals were soon followed by some ragged urchins who held fast to each other's arms as they timidly approached the barracks. Then a few old women with handkerchiefs tied about their heads and fastened under their chins appeared with thick rosaries in their hands, pretending to be at their prayers so that the soldiers would let them pass. When it was seen that one might walk about without being shot at, the men began to come out with assumed airs of indifference. First they limited their steps to the neighborhood of their houses, caressing their game-cocks, then they extended their stroll, stopping from time to time, until at last they stood in front of the town hall.

In a quarter of an hour other versions of the affair were in circulation. Ibarra with his servants had tried to kidnap Maria Clara, and Capitan Tiago had defended her, aided by the Civil Guard. The number of killed was now not fourteen but thirty. Capitan Tiago was wounded and would leave that very day with his family for Manila.

The arrival of two cuadrilleros carrying a human form on a covered stretcher and followed by a civil-guard produced a great sensation. It was conjectured that they came from the convento, and, from the shape of the feet, which were dangling over one end, some guessed who the dead man might be, some /one else a little distance away told who it was; further on the corpse was multiplied and the mystery of the Holy Trinity duplicated, later the miracle of the loaves and fishes was repeated — and the dead were then thirty and eight.

By half-past seven, when other guards arrived from neighboring towns, the current version was clear and detailed. "I've just come from the town hall, where I've seen Don Filipo and Don Crisostomo prisoners," a man told Sister Puté "I've talked with one of the cuadrilleros who are on guard. Well, Bruno, the son of that fellow who was flogged to death, confessed everything last night. As you know, Capitan Tiago is going to marry his daughter to the young Spaniard, so Don Crisostomo in his rage wanted to get revenge and tried to kill all the Spaniards, even the curate. Last night they attacked the barracks and the convento, but fortunately, by God's mercy, the curate was in Capitan Tiago's house. They say that a lot of them escaped. The civil-guards burned Don Crisostomo's house down, and if they had n't arrested him first they would have burned him also."

"They burned the house down?"

"All the servants are under arrest. Look, you can still see the smoke from here!" answered the narrator, approaching the window. "Those who come from there tell of many sad things."

All looked toward the place indicated. A thin column of smoke was still slowly rising toward the sky. All made comments, more or less pitying, more or less accusing.

"Poor youth!" exclaimed an old man, Puté's husband.

"Yes," she answered, "but look how he did n't order a mass said for the soul of his father, who undoubtedly needs it more than others."

"But, woman, have n't you any pity?"

"Pity for the excommunicated? It's a sin to take pity on the enemies of God, the curates say. Don't you remember? In the cemetery he walked about as if he was in a corral."

"But a corral and the cemetery are alike," replied the old man, "only that into the former only one kind of animal enters."

"Shut up!" cried Sister Puté. "You'll still defend those whom God has clearly punished. You'll see how they'll arrest you, too. You're upholding a falling house."

Her husband became silent before this argument.

"Yes," continued the old lady, "after striking Padre Damaso there was n't anything left for him to do but to kill Padre Salvi."

"But you can't deny that he was good when he was a little boy."

"Yes, he was good," replied the old woman, "but he went to Spain. All those that go to Spain become heretics, as the curates have said."

"Oho!" exclaimed her husband, seeing his chance for a retort, "and the curate, and all the curates, and the Archbishop, and the Pope, and the Virgin — are n't they from Spain? Are they also heretics? *Abá!*"

Happily for Sister Puté the arrival of a maidservant running, all pale and terrified, cut short this discussion.

"A man hanged in the next garden!" she cried breathlessly.

"A man hanged?" exclaimed all in stupefaction. The women crossed themselves. No one could move from his place.

"Yes, sir," went on the trembling servant; "I was going to pick peas — I looked into our neighbor's garden to see if it was — I saw a man swinging — I thought it was Teo, the servant who always gives me — I went nearer to — pick the peas, and I saw that it was n't Teo, but a dead man. I ran and I ran and —"

"Let's go see him," said the old man, rising. "Show us the way."

"Don't you go!" cried Sister Puté, catching hold of his camisa. "Something will happen to you! Is he hanged? Then the worse for him!"

"Let me see him, woman. You, Juan, go to the barracks and report it. Perhaps he's not dead yet."

So he proceeded to the garden with the servant, who kept behind him. The women, including even Sister Puté herself, followed after, filled with fear and curiosity.

"There he is, sir," said the servant, as she stopped and pointed with her finger.

The committee paused at a respectful distance and allowed the old man to go forward alone.

A human body hanging from the branch of a santol tree swung about gently in the breeze. The old man stared at it for a time and saw that the legs and arms were stiff, the clothing soiled, and the head doubled over.

"We must n't touch him until some officer of the law arrives," he said aloud. "He's already stiff, he's been dead for some time."

The women gradually moved closer.

"He's the fellow who lived in that little house there. He came here two weeks ago. Look at the scar on his face."

"*Ave Maria!*" exclaimed some of the women.

"Shall we pray for his soul?" asked a young woman, after she had finished staring and examining the body.

"Fool, heretic!" scolded Sister Puté. "Dou't you know what Padre Damaso said? It's tempting God to pray for one of the damned. Whoever commits suicide is irrevocably damned and therefore he is n't buried in holy ground."

Then she added, "I knew that this man was coming to a bad end; I never could find out how he lived."

"I saw him twice talking with the senior sacristan," observed a young woman.

"It would n't be to confess himself or to order a mass!"

Other neighbors came up until a large group surrounded the corpse, which was still swinging about. After half an hour, an alguazil and the directorcillo arrived with two cuadrilleros, who took the body down and placed it on a stretcher.

"People are getting in a hurry to die," remarked the directorcillo with a smile, as he took a pen from behind his ear.

He made captious inquiries, and took down the statement of the maidservant, whom he tried to confuse, now looking at her fiercely, now threatening her, now attributing to her things that she had not said, so much so that she, thinking that she would have to go to jail, began to cry and wound up by declaring that she was n't looking for peas but — and she called Teo as a witness.

While this was taking place, a rustic in a wide salakot

with a big bandage on his neck was examining the corpse and the rope. The face was not more livid than the rest of the body, two scratches and two red spots were to be seen above the noose, the strands of the rope were white and had no blood on them. The curious rustic carefully examined the camisa and pantaloons, and noticed that they were very dusty and freshly torn in some parts. But what most caught his attention were the seeds of *amores-secos* that were sticking on the camisa even up to the collar.

"What are you looking at?" the directorcillo asked him.

"I was looking, sir, to see if I could recognize him," stammered the rustic, partly uncovering, but in such a way that his salakot fell lower.

"But have n't you heard that it's a certain Lucas? Were you asleep?"

The crowd laughed, while the abashed rustic muttered a few words and moved away slowly with his head down.

"Here, where you going?" cried the old man after him. "That's not the way out. That's the way to the dead man's house."

"The fellow's still asleep," remarked the directorcillo facetiously. "Better pour some water over him."

Amid the laughter of the bystanders the rustic left the place where he had played such a ridiculous part and went toward the church. In the sacristy he asked for the senior sacristan.

"He's still asleep," was the rough answer. "Don't you know that the convento was assaulted last night?"

"Then I 'll wait till he wakes up." This with a stupid stare at the sacristans, such as is common to persons who are used to rough treatment.

In a corner which was still in shadow the one-eyed senior sacristan lay asleep in a big chair. His spectacles were placed on his forehead amid long locks of hair, while his thin, squalid chest, which was bare, rose and fell regularly.

The rustic took a seat near by, as if to wait patiently, but he dropped a piece of money and started to look for it with the aid of a candle under the senior sacristan's chair. He noticed seeds of *amores-secos* on the pantaloons and on the cuffs of the sleeper's camisa. The latter awoke, rubbed his one good eye, and began to scold the rustic with great ill-humor.

"I wanted to order a mass, sir," was the reply in a tone of excuse.

"The masses are already over," said the sacristan, sweetening his tone a little at this. "If you want it for to-morrow — is it for the souls in purgatory?"

"No, sir," answered the rustic, handing him a peso. Then gazing fixedly at the single eye, he added, "It's for a person who's going to die soon."

Hereupon he left the sacristy. "I could have caught him last night!" he sighed, as he took off the bandage and stood erect to recover the face and form of Elias.

CHAPTER LVII

VAE VICTIS!

Mi gozo en un pozo.

GUARDS with forbidding mien paced to and fro in front of the door of the town hall, threatening with their rifle-butts the bold urchins who rose on tiptoe or climbed up on one another to see through the bars.

The hall itself did not present that agreeable aspect it wore when the program of the fiesta was under discussion — now it was gloomy and rather ominous. The civil-guards and cuadrilleros who occupied it scarcely spoke and then with few words in low tones. At the table the directorcillo, two clerks, and several soldiers were rustling papers, while the alferez strode from one side to the other, at times gazing fiercely toward the door: prouder Themistocles could not have appeared in the Olympic games after the battle of Salamis. Doña Consolacion yawned in a corner, exhibiting a dirty mouth and jagged teeth, while she fixed her cold, sinister gaze on the door of the jail, which was covered with indecent drawings. She had succeeded in persuading her husband, whose victory had made him amiable, to let her witness the inquiry and perhaps the accompanying tortures. The hyena smelt the carrion and licked herself, wearied by the delay.

The gobernadorcillo was very compunctious. His seat, that large chair placed under his Majesty's portrait, was vacant, being apparently intended for some one else. About nine o'clock the curate arrived, pale and scowling.

"Well, you have n't kept yourself waiting!" the alferez greeted him.

VAE VICTIS!

"I should prefer not to be present," replied Padre Salvi in a low voice, paying no heed to the bitter tone of the alferez. "I'm very nervous."

"As no one else has come to fill the place, I judged that your presence — You know that they leave this afternoon."

"Young Ibarra and the teniente-mayor?"

The alferez pointed toward the jail. "There are eight there," he said. "Bruno died at midnight, but his statement is on record."

The curate saluted Doña Consolacion, who responded with a yawn, and took his seat in the big chair under his Majesty's portrait. "Let us begin," he announced.

"Bring out those two who are in the stocks," ordered the alferez in a tone that he tried to make as terrible as possible. Then turning to the curate he added with a change of tone, "They are fastened in by skipping two holes."

For the benefit of those who are not informed about these instruments of torture, we will say that the stocks are one of the most harmless. The holes in which the offender's legs are placed are a little more or less than a foot apart; by skipping two holes, the prisoner finds himself in a rather forced position with peculiar inconvenience to his ankles and a distance of about a yard between his lower extremities. It does not kill instantaneously, as may well be imagined.

The jailer, followed by four soldiers, pushed back the bolt and opened the door. A nauseating odor and currents of thick, damp air escaped from the darkness within at the same time that laments and sighs were heard. A soldier struck a match, but the flame was choked in such a foul atmosphere, and they had to wait until the air became fresher.

In the dim light of the candle several human forms became vaguely outlined: men hugging their knees or hiding their heads between them, some lying face downward, some standing, and some turned toward the wall. A blow and a creak were heard, accompanied by curses — the stocks were opened. Doña Consolacion bent forward with the muscles of her neck swelling and her bulging eyes fixed on the half-opened door.

A wretched figure, Tarsilo, Bruno's brother, came out between two soldiers. On his wrists were handcuffs and his clothing was in shreds, revealing quite a muscular body. He turned his eyes insolently on the alferez's woman.

"This is the one who defended himself with the most courage and told his companions to run," said the alferez to Padre Salvi.

Behind him came another of miserable aspect, moaning and weeping like a child. He limped along exposing pantaloons spotted with blood. "Mercy, sir, mercy! I'll not go back into the yard," he whimpered.

"He's a rogue," observed the alferez to the curate. "He tried to run, but he was wounded in the thigh. These are the only two that we took alive."

"What's your name?" the alferez asked Tarsilo.

"Tarsilo Alasigan."

"What did Don Crisostomo promise you for attacking the barracks?"

"Don Crisostomo never had anything to do with us."

"Don't deny it! That's why you tried to surprise us."

"You're mistaken. You beat our father to death and we were avenging him, nothing more. Look for your two associates."

The alferez gazed at the sergeant in surprise.

"They're over there in the gully where we threw them yesterday and where they'll rot. Now kill me, you'll not learn anything more."

General surprise and silence, broken by the alferez. "You are going to tell who your other accomplices are," he threatened, flourishing a rattan whip.

A smile of disdain curled the prisoner's lips. The alferez consulted with the curate in a low tone for a few moments, then turned to the soldiers. "Take him out where the corpses are," he commanded.

On a cart in a corner of the yard were heaped five corpses, partly covered with a filthy piece of torn matting. A soldier walked about near them, spitting at every moment.

"Do you know them?" asked the alferez, lifting up the matting.

Tarsilo did not answer. He saw the corpse of the madwoman's husband with two others: that of his brother, slashed with bayonet-thrusts, and that of Lucas with the halter still around his neck. His look became somber and a sigh seemed to escape from his breast.

"Do you know them?" he was again asked, but he still remained silent.

The air hissed and the rattan cut his shoulders. He shuddered, his muscles contracted. The blows were redoubled, but he remained unmoved.

"Whip him until he bursts or talks!" cried the exasperated alferez.

"Talk now," the directorcillo advised him. "They'll kill you anyhow."

They led him back into the hall where the other prisoner, with chattering teeth and quaking limbs, was calling upon the saints.

"Do you know this fellow?" asked Padre Salvi.

"This is the first time that I've ever seen him," replied Tarsilo with a look of pity at the other.

The alferez struck him with his fist and kicked him. "Tie him to the bench!"

Without taking off the handcuffs, which were covered with blood, they tied him to a wooden bench. The wretched boy looked about him as if seeking something and noticed Doña Consolacion, at sight of whom he smiled sardonically. In surprise the bystanders followed his glance and saw the señora, who was lightly gnawing at her lips.

"I've never seen an uglier woman!" exclaimed Tarsilo in the midst of a general silence. "I'd rather lie down on a bench as I do now than at her side as the alferez does."

The Muse turned pale.

"You're going to flog me to death, Señor Alferez," he went on, "but tonight your woman will revenge me by embracing you."

"Gag him!" yelled the furious alferez, trembling with wrath.

Tarsilo seemed to have desired the gag, for after it was put in place his eyes gleamed with satisfaction. At a signal from the alferez, a guard armed with a rattan whip began his gruesome task. Tarsilo's whole body contracted, and a stifled, prolonged cry escaped from him in spite of the piece of cloth which covered his mouth. His head drooped and his clothes became stained with blood.

Padre Salvi, pallid and with wandering looks, arose laboriously, made a sign with his hand, and left the hall with faltering steps. In the street he saw a young woman leaning with her shoulders against the wall, rigid, motionless, listening attentively, staring into space, her clenched hands stretched out along the wall. The sun beat down upon her fiercely. She seemed to be breathlessly counting those dry, dull strokes and those heartrending groans. It was Tarsilo's sister.

Meanwhile, the scene in the hall continued. The wretched boy, overcome with pain, silently waited for his executioners to become weary. At last the panting soldier let his arm fall, and the alferez, pale with anger and astonishment, made a sign for them to untie him. Doña Consolacion then arose and murmured a few words into the ear of her husband, who nodded his head in understanding.

"To the well with him!" he ordered.

The Filipinos know what this means: in Tagalog they call it *timbain*. We do not know who invented this procedure, but we judge that it must be quite ancient. Truth at the bottom of a well may perhaps be a sarcastic interpretation.

VAE VICTIS! 439

In the center of the yard rose the picturesque curb of a well, roughly fashioned from living rock. A rude apparatus of bamboo in the form of a well-sweep served for drawing up the thick, slimy, foul-smelling water. Broken pieces of pottery, manure, and other refuse were collected there, since this well was like the jail, being the place for what society rejected or found useless, and any object that fell into it, however good it might have been, was then a thing lost. Yet it was never closed up, and even at times the prisoners were condemned to go down and deepen it, not because there was any thought of getting anything useful out of such punishment, but because of the difficulties the work offered. A prisoner who once went down there would contract a fever from which he would surely die.

Tarsilo gazed upon all the preparations of the soldiers with a fixed look. He was pale, and his lips trembled or murmured a prayer. The haughtiness of his desperation seemed to have disappeared or, at least, to have weakened. Several times he bent his stiff neck and fixed his gaze on the ground as though resigned to his sufferings. They led him to the well-curb, followed by the smiling Doña Consolacion. In his misery he cast a glance of envy toward the heap of corpses and a sigh escaped from his breast.

"Talk now," the directorcillo again advised him. "They'll hang you anyhow. You'll at least die without suffering so much."

"You'll come out of this only to die," added a cuadrillero.

They took away the gag and hung him up by his feet, for he must go down head foremost and remain some time under the water, just as the bucket does, only that the man is left a longer time. While the alferez was gone to look for a watch to count the minutes, Tarsilo hung with his long hair streaming down and his eyes half closed.

"If you are Christians, if you have any heart," he begged in a low voice, "let me down quickly or make my head strike against the sides so that I'll die. God will reward you for this good deed — perhaps some day you may be as I am!"

The alferez returned, watch in hand, to superintend the lowering.

"Slowly, slowly!" cried Doña Consolacion, as she kept her gaze fixed on the wretch. "Be careful!"

The well-sweep moved gently downwards. Tarsilo rubbed against the jutting stones and filthy weeds that grew in the crevices. Then the sweep stopped while the alferez counted the seconds.

"Lift him up!" he ordered, at the end of a half-minute.

The silvery and harmonious tinkling of the drops of water falling back indicated the prisoner's return to the light. Now that the sweep was heavier he rose rapidly. Pieces of stone and pebbles torn from the walls fell noisily. His forehead and hair smeared with filthy slime, his face covered with cuts and bruises, his body wet and dripping, he appeared to the eyes of the silent crowd. The wind made him shiver with cold.

"Will you talk?" he was asked.

"Take care of my sister," murmured the unhappy boy as he gazed beseechingly toward one of the cuadrilleros.

The bamboo sweep again creaked, and the condemned boy once more disappeared. Doña Consolacion observed that the water remained quiet. The alferez counted a minute.

When Tarsilo again came up his features were contracted and livid. With his bloodshot eyes wide open, he looked at the bystanders.

"Are you going to talk?" the alferez again demanded in dismay.

Tarsilo shook his head, and they again lowered him. His eyelids were closing as the pupils continued to stare at the sky where the fleecy clouds floated; he doubled back his neck so that he might still see the light of day, but all too soon he had to go down into the water, and that foul curtain shut out the sight of the world from him forever.

A minute passed. The watchful Muse saw large bubbles

rise to the surface of the water. "He's thirsty," she commented with a laugh. The water again became still.

This time the alferez did not give the signal for a minute and a half. Tarsilo's features were now no longer contracted. The half-raised lids left the whites of his eyes showing, from his mouth poured muddy water streaked with blood, but his body did not tremble in the chill breeze.

Pale and terrified, the silent bystanders gazed at one another. The alferez made a sign that they should take the body down, and then moved away thoughtfully. Doña Consolacion applied the lighted end of her cigar to the bare legs, but the flesh did not twitch and the fire was extinguished.

"He strangled himself," murmured a cuadrillero. "Look how he turned his tongue back as if trying to swallow it."

The other prisoner, who had watched this scene, sweating and trembling, now stared like a lunatic in all directions. The alferez ordered the directorcillo to question him.

"Sir, sir," he groaned, "I'll tell everything you want me to."

"Good! Let's see, what's your name?"

"Andong,[1] sir!"

"Bernardo — Leonardo — Ricardo — Eduardo — Gerardo — or what?"

"Andong, sir!" repeated the imbecile.

"Put it down Bernardo, or whatever it may be," dictated the alferez.

"Surname?"

The man gazed at him in terror.

"What name have you that is added to the name Andong?"

"Ah, sir! Andong the Witless, sir!"

The bystanders could not restrain a smile. Even the alferez paused in his pacing about.

[1] A common nickname. See the Glossary, under *Nicknames.* —- TR.

"Occupation?"

"Pruner of coconut trees, sir, and servant of my mother-in-law."

"Who ordered you to attack the barracks?"

"No one, sir!"

"What, no one? Don't lie about it or into the well you go! Who ordered you? Say truly!"

"Truly, sir!"

"Who?"

"Who, sir!"

"I'm asking you who ordered you to start the revolution?"

"What revolution, sir?"

"This one, for you were in the yard by the barracks last night."

"Ah, sir!" exclaimed Andong, blushing.

"Who's guilty of that?"

"My mother-in-law, sir!"

Surprise and laughter followed these words. The alferez stopped and stared not unkindly at the wretch, who, thinking that his words had produced a good effect, went on with more spirit: "Yes, sir, my mother-in-law does n't give me anything to eat but what is rotten and unfit, so last night when I came by here with my belly aching I saw the yard of the barracks near and I said to myself, 'It's night-time, no one will see me.' I went in — and then many shots sounded — "

A blow from the rattan cut his speech short.

"To the jail," ordered the alferez. "This afternoon, to the capital!"

CHAPTER LVIII

THE ACCURSED

SOON the news spread through the town that the prisoners were about to set out. At first it was heard with terror; afterward came the weeping and wailing. The families of the prisoners ran about in distraction, going from the convento to the barracks, from the barracks to the town hall, and finding no consolation anywhere, filled the air with cries and groans. The curate had shut himself up on a plea of illness; the alferez had increased the guards, who received the supplicating women with the butts of their rifles; the gobernadorcillo, at best a useless creature, seemed to be more foolish and more useless than ever. In front of the jail the women who still had strength enough ran to and fro, while those who had not sat down on the ground and called upon the names of their beloved.

Although the sun beat down fiercely, not one of these unfortunates thought of going away. Doray, the erstwhile merry and happy wife of Don Filipo, wandered about dejectedly, carrying in her arms their infant son, both weeping. To the advice of friends that she go back home to avoid exposing her baby to an attack of fever, the disconsolate woman replied, "Why should he live, if he is n't going to have a father to rear him?"

"Your husband is innocent. Perhaps he'll come back."

"Yes, after we're all dead!"

Capitana Tinay wept and called upon her son Antonio. The courageous Capitana Maria gazed silently toward the small grating behind which were her twin-boys, her only sons.

There was present also the mother-in-law of the pruner

of coco-palms, but she was not weeping; instead, she paced back and forth, gesticulating with uplifted arms, and haranguing the crowd: "Did you ever see anything like it? To arrest my Andong, to shoot at him, to put him in the stocks, to take him to the capital, and only because — because he had a new pair of pantaloons! This calls for vengeance! The civil-guards are committing abuses! I swear that if I ever again catch one of them in my garden, as has often happened, I'll chop him up, I'll chop him up, or else — let him try to chop me up!" Few persons, however, joined in the protests of the Mussulmanish mother-in-law.

"Don Crisostomo is to blame for all this," sighed a woman.

The schoolmaster was also in the crowd, wandering about bewildered. Ñor Juan did not rub his hands, nor was he carrying his rule and plumb-bob; he was dressed in black, for he had heard the bad news and, true to his habit of looking upon the future as already assured, was in mourning for Ibarra's death.

At two o'clock in the afternoon an open cart drawn by two oxen stopped in front of the town hall. This was at once set upon by the people, who attempted to unhitch the oxen and destroy it. "Don't do that!" said Capitana Maria. "Do you want to make them walk?" This consideration acted as a restraint on the prisoners' relatives.

Twenty soldiers came out and surrounded the cart; then the prisoners appeared. The first was Don Filipo, bound. He greeted his wife smilingly, but Doray broke out into bitter weeping and two guards had difficulty in preventing her from embracing her husband. Antonio, the son of Capitana Tinay, appeared crying like a baby, which only added to the lamentations of his family. The witless Andong broke out into tears at sight of his mother-in-law, the cause of his misfortune. Albino, the quondam theological student, was also bound, as were Capitana Maria's twins. All three were grave and serious. The last to come

THE ACCURSED

out was Ibarra, unbound, but conducted between two guards. The pallid youth looked about him for a friendly face.

"He's the one that's to blame!" cried many voices. "He's to blame and he goes loose!"

"My son-in-law has n't done anything and he's got handcuffs on!"

Ibarra turned to the guards. "Bind me, and bind me well, elbow to elbow," he said.

"We have n't any order."

"Bind me!" And the soldiers obeyed.

The alferez appeared on horseback, armed to the teeth, ten or fifteen more soldiers following him.

Each prisoner had his family there to pray for him, to weep for him, to bestow on him the most endearing names — all save Ibarra, who had no one, even Ñor Juan and the schoolmaster having disappeared.

"Look what you've done to my husband and my son!" Doray cried to him. "Look at my poor son! You've robbed him of his father!"

So the sorrow of the families was converted into anger toward the young man, who was accused of having started the trouble. The alferez gave the order to set out.

"You're a coward!" the mother-in-law of Andong cried after Ibarra. "While others were fighting for you, you hid yourself, coward!"

"May you be accursed!" exclaimed an old man, running along beside him. "Accursed be the gold amassed by your family to disturb our peace! Accursed! Accursed!"

"May they hang you, heretic!" cried a relative of Albino's. Unable to restrain himself, he caught up a stone and threw it at the youth.

This example was quickly followed, and a rain of dirt and stones fell on the wretched young man. Without anger or complaint, impassively he bore the righteous vengeance of so many suffering hearts. This was the parting, the farewell, offered to him by the people among whom were all his affections. With bowed head, he was perhaps thinking of a man whipped through the streets of Manila, of an old woman falling dead at the sight of her son's head; perhaps Elias's history was passing before his eyes.

The alferez found it necessary to drive the crowd back, but the stone-throwing and the insults did not cease. One mother alone did not wreak vengeance on him for her sorrows, Capitana Maria. Motionless, with lips contracted and eyes full of silent tears, she saw her two sons move away; her firmness, her dumb grief surpassed that of the fabled Niobe.

So the procession moved on. Of the persons who appeared at the few open windows those who showed most pity for the youth were the indifferent and the curious. All his friends had hidden themselves, even Capitan Basilio himself, who forbade his daughter Sinang to weep.

Ibarra saw the smoking ruins of his house — the home of his fathers, where he was born, where clustered the fondest recollections of his childhood and his youth. Tears long repressed started into his eyes, and he bowed his head and wept without having the consolation of being able to hide his grief, tied as he was, nor of having any one in whom his sorrow awoke compassion. Now he had neither country, nor home, nor love, nor friends, nor future!

From a slight elevation a man gazed upon the sad procession. He was an old man, pale and emaciated, wrapped in a woolen blanket, supporting himself with difficulty on a staff. It was the old Sage, Tasio, who, on hearing of the event, had left his bed to be present, but his strength had not been sufficient to carry him to the town hall. The old man followed the cart with his gaze until it disappeared in the distance and then remained for some time afterward with his head bowed, deep in thought. Then he stood up and laboriously made his way toward his house, pausing to rest at every step. On the following day some herdsmen him dead on the very threshold of his solitary home.

CHAPTER LIX

PATRIOTISM AND PRIVATE INTERESTS

SECRETLY the telegraph transmitted the report to Manila, and thirty-six hours later the newspapers commented on it with great mystery and not a few dark hints — augmented, corrected, or mutilated by the censor. In the meantime, private reports, emanating from the convents, were the first to gain secret currency from mouth to mouth, to the great terror of those who heard them. The fact, distorted in a thousand ways, was believed with greater or less ease according to whether it was flattering or worked contrary to the passions and ways of thinking of each hearer.

Without public tranquillity seeming disturbed, at least outwardly, yet the peace of mind of each home was whirled about like the water in a pond: while the surface appears smooth and clear, in the depths the silent fishes swarm, dive about, and chase one another. For one part of the population crosses, decorations, epaulets, offices, prestige, power, importance, dignities began to whirl about like butterflies in a golden atmosphere. For the other part a dark cloud arose on the horizon, projecting from its gray depths, like black silhouettes, bars, chains, and even the fateful gibbet. In the air there seemed to be heard investigations, condemnations, and the cries from the torture chamber; Marianas[1] and Bagumbayan presented themselves wrapped in a torn and bloody veil, fishers and fished confused. Fate pictured the event to the imaginations of the Manilans like certain Chinese fans — one side painted

[1] The Marianas, or Ladrone Islands, were used as a place of banishment for political prisoners. — TR.

black, the other gilded with bright-colored birds and flowers.

In the convents the greatest excitement prevailed. Carriages were harnessed, the Provincials exchanged visits and held secret conferences; they presented themselves in the palaces to offer their aid to *the government in its perilous crisis*. Again there was talk of comets and omens.

"A *Te Deum!* A *Te Deum!*" cried a friar in one convent. "This time let no one be absent from the chorus! It's no small mercy from God to make it clear just now, especially in these hopeless times, how much we are worth!"

"The little general *Mal-Aguero*[1] can gnaw his lips over this lesson," responded another.

"What would have become of him if not for the religious corporations?"

"And to celebrate the fiesta better, serve notice on the cook and the refectioner. *Gaudeamus* for three days!"

"Amen!" "Viva Salvi!" "Amen!"

In another convent they talked differently.

"You see, now, that fellow is a pupil of the Jesuits. The filibusters come from the Ateneo.

"And the anti-friars."

"I told you so. The Jesuits are ruining the country, they're corrupting the youth, but they are tolerated because they trace a few scrawls on a piece of paper when there is an earthquake."

"And God knows how they are made!"

"Yes, but don't contradict them. When everything is shaking and moving about, who draws diagrams? Nothing, Padre Secchi —"[2]

---

[1] "Evil Omen," a nickname applied by the friars to General Joaquin Jovellar, who was governor of the Islands from 1883 to 1885. It fell to the lot of General Jovellar, a kindly old man, much more soldier than administrator, to attempt the introduction of certain salutary reforms tending toward progress, hence his disfavor with the holy fathers. The mention of "General J——" in the last part of the epilogue probably refers also to him. — TR.

[2] A celebrated Italian astronomer, member of the Jesuit Order. The Jesuits are still in charge of the Observatory of Manila. — TR.

PATRIOTISM AND PRIVATE INTERESTS

And they smiled with sovereign disdain.

"But what about the weather forecasts and the typhoons?" asked another ironically. "Are n't they divine?"

"Any fisherman foretells them!"

"When he who governs is a fool — tell me how your head is and I'll tell you how your foot is! But you'll see if the friends favor one another. The newspapers very nearly ask a miter for Padre Salvi."

"He's going to get it! He'll lick it right up!"

"Do you think so?"

"Why not! Nowadays they grant one for anything whatsoever. I know of a fellow who got one for less. He wrote a cheap little work demonstrating that the Indians are not capable of being anything but mechanics. Pshaw, old-fogyisms!"

"That's right! So much favoritism injures Religion!" exclaimed another. "If the miters only had eyes and could see what heads they were upon —"

"If the miters were natural objects," added another in a nasal tone, "*Natura abhorret vacuum.*"

"That's why they grab for them, their emptiness attracts!" responded another.

These and many more things were said in the convents, but we will spare our reader other comments of a political, metaphysical, or piquant nature and conduct him to a private house. As we have few acquaintances in Manila, let us enter the home of Capitan Tinong, the polite individual whom we saw so profusely inviting Ibarra to honor him with a visit.

In the rich and spacious sala of his Tondo house, Capitan Tinong was seated in a wide armchair, rubbing his hands in a gesture of despair over his face and the nape of his neck, while his wife, Capitana Tinchang, was weeping and preaching to him. From the corner their two daughters listened silently and stupidly, yet greatly affected.

"Ay, Virgin of Antipolo!" cried the woman. "Ay,

Virgin of the Rosary and of the Girdle![1] Ay, ay! Our Lady of Novaliches!"

"Mother!" responded the elder of the daughters.

"I told you so!" continued the wife in an accusing tone. "I told you so! Ay, Virgin of Carmen,[2] ay!"

"But you didn't tell me anything," Capitan Tinong dared to answer tearfully. "On the contrary, you told me that I was doing well to frequent Capitan Tiago's house and cultivate friendship with him, because he's rich — and you told me — "

"What! What did I tell you? I didn't tell you that, I didn't tell you anything! Ay, if you had only listened to me!"

"Now you're throwing the blame on me," he replied bitterly, slapping the arm of his chair. "Didn't you tell me that I had done well to invite him to dine with us, because he was wealthy? Didn't you say that we ought to have friends only among the wealthy? *Abá!*"

"It's true that I told you so, because — because there wasn't anything else for me to do. You did nothing but sing his praises: *Don Ibarra* here, *Don Ibarra* there, *Don Ibarra* everywhere. *Abaá!* But I didn't advise you to hunt him up and talk to him at that reception! You can't deny that!"

"Did I know that he was to be there, perhaps?"

"But you ought to have known it!"

"How so, if I didn't even know him?"

---

[1] "Our Lady of the Girdle" is the patroness of the Augustinian Order. — Tr.

[2] This image is in the six-million-peso steel church of St. Sebastian in Manila. Something of her early history is thus given by Fray Luis de Jesus in his *Historia* of the Recollect Order (1681): "A very holy image is revered there under the title of Carmen. Although that image is small in stature, it is a great and perennial spring of prodigies for those who invoke her. Our religious took it from Nueva España (Mexico), and even in that very navigation she was able to make herself known by her miracles. . . . That most holy image is daily frequented with vows, presents, and novenas, thank-offerings of the many who are daily favored by that queen of the skies." — Blair and Robertson, *The Philippine Islands*, Vol. XXI, p. 195.

"But you ought to have known him!"

"But, Tinchang, it was the first time that I ever saw him, that I ever heard him spoken of!"

"Well then, you ought to have known him before and heard him spoken of. That's what you're a man for and wear trousers and read *El Diario de Manila*,"[1] answered his unterrified spouse, casting on him a terrible look.

To this Capitan Tinong did not know what to reply. Capitana Tinchang, however, was not satisfied with this victory, but wished to silence him completely. So she approached him with clenched fists. "Is this what I've worked for, year after year, toiling and saving, that you by your stupidity may throw away the fruits of my labor?" she scolded. "Now they'll come to deport you, they'll take away all our property, just as they did from the wife of — Oh, if I were a man, if I were a man!"

Seeing that her husband bowed his head, she again fell to sobbing, but still repeating, "Ay, if I were a man, if I were a man!"

"Well, if you were a man," the provoked husband at length asked, "what would you do?"

"What would I do? Well — well — well, this very minute I'd go to the Captain-General and offer to fight against the rebels, this very minute!"

"But have n't you seen what the *Diario* says? Read it: 'The vile and infamous treason has been suppressed with energy, strength, and vigor, and soon the rebellious enemies of the Fatherland and their accomplices will feel all the weight and severity of the law.' Don't you see it? There is n't any more rebellion."

"That does n't matter! You ought to offer yourself as they did in '72;[2] they saved themselves."

[1] The oldest and most conservative newspaper in Manila at the time this work was written. — TR.
[2] Following closely upon the liberal administration of La Torre, there occurred in the Cavite arsenal in 1872 a mutiny which was construed as an incipient rebellion, and for alleged complicity in it three

"Yes, that's what was done by Padre Burg—"

But he was unable to finish this name, for his wife ran to him and slapped her hand over his mouth. "Shut up! Are you saying that name so that they may garrote you tomorrow on Bagumbayan? Don't you know that to pronounce it is enough to get yourself condemned without trial? Keep quiet!"

However Capitan Tinong may have felt about obeying her, he could hardly have done otherwise, for she had his mouth covered with both her hands, pressing his little head against the back of the chair, so that the poor fellow might have been smothered to death had not a new personage appeared on the scene. This was their cousin, Don Primitivo, who had memorized the "Amat," a man of some forty years, plump, big-paunched, and elegantly dressed.

"*Quid video?*" he exclaimed as he entered. "What's happening? *Quare?*"[1]

"Ay, cousin!" cried the woman, running toward him in tears, "I've sent for you because I don't know what's going to become of us. What do you advise? Speak, you've studied Latin and know how to argue."

"But first, *quid quaeritis? Nihil est in intellectu quod prius non fuerit in sensu; nihil volitum quin praecognitum.*"[2]

He sat down gravely and, just as if the Latin phrases had possessed a soothing virtue, the couple ceased weeping and drew nearer to him to hang upon the advice from his lips, as at one time the Greeks did before the words of salvation from the oracle that was to free them from the Persian invaders.

"Why do you weep? *Ubinam gentium sumus?*"[3]

---

native priests, Padres Burgos, Gomez, and Zamora, were garroted, while a number of prominent Manilans were deported. — TR.

[1] What do I see? . . . Wherefore?

[2] What do you wish? Nothing is in the intellect which has not first passed through the senses; nothing is willed that is not already in the mind.

[3] Where in the world are we?

"You've already heard of the uprising?"

"*Alzamentum Ibarrae ab alferesio Guardiae Civilis destructum? Et nunc?*[1] What! Does Don Crisostomo owe you anything?"

"No, but you know, Tinong invited him to dinner and spoke to him on the Bridge of Spain — in broad daylight! They'll say that he's a friend of his!"

"A friend of his!" exclaimed the startled Latinist, rising. "*Amice, amicus Plato sed magis amica veritas.* Birds of a feather flock together. *Malum est negotium et est timendum rerum istarum horrendissimum resultatum!*[2] Ahem!"

Capitan Tinong turned deathly pale at hearing so many words in *um;* such a sound presaged ill. His wife clasped her hands supplicatingly and said:

"Cousin, don't talk to us in Latin now. You know that we're not philosophers like you. Let's talk in Spanish or Tagalog. Give us some advice."

"It's a pity that you don't understand Latin, cousin. Truths in Latin are lies in Tagalog; for example, *contra principia negantem fustibus est arguendum*[3] in Latin is a truth like Noah's ark, but I put it into practise once and I was the one who got whipped. So, it's a pity that you don't know Latin. In Latin everything would be straightened out."

"We, too, know many *oremus, parcenobis,* and *Agnus Dei Catolis*,[4] but now we shouldn't understand one another. Provide Tinong with an argument so that they won't hang him!"

"You've done wrong, very wrong, cousin, in cultivating friendship with that young man," replied the Latinist.

[1] The uprising of Ibarra suppressed by the alferez of the Civil Guard? And now?
[2] Friend, Plato is dear but truth is dearer. . . . It's a bad business and a horrible result from these things is to be feared.
[3] Against him who denies the fundamentals, clubs should be used as arguments.
[4] Latin prayers. "Agnus Dei Catolis" for "Agnus Dei qui tollis" (John I. 29).

"The righteous suffer for the sinners. I was almost going to advise you to make your will. *Vae illis! Ubi est fumus ibi est ignis! Similis simili audet; atqui Ibarra ahorcatur, ergo ahorcaberis —*"[1] With this he shook his head from side to side disgustedly.

"Saturnino, what's the matter?" cried Capitana Tinchang in dismay. "Ay, he's dead! A doctor! Tinong, Tinongoy!"

The two daughters ran to her, and all three fell to weeping.

"It's nothing more than a swoon, cousin! I would have been more pleased that — that — but unfortunately it's only a swoon. *Non timeo mortem in catre sed super espaldonem Bagumbayanis.*[2] Get some water!"

"Don't die!" sobbed the wife. "Don't die, for they'll come and arrest you! Ay, if you die and the soldiers come, ay, ay!"

The learned cousin rubbed the victim's face with water until he recovered consciousness. "Come, don't cry. *Inveni remedium:* I've found a remedy. Let's carry him to bed. Come, take courage! Here I am with you — and all the wisdom of the ancients. Call a doctor, and you, cousin, go right away to the Captain-General and take him a present — a gold ring, a chain. *Dadivae quebrantant peñas.*[3] Say that it's a Christmas gift. Close the windows, the doors, and if any one asks for my cousin, say that he is seriously ill. Meanwhile, I'll burn all his letters, papers, and books, so that they can't find anything, just as Don Crisostomo did. *Scripti testes sunt! Quod medicamenta non sanant, ferrum sanat, quod ferrum non sanat, ignis sanat.*"[4]

"Yes, do so, cousin, burn everything!" said Capitana

---

[1] Woe unto them! Where there's smoke there's fire! Like seeks like; and if Ibarra is hanged, therefore you will be hanged.

[2] I do not fear death in bed, but upon the mount of Bagumbayan.

[3] The first part of a Spanish proverb: "Gifts break rocks, and enter without gimlets."

[4] What is written is evidence! What medicines do not cure, iron cures; what iron does not cure, fire cures.

PATRIOTISM AND PRIVATE INTERESTS 455

Tinchang. "Here are the keys, here are the letters from Capitan Tiago. Burn them! Don't leave a single European newspaper, for they're very dangerous. Here are the copies of *The Times* that I've kept for wrapping up soap and old clothes. Here are the books."

"Go to the Captain-General, cousin," said Don Primitivo, "and leave us alone. *In extremis extrema.*[1] Give me the authority of a Roman dictator, and you'll see how soon I'll save the coun— I mean, my cousin."

He began to give orders and more orders, to upset bookcases, to tear up papers, books, and letters. Soon a big fire was burning in the kitchen. Old shotguns were smashed with axes, rusty revolvers were thrown away. The maidservant who wanted to keep the barrel of one for a blowpipe received a reprimand:

"*Conservare etiam sperasti, perfida?*[2] Into the fire!"

So he continued his auto da fé. Seeing an old volume in vellum, he read the title, *Revolutions of the Celestial Globes*, by Copernicus. Whew! *Ite, maledicti, in ignem kalanis!*"[3] he exclaimed, hurling it into the flames. "Revolutions and Copernicus! Crimes on crimes! If I had n't come in time! *Liberty in the Philippines!* Ta, ta, ta! What books! Into the fire!"

Harmless books, written by simple authors, were burned; not even the most innocent work escaped. Cousin Primitivo was right: the righteous suffer for the sinners.

Four or five hours later, at a pretentious reception in the Walled City, current events were being commented upon. There were present a lot of old women and maidens of marriageable age, the wives and daughters of government employees, dressed in loose gowns, fanning themselves and yawning. Among the men, who, like the women, showed in their faces their education and origin, was an elderly gentleman, small and one-armed, whom the others treated

---

[1] In extreme cases, extreme measures.
[2] Do you wish to keep it also, traitress?
[3] Go, accursed, into the fire of the kalan.

with great respect. He himself maintained a disdainful silence.

"To tell the truth, formerly I could n't endure the friars and the civil-guards, they 're so rude," said a corpulent dame, "but now that I see their usefulness and their services, I would almost marry any one of them gladly. I 'm a patriot."

"That 's what I say!" added a thin lady. "What a pity that we have n't our former governor. He would leave the country as clean as a platter."

"And the whole race of filibusters would be exterminated!"

"Don't they say that there are still a lot of islands to be populated? Why don't they deport all these crazy Indians to them? If I were the Captain-General—"

"Señoras," interrupted the one-armed individual, "the Captain-General knows his duty. As I 've heard, he 's very much irritated, for he had heaped favors on that Ibarra."

"Heaped favors on him!" echoed the thin lady, fanning herself furiously. "Look how ungrateful these Indians are! Is it possible to treat them as if they were human beings? *Jesús!*"

"Do you know what I 've heard?" asked a military official.

"What 's that?"

"Let 's hear it!"

"What do they say?"

"Reputable persons," replied the officer in the midst of a profound silence, "state that this agitation for building a schoolhouse was a pure fairy tale."

"*Jesús!* Just see that!" the señoras exclaimed, already believing in the trick.

"The school was a pretext. What he wanted to build was a fort from which he could safely defend himself when we should come to attack him."

"What infamy! Only an Indian is capable of such cowardly thoughts," exclaimed the fat lady. "If I were the

PATRIOTISM AND PRIVATE INTERESTS 457

Captain-General they would soon see — they would soon see —"

"That's what I say!" exclaimed the thin lady, turning to the one-armed man. "Arrest all the little lawyers, priestlings, merchants, and without trial banish or deport them! Tear out the evil by the roots!"

"But it's said that this filibuster is the descendant of Spaniards," observed the one-armed man, without looking at any one in particular.

"Oh, yes!" exclaimed the fat lady, unterrified. "It's always the creoles! No Indian knows anything about revolution! Rear crows, rear crows!"[1]

"Do you know what I've heard?" asked a creole lady, to change the topic of conversation. "The wife of Capitan Tinong, you remember her, the woman in whose house we danced and dined during the fiesta of Tondo —"

"The one who has two daughters? What about her?"

"Well, that woman just this afternoon presented the Captain-General with a ring worth a thousand pesos!"

The one-armed man turned around. "Is that so? Why?" he asked with shining eyes.

"She said that it was a Christmas gift —"

"But Christmas does n't come for a month yet!"

"Perhaps she's afraid the storm is blowing her way," observed the fat lady.

"And is getting under cover," added the thin señora.

"When no return is asked, it's a confession of guilt."

"This must be carefully looked into," declared the one-armed man thoughtfully. "I fear that there's a cat in the bag."

"A cat in the bag, yes! That's just what I was going to say," echoed the thin lady.

"And so was I," said the other, taking the words out of her mouth, "the wife of Capitan Tinong is so stingy — she has n't yet sent us any present and that after we've been

[1] The first part of a Spanish proverb: "Cría cuervos y te sacarán los ojos," "Rear crows and they will pick your eyes out."— TR.

in her house. So, when such a grasping and covetous woman lets go of a little present worth a thousand pesos — "

"But, is it a fact?" inquired the one-armed man.

"Certainly! Most certainly! My cousin's sweetheart, his Excellency's adjutant, told her so. And I'm of the opinion that it's the very same ring that the older daughter wore on the day of the fiesta. She's always covered with diamonds."

"A walking show-case!"

"A way of attracting attention, like any other! Instead of buying a fashion plate or paying a dressmaker — "

Giving some pretext, the one-armed man left the gathering. Two hours later, when the world slept, various residents of Tondo received an invitation through some soldiers. The authorities could not consent to having certain persons of position and property sleep in such poorly guarded and badly ventilated houses — in Fort Santiago and other government buildings their sleep would be calmer and more refreshing. Among these favored persons was included the unfortunate Capitan Tinong.

CHAPTER LX

MARIA CLARA WEDS

CAPITAN TIAGO was very happy, for in all this terrible storm no one had taken any notice of him. He had not been arrested, nor had he been subjected to solitary confinement, investigations, electric machines, continuous foot-baths in underground cells, or other pleasantries that are well-known to certain folk who call themselves civilized. His friends, that is, those who had been his friends — for the good man had denied all his Filipino friends from the instant when they were suspected by the government — had also returned to their homes after a few days' vacation in the state edifices. The Captain-General himself had ordered that they be cast out from his precincts, not considering them worthy of remaining therein, to the great disgust of the one-armed individual, who had hoped to celebrate the approaching Christmas in their abundant and opulent company.

Capitan Tinong had returned to his home sick, pale, and swollen; the excursion had not done him good. He was so changed that he said not a word, nor even greeted his family, who wept, laughed, chattered, and almost went mad with joy. The poor man no longer ventured out of his house for fear of running the risk of saying good-day to a filibuster. Not even Don Primitivo himself, with all the wisdom of the ancients, could draw him out of his silence.

"*Crede, prime,*" the Latinist told him, "if I had n't got here to burn all your papers, they would have squeezed your neck; and if I had burned the whole house they would n't have touched a hair of your head. But *quod eventum, eventum; gratias agamus Domino Deo quia non in Marianis Insulis es, camotes seminando.*"[1]

Stories similar to Capitan Tinong's were not unknown to Capitan Tiago, so he bubbled over with gratitude, without knowing exactly to whom he owed such signal favors. Aunt Isabel attributed the miracle to the Virgin of Antipolo, to the Virgin of the Rosary, or at least to the Virgin of Carmen, and at the very, very least that she was willing to concede, to Our Lady of the Girdle; according to her the miracle could not get beyond that.

Capitan Tiago did not deny the miracle, but added: " I think so, Isabel, but the Virgin of Antipolo could n't have done it alone. My friends have helped, my future son-in-law, Señor Linares, who, as you know, joked with Señor Antonio Canovas himself, the premier whose portrait appears in the *Ilustración*, he who does n't condescend to show more than half his face to the people."

So the good man could not repress a smile of satisfaction every time that he heard any important news. And there was plenty of news: it was whispered about in secret that Ibarra would be hanged; that, while many proofs of his guilt had been lacking, at last some one had appeared to sustain the accusation; that experts had declared that in fact the work on the schoolhouse could pass for a bulwark of fortification, although somewhat defective, as was only to be expected of ignorant Indians. These rumors calmed him and made him smile.

In the same way that Capitan Tiago and his cousin diverged in their opinions, the friends of the family were also divided into two parties, — one miraculous, the other governmental, although this latter was insignificant. The miraculous party was again subdivided: the senior sacristan of Binondo, the candle-woman, and the leader of the Broth-

---

[1] Believe me, cousin . . . what has happened, has happened; let us give thanks to God that you are not in the Marianas Islands, planting camotes. (It may be observed that here, as in some of his other speeches, Don Primitivo's Latin is rather Philippinized.) — TR.

erhood saw the hand of God directed by the Virgin of the Rosary; while the Chinese wax-chandler, his caterer on his visits to Antipolo, said, as he fanned himself and shook his leg:

"Don't fool yourself — it's the Virgin of Antipolo! She can do more than all the rest — don't fool yourself!"[1]

Capitan Tiago had great respect for this Chinese, who passed himself off as a prophet and a physician. Examining the palm of the deceased lady just before her daughter was born, he had prognosticated: "If it's not a boy and does n't die, it'll be a fine girl!"[2] and Maria Clara had come into the world to fulfill the infidel's prophecy.

Capitan Tiago, then, as a prudent and cautious man, could not decide so easily as Trojan Paris — he could not so lightly give the preference to one Virgin for fear of offending another, a situation that might be fraught with grave consequences. "Prudence!" he said to himself. "Let's not go and spoil it all now."

He was still in the midst of these doubts when the governmental party arrived, — Doña Victorina, Don Tiburcio, and Linares. Doña Victorina did the talking for the three men as well as for herself. She mentioned Linares' visits to the Captain-General and repeatedly insinuated the advantages of a relative of "quality." "Now," she concluded, "as we was zaying: he who zhelterz himzelf well, builds a good roof."

"T-the other w-way, w-woman!" corrected the doctor.

For some days now she had been endeavoring to *Andalusize* her speech, and no one had been able to get this idea out of her head — she would sooner have first let them tear off her false frizzes.

"Yez," she went on, speaking of Ibarra, "he deserves

[1] The original is in the *lingua franca* of the Philippine Chinese, a medium of expression *sui generis*, being, like Ulysses, "a part of all that he has met," and defying characteristic translation: "No siya ostí gongon; miligen li Antipolo esi! Esi pueli más con tolo; no siya ostí gongong!" — TR.

[2] "Si esi no hómole y no pataylo, mujé juete-juete!"

it all. I told you zo when I first zaw him, he's a filibuzter. What did the General zay to you, cousin? What did he zay? What news did he tell you about thiz Ibarra?"

Seeing that her cousin was slow in answering, she continued, directing her remarks to Capitan Tiago, "Believe me, if they zentenz him to death, as is to be hoped, it'll be on account of my cousin."

"Señora, señora!" protested Linares.

But she gave him no time for objections. "How diplomatic you have become! We know that you're the adviser of the General, that he couldn't live without you. Ah, Clarita, what a pleasure to zee you!"

Maria Clara was still pale, although now quite recovered from her illness. Her long hair was tied up with a light blue silk ribbon. With a timid bow and a sad smile she went up to Doña Victorina for the ceremonial kiss.

After the usual conventional remarks, the pseudo-Andalusian continued: "We've come to visit you. You've been zaved, thankz to your relations." This was said with a significant glance toward Linares.

"God has protected my father," replied the girl in a low voice.

"Yez, Clarita, but the time of the miracles is pazt. We Zpaniards zay: 'Truzt in the Virgin and take to your heels.'"

"T-the other w-way!"

Capitan Tiago, who had up to this point had no chance to speak, now made bold enough to ask, while he threw himself into an attitude of strict attention, "So you, Doña Victorina, think that the Virgin—"

"We've come ezpezially to talk with you about the virgin," she answered mysteriously, making a sign toward Maria Clara. "We've come to talk business."

The maiden understood that she was expected to retire, so with an excuse she went away, supporting herself on the furniture.

MARIA CLARA WEDS 463

What was said and what was agreed upon in this conference was so sordid and mean that we prefer not to recount it. It is enough to record that as they took their leave they were all merry, and that afterwards Capitan Tiago said to Aunt Isabel:

"Notify the restaurant that we'll have a fiesta tomorrow. Get Maria ready, for we're going to marry her off before long."

Aunt Isabel stared at him in consternation.

"You'll see! When Señor Linares is our son-in-law we'll get into all the palaces. Every one will envy us, every one will die of envy!"

Thus it happened that at eight o'clock on the following evening the house of Capitan Tiago was once again filled, but this time his guests were only Spaniards and Chinese. The fair sex was represented by Peninsular and Philippine-Spanish ladies.

There were present the greater part of our acquaintances: Padre Sibyla and Padre Salvi among various Franciscans and Dominicans; the old lieutenant of the Civil Guard, Señor Guevara, gloomier than ever; the alferez, who was for the thousandth time describing his battle and gazing over his shoulders at every one, believing himself to be a Don John of Austria, for he was now a major; De Espadaña, who looked at the alferez with respect and fear, and avoided his gaze; and Doña Victorina, swelling with indignation. Linares had not yet come; as a personage of importance, he had to arrive later than the others. There are creatures so simple that by being an hour behind time they transform themselves into great men.

In the group of women Maria Clara was the subject of a murmured conversation. The maiden had welcomed them all ceremoniously, without losing her air of sadness.

"Pish!" remarked one young woman. "The proud little thing!"

"Pretty little thing!" responded another. "But he

might have picked out some other girl with a less foolish face."

"The gold, child! The good youth is selling himself."

In another part the comments ran thus:

"To get married when her first fiancé is about to be hanged!"

"That's what's called prudence, having a substitute ready."

"Well, when she gets to be a widow—"

Maria Clara was seated in a chair arranging a salver of flowers and doubtless heard all these remarks, for her hand trembled, she turned pale, and several times bit her lips.

In the circle of men the conversation was carried on in loud tones and, naturally, turned upon recent events. All were talking, even Don Tiburcio, with the exception of Padre Sibyla, who maintained his usual disdainful silence.

"I've heard it said that your Reverence is leaving the town, Padre Salvi?" inquired the new major, whose fresh star had made him more amiable.

"I have nothing more to do there. I'm going to stay permanently in Manila. And you?"

"I'm also leaving the town," answered the ex-alferez, swelling up. "The government needs me to command a flying column to clean the provinces of filibusters."

Fray Sibyla looked him over rapidly from head to foot and then turned his back completely.

"Is it known for certain what will become of the ringleader, the filibuster?" inquired a government employee.

"Do you mean Crisostomo Ibarra?" asked another. "The most likely and most just thing is that he will be hanged, like those of '72."

"He's going to be deported," remarked the old lieutenant, dryly.

"Deported! Nothing more than deported? But it will be a perpetual deportation!" exclaimed several voices at the same time.

"If that young man," continued the lieutenant, Guevara, in a loud and severe tone, "had been more cautious, if he had confided less in certain persons with whom he corresponded, if our prosecutors did not know how to interpret so subtly what is written, that young man would surely have been acquitted."

This declaration on the part of the old lieutenant and the tone of his voice produced great surprise among his hearers, who were apparently at a loss to know what to say. Padre Salvi stared in another direction, perhaps to avoid the gloomy look that the old soldier turned on him. Maria Clara let her flowers fall and remained motionless. Padre Sibyla, who knew so well how to be silent, seemed also to be the only one who knew how to ask a question.

"You're speaking of letters, Señor Guevara?"

"I'm speaking of what was told me by his lawyer, who looked after the case with interest and zeal. Outside of some ambiguous lines which this youth wrote to a woman before he left for Europe, lines in which the government's attorney saw a plot and a threat against the government, and which he acknowledged to be his, there was n't anything found to accuse him of."

"But the declaration of the outlaw before he died?"

"His lawyer had that thrown out because, according to the outlaw himself, they had never communicated with the young man, but with a certain Lucas, who was an enemy of his, as could be proved, and who committed suicide, perhaps from remorse. It was proved that the papers found on the corpse were forged, since the handwriting was like that of Señor Ibarra's seven years ago, but not like his now, which leads to the belief that the model for them may have been that incriminating letter. Besides, the lawyer says that if Señor Ibarra had refused to acknowledge the letter, he might have been able to do a great deal for him — but at sight of the letter he turned pale, lost his courage, and confirmed everything written in it."

"Did you say that the letter was directed to a woman?" asked a Franciscan. "How did it get into the hands of the prosecutor?"

The lieutenant did not answer. He stared for a moment at Padre Salvi and then moved away, nervously twisting the sharp point of his gray beard. The others made their comments.

"There is seen the hand of God!" remarked one. "Even the women hate him."

"He had his house burned down, thinking in that way to save himself, but he did n't count on the guest, on his *querida*, his *babaye*," added another, laughing. "It's the work of God! *Santiago y cierra España!*"[1]

Meanwhile the old soldier paused in his pacing about and approached Maria Clara, who was listening to the conversation, motionless in her chair, with the flowers scattered at her feet.

"You are a very prudent girl," the old officer whispered to her. "You did well to give up the letter. You have thus assured yourself an untroubled future."

With startled eyes she watched him move away from her, and bit her lip. Fortunately, Aunt Isabel came along, and she had sufficient strength left to catch hold of the old lady's skirt.

"Aunt!" she murmured.

"What's the matter?" asked the old lady, frightened by the look on the girl's face.

"Take me to my room!" she pleaded, grasping her aunt's arm in order to rise.

"Are you sick, daughter? You look as if you'd lost your bones! What's the matter?"

"A fainting spell — the people in the room — so many lights — I need to rest. Tell father that I'm going to sleep."

"You're cold. Do you want some tea?"

Maria Clara shook her head, entered and locked the

[1] The Spanish battle-cry: "St. James, and charge, Spain!" — TR.

door of her chamber, and then, her strength failing her, she fell sobbing to the floor at the feet of an image.

"Mother, mother, mother mine!" she sobbed.

Through the window and a door that opened on the azotea the moonlight entered. The musicians continued to play merry waltzes, laughter and the hum of voices penetrated into the chamber, several times her father, Aunt Isabel, Doña Victorina, and even Linares knocked at the door, but Maria did not move. Heavy sobs shook her breast.

Hours passed — the pleasures of the dinner-table ended, the sound of singing and dancing was heard, the candle burned itself out, but the maiden still remained motionless on the moonlit floor at the feet of an image of the Mother of Jesus.

Gradually the house became quiet again, the lights were extinguished, and Aunt Isabel once more knocked at the door.

"Well, she's gone to sleep," said the old woman, aloud. "As she's young and has no cares, she sleeps like a corpse."

When all was silence she raised herself slowly and threw a look about her. She saw the azotea with its little arbors bathed in the ghostly light of the moon.

"An untroubled future! She sleeps like a corpse!" she repeated in a low voice as she made her way out to the azotea.

The city slept. Only from time to time there was heard the noise of a carriage crossing the wooden bridge over the river, whose undisturbed waters reflected smoothly the light of the moon. The young woman raised her eyes toward a sky as clear as sapphire. Slowly she took the rings from her fingers and from her ears and removed the combs from her hair. Placing them on the balustrade of the azotea, she gazed toward the river.

A small banka loaded with zacate stopped at the foot of the landing such as every house on the bank of the river has.

One of two men who were in it ran up the stone stairway and jumped over the wall, and a few seconds later his footsteps were heard on the stairs leading to the azotea.

Maria Clara saw him pause on discovering her, but only for a moment. Then he advanced slowly and stopped within a few paces of her. Maria Clara recoiled.

"Crisostomo!" she murmured, overcome with fright.

"Yes, I am Crisostomo," replied the young man gravely. "An enemy, a man who has every reason for hating me, Elias, has rescued me from the prison into which my friends threw me."

A sad silence followed these words. Maria Clara bowed her head and let her arms fall.

Ibarra went on: "Beside my mother's corpse I swore that I would make you happy, whatever might be my destiny! You can have been faithless to your oath, for she was not your mother; but I, I who am her son, hold her memory so sacred that in spite of a thousand difficulties I have come here to carry mine out, and fate has willed that I should speak to you yourself. Maria, we shall never see each other again — you are young and perhaps some day your conscience may reproach you — I have come to tell you, before I go away forever, that I forgive you. Now, may you be happy and — farewell!"

Ibarra started to move away, but the girl stopped him.

"Crisostomo," she said, "God has sent you to save me from desperation. Hear me and then judge me!"

Ibarra tried gently to draw away from her. "I didn't come to call you to account! I came to give you peace!"

"I don't want that peace which you bring me. Peace I will give myself. You despise me and your contempt will embitter all the rest of my life."

Ibarra read the despair and sorrow depicted in the suffering girl's face and asked her what she wished.

"That you believe that I have always loved you!"

At this he smiled bitterly.

"Ah, you doubt me! You doubt the friend of your

childhood, who has never hidden a single thought from
you!" the maiden exclaimed sorrowfully. "I understand
now! But when you hear my story, the sad story that was revealed to me during my illness, you will have mercy on
me, you will not have that smile for my sorrow. Why did
you not let me die in the hands of my ignorant physician?
You and I both would have been happier!"

Resting a moment, she then went on: "You have desired it, you have doubted me! But may my mother forgive me! On one of the sorrowfulest of my nights of
suffering, a man revealed to me the name of my real father
and forbade me to love you — except that my father himself should pardon the injury you had done him."

Ibarra recoiled a pace and gazed fearfully at her.

"Yes," she continued, "that man told me that he could
not permit our union, since his conscience would forbid it,
and that he would be obliged to reveal the name of my real
father at the risk of causing a great scandal, for my father
is — " And she murmured into the youth's ear a name
in so low a tone that only he could have heard it.

"What was I to do? Must I sacrifice to my love the
memory of my mother, the honor of my supposed father,
and the good name of the real one? Could I have done that
without having even you despise me?"

"But the proof! Had you any proof? You needed
proofs!" exclaimed Ibarra, trembling with emotion.

The maiden snatched two papers from her bosom.

"Two letters of my mother's, two letters written in the
midst of her remorse, while I was yet unborn! Take them,
read them, and you will see how she cursed me and wished
for my death, which my father vainly tried to bring about
with drugs. These letters he had forgotten in a building
where he had lived; the other man found and preserved
them and only gave them up to me in exchange for your
letter, in order to assure himself, so he said, that I would
not marry you without the consent of my father. Since I
have been carrying them about with me, in place of your

letter, I have felt the chill in my heart. I sacrificed you, I sacrificed my love! What else could one do for a dead mother and two living fathers? Could I have suspected the use that was to be made of your letter?"

Ibarra stood appalled, while she continued: "What more was left for me to do? Could I perhaps tell you who my father was, could I tell you that you should beg forgiveness of him who made your father suffer so much? Could I ask my father that he forgive you, could I tell him that I knew that I was his daughter — him, who desired my death so eagerly? It was only left to me to suffer, to guard the secret, and to die suffering! Now, my friend, now that you know the sad history of your poor Maria, will you still have for her that disdainful smile?"

"Maria, you are an angel!"

"Then I am happy, since you believe me —"

"But yet," added the youth with a change of tone, "I've heard that you are going to be married."

"Yes," sobbed the girl, "my father demands this sacrifice. He has loved me and cared for me when it was not his duty to do so, and I will pay this debt of gratitude to assure his peace, by means of this new relationship, but —"

"But what?"

"I will never forget the vows of faithfulness that I have made to you."

'What are you thinking of doing?" asked Ibarra, trying to read the look in her eyes.

"The future is dark and my destiny is wrapped in gloom! I don't know what I should do. But know, that I have loved but once and that without love I will never belong to any man. And you, what is going to become of you?"

"I am only a fugitive, I am fleeing. In a little while my flight will have been discovered. Maria —"

Maria Clara caught the youth's head in her hands and kissed him repeatedly on the lips, embraced him, and drew abruptly away. "Go, go!" she cried. "Go, and farewell!"

MARIA CLARA WEDS

Ibarra gazed at her with shining eyes, but at a gesture from her moved away — intoxicated, wavering.

Once again he leaped over the wall and stepped into the banka. Maria Clara, leaning over the balustrade, watched him depart. Elias took off his hat and bowed to her profoundly.

CHAPTER LXI

THE CHASE ON THE LAKE

"LISTEN, sir, to the plan that I have worked out," said Elias thoughtfully, as they moved in the direction of San Gabriel. "I'll hide you now in the house of a friend of mine in Mandaluyong. I'll bring you all your money, which I saved and buried at the foot of the balete in the mysterious tomb of your grandfather. Then you will leave the country."

"To go abroad?" inquired Ibarra.

"To live out in peace the days of life that remain to you. You have friends in Spain, you are rich, you can get yourself pardoned. In every way a foreign country is for us a better fatherland than our own."

Crisostomo did not answer, but meditated in silence. At that moment they reached the Pasig and the banka began to ascend the current. Over the Bridge of Spain a horseman galloped rapidly, while a shrill, prolonged whistle was heard.

"Elias," said Ibarra, "you owe your misfortunes to my family, you have saved my life twice, and I owe you not only gratitude but also the restitution of your fortune. You advise me to go abroad — then come with me and we will live like brothers. Here you also are wretched."

Elias shook his head sadly and answered: "Impossible! It's true that I cannot love or be happy in my country, but I can suffer and die in it, and perhaps for it — that is always something. May the misfortunes of my native land be my own misfortunes and, although no noble sentiment unites us, although our hearts do not beat to a single name, at least may the common calamity bind me to my countrymen, at least may I weep over our sorrows with them, may the same hard fate oppress all our hearts alike!"

"Then why do you advise me to go away?"

"Because in some other country you could be happy while I could not, because you are not made to suffer, and because you would hate your country if some day you should see yourself ruined in its cause, and to hate one's native land is the greatest of calamities."

"You are unfair to me!" exclaimed Ibarra with bitter reproach. "You forget that scarcely had I arrived here when I set myself to seek its welfare."

"Don't be offended, sir, I was not reproaching you at all. Would that all of us could imitate you! But I do not ask impossibilities of you and I mean no offense when I say that your heart deceives you. You loved your country because your father taught you to do so; you loved it because in it you had affection, fortune, youth, because everything smiled on you, your country had done you no injustice; you loved it as we love anything that makes us happy. But the day in which you see yourself poor and hungry, persecuted, betrayed, and sold by your own countrymen, on that day you will disown yourself, your country, and all mankind."

"Your words pain me," said Ibarra resentfully.

Elias bowed his head and meditated before replying. "I wish to disillusion you, sir, and save you from a sad future. Recall that night when I talked to you in this same banka under the light of this same moon, not a month ago. Then you were happy, the plea of the unfortunates did not touch you; you disdained their complaints because they were the complaints of criminals; you paid more attention to their enemies, and in spite of my arguments and petitions, you placed yourself on the side of their oppressors. On you then depended whether I should turn criminal or allow myself to be killed in order to carry out a sacred pledge, but God has not permitted this because the old chief of the outlaws is dead. A month has hardly passed and you think otherwise."

"You're right, Elias, but man is a creature of circumstances! Then I was blind, annoyed — what did I know? Now misfortune has torn the bandage from my eyes; the solitude and misery of my prison have taught me; now I see the horrible cancer which feeds upon this society, which clutches its flesh, and which demands a violent rooting out. They have opened my eyes, they have made me see the sore, and they force me to be a criminal! Since they wish it, I will be a filibuster, a real filibuster, I mean. I will call together all the unfortunates, all who feel a heart beat in their breasts, all those who were sending you to me. No, I will not be a criminal, never is he such who fights for his native land, but quite the reverse! We, during three centuries, have extended them our hands, we have asked love of them, we have yearned to call them brothers, and how do they answer us? With insults and jests, denying us even the chance character of human beings. There is no God, there is no hope, there is no humanity; there is nothing but the right of might!" Ibarra was nervous, his whole body trembled.

As they passed in front of the Captain-General's palace they thought that they could discern movement and excitement among the guards.

"Can they have discovered your flight?" murmured Elias. "Lie down, sir, so that I can cover you with zacate. Since we shall pass near the powder-magazine it may seem suspicious to the sentinel that there are two of us."

The banka was one of those small, narrow canoes that do not seem to float but rather to glide over the top of the water. As Elias had foreseen, the sentinel stopped him and inquired whence he came.

"From Manila, to carry zacate to the judges and curates," he answered, imitating the accent of the people of Pandakan.

A sergeant came out to learn what was happening. "Move on!" he said to Elias. "But I warn you not to take anybody into your banka. A prisoner has just escaped. If you capture him and turn him over to me I'll give you a good tip."

"All right, sir. What's his description?"

"He wears a sack coat and talks Spanish. So look out!"

The banka moved away. Elias looked back and watched the silhouette of the sentinel standing on the bank of the river.

"We'll lose a few minutes' time," he said in a low voice. "We must go into the Beata River to pretend that I'm from Peñafrancia. You will see the river of which Francisco Baltazar sang."

The town slept in the moonlight, and Crisostomo rose up to admire the sepulchral peace of nature. The river was narrow and the level land on either side covered with grass. Elias threw his cargo out on the bank and, after removing a large piece of bamboo, took from under the grass some empty palm-leaf sacks. Then they continued on their way.

"You are the master of your own will, sir, and of your future," he said to Crisostomo, who had remained silent. "But if you will allow me an observation, I would say: think well what you are planning to do — you are going to light the flames of war, since you have money and brains, and you will quickly find many to join you, for unfortunately there are plenty of malcontents. But in this struggle which you are going to undertake, those who will suffer most will be the defenseless and the innocent. The same sentiments that a month ago impelled me to appeal to you asking for reforms are those that move me now to urge you to think well. The country, sir, does not think of separating from the mother country; it only asks for a little freedom, justice, and affection. You will be supported by the malcontents, the criminals, the desperate, but the people will hold aloof. You are mistaken if, seeing all dark, you think that the country is desperate. The country suffers, yes, but it still hopes and trusts and will only rebel when it has lost its patience, that is, when those who govern it wish it to do so, and that time is yet distant. I myself will not follow you, never will I resort to such extreme measures while I see hope in men."

"Then I'll go on without you!" responded Ibarra resolutely.

"Is your decision final?"

"Final and firm; let the memory of my mother bear witness! I will not let peace and happiness be torn away from me with impunity, I who desired only what was good, I who have respected everything and endured everything out of love for a hypocritical religion and out of love of country. How have they answered me? By burying me in an infamous dungeon and robbing me of my intended wife! No, not to avenge myself would be a crime, it would be encouraging them to new acts of injustice! No, it would be cowardice, pusillanimity, to groan and weep when there is blood and life left, when to insult and menace is added mockery. I will call out these ignorant people, I will make them see their misery. I will teach them to think not of brotherhood but only that they are wolves for devouring, I will urge them to rise against this oppression and proclaim the eternal right of man to win his freedom!"

"But innocent people will suffer!"

"So much the better! Can you take me to the mountains?"

"Until you are in safety," replied Elias.

Again they moved out into the Pasig, talking from time to time of indifferent matters.

"Santa Ana!" murmured Ibarra. "Do you recognize this building?" They were passing in front of the country-house of the Jesuits.

"There I spent many pleasant and happy days!" sighed Elias. "In my time we came every month. Then I was like others, I had a fortune, family, I dreamed, I looked forward to a future. In those days I saw my sister in the near-by college, she presented me with a piece of her own embroidery-work. A friend used to accompany her, a beautiful girl. All that has passed like a dream."

They remained silent until they reached Malapad-na-bato.[1] Those who have ever made their way by night up the Pasig, on one of those magical nights that the Philippines offers, when the moon pours out from the limpid blue her melancholy light, when the shadows hide the miseries of man and the silence is unbroken by the sordid accents of his voice, when only Nature speaks — they will understand the thoughts of both these youths.

At Malapad-na-bato the carbineer was sleepy and, seeing that the banka was empty and offered no booty which he might seize, according to the traditional usage of his corps and the custom of that post, he easily let them pass on. Nor did the civil-guard at Pasig suspect anything, so they were not molested.

Day was beginning to break when they reached the lake, still and calm like a gigantic mirror. The moon paled and the east was dyed in rosy tints. Some distance away they perceived a gray mass advancing slowly toward them.

"The police boat is coming," murmured Elias. "Lie down and I'll cover you with these sacks."

The outlines of the boat became clearer and plainer.

"It's getting between us and the shore," observed Elias uneasily.

Gradually he changed the course of his banka, rowing toward Binangonan. To his great surprise he noticed that the boat also changed its course, while a voice called to him.

Elias stopped rowing and reflected. The shore was still far away and they would soon be within range of the

[1] The "wide rock" that formerly jutted out into the river just below the place where the streams from the Lake of Bay join the Mariquina to form the Pasig proper. This spot was celebrated in the demonology of the primitive Tagalogs and later, after the tutelar devils had been duly exorcised by the Spanish padres, converted into a revenue station. The name is preserved in that of the little barrio on the river bank near Fort McKinley. — TR.

rifles on the police boat. He thought of returning to
Pasig, for his banka was the swifter of the two boats, but
unluckily he saw another boat coming from the river and
made out the gleam of caps and bayonets of the Civil
Guard.

"We're caught!" he muttered, turning pale.

He gazed at his robust arms and, adopting the only
course left, began to row with all his might toward Talim
Island, just as the sun was rising.

The banka slipped rapidly along. Elias saw standing
on the boat, which had veered about, some men making
signals to him.

"Do you know how to manage a banka?" he asked
Ibarra.

"Yes, why?"

"Because we are lost if I don't jump into the water
and throw them off the track. They will pursue me, but
I swim and dive well. I'll draw them away from you
and then you can save yourself."

"No, stay here, and we'll sell our lives dearly!"

"That would be useless. We have no arms and with
their rifles they would shoot us down like birds."

At that instant the water gave forth a hiss such as is
caused by the falling of hot metal into it, followed instantaneously by a loud report.

"You see!" said Elias, placing the paddle in the boat.
"We'll see each other on Christmas Eve at the tomb of
your grandfather. Save yourself."

"And you?"

"God has carried me safely through greater perils."

As Elias took off his camisa a bullet tore it from his
hands and two loud reports were heard. Calmly he
clasped the hand of Ibarra, who was still stretched out
in the bottom of the banka. Then he arose and leaped into
the water, at the same time pushing the little craft away
from him with his foot.

Cries resounded, and soon some distance away the

youth's head appeared, as if for breathing, then instantly disappeared.

"There, there he is!" cried several voices, and again the bullets whistled.

The police boat and the boat from the Pasig now started in pursuit of him. A light track indicated his passage through the water as he drew farther and farther away from Ibarra's banka, which floated about as if abandoned. Every time the swimmer lifted his head above the water to breathe, the guards in both boats shot at him.

So the chase continued. Ibarra's little banka was now far away and the swimmer was approaching the shore, distant some thirty yards. The rowers were tired, but Elias was in the same condition, for he showed his head oftener, and each time in a different direction, as if to disconcert his pursuers. No longer did the treacherous track indicate the position of the diver. They saw him for the last time when he was some ten yards from the shore, and fired. Then minute after minute passed, but nothing again appeared above the still and solitary surface of the lake.

Half an hour afterwards one of the rowers claimed that he could distinguish in the water near the shore traces of blood, but his companions shook their heads dubiously.

CHAPTER LXII

PADRE DAMASO EXPLAINS

VAINLY were the rich wedding presents heaped upon a table; neither the diamonds in their cases of blue velvet, nor the piña embroideries, nor the rolls of silk, drew the gaze of Maria Clara. Without reading or even seeing it the maiden sat staring at the newspaper which gave an account of the death of Ibarra, drowned in the lake.

Suddenly she felt two hands placed over her eyes to hold her fast and heard Padre Damaso's voice ask merrily, "Who am I? Who am I?"

Maria Clara sprang from her seat and gazed at him in terror.

"Foolish little girl, you're not afraid, are you? You were n't expecting me, eh? Well, I've come in from the provinces to attend your wedding."

He smiled with satisfaction as he drew nearer to her and held out his hand for her to kiss. Maria Clara approached him tremblingly and touched his hand respectfully to her lips.

"What's the matter with you, Maria?" asked the Franciscan, losing his merry smile and becoming uneasy. "Your hand is cold, you're pale. Are you ill, little girl?"

Padre Damaso drew her toward himself with a tenderness that one would hardly have thought him capable of, and catching both her hands in his questioned her with his gaze.

"Don't you have confidence in your godfather any more?" he asked reproachfully. "Come, sit down and tell me your little troubles as you used to do when you were a child, when you wanted tapers to make wax dolls. You know that I've always loved you, I've never been cross with you."

His voice was now no longer brusque, and even became tenderly modulated. Maria Clara began to weep.

"You're crying, little girl? Why do you cry? Have you quarreled with Linares?"

Maria Clara covered her ears. "Don't speak of him — not now!" she cried.

Padre Damaso gazed at her in startled wonder.

"Won't you trust me with your secrets? Haven't I always tried to satisfy your lightest whim?"

The maiden raised eyes filled with tears and stared at him for a long time, then again fell to weeping bitterly.

"Don't cry so, little girl. Your tears hurt me. Tell me your troubles, and you'll see how your godfather loves you!"

Maria Clara approached him slowly, fell upon her knees, and raising her tear-stained face toward his asked in a low, scarcely audible tone, "Do you still love me?"

"Child!"

"Then, protect my father and break off my marriage!"

Here the maiden told of her last interview with Ibarra, concealing only her knowledge of the secret of her birth. Padre Damaso could scarcely credit his ears.

"While he lived," the girl continued, "I thought of struggling, I was hoping, trusting! I wanted to live so that I might hear of him, but now that they have killed him, now there is no reason why I should live and suffer." She spoke in low, measured tones, calmly, tearlessly.

"But, foolish girl, isn't Linares a thousand times better than — "

"While he lived, I could have married — I thought of running away afterwards — my father wants only the relationship! But now that he is dead, no other man shall call me wife! While he was alive I could debase myself, for there would have remained the consolation that he lived and perhaps thought of me, but now that he is dead — the nunnery or the tomb!"

The girl's voice had a ring of firmness in it such that Padre Damaso lost his merry air and became very thoughtful.

"Did you love him as much as that?" he stammered.

Maria Clara did not answer. Padre Damaso dropped his head on his chest and remained silent for a long time.

"Daughter in God," he exclaimed at length in a broken voice, "forgive me for having made you unhappy without knowing it. I was thinking of your future, I desired your happiness. How could I permit you to marry a native of the country, to see you an unhappy wife and a wretched mother? I could n't get that love out of your head even though I opposed it with all my might. I committed wrongs, for you, solely for you. If you had become his wife you would have mourned afterwards over the condition of your husband, exposed to all kinds of vexations without means of defense. As a mother you would have mourned the fate of your sons: if you had educated them, you would have prepared for them a sad future, for they would have become enemies of Religion and you would have seen them garroted or exiled; if you had kept them ignorant, you would have seen them tyrannized over and degraded. I could not consent to it! For this reason I sought for you a husband that could make you the happy mother of sons who would command and not obey, who would punish and not suffer. I knew that the friend of your childhood was good, I liked him as well as his father, but I have hated them both since I saw that they were going to bring about your unhappiness, because I love you, I adore you, I love you as one loves his own daughter! Yours is my only affection; I have seen you grow — not an hour has passed that I have not thought of you — I dreamed of you — you have been my only joy!"

Here Padre Damaso himself broke out into tears like a child.

PADRE DAMASO EXPLAINS

"Then, as you love me, don't make me eternally wretched. He no longer lives, so I want to be a nun!"

The old priest rested his forehead on his hand. "To be a nun, a nun!" he repeated. "You don't know, child, what the life is, the mystery that is hidden behind the walls of the nunnery, you don't know! A thousand times would I prefer to see you unhappy in the world rather than in the cloister. Here your complaints can be heard, there you will have only the walls. You are beautiful, very beautiful, and you were not born for that — to be a bride of Christ! Believe me, little girl, time will wipe away everything. Later on you will forget, you will love, you will love your husband — Linares."

"The nunnery or — death!"

"The nunnery, the nunnery, or death!" exclaimed Padre Damaso. "Maria, I am now an old man, I shall not be able much longer to watch over you and your welfare. Choose something else, seek another love, some other man, whoever he may be — anything but the nunnery."

"The nunnery or death!"

"My God, my God!" cried the priest, covering his head with his hands, "Thou chastisest me, so let it be! But watch over my daughter!"

Then, turning again to the young woman, he said, "You wish to be a nun, and it shall be so. I don't want you to die."

Maria Clara caught both his hands in hers, clasping and kissing them as she fell upon her knees, repeating over and over, "My godfather, I thank you, my godfather!"

With bowed head Fray Damaso went away, sad and sighing. "God, Thou dost exist, since Thou chastisest! But let Thy vengeance fall on me, harm not the innocent. Save Thou my daughter!"

CHAPTER LXIII

CHRISTMAS EVE

HIGH up on the slope of the mountain near a roaring stream a hut built on the gnarled logs hides itself among the trees. Over its kogon thatch clambers the branching gourd-vine, laden with flowers and fruit. Deer antlers and skulls of wild boar, some with long tusks, adorn this mountain home, where lives a Tagalog family engaged in hunting and cutting firewood.

In the shade of a tree the grandsire was making brooms from the fibers of palm leaves, while a young woman was placing eggs, limes, and some vegetables in a wide basket. Two children, a boy and a girl, were playing by the side of another, who, pale and sad, with large eyes and a deep gaze, was seated on a fallen tree-trunk. In his thinned features we recognize Sisa's son, Basilio, the brother of Crispin.

"When your foot gets well," the little girl was saying to him, "we'll play hide-and-seek. I'll be the leader."

"You'll go up to the top of the mountain with us," added the little boy, "and drink deer blood with lime-juice and you'll get fat, and then I'll teach you how to jump from rock to rock above the torrent."

Basilio smiled sadly, stared at the sore on his foot, and then turned his gaze toward the sun, which shone resplendently.

"Sell these brooms," said the grandfather to the young woman, "and buy something for the children, for tomorrow is Christmas."

"Firecrackers, I want some firecrackers!" exclaimed the boy.

"I want a head for my doll," cried the little girl, catching hold of her sister's tapis.

"And you, what do you want?" the grandfather asked Basilio, who at the question arose laboriously and approached the old man.

"Sir," he said, "I've been sick more than a month now, have n't I?"

"Since we found you lifeless and covered with wounds, two moons have come and gone. We thought you were going to die."

"May God reward you, for we are very poor," replied Basilio. "But now that tomorrow is Christmas I want to go to the town to see my mother and my little brother. They will be seeking for me."

"But, my son, you 're not yet well, and your town is far away. You won't get there by midnight."

"That does n't matter, sir. My mother and my little brother must be very sad. Every year we spend this holiday together. Last year the three of us had a whole fish to eat. My mother will have been mourning and looking for me."

"You won't get to the town alive, boy! Tonight we 're going to have chicken and wild boar's meat. My sons will ask for you when they come from the field."

"You have many sons while my mother has only us two. Perhaps she already believes that I 'm dead! Tonight I want to give her a pleasant surprise, a Christmas gift, a son."

The old man felt the tears springing up into his eyes, so, placing his hands on the boy's head, he said with emotion: "You 're like an old man! Go, look for your mother, give her the Christmas gift — from God, as you say. If I had known the name of your town I would have gone there when you were sick. Go, my son, and may God and the Lord Jesus go with you. Lucia, my granddaughter, will go with you to the nearest town."

"What! You 're going away?" the little boy asked him.

"Down there are soldiers and many robbers. Don't you want to see my firecrackers? Boom, boom, boom!"

"Don't you want to play hide-and-seek?" asked the little girl. "Have you ever played it? Surely there's nothing any more fun than to be chased and hide yourself?"

Basilio smiled, but with tears in his eyes, and caught up his staff. "I'll come back soon," he answered. "I'll bring my little brother, you'll see him and play with him. He's just about as big as you are."

"Does he walk lame, too?" asked the little girl. "Then we'll make him 'it' when we play hide-and-seek."

"Don't forget us," the old man said to him. "Take this dried meat as a present to your mother."

The children accompanied him to the bamboo bridge swung over the noisy course of the stream. Lucia made him support himself on her arm, and thus they disappeared from the children's sight, Basilio walking along nimbly in spite of his bandaged leg.

The north wind whistled by, making the inhabitants of San Diego shiver with cold. It was Christmas Eve and yet the town was wrapped in gloom. Not a paper lantern hung from the windows nor did a single sound in the houses indicate the rejoicing of other years.

In the house of Capitan Basilio, he and Don Filipo — for the misfortunes of the latter had made them friendly — were standing by a window-grating and talking, while at another were Sinang, her cousin Victoria, and the beautiful Iday, looking toward the street.

The waning moon began to shine over the horizon, illumining the clouds and making the trees and houses cast long, fantastic shadows.

"Yours is not a little good fortune, to get off free in these times!" said Capitan Basilio to Don Filipo. "They've burned your books, yes, but others have lost more."

A woman approached the grating and gazed into the interior. Her eyes glittered, her features were emaciated, her hair loose and dishevelled. The moonlight gave her a weird aspect.

"Sisa!" exclaimed Don Filipo in surprise. Then turning to Capitan Basilio, as the madwoman ran away, he asked, "Wasn't she in the house of a physician? Has she been cured?"

Capitan Basilio smiled bitterly. "The physician was afraid they would accuse him of being a friend of Don Crisostomo's, so he drove her from his house. Now she wanders about again as crazy as ever, singing, harming no one, and living in the woods."

"What else has happened in the town since we left it? I know that we have a new curate and another alferez."

"These are terrible times, humanity is retrograding," murmured Capitan Basilio, thinking of the past. "The day after you left they found the senior sacristan dead, hanging from a rafter in his own house. Padre Salvi was greatly affected by his death and took possession of all his papers. Ah, yes, the old Sage, Tasio, also died and was buried in the Chinese cemetery."

"Poor old man!" sighed Don Filipo. "What became of his books?"

"They were burned by the pious, who thought thus to please God. I was unable to save anything, not even Cicero's works. The gobernadorcillo did nothing to prevent it."

Both became silent. At that moment the sad and melancholy song of the madwoman was heard.

"Do you know when Maria Clara is to be married?" Iday asked Sinang.

"I don't know," answered the latter. "I received a letter from her but haven't opened it for fear of finding out. Poor Crisostomo!"

"They say that if it were not for Linares, they would hang Capitan Tiago, so what was Maria Clara going to do?" observed Victoria.

A boy limped by, running toward the plaza, whence

came the notes of Sisa's song. It was Basilio, who had found his home deserted and in ruins. After many inquiries he had only learned that his mother was insane and wandering about the town — of Crispin not a word.

Basilio choked back his tears, stifled any expression of his sorrow, and without resting had started in search of his mother. On reaching the town he was just asking about her when her song struck his ears. The unhappy boy overcame the trembling in his limbs and ran to throw himself into his mother's arms.

The madwoman left the plaza and stopped in front of the house of the new alferez. Now, as formerly, there was a sentinel before the door, and a woman's head appeared at the window, only it was not the Medusa's but that of a comely young woman: alferez and unfortunate are not synonymous terms.

Sisa began to sing before the house with her gaze fixed on the moon, which soared majestically in the blue heavens among golden clouds. Basilio saw her, but did not dare to approach her. Walking back and forth, but taking care not to get near the barracks, he waited for the time when she would leave that place.

The young woman who was at the window listening attentively to the madwoman's song ordered the sentinel to bring her inside, but when Sisa saw the soldier approach her and heard his voice she was filled with terror and took to flight at a speed of which only a demented person is capable. Basilio, fearing to lose her, ran after her, forgetful of the pains in his feet.

"Look how that boy's chasing the madwoman!" indignantly exclaimed a woman in the street. Seeing that he continued to pursue her, she picked up a stone and threw it at him, saying, "Take that! It's a pity that the dog is tied up!"

Basilio felt a blow on his head, but paid no attention to it as he continued running. Dogs barked, geese cackled, several windows opened to let out curious faces but

CHRISTMAS EVE 489

quickly closed again from fear of another night of terror.

Soon they were outside of the town. Sisa began to moderate her flight, but still a great distance separated her from her pursuer.

"Mother!" he called to her when he caught sight of her.

Scarcely had the madwoman heard his voice when she again took to flight.

"Mother, it's I!" cried the boy in desperation, but the madwoman did not heed him, so he followed panting. They had now passed the cultivated fields and were near the wood; Basilio saw his mother enter it and he also went in. The bushes and shrubs, the thorny vines and projecting roots of trees, hindered the movements of both. The son followed his mother's shadowy form as it was revealed from time to time by the moonlight that penetrated through the foliage and into the open spaces. They were in the mysterious wood of the Ibarra family.

The boy stumbled and fell several times, but rose again, each time without feeling pain. All his soul was centered in his eyes, following the beloved figure. They crossed the sweetly murmuring brook where sharp thorns of bamboo that had fallen on the sand at its margin pierced his bare feet, but he did not stop to pull them out.

To his great surprise he saw that his mother had plunged into the thick undergrowth and was going through the wooden gateway that opened into the tomb of the old Spaniard at the foot of the balete. Basilio tried to follow her in, but found the gate fastened. The madwoman defended the entrance with her emaciated arms and disheveled head, holding the gate shut with all her might.

"Mother, it's I, it's I! I'm Basilio, your son!" cried the boy as he let himself fall weakly.

But the madwoman did not yield. Bracing herself with her feet on the ground, she offered an energetic resistance. Basilio beat the gate with his fists, with his blood-stained head, he wept, but in vain. Painfully he arose and examined the wall, thinking to scale it, but found no way to do so. He then walked around it and noticed that a branch of the fateful balete was crossed with one from another tree. This he climbed and, his filial love working miracles, made his way from branch to branch to the balete, from which he saw his mother still holding the gate shut with her head.

The noise made by him among the branches attracted Sisa's attention. She turned and tried to run, but her son, letting himself fall from the tree, caught her in his arms and covered her with kisses, losing consciousness as he did so.

Sisa saw his blood-stained forehead and bent over him. Her eyes seemed to start from their sockets as she peered into his face. Those pale features stirred the sleeping cells of her brain, so that something like a spark of intelligence flashed up in her mind and she recognized her son. With a terrible cry she fell upon the insensible body of the boy, embracing and kissing him. Mother and son remained motionless.

When Basilio recovered consciousness he found his mother lifeless. He called to her with the tenderest names, but she did not awake. Noticing that she was not even breathing, he arose and went to the neighboring brook to get some water in a banana leaf, with which to rub the pallid face of his mother, but the madwoman made not the least movement and her eyes remained closed.

Basilio gazed at her in terror. He placed his ear over her heart, but the thin, faded breast was cold, and her heart no longer beat. He put his lips to hers, but felt no breathing. The miserable boy threw his arms about the corpse and wept bitterly.

The moon gleamed majestically in the sky, the wandering breezes sighed, and down in the grass the crickets chirped. The night of light and joy for so many children, who in the warm bosom of the family celebrate this feast of sweetest memories — the feast which commemorates the first look of love that Heaven sent to earth — this night when in all Christian families they eat, drink, dance, sing, laugh, play, caress, and kiss one another — this night, which in cold countries holds such magic for childhood with its traditional pine-tree covered with lights, dolls, candies, and tinsel, whereon gaze the round, staring eyes in which innocence alone is reflected — this night brought to Basilio only orphanhood. Who knows but that perhaps in the home whence came the taciturn Padre Salvi children also played, perhaps they sang

"La Nochebuena se viene,
La Nochebuena se va."[1]

For a long time the boy wept and moaned. When at last he raised his head he saw a man standing over him, gazing at the scene in silence.

"Are you her son?" asked the unknown in a low voice.

The boy nodded.

"What do you expect to do?"

"Bury her!"

"In the cemetery?"

"I have n't any money and, besides, the curate would n't allow it."

"Then?"

"If you would help me —"

"I 'm very weak," answered the unknown as he sank slowly to the ground, supporting himself with both hands. "I 'm wounded. For two days I have n't eaten or slept. Has no one come here tonight?"

The man thoughtfully contemplated the attractive features of the boy, then went on in a still weaker voice, "Listen! I, too, shall be dead before the day comes. Twenty paces from here, on the other side of the brook, there is a big pile of firewood. Bring it here, make a pyre, put our bodies upon it, cover them over, and set fire to the whole — fire, until we are reduced to ashes!"

[1] A Christmas carol: "Christmas night is coming, Christmas night is going." — TR.

Basilio listened attentively.

"Afterwards, if no one comes, dig here. You will find a lot of gold and it will all be yours. Take it and go to school."

The voice of the unknown was becoming every moment more unintelligible. "Go, get the firewood. I want to help you."

As Basilio moved away, the unknown turned his face toward the east and murmured, as though praying:

"I die without seeing the dawn brighten over my native land! You, who have it to see, welcome it — and forget not those who have fallen during the night!"

He raised his eyes to the sky and his lips continued to move, as if uttering a prayer. Then he bowed his head and sank slowly to the earth.

Two hours later Sister Rufa was on the back veranda of her house making her morning ablutions in order to attend mass. The pious woman gazed at the adjacent wood and saw a thick column of smoke rising from it. Filled with holy indignation, she knitted her eyebrows and exclaimed:

"What heretic is making a clearing on a holy day? That's why so many calamities come! You ought to go to purgatory and see if you could get out of there, savage!"

EPILOGUE

Since some of our characters are still living and others have been lost sight of, a real epilogue is impossible. For the satisfaction of the groundlings we should gladly kill off all of them, beginning with Padre Salvi and ending with Doña Victorina, but this is not possible. Let them live! Anyhow, the country, not ourselves, has to support them.

After Maria Clara entered the nunnery, Padre Damaso left his town to live in Manila, as did also Padre Salvi, who, while he awaits a vacant miter, preaches sometimes in the church of St. Clara, in whose nunnery he discharges the duties of an important office. Not many months had passed when Padre Damaso received an order from the Very Reverend Father Provincial to occupy a curacy in a remote province. It is related that he was so grievously affected by this that on the following day he was found dead in his bedchamber. Some said that he had died of an apoplectic stroke, others of a nightmare, but his physician dissipated all doubts by declaring that he had died suddenly.

None of our readers would now recognize Capitan Tiago. Weeks before Maria Clara took the vows he fell into a state of depression so great that he grew sad and thin, and became pensive and distrustful, like his former friend, Capitan Tinong. As soon as the doors of the nunnery closed he ordered his disconsolate cousin, Aunt Isabel, to collect whatever had belonged to his daughter and his dead wife and to go to make her home in Malabon or San Diego, since he wished to live alone thenceforward. He then devoted himself passionately to *liam-pó* and the cockpit, and began to smoke opium. He no longer goes to Antipolo nor does he order any more masses, so Doña Patrocinia, his old rival, celebrates her triumph piously by snoring during the sermons. If at any time during the late afternoon you should walk along Calle Santo Cristo, you would see seated in a Chinese shop a small man, yellow, thin, and bent, with stained and dirty finger nails, gazing through dreamy, sunken eyes at the passers-by as if he did not see them. At nightfall you would see him rise with difficulty and, supporting himself on his cane, make his way to a narrow little by-street to enter a grimy building over the door of which may be seen in large red letters: FUMADERO PUBLICO DE ANFION.[1] This is that Capitan Tiago who was so celebrated, but who is now completely forgotten, even by the very senior sacristan himself.

Doña Victorina has added to her false frizzes and to her *Andalusization,* if we may be permitted the term, the new custom of driving the carriage horses herself, obliging Don Tiburcio to remain quiet. Since many unfortunate accidents occurred on account of the weakness of her eyes, she has taken to wearing spectacles, which give her a marvelous appearance. The doctor has never been called upon again to attend any one and the servants see him many days in the week without teeth, which, as our readers know, is a very bad sign. Linares, the only defender of the hapless doctor, has long been at rest in Paco cemetery, the victim of dysentery and the harsh treatment of his cousin-in-law.

The victorious alferez returned to Spain a major, leaving his amiable spouse in her flannel camisa, the color of which is now indescribable. The poor Ariadne, finding herself thus abandoned, also devoted herself, as did the daughter of Minos, to the cult of Bacchus and the cultivation of tobacco; she drinks and smokes with such fury that now not only the girls but even the old women and little children fear her.

Probably our acquaintances of the town of San Diego are still alive, if they did not perish in the explosion of the steamer "Lipa," which was making a trip to the province.

[1] Public Opium-Smoking Room.

EPILOGUE

Since no one bothered himself to learn who the unfortunates were that perished in that catastrophe or to whom belonged the legs and arms left neglected on Convalescence Island and the banks of the river, we have no idea whether any acquaintance of our readers was among them or not. Along with the government and the press at the time, we are satisfied with the information that the only friar who was on the steamer was saved, and we do not ask for more. The principal thing for us is the existence of the virtuous priests, whose reign in the Philippines may God conserve for the good of our souls.[1]

Of Maria Clara nothing more is known except that the sepulcher seems to guard her in its bosom. We have asked several persons of great influence in the holy nunnery of St. Clara, but no one has been willing to tell us a single word, not even the talkative devotees who receive the famous fried chicken-livers and the even more famous sauce known as that " of the nuns," prepared by the intelligent cook of the Virgins of the Lord.

Nevertheless: On a night in September the hurricane raged over Manila, lashing the buildings with its gigantic wings. The thunder crashed continuously. Lightning flashes momentarily revealed the havoc wrought by the blast and threw the inhabitants into wild terror. The rain fell in torrents. Each flash of the forked lightning showed a piece of roofing or a window-blind flying through the air to fall with a horrible crash. Not a person or a carriage moved through the streets. When the hoarse reverberations of the thunder, a hundred times re-echoed, lost themselves in the distance, there was heard the soughing of the wind as it drove the raindrops with a continuous tick-tack against the concha-panes of the closed windows.

Two patrolmen sheltered themselves under the eaves of a building near the nunnery, one a private and the other a *distinguido*.

" What's the use of our staying here ? " said the private.

---

[1] January 2, 1883. — *Author's note.*

"No one is moving about the streets. We ought to get into a house. My *querida* lives in Calle Arzobispo."

"From here over there is quite a distance and we'll get wet," answered the *distinguido*.

"What does that matter just so the lightning doesn't strike us?"

"Bah, don't worry! The nuns surely have a lightning-rod to protect them."

"Yes," observed the private, "but of what use is it when the night is so dark?"

As he said this he looked upward to stare into the darkness. At that moment a prolonged streak of lightning flashed, followed by a terrific roar.

"*Nakú! Susmariosep!*" exclaimed the private, crossing himself and catching hold of his companion. "Let's get away from here."

"What's happened?"

"Come, come away from here," he repeated with his teeth rattling from fear.

"What have you seen?"

"A specter!" he murmured, trembling with fright.

"A specter?"

"On the roof there. It must be the nun who practises magic during the night."

The *distinguido* thrust his head out to look, just as a flash of lightning furrowed the heavens with a vein of fire and sent a horrible crash earthwards. "*Jesús!*" he exclaimed, also crossing himself.

In the brilliant glare of the celestial light he had seen a white figure standing almost on the ridge of the roof with arms and face raised toward the sky as if praying to it. The heavens responded with lightning and thunderbolts!

As the sound of the thunder rolled away a sad plaint was heard.

"That's not the wind, it's the specter," murmured the private, as if in response to the pressure of his companion's hand.

"Ay! Ay!" came through the air, rising above the noise of the rain, nor could the whistling wind drown that sweet and mournful voice charged with affliction.

Again the lightning flashed with dazzling intensity.

"No, it's not a specter!" exclaimed the *distinguido*. "I've seen her before. She's beautiful, like the Virgin! Let's get away from here and report it."

The private did not wait for him to repeat the invitation, and both disappeared.

Who was moaning in the middle of the night in spite of the wind and rain and storm? Who was the timid maiden, the bride of Christ, who defied the unchained elements and chose such a fearful night under the open sky to breathe forth from so perilous a height her complaints to God? Had the Lord abandoned his altar in the nunnery so that He no longer heard her supplications? Did its arches perhaps prevent the longings of the soul from rising up to the throne of the Most Merciful?

The tempest raged furiously nearly the whole night, nor did a single star shine through the darkness. The despairing plaints continued to mingle with the soughing of the wind, but they found Nature and man alike deaf; God had hidden himself and heard not.

On the following day, after the dark clouds had cleared away and the sun shone again brightly in the limpid sky, there stopped at the door of the nunnery of St. Clara a carriage, from which alighted a man who made himself known as a representative of the authorities. He asked to be allowed to speak immediately with the abbess and to see all the nuns.

It is said that one of these, who appeared in a gown all wet and torn, with tears and tales of horror begged the man's protection against the outrages of hypocrisy. It is also said that she was very beautiful and had the most lovely and expressive eyes that were ever seen.

The representative of the authorities did not accede to her request, but, after talking with the abbess, left her there in spite of her tears and pleadings. The youthful nun saw the door close behind him as a condemned person might look upon the portals of Heaven closing against him, if ever Heaven should come to be as cruel and unfeeling as men are. The abbess said that she was a madwoman. The man may not have known that there is in Manila a home for the demented; or perhaps he looked upon the nunnery itself as an insane asylum, although it is claimed that he was quite ignorant, especially in a matter of deciding whether a person is of sound mind.

It is also reported that General J—— thought otherwise, when the matter reached his ears. He wished to protect the madwoman and asked for her. But this time no beautiful and unprotected maiden appeared, nor would the abbess permit a visit to the cloister, forbidding it in the name of Religion and the Holy Statutes. Nothing more was said of the affair, nor of the ill-starred Maria Clara.

GLOSSARY

abá: A Tagalog exclamation of wonder, surprise, etc., often used to introduce or emphasize a contradictory statement.

abaka: "Manila hemp," the fiber of a plant of the banana family.

achara: Pickles made from the tender shoots of bamboo, green papayas, etc.

alcalde: Governor of a province or district with both executive and judicial authority.

alferez: Junior officer of the Civil Guard, ranking next below a lieutenant.

alibambang: A leguminous plant whose acid leaves are used in cooking.

alpay: A variety of nephelium, similar but inferior to the Chinese lichi.

among: Term used by the natives in addressing a priest, especially a friar: from the Spanish amo, master.

amores-secos: "Barren loves," a low-growing weed whose small, angular pods adhere to clothing.

andas: A platform with handles, on which an image is borne in a procession.

asuang: A malignant devil reputed to feed upon human flesh, being especially fond of new-born babes.

até: The sweet-sop.

Audiencia: The administrative council and supreme court of the Spanish régime.

Ayuntamiento: A city corporation or council, and by extension the building in which it has its offices; specifically, in Manila, the capitol.

azotea: The flat roof of a house or any similar platform; a roof-garden.

babaye: Woman (the general Malay term).

baguio: The local name for the typhoon or hurricane.

bailúhan: Native dance and feast: from the Spanish baile.

balete: The Philippine banyan, a tree sacred in Malay folk-lore.

banka: A dugout canoe with bamboo supports or outriggers.

Bilibid: The general penitentiary at Manila.

buyo: The masticatory prepared by wrapping a piece of areca-nut with a little shell-lime in a betel-leaf: the pan of British India.

cabeza de barangay: Headman and tax collector for a group of about fifty families, for whose "tribute" he was personally responsible.

calle: Street.

camisa: 1. A loose, collarless shirt of transparent material worn by men outside the trousers.

2. A thin, transparent waist with flowing sleeves, worn by women.

GLOSSARY

camote: A variety of sweet potato.
capitan: "Captain," a title used in addressing or referring to the gobernadorcillo or a former occupant of that office.
carambas: A Spanish exclamation denoting surprise or displeasure.
carbineer: Internal-revenue guard.
cedula: Certificate of registration and receipt for poll-tax.
chico: The sapodilla plum.
Civil Guard: Internal quasi-military police force of Spanish officers and native soldiers.
cochero: Carriage driver: coachman.
Consul: A wealthy merchant; originally, a member of the **Consulado,** the tribunal, or corporation, controlling the galleon trade.
cuadrillero: Municipal guard.
cuarto: A copper coin, one hundred and sixty of which were equal in value to a silver peso.
cuidao: "Take care!" "Look out!" A common exclamation, from the Spanish cuidado.
dálag: The Philippine Ophiocephalus, the curious walking mudfish that abounds in the paddy-fields during the rainy season.
dalaga: Maiden, woman of marriageable age.
dinding: House-wall or partition of plaited bamboo wattle.
director, directorcillo: The town secretary and clerk of the gobernadorcillo.
distinguido: A person of rank serving as a private soldier but exempted from menial duties and in promotions preferred to others of equal merit.
escribano: Clerk of court and official notary.
filibuster: A native of the Philippines who was accused of advocating their separation from Spain.
gobernadorcillo: "Petty governor," the principal municipal official.
gogo: A climbing, woody vine whose macerated stems are used as soap; "soap-vine."
guingón: Dungaree, a coarse blue cotton cloth.
hermano mayor: The manager of a fiesta.
husi: A fine cloth made of silk interwoven with cotton, abaka, or pineapple-leaf fibers.
ilang-ilang: The Malay "flower of flowers," from which the well-known essence is obtained.
Indian: The Spanish designation for the Christianized Malay of the Philippines was indio (Indian), a term used rather contemptuously, the name Filipino being generally applied in a restricted sense to the children of Spaniards born in the Islands.
kaingin: A woodland clearing made by burning off the trees and underbrush, for planting upland rice or camotes.
kalan: The small, portable, open, clay fireplace commonly used in cooking.
kalao: The Philippine hornbill. As in all Malay countries, this bird is the object of curious superstitions. Its raucous cry, which may be faintly characterized as hideous, is said to mark the hours and, in the night-time, to presage death or other disaster.
kalikut: A short section of bamboo in which the buyo is mixed; a primitive betel-box.

GLOSSARY

kamagon: A tree of the ebony family, from which fine cabinet-wood is obtained. Its fruit is the mabolo, or date-plum.

kasamá: Tenants on the land of another, to whom they render payment in produce or by certain specified services.

kogon: A tall, rank grass used for thatch.

kris: A Moro dagger or short sword with a serpentine blade.

kundíman: A native song.

kupang: A large tree of the Mimosa family.

kuriput: Miser, "skinflint."

lanson: The langsa, a delicious cream-colored fruit about the size of a plum. In the Philippines, its special habitat is the country around the Lake of Bay.

liam-pó: A Chinese game of chance (?).

lomboy: The jambolana, a small, blue fruit with a large stone.

Malacañang: The palace of the Captain-General in Manila: from the vernacular name of the place where it stands, "fishermen's resort."

mankukúlan: An evil spirit causing sickness and other misfortunes, and a person possessed of such a demon.

morisqueta: Rice boiled without salt until dry, the staple food of the Filipinos.

Moro: Mohammedan Malay of southern Mindanao and Sulu.

mutya: Some object with talismanic properties, "rabbit's foot."

nakú: A Tagalog exclamation of surprise, wonder, etc.

nipa: Swamp-palm, with the imbricated leaves of which the roots and sides of the common Filipino houses are constructed.

nito: A climbing fern whose glossy, wiry leaves are used for making fine hats, cigar-cases, etc.

novena: A devotion consisting of prayers recited on nine consecutive days, asking for some special favor; also, a booklet of these prayers.

oy: An exclamation to attract attention, used toward inferiors and in familiar intercourse: probably a contraction of the Spanish imperative, oye, "listen!"

pakó: An edible fern.

palasán: A thick, stout variety of rattan, used for walking-sticks.

pandakaki: A low tree or shrub with small, star-like flowers.

pañuelo: A starched neckerchief folded stiffly over the shoulders, fastened in front and falling in a point behind: the most distinctive portion of the customary dress of the Filipino women.

papaya: The tropical papaw, fruit of the "melon-tree."

paracmason: Freemason, the *bête noire* of the Philippine friar.

peseta: A silver coin, in value one-fifth of a peso or thirty-two cuartos.

peso: A silver coin, either the Spanish peso or the Mexican dollar, about the size of an American dollar and of approximately half its value.

piña: Fine cloth made from pineapple-leaf fibers.

proper names: The author has given a simple and sympathetic touch to his story throughout by using the familiar names commonly employed among the Filipinos in their home-life. Some of these are nicknames or pet names, such as Andong, Andoy, Choy, Neneng ("Baby"), Puté, Tinchang, and Yeyeng. Others are abbreviations or corruptions of the Christian names, often with the particle ng or ay added, which is a common practice: Andeng, Andrea; Doray, Teodora; Iday, Brigida (Bridget);

GLOSSARY

Sinang, Lucinda (Lucy); Sipa, Josefa; Sisa, Narcisa; Teo, Teodoro (Theodore); Tiago, Santiago (James); Tasio, Anastasio; Tiká, Escolastica; Tinay, Quintina; Tinong, Saturnino.

Provincial: Head of a religious order in the Philippines.
querida: Paramour, mistress: from the Spanish, "beloved."
real: One-eighth of a peso, twenty cuartos.
sala: The principal room in the more pretentious Philippine houses.
salabat: An infusion of ginger.
salakot: Wide hat of palm or bamboo and rattan, distinctively Filipino.
sampaguita: The Arabian jasmine: a small, white, very fragrant flower, extensively cultivated, and worn in chaplets and rosaries by the women and girls — the typical Philippine flower.
santol: The Philippine sandal-tree.
sawali: Plaited bamboo wattle.
sinamay: A transparent cloth woven from abaka fibers.
sinigang: Water with vegetables or some acid fruit, in which fish are boiled; "fish soup."
Susmariosep: A common exclamation: contraction of the Spanish, Jesús, María, y José, the Holy Family.
tabí: The cry of carriage drivers to warn pedestrians.
talibon: A short sword, the "war bolo."
tapa: Jerked meat.
tápis: A piece of dark cloth or lace, often richly worked or embroidered, worn at the waist somewhat in the fashion of an apron: a distinctive portion of the native women's attire, especially among the Tagalogs.
tarambulo: A low weed whose leaves and fruit pedicles are covered with short, sharp spines.
teniente-mayor: Senior lieutenant, the senior member of the town council and substitute for the gobernadorcillo.
tikas-tikas: A variety of canna bearing bright red flowers.
tertiary brethren: Members of a lay society affiliated with a regular monastic order, especially the Venerable Tertiary Order of the Franciscans.
timbaín: The "water-cure," and hence, any kind of torture. The primary meaning is "to draw water from a well," from timba, pail.
tikbalang: An evil spirit, capable of assuming various forms, but said to appear usually in the shape of a tall black man with disproportionately long legs: the "bogey man" of Tagalog children.
tulisan: Outlaw, bandit. Under the old régime in the Philippines the tulisanes were those who, on account of real or fancied grievances against the authorities, or from fear of punishment for crime, or from an instinctive desire to return to primitive simplicity, foreswore life in the towns "under the bell," and made their homes in the mountains or other remote places. Gathered in small bands with such arms as they could secure, they sustained themselves by highway robbery and the levying of blackmail from the country folk.
zacate: Native grass used for feeding livestock.

Lightning Source UK Ltd.
Milton Keynes UK
UKOW06f0857270317
297590UK00020B/579/P